THE INNER MAN

The Inner Man

A NOVEL BY

MARTIN
WALSER

TRANSLATED FROM

THE GERMAN BY

LEILA VENNEWITZ

Holt, Rinehart and Winston *New York*

Copyright © 1979 by Suhrkamp Verlag
Frankfurt am Main
Translation copyright © 1984
by Martin Walser and Leila Vennewitz
All rights reserved, including the right to reproduce
this book or portions thereof in any form.
First published in the United States in 1985
by Holt, Rinehart and Winston, 383 Madison Avenue,
New York, New York 10017.
Published simultaneously in Canada
by Holt, Rinehart and Winston
of Canada, Limited.
Originally published in the Federal Republic of
Germany under the title *Seelenarbeit*.

Library of Congress Cataloging in Publication Data
Walser, Martin, 1927–
The inner man.
Translation of: Seelenarbeit.
I. Title.
PT2685.A48S413   1985   833'.914   84-672
ISBN: 0-03-059373-5

First American Edition

Designer: Margaret M. Wagner

Printed in the United States of America
1 3 5 7 9 10 8 6 4 2

ISBN 0-03-059373-5

TRANSLATOR'S
ACKNOWLEDGMENT

*My husband, William, has been generous in
contributing his knowledge, skills, and
energy toward the translating of this book,
and for this I am deeply indebted to him.*

—Leila Vennewitz

For Käthe

May

1

XAVER reached for the subdued, unbearable sound of the alarm clock and turned it off. From behind, his wife placed her hand on his shoulder to complete the work of the alarm clock. Xaver felt himself contracting, forehead and knees trying to come together. His wife's hand slid down his back. In a whisper she asked: "What's the matter?" He grasped her hand. He couldn't speak.

I have a *stomachache*. He hated those words. Those childish words. I'm in pain. That sounded too big. Agnes would be scared. You-really-must-see-the-doctor. What else could she say? And what could the doctor say? The first question Dr. Meichle asked anyone who sat down on the white chair by his desk was: "Do you feel ill?" Almost everyone who worked at Gleitze's was familiar with the Dr. Meichle question, Do-you-feel-ill? People called it out to one another as a joke, in Dr. Meichle's exact intonation: *ill* had to be pronounced in such a way that the *i* practically disappeared, while the *'ll* had to be a long, full nasal tone.

As soon as one found oneself sitting once again across from Dr. Meichle and hearing his Do-you-feel-ill? one had to admit that all imitations of that phrase were totally inadequate. One sat there as if one had never heard the question before, aware of the responsibility inherent in replying. If, for instance, one merely had a stomachache but otherwise felt in good health, the only answer to the doctor's question was no. Any attempt at hesitation was ignored by Dr. Meichle. Presumably experience had shown him that it was best for the patient if the treatment was based on either a yes or a no. Needless to say, Xaver had once answered the doctor's question with I-have-a-stomach-ache, whereupon Dr. Meichle had said: "We'll talk about that later, first please answer my question," and repeated with the familiar severity: "Do you feel ill?"

At the touch of Agnes's hand for the second time on his shoulder, Xaver nodded and got up. He drew back the heavy, dark green curtains, pushed out the shutter, and looked down onto the empty parking lot of the inn, the Happy Prospect. At this hour the parking lot was empty. He had heard the cars driving off one by one. At a quarter past two he had heard the last engine starting up, the last churning of the wheels on the gravel surface as the driver took off. The twenty-two fir trees he had planted along the edge of his property were now more than shoulder-high. But no planting can keep out the sound of voices. Let alone Margot's voice. Twenty years ago he had sung with Margot in the church choir. Then when she didn't marry him he realized he had always taken it for granted that one day she would be his wife. Whenever she called out to the customers at night, Thank-you-for-coming-drive-carefully-and-come-back-soon! he had the same thought: that she had a voice one could not only hear but actually see. Margot had a shining voice.

Each time he heard a car there was no way of telling whether that was really the last customer. So he would wait. The worst noises were the unexpected ones. They scored a direct hit. In his stomach. It was as if he had no ears, only a stomach. The next sound never came from where it was expected, never where the previous sound had come from. One had adjusted one's hearing to a certain distance, and suddenly footsteps crunched so close by that the next step must surely land in the pit of one's stomach. The night is a barrel from which there is no getting out, thought Xaver. When the noises wakened him that night, he had just been dreaming that he was lying stretched out on his

back. In a very special cage: a flat strip of rusty iron, three or
four inches wide, had been wound round and round him about
two inches from his body, so that he could scarcely move. It was
two-thirty A.M. Perhaps the laxative was starting to work. He
only took a laxative when he had a long drive ahead of him the
next day. This time they were going to Düsseldorf. Two-thirty
P.M. at the Savoy. Obviously Dr. Gleitze wouldn't want to stop
on the way. So Xaver had to make sure. He sat for a while on the
toilet, then crept back into bed with the thought that his bowels
still had another three hours in which to perform. He had no
idea how he was going to fall asleep again. At five his alarm
went off.

On days after such nights he would have preferred not to have
to straighten up entirely for a single second. He would much
rather have associated with animals than with humans. It made
him feel good just to go into the empty stable and be glad that
he kept troughs and gutters in good running order. It would
have been even nicer to walk between cows and run his hand
along their warm, solid necks. He didn't seriously regret that
his brother had taken the fields and he the farm buildings. He
had never wanted to be a farmer. But on such days he felt drawn
to the stable. On such days he responded with special warmth to
the morning greetings of his dog Tell. And Dorle the cat was
allowed to lie on his lap while he was having breakfast. On days
after such nights he was glad when the business of driving up to
the door, saying good morning, holding the door open, helping
his boss into the car, and driving off was over. Regardless of the
weather, on such days Xaver wore sunglasses as he drove up to
Tettnang-Oberhof to pick up Dr. Gleitze at the Villa Säntis
View.

Even before sitting down at the round kitchen table, Xaver
drove the Mercedes 450 out of the garage. Xaver enjoyed noting
how his 450 made everything about the farm look even smaller.
He didn't mind the inhabitants of Wigratsweiler observing this

contrast. He had driven the car home last night because today he had to pick up not only his boss but also one of the directors, Mr. Trummel, who lived at Lake Deger, a few hills beyond Wigratsweiler. Xaver parked the car between the house and the former manure pile, of which only the container remained, an empty, open concrete box.

After breakfast Xaver made one last trip to the toilet, although he already knew that the laxative hadn't yet taken effect. He stayed longer than necessary and flushed the toilet so Agnes wouldn't bother him with questions. Then he picked up his overnight bag, kissed Agnes on the neck, and got into the car. "Say hello to the kids!" His lips quickly formed a kiss that he tossed into the air with a jerk of his head. Then he turned down onto the village street and drove up over the ridge and down the other side between the blossoming meadows, toward Lake Deger.

Xaver enjoyed the sound made by the big tires as the car moved slowly along the unpaved road. A good wheel sings, someone had said on Saturday in that Western about the Mormons. Every now and again a stone was flicked aside by the edge of a tire with a high ringing sound. The stones that came directly under the tires and were thus pressed into the tread contributed a murmuring sound as a kind of continuo. And the tall drooping May grass brushed against the car's metal flanks on both sides, producing a kind of swishing, chirping sound. As he drove, Xaver pulled a long blade of grass out of its shaft, put the whitish-green end into his mouth, and sucked and chewed the sweetness out of it. Odd, how bare and empty the hop poles and wires look in their lush Maytime surroundings.

By the time Xaver had turned the car, Mr. Trummel was already coming down the long flight of steps from his villa, which stood high and isolated on the slope above Lake Deger. He acknowledged Xaver with a smile—i.e., his moustache moved enough to reveal his teeth. Trummel was also wearing sunglasses. He always wore them. They had round lenses and an old-fashioned-looking gold frame. He immediately opened his attaché case and began to study some papers.

Xaver had instructions not to drive up to the house in Tettnang-Oberhof but merely to pick up Dr. Gleitze's luggage. Aloisia handed him the suitcase; she would bring the coat, umbrella, and hat to the car herself. Xaver walked over to the studio. It was a cottage at the edge of the property, overgrown on three sides with a pelt of shrubs and wild vines. The fourth side, facing south, was of wood and glass. Xaver usually had to fetch the boss from this studio. And he was always already at work. It was only when he came for him before six in the morning that he had to pick him up at the house. When Mrs. Gleitze came along or he had to pick her up alone, he was told to open the garden gate and drive right up to the front door. She had explained to him why. He mustn't think she was too lazy to walk from the house to the street! It was just that she didn't like getting into a car in front of other people. Perhaps because she was so tall. For a long time she'd had the feeling that, when she was getting into a car, every passerby was looking up her skirt. She was almost a head taller than her husband. Xaver had not believed her explanation, but he was pleased she had given it to him. She seemed to dislike physical movement. Quite often she would call him away from painting a fence, pruning the roses, digging over the soil, or trimming a hedge, to come into the house or onto the terrace to hand her something that, though not within her reach, wasn't more than ten or twelve feet beyond it. She would point to the cigarette lighter or book and say: "Would you mind, Xaver, handing me that book over there, please?" And the way she said "over there" conveyed how far that spot, less than ten feet away, appeared to her. Xaver felt that her general helpfulness was also associated with her reluctance to move. She was forever organizing good deeds and helpful actions. What this meant was that she was forever making someone do something for someone else. Whatever she could do from her chair or just sitting down, by giving instructions or making phone calls, she would do. On every trip she encouraged Xaver please to take advantage of the trip for himself, for his wife and the children. She would make detailed suggestions about gifts he could take home from Salzburg or Basel or Strasbourg for Agnes and the girls. She didn't mind one bit if the impression arose that this trip to Salzburg or Basel or Strasbourg was being made less for his employers' benefit than for Xaver's.

Aloisia simply said: "She's so lazy it stinks." Xaver said: "You can't put it like that, it's not as simple as all that."

In Markdorf, just beyond the intersection, Mr. Ruckhaberle, the engineer, stood waiting. Ruckhaberle lifted his attaché case into the trunk of the Mercedes as if it weighed a ton, said a sleepy good morning, sat down beside Xaver, and was asleep before they reached Stockach. Xaver admired the plump, flaxen-haired giant. Scarcely thirty, and flops down and falls asleep. Ruckhaberle woke up two or three times, asking "Where are we?"; Xaver would answer and Ruckhaberle would let his head fall forward again, and go on sleeping. Quite often he would even snore. The other men noticed it, too. With disapproval. Ought Xaver to nudge the fellow? Was that permitted? So long as he doesn't start farting, too, Xaver thought. That was really the worst, when one of his passengers let out a smell and all the others thought it was Xaver. Xaver anxiously observed the men behind him.

Actually they both have children's faces, thought Xaver. Trummel's roundish face, framed by long, straight dark hair, looked like that of an ageless girl. After Trummel had been with the company for five years, a huge puppet representing him was carried along in the Markdorf Carnival procession; the banner stretched across the float bore the words: MONA LISA WITH GALLSTONES.

Today they were taking the alternate route to the autobahn,

along highways 14 and 27. Xaver could never drive up the hill
out of Stockach without looking for his boss in the rearview
mirror. The first time he had driven up this hill, the boss had
said from the backseat: "Schorsch always got to the top without
shifting down." Xaver was startled. Got to the top! That sounded as if Xaver couldn't manage something that Schorsch had
managed. Actually he had wanted to say something about
torque, r.p.m., and performance, and that Schorsch had been a
fool not to shift down here; he, personally, always tried to spare
the engine as much as possible and to shift when the gear the car
happened to be in no longer produced the necessary r.p.m. for
the required performance. But he couldn't say a word. He had
shifted up again a little too soon. That had made him feel as if he
were admitting an error. Should he try to justify himself? That
would have meant saying something against Schorsch, who had
just been transferred to the warehouse because of a couple of
beers. Since then, Xaver had never driven up this hill without
watching Dr. Gleitze in the rearview mirror. Usually Dr.
Gleitze was wearing his headset or reading or sleeping. He'd
forgotten all about it. By now they had been driving for years
with automatic transmission, and that also shifted down on this
hill. Xaver would have liked to point out to the boss that the
automatic transmission reacted exactly as Xaver always had.
Surely that must convey something to the boss, who had a doc-
torate in engineering science.

Suddenly the two men in the back of the car started to laugh.
Since Xaver hadn't been trying to listen in on their conversation, he didn't know why they were laughing. It was more of a
snicker than a laugh. The high whinnying snicker of the two
men got on Xaver's nerves. As soon as the men had started to
snicker, Xaver felt he must restrain himself. That was by this
time second nature. It was the first thing one learned on this
job, to keep one's face under control. When the employers tell
jokes, not to join in the laughter. When they are bogged down

in problems, not to look worried. But also to be careful not to have a sudden thought that might prompt a grin. As for this snickering, he felt quite defenseless. He had the sensation of falling. He could feel nausea rising from his stomach and settling somewhere between stomach and palate. Let's hope to God nothing else happens now, thought Xaver.

Rounding the curve that leads sharply down through the forest into Tuttlingen, he was reminded of that morning of April 17 thirteen years ago. Since until the moment they reached this curve the roads had been completely dry and free of snow, he had been driving at normal speed. On reaching the curve—it had been six-thirty A.M. and they were driving to Göttingen—he suddenly saw that the entire surface of the road was snow-white with frost or a combination of ice and frost. There had been no time to think. The car was already skidding. Xaver had taken his feet off the pedals. He barely touched the steering wheel, as if it were a hot potato. The car had responded to his turn to the left but not the one to the right that immediately followed. They skidded straight through the white right curve. It was only when they seemed about to fly into the ditch and smash against the trees that Xaver could feel firm ground under the tires again; he turned a little more sharply toward the right and stepped lightly on the brake. It was no more than a hint of braking. They had made it.

The boss, who had been fully aware of all that was happening, told Xaver to stop at the next parking bay. Xaver was told to get out. Walking closely side by side, they paced up and down the parking bay; the streamers of their breath intermingled; they walked almost as close together as they had on that spring evening two years later on the suburban street in Frankfurt; from time to time Dr. Gleitze even grasped Xaver's arm. They were almost running—or rather, the boss was almost running—from excitement; and Xaver had to keep up with him, though he felt more like collapsing. It felt as if he didn't have a single drop of blood left in his body.

Dr. Gleitze explained to Xaver that, although he was an engineer, he could never travel by plane. There was no need to go into all the reasons right now, but this much he could say: that he fully intended to see out the century. And for the following reason: he had decided to attend every performance of a Mozart opera to be staged during the second half of the century in any leading opera house in Europe because he intended to write a book on the principal performances. The electrical circuits he had constructed in his youth had been so advanced compared to all the competitive designs that, due also to his brother Friedhelm's universal technical competence, he could now run the Gleitze works with his left hand only. His right hand belonged to the history of Mozart operas in the second half of the twentieth century. He felt this was a task that no one but himself could carry out, so it was up to him to do it. Even to someone who knew nothing about Mozart's operas, surely it must be obvious that the essential condition for the achievement of his labors was to cross over the threshold of the century while still alive. One year after that—at age seventy-six—he would have completed his work and presented it to the public. He was sure Xaver would understand that under such circumstances a chauffeur bore a unique responsibility. So a situation such as the one just before the curve must never occur again. This must be clearly understood: never, never, never again. Perhaps it had not been possible to foresee that slithery white spot. On the other hand, on his, Dr. Gleitze's instructions, Xaver had been picked from the garage workshop just because what Köberle, the foreman, had been able to find out and tell him about Xaver had sufficed to convince him, even without knowing Xaver, of his absolute reliability. Because Xaver neither drank nor smoked. Because he had once been German champion in small-bore shooting. Not that he wanted to boast about Xaver's championship, but because he, Dr. Gleitze, knew that in no other sport did character play such a crucial role as it did in shooting. To be a champion in that meant having a champion character. And that was the very thing he had learned to appreciate in Xaver. His wholesome, natural, open, unspoiled quality. Xaver's calmness. His poise. His alert but never rash behavior. An incident such as the one on the icy curve could result in either immediate dismissal or a lifetime pact. "I noticed how gently and tactfully you responded to the lethal challenge of that icy curve. I would like to make a pact with you for many years to come. You have my confidence."

Finally Dr. Gleitze had actually stopped in front of Xaver and, as was his way, looked at him with his face thrust too far forward and turned slightly to one side. He never looked anyone straight in the face. He always turned his face a little bit away, so that he seemed to be looking past one. But then he would turn his eyes toward one. And since he would often not only turn his head as if to look past one but also bend or rather lower it, he would end by looking up at one at an angle. Up and across. With lowered head. Sometimes it looked as if he were trying to shake water out of his right ear.

Dr. Gleitze had offered Xaver one of his soft hands, which always seemed to be drowning a bit in his shirt sleeves. To Xaver it felt like being sworn in. There was nothing for him to say. First a near-accident, then this scene. More than anything else Xaver wanted to say that Master Köberle had obviously reported incorrectly. Although Xaver had been a member of the rifle club and had participated three times in regional championships, he had never been German champion. His brother Jakob, reported missing in Karelia—he was the one who in 1941 had taken part in the national championships in Berlin; it was he who had narrowly missed becoming national champion. But at the end they found only fifty-nine shots on his targets, and on the one beside it sixty-one. His competitor had his worst shot deducted, while Jakob's worst shot was added to his own score. So much for the championship, sir! But he couldn't get it out. Not even later. Never. He had always wanted to rectify this mistake. But it was never the right moment.

Mr. Trummel handed the boss a document and, while the boss was reading it, Trummel read what appeared to be a carbon copy. Xaver could hear that it concerned someone in alarm-systems sales with whom the director of sales, Mr. Trummel, was no longer satisfied. Since a cousin of Xaver's was working in alarm systems, a cousin, in fact, who had already been causing the family some concern, Xaver tried to overhear whether the employee in question might not indeed be his cousin Konrad. Dr. Gleitze interrupted his reading to ask Trummel about the wife of the man the document was about. Trummel's reply: "She must be quite a woman if she can get that nonstarter to do anything." Dr. Gleitze nodded, went on reading. Trummel added: "I just wanted to point up his general attitude." After silently reading a few more lines he made sure by a sidelong glance that the boss had reached the crucial spot, and said: "And anyway, what kind of a fool does he take me for?"

Xaver was now almost certain they were discussing Konrad. Dr. Gleitze finished reading and said: "A very generous report."

"Well, I agreed with your brother," replied Trummel, "that we shouldn't go all out right now."

Dr. Gleitze: "Quite right! Either he gets the message or . . ."

Because of an oncoming truck Xaver managed to pick up only the end of Gleitze's sentence: ". . . we'll just have to come down a bit harder on him in July at the latest."

Trummel: "Good and hard. Either he'll break down completely or he'll toe the line. I gave him a good grilling. You know, he has never yet taken his area chart home over the weekend."

Dr. Gleitze had a softer voice than Trummel, and Xaver understood only the words "sample delivery slip."

Trummel: "If he used his head and tried to get organized he could save himself a lot of work. I tried to explain that to him too, but he spends all his evenings at the tavern and simply shuts out the world."

Konrad, who else!

"If he'd only give it half an hour's thought, the next day he would . . ." A truck. Xaver could see only the boss in his mirror: "That's typical, doesn't do a stroke and is already off on another vacation."

Trummel: "He claims his car was totaled there. But then from Friday to Saturday, off to Isny, putting it down as a business trip. That's when I had him on the mat."

Dr. Gleitze: "A pretty sloppy attitude."

Trummel: "Anyone can make a mistake, but with Ehrle— the very sight of the fellow makes me retch."

Although Xaver had been pretty sure they were talking about his cousin, the name now cut like a dagger into his guts. His mother's maiden name, spat out contemptuously from the lipless mouth of Mr. Trummel. He saw Dr. Gleitze nod and hand back the document. Trummel then supplied the boss with a new sheet of paper. This time it seemed to be a technical drawing. In preparation for the meeting in Düsseldorf.

So, down to Efrizweiler as soon as possible, to warn Konrad. He hoped neither of the men knew that Konrad was Xaver's cousin. But if he were to tell Konrad exactly what he had just heard, Konrad would simply laugh and make some boastful crack. Xaver and his slave nature! The old scaredy-cat! The typical Get-going-now who sits up and begs when commanded! That's the way Konrad talked, especially if there was a woman around. When he was alone with Xaver he didn't sound off quite as much. So he must be sure there was no woman around when he told Konrad about the conversation between Trummel and Gleitze. In the presence of a woman Konrad could be relied upon to react in a way least likely to do him any good. But even if Xaver were alone with Konrad and passed on the remarks he had just heard, Konrad would react with boastful counter-phrases, as if he could well afford them. He always behaved as though he were on an equal footing with everybody. As if no one had any power over him. He was constantly playing up his inde-pendence, that of a man who can afford to do anything. No one can push me around! That was one of his stock phrases. Or: We'll have to see about *that!* Or: Not to me, they can't! Or: Looks as if I'll have to straighten those guys out! What the hell's this s'posed to mean? Now I've seen everything! Would you believe it? That'd be a nice mess! That'd make fools of the experts! I'll show them a thing or two! He had a seemingly inex-haustible supply of such belligerent clichés. The veins in his neck would swell when he became belligerent, the sweat stand out on his temples. His clichés seemed to put a strain on him.

Xaver would have to tone down what he had heard. A tenth of it was probably more than Konrad could stomach. Konrad still smoked forty cigarettes a day and had five kids. He had first trained as a landscape gardener. Then he had been with the para-troopers. Then he had grown his moustache and sideburns and joined an insurance company. Since then, whenever he came to Wigratsweiler he always stopped first at the Happy Prospect and asked Margot to phone across to say Konrad was there. In the days when Konrad had still been selling insurance, Xaver had once spent his vacation driving him around the uplands. That had been a typical Konrad idea, to pass himself off as a regional agent complete with chauffeur. Even when they went to a tavern in the evening, they would still call each other Mis-ter; and when Konrad entered a place even for the first time he would promptly sit down at the table reserved for regulars. He could strike up a conversation with anybody. A visit to him at his home in Efrizweiler was immediately taken as an excuse to go to the tavern. His wife would call out after him, admonishing, pleading, imploring, as long as they were within earshot. Konrad would only answer Yes-yes-yes-yeeees.

In the taverns he always drank more than anyone else who happened at that moment to be present. He couldn't have borne not to be the one who drank the most and talked the most and the loudest. Everything he said was obviously intended as self-glorification. As far as Xaver could see, Konrad's uninhibited self-glorification didn't actually glorify him at all. Instead, Konrad seemed to him more of a desperate man, if only because he sweated so fast and so visibly. Xaver never drank alcohol in taverns. So, cold sober, he had had to watch Konrad become increasingly noisy and incoherent. It embarrassed Xaver that, on that drive through the uplands, Konrad had repeated the same stories over and over again in every tavern. The repetition made everything he said sound less true. Xaver would have liked to tell Konrad he needn't mind on his account. He fully understood that Konrad couldn't come up with something new every evening. Konrad Ehrle, the Saint George of the insurance business! At the time, that was Konrad's set piece.

Every other insurance salesman was a low-down, work-shy, self-serving louse of an agent out to exploit the ignorance of simple folk who hadn't yet been sucked up to by the insurance business. Not so Konrad Ehrle! And every insurance company was nothing but a supermodern, mathematically-logistically-mechanically equipped defrauding company. Not so the company that Konrad represented! But even it wants to make a profit. And it is to prevent even this that Konrad Ehrle has entered the fray. "I'm here to save you money," he always told his listeners. Quite often there were men among them with whom he had signed policies earlier in the day. He always made a point of inviting them for a drink. "Never let it be said," he would say, "that I failed to buy a drink for a customer." If they really wanted to know, he wouldn't be carrying off a single pitiful penny from this village. On the contrary. Would all those who are old customers of his company please stand up? Let them confirm what he has done for them today! Reducing premiums! What else! In the face of spiraling medical and hospital costs, Konrad Ehrle is driving through villages and towns to clean up the mess left behind by those wicked agents who had come this way. Additional insurance for kids! When kids are only put into the children's wards anyway! And foreign-travel insurance for people whose only travel is an annual visit to Aunt Berta somewhere in the next county! Of course—and this is just where the problem starts—now that the chief surgeon has to hand over 60 rather than 30 percent to the hospital, he is charging whatever maximum the fee scale for doctors will allow. He's entitled to charge anywhere between the minimum and ten times the minimum, fellas! In the hospital! The doctor on the outside can only go as high as six times. So five thousand for a perforated appendix isn't out of the way these days, fellas! And that's more than the national health service can cough up, fellas! That's why additional insurance is actually not a bad idea, fellas! Just in case a person would rather be operated on by the chief surgeon than by the janitor. His insurance company pays out over two million marks every day! It's all a matter of bigness. Bigness is the advantage, fellas! Just bigness. If you roll dice a hundred times, you'll win fifty times. If you roll two hundred times, you won't win a hundred times but only sixty to seventy times, that's insurance math, fellas! So: the more shoulders, the less burden for the individual, to put it in simple terms. So much for the insurance business, fellas! Once you know these things, you understand it all much better. And the fact that he is working *for* people rather than against them—well, the best proof of that is his annual statement. Here, he'll put it on the table, anyone's welcome to read it who can read—here, premium increase as against reduced premiums: a trade-off. So no success. The higher-ups are querying that, and no wonder. But he doesn't mind

telling them off. In the long run his method will pay off. The
uplands are bound to gain confidence in him. And through him
in his company! And isn't confidence everything? He still has a
hard struggle ahead. The company supervisor is practically
looking over his shoulder. In four weeks at most the supervisor'll turn up here waving the policies around and point for
point saying the exact opposite of what he, Konrad Ehrle, is
now saying. Then it's up to you, fellas! What usually happens is
that the good folks cave in and let themselves be bamboozled yet
again by the supervisor. Serve 'em right. So they can go on paying through the nose. That's fine with him. If folks are that
dumb! All he can say is, anyone who caves in has only himself to
blame, there's nothing more he can do to help him. If those guys
want to kiss the supervisor's ass, go ahead! In this corner, Konrad Ehrle, in that corner the supervisor. Take your pick!

Oh, Cousin Konrad! thought Xaver. It looked as if he had
wrecked his car again. Konrad didn't dare have a drink at home.
With Xaver it was the other way around. Since on the basis of
Köberle's flattering report his boss took him for a teetotaler, he
never risked having any alcohol in a restaurant. The likelihood
of Dr. Gleitze's coming into a place where Xaver would be having a beer or a glass of wine was slight. But he might find out
about it. There are inconceivable coincidences, everyone knows
that. When Konrad started working for Gleitze, he stopped
drinking. He had even taken over the coaching of the company's
junior soccer team. He used to play the game himself, in Bibe-
rach and Ulm. Suddenly he was no longer allowed to coach.
Whether he started drinking again and for that reason was no
longer allowed to coach, or whether he was no longer allowed to
coach and for that reason started drinking again, was something
Xaver never found out. Genesis unclear, thought Xaver. He
happened to feel like using the word *genesis*. It was one of the
exotic words that Konrad often used in his drunken tirades, invariably explaining it. The genesis of the disease was what Kon-

rad had always said, that's what counts. If you can't lay your hand on the genesis, no doctor can help you. The genesis, fellas, look for the genesis! In all of Konrad's alcoholic harangues there was also something about alcoholism being caused 90 percent by the environment and only 5 percent by heredity. Konrad never said for what cause the remaining 5 percent was reserved, if 90 percent belonged to environment and 5 percent to heredity. And never yet had any of his listeners in the taverns asked about that last 5 percent. Konrad usually ended up expounding on his own gift for psychology. It was none of *his* doing, he just happened to have this gift. And it was the luck of the draw, he'd say, that this gift for psychology he had was the determining factor in his profession. Konrad was a true Ehrle.

As Xaver drove through the railway underpass beyond Tuttlingen, he was suddenly afraid he wouldn't have enough willpower to turn the steering wheel as sharply to the right as was required by the curve that came right after the underpass. He was a bit disappointed to find that he managed the curve, as always, quite correctly. How many such underpasses were there between Stockach and Stuttgart? Crashing, getting stuck in the hedge, wheels spinning: these were images better suited to the steady dull pressure in his stomach than flowing, adroit, invariably successful movements. He wasn't driving Dr. Gleitze, Mr. Trummel, and Mr. Ruckhaberle, he was driving his stomachache. Now he could have used a toilet.

Before reaching Rottweil he swung off the highway, taking the shortcut via Wellendingen so as to pick up federal highway 27 in Schömberg. This was in defiance of Dr. Gleitze's principle: the better road takes priority over the shorter. But knowing that he would now have his fluctuating bowel pressure all the way to Düsseldorf, he wanted to speed up the journey as discreetly as possible. Privately, he called this fluctuating pressure his labor pains. But he mustn't encourage these labor pains, he must suppress them. From now until Düsseldorf he would be solely preoccupied with his bowels. It would be a struggle. To throttle his bowels back entirely would be too painful. To yield by even a fraction would mean losing control over them.

It had been like that even in his schooldays. He had had a teacher who believed that students didn't really have to leave the room. They only asked to leave, the teacher would say, in order to skip five minutes of class. Digestive processes were something that should be attended to before coming to school. We do Number Two at home, he would say. Number One in school: for that no more than a minute was required. Please may I leave the room? Xaver had envied any boy who had dared stand up and pronounce those words, since it meant standing up and asking for permission to skip five minutes of class. Xaver had never dared speak up. So he sat on what he hadn't been able to hold back. This meant that at recess he couldn't jump up and run outside with the others. Pressing his buttocks together he had to walk stiff-legged out of the room so as not to lose his feces on the way. The teacher would already be standing impatiently by his desk, calling: "Come on, Xaver, outside, fresh air!" "Yes, sir," Xaver would say, pretending to look for something in his satchel.

"Travel irregularity" was what Dr. Meichle called Xaver's complaint. "We all suffer from constipation when we travel," said Dr. Meichle. Xaver felt that the doctor had forgotten he was talking to a professional driver, in other words to someone almost constantly on the move. On the other hand Xaver was glad that Dr. Meichle had advised against laxatives. "It's a matter of attitude," Dr. Meichle had said. "And training. Think kindly of your bowels. There are exceptions, of course. But don't get used to external aids, that's the last thing you should do." For years Xaver had been waiting for Dr. Gleitze to say just once: Stop the next chance you get, please—I need to go behind a tree. Not once had Dr. Gleitze said any such thing. He never seemed to need to relieve himself in any way. In Xaver's eyes that made him an object of admiration. The result was, of course, that Xaver couldn't bring up the subject himself and say: I have to get out for a moment, sir. He was quite sure that Dr. Gleitze would say exactly what the teacher said, that Number Two should be attended to before coming to work.

Only Mrs. Gleitze spoke frequently and freely in the morning of her digestion. When she came along on an extended trip, it always seemed to occur to her after about an hour how pleasant it was to be sitting like this in a car and to know that she'd already been to the toilet that day. Her ability to come out with it might have been due to her Viennese dialect. She spoke with such a broad accent that Xaver felt she must be putting it on. She took, so she always said, bran soaked in water. The way she said *bra-an* actually made the adjective *soaked* superfluous. It was the only thing that worked with her, she would say. If she took bran soaked in water, she said, her digestion worked perfectly. Nothing else did a thing for her. But that worked, bran soaked in water. It did the trick. Bran soaked in water didn't taste very nice, but an effortless bowel movement was more important to her. It had occasionally crossed Xaver's mind that she might have been asked by Dr. Meichle to bring up the topic of constipation and bowel movements in the car. After all, Dr. Meichle maintained that Xaver didn't have the correct attitude toward his digestion. Perhaps Mrs. Gleitze was supposed to have some influence there. But then he realized that it was a kind of megalomania on his part to think that, when Dr. Meichle and Mrs. Gleitze met on the tennis court or at the Inselhotel in Konstanz or while skiing in Davos, they could think of nothing better to talk about than Xaver Zürn, and in particular about Xaver Zürn's digestion. So don't get carried away, okay?

Now as they drove through the lonely forests of the secondary road he was aware that he had turned off highway 14 because with every second this gently rolling, lonely stretch offered him an opportunity to relieve himself. How he loved the sound of that word! But he couldn't imagine himself stopping at this point, asking the gentlemen if they'd mind waiting five minutes, disappearing into the forest, and leaving behind a boss and a type like Trummel who would sit there discussing Xaver's bowel movement, imagining him . . . Horrible. He might have said it, if at all, when driving alone with Dr. Gleitze. But even that was unimaginable. Dr. Gleitze was too refined a person. And too pure. A very mild man, and sensitive, somehow. Trummel, on the other hand, seemed tough. In spite of the girlish face framed by that hair. That flesh might just as well be stone. Everything one heard about him was intimidating. Through the sunglasses, which he never took off, one saw oneself being looked at by a reptile. In spite of that, Trummel, too, seemed mild. Mild but tough. One always thinks, Now he's going to smile, and then he doesn't.

Last week, on the way back from Vienna, Dr. Gleitze had for once looked angry. And talked louder than ever before. Mrs. Gleitze had given her answers in a pointedly lowered voice; this meant that Xaver wasn't supposed to catch what she was saying. Since Dr. Gleitze spoke without such precautions, Xaver naturally took his side immediately. He even felt that, because Dr. Gleitze was speaking so loudly and uninhibitedly, he was being called as a witness to what his boss was saying. Xaver really had to restrain himself from nodding at each of his boss's sentences. It seemed that Mrs. Gleitze's father had once been a high-ranking judge and was now living in retirement in Vienna; but, in Mrs. Gleitze's opinion, her father and mother couldn't live on that pension: not as befitted their situation. Dr. Gleitze didn't mind letting her parents have some money as often as they needed it, but he didn't want that to be regarded as an obligation. Surely she must have realized long ago, he told his wife, that he would give whatever was asked of him provided there was no attempt to force him, to blackmail him. "Don't ever say that again!" she said in a low, sharp tone. He *would* say it again, said the boss. And he did: blackmail. Quite apart from that, he thought it was rather odd of his wife to maintain that her parents couldn't live on their pension as befitted their station. Surely even she couldn't expect her father to receive a bonus for every death sentence he had rendered for the benefit of the old regime! Well, she said in a venomous whisper, at least her father hadn't been one of Hitler's *commis voyageurs*. Whereupon he had snatched up his headset. Not another word all the way to the Villa Säntis View in Tettnang-Oberhof. She looked out the window as if profoundly interested in the steaming countryside around Lake Chiem.

After Heidelberg, Xaver's battle with his bowels became a battle with a wild beast. It became a battle of wits. A battle in which everything depended on there being no victor. Once again he swore to himself never to take another laxative. He'd rather have his stool petrify. His bowels were now assaulting him with piercing cramps. All the way up his spine into his brain, a biting, searing pain. There was no way he could fight that. All he could do was try not to capitulate outright to this pain. But any attempt to fight the pain would only increase it. And the slightest yielding might lead to disaster. Xaver had read descriptions of battles during the Peasants' War. Whenever the horde of peasants yielded a mere fraction at only one point, the enemy forces always became imbued with such a sensation of power that they would actually intensify the pressure quite disproportionately, and the horde that had yielded a mere fraction at a single point would be swept away in headlong flight and usually wiped out.

Fortunately he had had some experience. It wasn't the first time he'd taken a laxative that started working at the wrong moment. Those manufacturers should all be blown sky high. You must hold on. You must. You will. You won't let the dragon out of its lair. Not by so much as a fraction. But neither will you drive it back too brutally. That would only make it want to

break out more fiercely than ever. You must achieve a stalemate. Pressure and counterpressure. An immobilized pain. Although you don't know how you're going to do this, you must
manage it. It is a thousand times stronger than you are. It won't
permit any stalemate, any immobilization. The moment you
cease your counterpressure, it will swing back its giant fist and
attack you out of your innermost self. Then you must instantly
check it. Even if that intensifies the pain to the point of its becoming unbearable. Think of Jesus Christ. This afternoon you
will be granted deliverance.

At the sight of the first industrial plants showing up left and
right of the autobahn, Xaver felt better. The maze of steel pip-
ing of the chemical factories looked like a blown-up picture of
his intestinal scenario. When at last at last at last he watched the
two bosses, followed by the young engineer, disappear into the
Savoy in Düsseldorf and wasn't allowed to enter the public
building with its hundred toilets because there was nowhere to
park and he wasn't staying at this hotel, he wanted to give a
great howl like some creature at death's door. He had to find a
place to park. But don't step too hard on the gas. He drove off
toward the station. At six he was to pick the men up again; the
night was to be spent in Cologne. In every city, the railway stations were his salvation. Nowhere else can a man rely so absolutely on being decently received when Nature calls as in
German railway stations. It always infuriated Xaver when some
industry-oriented group lashed out on TV against the deficit of
the Federal Railway. If only because of its public and almost
always spotless toilets, he was happy to concede however many
billions of marks were required by the Federal Railway. In the
best hotel as well as in the most remote railway station, he always covered the edge of the seat with toilet paper. Then when
he was free to let the dark snake spiral down into the white
bowl, his triumph was complete. He whistled as he walked
through Düsseldorf station. If an inner voice hadn't at the last

moment said no, he would have hurried straight to one of the kiosks and bought something. Cufflinks. Or better still, a knife. Although he already had one. In the glove compartment. And five at home. Daggers, stilettos, switchblades.

More and more often he was having to resist the impulse to buy a knife. Sometimes he succumbed to the temptation. He made a little skip. Because he knew he didn't look like someone who skips, his skipping was more internal. He didn't leave the ground. But he whistled. He felt an urge to yodel. He was happy that his car was such a nice shade of pale green. He was proud of his car. He felt as if everyone must notice that he was in Düsseldorf. He took it for granted that they all regarded the Mercedes 450 SEL as his car. Not that he felt it essential to be taken for the owner. But everybody could see that this was his car. And it was his car. Whose car was it, then, if not his? To whom did this car respond, then, if not to him? To whom, if not to him, was this machine accustomed? It was his, his, his car! And it was *the* best car in the world. To doubt this was to understand nothing about cars. He felt happy. Düsseldorf! And it was May!

After finding a parking spot near Breite-Strasse, he picked up his briefcase and walked along Königsallee looking for an empty chair beside the torpid water. From his lunchbox he took the bread Agnes had baked from the flour she had ground from the wheat they had picked up from his brother-in-law's farm in Schmalegg. With it he drank some of the herbal tea Agnes had made from yarrow and balm mint. An old man holding his hat on his knee said to Xaver: "Today the chestnuts are coming into bloom." Xaver nodded. "And the plane trees have their leaves," said the man. Xaver nodded more vigorously and made a face intended to express admiration for what Nature had to offer in the heart of Düsseldorf. "The pink hawthorn is the last," said the old man. "When the pink hawthorn is in bloom, the best time is over." Xaver suddenly felt such pity for the old man that he couldn't go on eating. Couldn't they at least have moved the old people out into the country? Surely they had stood it long enough in the city!

He could almost have run to the mayor and yelled right into his face, for Chrissake.

Just before six he was in the lobby of the hotel. Right behind him a rack of dresses was being pushed into the lobby. A man followed with an armful of skirts on hangers. A young woman in a long skirt and fur jacket, all dressed up for the opera, was walking with her husband from the elevator to the exit. At each step her foot turned over slightly. Then when she tried to hurry across the street outside, her foot turned over sharply at each step. From an open telephone booth a man's loud voice could be heard: "It's a matter of details now, whether the carload's going to Prague, or some such thing." When he had finished, the man went to the counter, tossed down a coin, said "Thank you," and hurried outside. These are the things you miss when you walk up the slope in the evening through the berry patch. Suddenly the contentment that at home often welled up in him for a few seconds among his currant bushes seemed terrible. I can be glad, he thought, that I'm in Düsseldorf, experiencing all this. Involuntarily he thought of Mrs. Gleitze, who was always hinting at how grateful Xaver should be for getting around so much.

At six-fifteen Trummel emerged from the restaurant to say they weren't ready yet. Xaver followed Trummel into the restaurant, where everything was done up in tobacco-brown leather. Only one table was occupied. In the farthest corner. Without looking back again, Trummel walked to that table. Three other men were sitting there with Dr. Gleitze and Mr. Ruckhaberle. Xaver sat down at the first convenient table by the door and ordered some mineral water from the waiter. At first he looked fixedly across at the other table. Somehow he wanted to wave to Dr. Gleitze or at least nod to him. After all, they hadn't seen each other for several hours. And they were far from home, too. Xaver had driven the car from Wigratsweiler via Lake Deger, Tettnang-Oberhof, Markdorf, highways 14 and 27, and various autobahns to Düsseldorf. Of course, anyone else would have done the same, obviously. How typical—there he was expecting the boss to interrupt the discussions for whose sake they had driven all this way, to embrace him, the chauffeur. Agnes was right, he craved recognition.

He always admired Agnes when he watched her at work in the garden or the vegetable patch or in the house. How she would kneel down by the sink to clean out the last traces of dirt from some almost inaccessible corner. When she went to get parsley from the garden, she would make use of the trip to remove a withered twig from a rosebush and to bring in a candle left behind by Julia on a windowsill. She did everything because it seemed necessary to her, because she felt it had to be done. Every one of her movements was work. She appeared to be totally independent of praise or recognition. There must be something in work itself that rewarded her. And the work was not inconsiderable. The fields had gone to Georg, of course, who was married and living in Nitzenweiler, but they had kept the slope behind the barn, with its forty apple trees, ten pear trees, eight cherry trees, and countless plum, mirabelle, and greengage trees. And a berry patch extending from the bottom of the slope to the top. And bordering the driveway down to the road, their flower and vegetable gardens. Xaver helped as often as he could, but she did most of the work. Magdalena and Julia hated working in the garden even more than in the house. Agnes demanded practically nothing of the children. "They're going to school," Agnes would say. "That's work too." After supper she even worked away at the girls' math problems. To everyone's amazement, she was always able to help. When Xaver went off with Julia into the front room to watch TV, she would stay behind at the round kitchen table and do math problems. She, who had never gone to high school, wanted to be able to keep pace with her daughters in math until they graduated. But this mathematical zeal of hers had only developed when it turned out that Magdalena's and Julia's school careers might be threatened by mathematics and subsequently by chemistry and physics. "We'll see about that," Agnes had said, and had never stopped saying it since. But in this, too, the last thing she was looking for was recognition. She attributed everything she achieved to common sense. The extent of Agnes's selflessness was always a mystery to Xaver. The only thing she wanted to be praised for was her cooking. If she wasn't praised once a day at a meal for that meal, she would have no inspiration for the next one, she would say. She claimed not to like cooking.

Xaver was already hoping the waiter would be carrying the ice cream past him into the lobby, but the waiter put it down in front of him, indicating by a gesture that one of the gentlemen at the table in the far corner had ordered the ice cream for Xaver. Xaver looked across. He knew that Dr. Gleitze had sent him the ice cream. He wanted to thank him by a nod. But Dr. Gleitze was engrossed in the discussion. Xaver knew quite well what the boss was implying when he treated him to ice cream. Wherever they went, the boss would invariably order some ice cream for him. This was to convey to Xaver that he appreciated his abstinence from nicotine and alcohol. At least, that was how Xaver interpreted it when he sat waiting in some hotel and the waiter arrived with ice cream from the boss. He would rather have had a beer. Sometimes it infuriated him when that stupid ice cream was set down in front of him as if he were a little child. That ice cream reminded him that the boss thought of him as being opposed to beer. And anyone who hates beer must like this sweet, sticky, colored concoction! Some day—he had decided this long ago—he must disabuse the boss of this false conclusion. But as long as the opportunity didn't arise, he had to put on a grateful expression and spoon up the stuff. As if a glass of beer could have impaired his driving efficiency! The boss is an asshole, he thought, and ate enough of the ice cream so that the boss, when he looked across, would think Xaver had eaten it all.

The gentlemen formed a group of six at the table in the far corner. An old headwaiter and two waiters were looking after them. Xaver thought the three other men must be Spanish. One of them spoke German the way Xaver had heard refugees speak it. His wife was Prussian, he said, from Gleiwitz. "What do you mean, Prussian?" asked Mr. Ruckhaberle. The Spanish gentleman: "Gleiwitz is in Prussia." Suddenly it became quite dark in the brown room, no doubt because outside the sun had disappeared. It seemed to Xaver that the room had suddenly become much larger through this sudden darkening. He felt much farther away from the six gentlemen in the corner. The headwaiter took away the salad that belonged to the Spanish gentleman who spoke German. "Would you prefer some other kind of dressing?" asked the waiter. "I know people from Spain don't like cream dressings." Aha, thought Xaver, and felt a surge of happiness because he had immediately guessed that they were Spanish. And guessed it from the sound of their speech. That proved to him once again that he had done the right thing in taking up English and French. Without that training he would never have recognized them as being Spanish.

The headwaiter handed the salad to one of the waiters: "Take that over and say, French dressing!" The waiter stood there staring. "French dressing!" repeated the headwaiter in some desperation. "*Salsa*," he then said in a resigned voice, shook his head, and remarked to the table at large: "They all understand Italian better than German." Xaver admired the quiet and skillful way the two waiters went about their work although the old headwaiter was continually finding fault with them. Xaver could feel a knot forming in his intestines. Through contraction. He was tempted to call out to the headwaiter not to humiliate his helpers in front of customers. He tried to rub away the knot, which was beginning to hurt a little.

Mr. Ruckhaberle hadn't put aside his papers even during the meal. "We'll soon be through," he said. "Section 2-4 is out," he went on. Xaver gathered that they were discussing the electrical circuits for a garment-manufacturing plant. "Here the conveyor line moves four meters from axle to axle; the question is whether it's feasible in your case—I didn't know where your machine stops." The Spaniard showed him. Ruckhaberle: "No problem. Just a moment." He used his pocket calculator. Next came the circuits for the transverse tipping conveyor. Dr. Gleitze suddenly asked: "Where are we?" Ruckhaberle: "2-5." The headwaiter called out to one of the waiters: "No, no. They already phoned twice yesterday, but they have no hard currency! The Finnish mark is weaker than my grandmother, for God's sake!" Mr. Trummel said: "Here's what we'll do: twenty percent on confirmation of order, then four further payments, twenty percent on start-up—" "Just a moment," said the Spaniard. "Confirmation of order is in effect when we have our import license." Mr. Trummel: "Twenty percent six months after start-up, twenty percent twelve months after start-up—" The Spaniard: "The first thing we have to know from you now is the percentage—we don't pay duty on those." Mr. Trummel went on to explain that payments could only be accepted through one of the Dresdner Bank's correspondents. When the bill was slow in arriving, Trummel said: "That's the limit, that *is* the limit."

Ruckhaberle suddenly came across to Xaver and said: "Come on, come on, we'll barely make the train. Bring the car around." Xaver ran. Drove up. On the way to the station Ruckhaberle didn't speak to Xaver. He still seemed preoccupied with the problems of the Spanish contract. As Xaver drove up to the station, Ruckhaberle looked at his watch and said: "Just made it!"

Xaver enviously watched the knock-kneed engineer hurriedly waddling into the station. He'll be home tomorrow morning, he thought. There's nothing nicer than to come home on an early May morning while the birds are singing. He picked up the two bosses and drove them to the Dom-Hotel in Cologne, then drove on to his hotel, the Drei Kronen. Room 36. He immediately opened the window but noticed that this did nothing to reduce the stale smell. He sat in the little armchair, reluctant to move at all because every movement required deeper breathing, thus making the stale smell in the room even more noticeable. He looked down on his stiffly outstretched legs. It feels good to stare at one spot. But Thursday seemed such a long way off. Thursday.

From outside he heard a voice quietly asking: "So whadidya bring?" And another voice answering just as quietly: "Camping boxes 'n stuff." Xaver was quite sure he had heard that question and that answer once before, in exactly the same words. Also through a hotel window. A year ago? Or how many years ago? But in Münster. In the Rheinischer Hof. But instead of in room 36, in room 37. That was the only difference. And there old roofs crowded outside the window. And the top of a birch tree, which seemed improbable at that height, had been so shaken by the wind that one expected to hear the leaves rattling. And down below in the alleys, impatient motorcyclists had been revving up. And someone had asked: "What did you bring?" And then the answer: "Camping boxes and stuff." If only he could have bet ten marks right then and there! But of course there was no one around who would doubt that he had heard that question and that answer once before. He had never won a bet. Probably there was no one around there because he could now offer a bet that he was sure to win. But how could he prove that he had heard that question and that answer years ago in Münster? There was no way of proving it. No one would accept such a bet. Only when he had bets to offer that he lost—then hands reached out from all sides. Konrad, for example. Konrad won all his bets.

Although he was very quick to bet, giving the impression that he was acting without thought, as soon as the bet was made Konrad would quietly produce his proof.

He felt like calling home now. But he had only been gone since this morning. And in hotels they charge whatever they like for a phone call. Cologne was a long way from home. He would phone tomorrow from Giessen. He got out the book he happened to be reading. *Tortured for Christ* by Richard Wurmbrand, *A Report on the Sufferings and Faith of the Suppressed Church in Countries Behind the Iron Curtain.*

All his life his favorite reading had been tales about persecuted Christians. He read his English and French thrillers mainly so as not entirely to forget the two foreign languages he had worked so hard to learn.

Fortunately there were still some books in the house that had belonged to his brother Johann, killed during the war in Königsberg. Johann had spent seven years in Wurzach. In the cloister school. If it hadn't been for those wonderful school reports left behind by Johann, he'd never have had the nerve to send his kids every day from Wigratsweiler to school in Friedrichshafen. He was now twice as old as Johann had been when he was killed in Königsberg. He still looked up to Johann's rigid photograph face as one looks up to an older brother, although the picture showed a child in a black uniform. In languages Johann had always had straight A's.

Xaver wondered whether a thriller wouldn't appeal to him more now than the tortured Christians in Romania. After all, his mother was no longer alive. How long was he supposed to go on reading books that she would have liked to see in his hands? As soon as he read martyrs' tales he could feel his mother's joyous gaze upon him. In the days when she was still alive, he used to notice that, as he read, she would stop and look up from her work merely to watch him sitting at the round kitchen table reading the legends, and he had been unable to go on reading as long as he felt her gaze upon him. The line his eyes happened to be fixed upon would begin to waver, to flicker. If, in spite of himself, he looked up, he would meet his mother's gaze. He would blush and quickly look down again at the coarse, yellowish paper of those legends. Now he realized that his mother had been inordinately pleased with him whenever he read pious works. Never since then had anyone approved of him as much as his mother had at the sight of him reading those legends. And why had he never been able to endure her gaze for longer than a quarter of a second? Because he was embarrassed by so much approval? Approval, but fear too. He could still see her standing there. He could study her expression at leisure. He could practically hear what she was thinking while she gazed at him. Yes, you're reading the legends, she had thought, and that's the best thing possible for you to do, but it won't help you one bit, you'll never make it, you're to be pitied. Yes, that's how she had gazed at him. Devoid of hope.

He tried to read. The fact that present-day Romanian Christians loved their tormentors to the same excessive degree that his legendary figures had done certainly fascinated him. It made him feel as if his mother were still alive. No, the more distinctly something reminded him of her, the more palpable was the feeling that she was no longer alive. The more alive she was in his imagination, the more acutely he felt that she was dead. Since that time he had never had another attack of tonsillitis. Is that true? Nonsense, of course not. Things go through one's head that are completely untrue. When was that, two or three years ago, also in May, in fact right here in the Drei Kronen, he had picked up quite a nasty cold. In the breakfast room. Too bad the other place no longer existed, where he had been staying regularly for almost ten years. A bit farther down in the old part of town. If only he could remember the name of that hotel! People had known him there. Greeted him. And he had forgotten its name. Here in the Drei Kronen no one greeted him. Here they

let him sit in the draft. The windows facing down toward the
Rhine had been open, as had the front entrance facing the town.
Since the other people having breakfast apparently didn't mind
the draft, he hadn't liked to ask for the door or window to be
closed. So there he had sat with damp hair in the draft. For
weeks he had tried to get rid of that cold. They'd better watch
out, those bastards, if at breakfast time tomorrow door and windows have been left open again! He would slam the door shut
with his own hand! He was fed up with consideration for others,
fed up, fed up! First, ten days of sore throat, then four weeks of
coughing! He could feel a knot forming in his stomach at the
thought of the staff at this hotel who let their guests have breakfast sitting in a terrible draft. One of those peroxide blondes
whose beehive hairdo was higher than her miniskirt was long!
One should complain to the Chamber of Commerce. Even be
prepared to sue! General damages, compensation for pain and
suffering. Five weeks of acute distress. Surely that's a form of
bodily injury. At least throw an ashtray, right now, at the glass
of that Mediterranean painting, and when they come and ask
him, shout right into their faces. Must he really take everything
lying down? And when, when would he finally put an end to it?
Hit back! Hit out, punch the next person in the nose, for Chrissake! Forever having to swallow everything. Everything. Forever. How long must this go on?

   With thumb and forefinger Xaver pressed his eyelids shut. In
his mind's eye flashed the knife he kept in the glove compartment. He had put down his book. He couldn't stay in the room.
He had to go out. He could barely stop himself from running.
He had the feeling that this time it was almost impossible to
breathe the air in Cologne. So hot and stifling. It's like in an
unaired barber shop where last year's cabbage has been stored!
He left the hotel. He wanted to go and see what was now at the
site of his former hotel, the one where he had been greeted by
name. He couldn't identify the site. When he went back up to

his room and noticed that it was still full of the same stale smell, he felt personally defeated. He quickly went to bed so as not to have to move anymore. Not to move anymore, become rigid, that was what he really wanted.

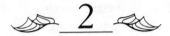

2

N E X T day it was raining. That made for a cozy atmosphere in the car. The boss had been to the opera the previous evening. Mr. Trummel had carried on business discussions with a Dutch manufacturer that had lasted until midnight. Xaver had acquired the habit of mentally participating in such backseat conversations. He contributed his comments, noted the reactions. He could practically hear himself being asked how he had spent the evening in Cologne. Oh, you know, he heard himself say, I'm really glad when I have a whole evening to read undisturbed. Opera, that's not my cup of tea, he heard himself say. Although there's nothing I enjoy listening to as much as singing, opera wouldn't be for me, he heard himself say. And the boss found an inconsistency in that and asked what he meant. And Xaver was glad to explain: It strikes me as comical when a person opens a door and sings at the same time. And supposing he doesn't open a door? he imagined his boss asking. Well, what he liked best was yodeling. Someone sings, and that's it. There's nothing finer than yodeling, he heard himself say. He was by no means as certain as he pretended to be. But so what, let the boss contradict him, so what! Xaver knew just as much about singing as that tough guy Trummel. How could the boss stand that Trummel anyway! Want to bet the boss never looks at a Western? Otherwise he'd know the type. That little toothy smile under a sparse moustache. That ice-cold girlish face framed by the straight hair. He does everything when it's trendy. He's just waiting for the chance! Whenever anybody at the plant had a grievance, it was sure to have something to do with Mr. Trummel. Who else! That would be a part for Richard Widmark.

In Giessen, Xaver drove the men to the Hotel Kübel. Since there was only a girl at the reception desk, he took charge of the boss's key and carried his luggage up to room 502. Trummel gave his tiny suitcase to the girl to carry. Xaver was pleased to find that room 502 was a suite. At a glance he saw three glass-topped tables with curvy gilt wrought-iron legs. He could leave the luggage in the living area and didn't need to go into the boss's bedroom. One morning in Nuremberg he had had to buy a cord for his boss's electric shaver and take it to the Carlton. The boss had still been in bed—not on his back but on his side—and had told Xaver to put the cord in the bathroom. So Xaver had had to go into the bathroom too. On leaving, he had avoided looking toward the boss again. Lying there like that on his side, he had seemed to him an object of pity. Like an animal destined for slaughter. The boss had been wearing white pajamas. Of some shiny white material.

Xaver drove to the little pension on Frankfurter-Strasse. A room fit only for sleeping. He walked to the inner city. Walked up and down the pedestrian mall. Walked all around it on the outside. What he enjoyed most was standing outside the windows of porn shops. That was the quickest way of passing the time. He wondered why he didn't enter one of those places. Or one of those movies. There was nothing that attracted him more than those pictures, those objects, those movies. He felt he could stand longer outside those places in the rain than if the weather had been fine. After a time the throbbing in his neck subsided. While studying those offerings, he felt how little his life was worth. How enormous reality was, or the world. And how insignificant his own share of it. Most of what there was he would never experience. Maybe not even hear of. But certainly never experience.

Sometimes he did go into one of those movies. If he could bring himself to. Look at the pictures, that much he could manage. But to go in like a person who needs it, very rarely could he manage that. Yet he did need it. There was nothing he needed more. But he mustn't admit that. Usually he just hung around outside. Till he was exhausted. Agnes wasn't interested in such things. In fact that was pretty well the way things were: his excessive interest in something was matched by her excessive lack of interest. To the same degree that it attracted him, it repelled her. He had to hide his true interest from her. Sometimes he believed he had come to terms with this. But when, as now in Giessen, he stood in front of such depictions and apparatus he realized he hadn't come to terms with it at all. The knowledge that he would never be able to explore the field of pornography with Agnes expanded within him like a disaster. To live just once with these women, the way it was shown and promised here! And if Agnes happened not to want to join in— well, it would've been nice, terrific in fact—then without her. But now Magdalena and Julia rose up in his mind. If they ever found out! If they could as much as imagine that their father was involved in anything like that, he'd wish he'd never been born. It seemed to him that Magdalena and Julia would never dream of their father being involved in such sexual matters as long as he genuinely abstained from them or was only mentally occupied with them. The more he tried to participate in something like that, the more easily they would be able to connect him with such things. That was the notion that prevailed in him.

But there was no prospect for him anyway. All he could do was think about it. And so he did. Almost to the point of mania. If you don't have all that, you're not alive. And you're not alive anyway. You drive from here to there, and back again. But Jakob and Johann would give a lot to be able to stand for hours in Giessen in front of such pictures. That's how he brought himself back to earth. He thought of the coat Johann had left behind, the one Xaver had worn for ten years after the war when going off to a dance in winter. His mother had told him it was an ulster. A light pinkish-gray with russet checks. And a belt. And a lining, so smooth that one had only to put one's hand in a sleeve and the coat was on. If Johann had come back, Xaver wouldn't have had that coat. He often thought of that.

Xaver ended up in the churchlike or castlelike or church-castlelike railway station, sat down in the station restaurant, and watched the young fellows who had that day been discharged from their military service. They were trying to get in as much boozing and singing as they could before having to disperse forever in their various trains. On their straw hats they wore the colors of the Federal Republic and wobbly gewgaws: plastic miniatures of fir trees, heather, vegetables. They had walking sticks with gaudy ring patterns; instead of crooks, triple-toned hooters. They bellowed: *"Germany is ours today, tomorrow we'll own the world!"* If anyone asked them to pipe down, they would shout: "This isn't East Germany, is it?"

Sitting at Xaver's table was an elderly man who never once looked in the direction from which the racket was coming. Without looking up he had told the waiter: "An orangeade and a sandwich." The waiter, impatiently: "What kind of san'wich, ham or—" "Ham," the man said, with admirable calm cutting off the waiter's impatient words. Only when he had the orangeade and the sandwich in front of him and he used his left hand to pick up the glass and the sandwich alternately did Xaver notice that the man's right arm was missing from the shoulder. Instinctively Xaver's right hand felt for his left ring finger. There was no ring. He had stopped wearing a wedding ring years ago. At the time, when he had been having circulatory problems, anything on his left side had bothered him. His ring, his wristwatch. He had bought himself a pocketwatch, and even after recovering from his problems he had never put the ring on again. Now suddenly he missed it. For the first time, come to think of it.

The discharged conscripts were singing *Oh Susanna, it's good to be alive!* Each vied to be the loudest. Each wanted to talk and sing and booze without interruption. Each of them a Konrad Ehrle. When one of them had a glass to his lips, he went on gesticulating. Suddenly one of them grabbed another man by the arm, wanting to drag him out—the train was already pulling in to the station—but the one being dragged wouldn't, couldn't possibly, go without taking along a third man, who in turn felt responsible for a fourth, who had to give a parting embrace to a fifth whose train hadn't yet arrived. It was a miracle that, with all that singing and pulling about, they still managed to catch their train. The ones left behind tried to replace their vanished comrades, seemingly gone forever, by louder singing and wilder gestures. Then suddenly it was time for them to leave too. After that, there was a deathly hush under the churchlike, vaulted ceiling. Until at last one man sitting alone at a table stood up and brandished his beer glass as if he were conducting a vast orchestra. After the orchestra had concluded the overture, he began, while still continuing to conduct, to sing: *Where'er I go I carry/A sturdy watch with me.* Xaver could feel the tears welling up in his eyes. He had to swallow and swallow again. That was one of his favorite songs.

Suddenly the man banged his glass down on the table and stopped singing. He muttered some mumbling, grinding sounds. Then he collapsed onto his chair and fell silent. Xaver felt happy. Everything was going exactly the way he wanted it to. That was just how it should happen. He was pretty sure there would always be something going on in this station restaurant that would give him pleasure. He called the waiter and said cockily: "An orangeade and a sandwich." The waiter, impatiently: "What kind of san'wich, ham or—" "Ham," said

Xaver, a little too quickly. His elderly one-armed neighbor gave no sign of having noticed what Xaver said. Xaver liked that. He stretched his arms as far as he could across the table and pushed his rear end back until he felt the chair's resistance. What a fabulous place, this Giessen, for Chrissake! Then he suddenly pulled back both hands as fast as he could and hid them under the table. How tactless to sprawl both his arms across a table like that while sitting beside a one-armed man! He paid his bill, left, and crawled into his clammy bed in the pension. The mattress sagged so badly that when he lay on his back he felt like a V.

The approach to the Europäischer Hof in Heidelberg was impeded by a construction site. It was not yet ten o'clock. Xaver was told to inquire at one o'clock whether they were to drive on that day. At one he was told that they wouldn't be leaving until the next day at eleven. "I won't be needing you anymore today," said Dr. Gleitze. That meant that Xaver could look for a room outside the city. If Dr. Gleitze said nothing, Xaver had to spend the night in town. Xaver drove to Ungstein. Mrs. Gleitze had asked him, if her husband happened to spend the night in Heidelberg, to pick up two cases of wine for her from the Isegrim-Hof winery in Ungstein.

Xaver found the village in the Palatinate on the other side of the Rhine. He thought of the hamlets close to home on their steep slopes. Here the plain apparently had to dip into hollows before there could be any kind of a rise. The sun shone down on the Palatinate. He was glad to be out of the muggy, lukewarm air of Heidelberg. Hotel Bettelhaus, room 33. He went for a stroll through the village. Here the street paving goes right up to the walls and doors of the houses. Each house is connected to the next by a courtyard wall. The big gates in these walls are closed. So the village street is a ravine. If a gate happens to be open because a tractor is driving through, one sees that the interior is cramped, too. Rabbit hutches, cats, plows, farm girls, containers . . . and already the gate was being closed again. Xaver compared these walled-in farms to the ones at home that lay open on the hillsides.

He found a phone booth at the south end of the village. He hadn't phoned home yet, nor from Giessen either. He always preferred to call on the last day. First Julia came to the phone. Most calls were for her anyway. When Agnes came, Xaver couldn't say much more than I'll-be-back-tomorrow. How was the weather there? she asked. They were in the midst of a terrific thunderstorm, could he hear it, now . . . had he heard it, that was pretty close, could he hear the rain, she'd even been afraid it would hail, it had been that sultry ever since he'd been gone, getting worse every day, she'd better stop now or lightning might strike the phone. "I doubt it," said Xaver. In Cologne, he said, it had been sultry too, and in Heidelberg today, too, but here the weather was fine. She couldn't understand a word he was saying, she said, lightning seemed to be striking right and left of the house. "You're having a fine time!" said Xaver. Agnes laughed. "Well then," she said. "Hey, wait a minute," said Xaver, "there's still seventy pfennigs to go." For a moment there was silence. Xaver could hear the telephone timer counting his money. "Okay, so I'll be back tomorrow." "Fine!" said Agnes. "We're looking forward to it." He would rather she had said: "I'm looking forward to it." "Well then—my love to the kids." "Right," said Agnes. Julia wanted to go to Bregenz today, with Herbert, but she—Agnes—had said, Julia couldn't go without first—Time was up. Xaver left the booth. He felt sick. He was almost furious. He would have liked to be really furious with Agnes. She hadn't said what he wanted to hear. Invariably when he called her from someplace she began talking about the kids. As if that interested him most, for Chrissake.

He found the Isegrim winery and told them he'd be back in a few minutes to pick up the cases for Mrs. Gleitze. That job done, he sat down in the village inn. Of the five people at the next table, four were wearing glasses. Inside the inn, all the wrought-ironwork reconfirmed that this was a wine-country village. The waitress impressed him. A fine figure of a woman. No doubt she was a waitress only on the side, so vastly did she seem to transcend her occupation. A man was sent off by his wife to follow the waitress to the counter and correct an order that the waitress was already writing up. The wife called out after her husband, who had almost caught up with the waitress: "Daddy, tell her we don't want the bread too fresh!" Xaver gave the wife a furious look. What a stupid cow. Couldn't she *feel* how she was insulting the waitress who was a waitress only on the side? Xaver felt like jumping up and smashing a glass in front of this impossible person and even spitting at her feet. He could feel a knot forming in his stomach. Couldn't the woman wait till she got the bread? Maybe it wasn't too fresh at all! And if it *was* fresh, what could the waitress do about it? To send her husband there like a flunky! Like a feebleminded flunky! Daddy . . . ! She couldn't have chosen a more fatuous word! And she was doing all this only to humiliate that gorgeous waitress. Probably she had noticed Xaver's admiration for this phenomenal woman and that in placing his order he had tried to display a kind of humility, and this had annoyed her, since no one was paying any attention to her, so now she had to try to insult that superb woman. He felt like dashing outside. Here, to have to eat in the same room as that person, it . . . it . . . Xaver drummed his fingers on the table. Suddenly he stood up, met the returning Daddy, halted behind the waitress until she noticed he was there, and asked him what he wanted; he told her to bring him a carafe of wine after all, he had changed his mind. And he insisted she choose the wine.

Later, on going up to his room, he stopped upstairs in the corridor in front of a watercolor picture. "German Winery Gate in Schweigen." A woman was driving a team of oxen past this gate. Xaver made a face. He was bitterly disappointed that the woman wasn't driving her team of oxen through the gate. And of course they had to hang the picture in such a way that a person approaching the door of room 33 couldn't avoid looking at it. Room 33 was the last door on the right. The picture hung on the end wall of the corridor. So there. And 33 was his, of course. If he had been given a room not so far along the corridor, he would never even have noticed this wretched winery-gate picture. But no, they had to put him in room 33, of course, so that he was forced to look at this intensely annoying picture.

Xaver undressed and lay down on the bed under the sloping wall. Actually he had wanted to tell Agnes that he had a present for her. That would have been the most important thing. In Heidelberg, in a store selling East Indian goods, he had bought her three little vials of Indian perfume. The salesgirl had opened all three vials for him. Xaver had been quite dazed by the heavy sweet scents. And they hadn't been that expensive, either. Considering they came all the way from India! He had meant to tell Agnes that he had a present for her. And the way he had meant to tell it should have made Agnes ask him tomorrow night, when the kids were in bed, what the present was. Ever since this morning he had been on his homecoming schedule. He was already anticipating the moment that meant so much to him. The kids in bed. Himself alone with Agnes. To say, I've got a present for you, while standing in front of her, seemed stupid to him. She had to ask! But for that she had to be prepared. And he had missed the opportunity. He felt that tonight he was going to have trouble falling asleep.

He remembered that the tiny stab he was now feeling under his right rib cage was nothing new to him. The stab was there. Permanently, it seemed. It had a uniquely fine point. It was like the stab of a hair. In other words, so fine as to make the pain almost ridiculous. It was only its permanence that made it noticeable, its unchanging quality. Xaver began to analyze what it might be. He couldn't imagine anything that pointed and fine which could have caused this stabbing. And anyway it was ridiculous to waste time on something like that.

At breakfast in the Drei Kronen, a man at the next table had been telling another man that a week ago his boss had been hit by a car in London and actually flung up into the air, then left bleeding and unconscious on the ground. He had told all this in Rhenish dialect. To Xaver's ears this sounded as if he were telling something amusing. Probably due to watching TV. It was still uncertain whether the boss would recover.

Although it was almost dark in his room, Xaver had quickly to press both eyelids firmly shut with thumb and forefinger. He felt that even the minutest dram of light would be totally unbearable. He simply must not visualize the boss actually flying through the air in London. He already knew that the accident in Münsingen would haunt him from now on. They had had to drive via Zweifalten to Stuttgart. On the uplands between Zweifalten and Münsingen, a car had emerged from a cart track onto the highway and driven straight into the path of a motorcyclist just ahead of Xaver, so that the motorcycle crashed head on into the hood of the car, and the driver and the girl on his pillion seat were tossed high up into the air and over the car like two leather dummies. Xaver had had time to avoid them. He saw the girl lying motionless on the ground. The motorcyclist tried to stand up, collapsed, pulled himself up again—his instinct was to get off the highway—but before he reached the edge of the road he collapsed again. Dr. Gleitze had said: "Don't stop." Xaver saw that the cars behind him were stopping. But the person who had had the best view was himself, Xaver. Dr. Gleitze said he couldn't bear looking at such sights. And that there were plenty of witnesses. The car driver who had been responsible for it all was an old man with a purplish face who was apparently unhurt. Xaver had said nothing. But he had shaken his head. And again he had to shake his head a few more times. Dr. Gleitze had been on his way to the opera. And they hadn't had

all that much time. Even so Xaver had shaken his head, and
shaken it again, to let his boss know that he didn't approve. But
the boss had ignored Xaver's compulsive head-shaking. The
next day they had driven home via Ulm. All the time he was
driving, Xaver had waited for Dr. Gleitze to bring up the subject of the accident. He had hardly been able to stand it. When
he drove up the hill on the autobahn, when he drove through the
tunnel, when he was on a level with Münsingen—he wanted
just to drive off onto the right shoulder, step on the brake, and
shout: I can't go on! You can kiss my ass, sir! You . . . You . . .
You . . . Xaver had sweated. He had glanced back. But Dr.
Gleitze was sitting between his earphones, in that seemingly
boneless posture in which he always sat when he listened to his
music.

A few months later, when he had to drive the boss to a seafood
restaurant in Hamburg, he had seen some daggers in the window of a junk store on a street that sloped down to the harbor.
As soon as he had dropped the boss off he had driven straight
back to the store and for forty-seven marks bought an Oriental
dagger that he had kept in the glove compartment ever since.
And he still clearly remembered that, while buying the knife,
he had been thinking solely of the leather figure flying through
the air, picking itself up a few times, and then lying inert.

The rage that choked him whenever he thought of the accident up there on the heights was directed against himself rather
than against the boss. It was four years ago now. Those figures
were still whirling through the air. As if released by pressing a
button. He should have stopped, regardless, for Chrissake. Dr.
Gleitze couldn't know that.

On the dot of eleven, Xaver entered the lobby of the Europäischer Hof. He chose a chair from which he could see the
whole lobby. The gentlemen arrived with a lady. Mrs. Trummel. So she was coming along too. Her clothes and jewelry were
always such that one felt an immediate comment on them was

expected. Then her makeup always seemed as if intended to convey a very particular message. And the same went for her hairdo. Her hat. Her handbag. Her perfume. Pungent and exquisite, that perfume. The thought of his little Indian bottles embarrassed him. What a woman. Like the ones in magazines. And she belonged to that vicious Trummel, who sat down in the car beside Xaver. Xaver couldn't breathe normally until he had used all his willpower to erect a sort of glass wall between himself and that ice-cold, cheesy face.

As soon as they were on the autobahn, Xaver tried to catch glimpses of Mrs. Trummel in the rearview mirror. Eyes, forehead, neck . . . they were all beautiful. All right, now look away and imagine her. See? Now you know you haven't seen a thing. Oh yes, you have. Just a girl's face. But only for a tenth of a second, then it's covered up again by that beauty. Try again. Imagine it without makeup. You can't do it a second time. But you remember how it looked, before. For a fraction of a second you have seen a very ordinary, pleasant girl's face. Now you can't get through anymore. Only the strangely flaring nostrils are a reminder of the girl's face. What she has made of her face is beautiful. She looks like abundance personified. It's all there. Does that mean you'd like to have her? No. No, really he wouldn't. He couldn't believe himself. Not right away. It took a while for him to realize what he felt when he sized up Mrs. Trummel. The beautiful Mrs. Trummel was ugly. No. He wasn't going to pretend that. But she was repulsive. He had another look. He had to look away at once for fear his expression would show how repulsive he found her. It wasn't imagination. He felt it with absolute clarity: there was nothing more repulsive than Mrs. Trummel's beauty.

Naturally he thought of Agnes. There was nothing about Agnes that didn't betray struggle. Her grim struggle with the kids, her confrontations with himself. And with all that she wanted to be beautiful! Would suddenly drive off to Ravensburg to buy blouses, slacks, sweaters, hair clips, shoes that at home failed to live up to the promises they had made in the store; besides, they had been far too expensive. On the way home the price always asserted itself. By the time Agnes reached home, she was despondent. Sad about her defeat. Xaver had to admire the purchase in great detail and thus accord it the highest possible value, so that the purchase price no longer seemed all that terrible. Never had he found his wife as beautiful as on this drive between Heidelberg and Stuttgart. Agnes's beauty lay in that incessant conflict between impairment and the will to beauty. But the will to beauty never asserted itself. Generally speaking, she remained as she was. The fact that she wasn't all that beautiful was what was beautiful about her. Truly! It was infinitely beautiful. What one saw in her, one remembered. She had suffered over the years, one could tell. One could see the traces of her struggles. One could see the once unmarked face showing through the one marked by struggle. He hadn't realized Agnes was so beautiful. It only dawned on him when he looked at the repulsive beauty of Mrs. Trummel. Agnes was ravaged. Of course. So was he. But, in the ravaged woman, the unravaged woman of earlier days was still visible. And this unravaged woman who now looked out of the ravaged one was more beautiful than she had ever been as a merely still unravaged woman. Xaver felt blissful. He felt as if Agnes had shared all his thoughts during the last half hour. A little bit of those thoughts had, after all, been for her sake. If this revulsion at so much perfection persisted, he had triumphed and things would be easier from now on. He hoped the revulsion would persist. Agnes, Agnes, he thought, if only you knew how I'm hurrying toward you! Unless Mrs. Gleitze invents some make-work, something one must always expect of her, of course, he can be home in four or five hours.

Just before the Feuerbach exit, Dr. Gleitze asked Xaver to drive into Stuttgart; they were dropping off the Trummels at the station there, he and Xaver would go on to Munich. Xaver could only nod. His well-trained, never-failing nod. To Munich. I see. To Munich. Aha. So we're going on to Munich. Hm-hm. So we're bound to be a little late. Okay. If they reached Munich by noon, Dr. Gleitze could be through by five, six at the latest, so they would simply be home by nine or ten. Or eleven. Why not? The kids would be in bed by then. The kids always seemed in the way when he got home anyway. So okay. By all means. Certainly, sir. Let's drive on to Munich. With this car there's nothing to it! And it's nicer anyway without those Trummels. You and I, sir, are driving home via Munich, no problem at all. For all I care, via Salzburg or Innsbruck. . . .

When he opened the car door for the Trummels in Stuttgart and looked at Mrs. Trummel, he had to look away immediately, simply for fear that his expression would betray the fact that it gave him a kind of pain to look at her.

Alone with the boss in the car. It was raining. He wished he could drive at 250 kilometers an hour. He felt equal to any challenge. To be allowed to shoot up the slopes of Stuttgart so that at the top they would take off into the air, that would really be something. He had to keep a tight hold on himself. But at least he enjoyed the sharper hiss of the tires on the wet road surface. The boss was not listening to music, he was studying one of his pale green scores. Xaver kept glancing back. He much preferred it when the boss read or wrote or slept. Xaver hated the earphones. For some reason it annoyed him when the boss put on those huge things. To Xaver's eyes, they put the finishing touch to the boss's babylike appearance, and not only because of the boneless posture he sank into when listening to music. Even his lip movements became like those of a baby.

When the boss wasn't listening to music, one might have been able to talk. His imaginary conversation with his boss didn't get off the ground so easily when the boss was listening to music. On the way to Munich it did. In his imagination Xaver discussed with him the evening in Frankfurt. More than ten years ago. Also in May. When he had picked up the boss at the Frankfurter Hof. And after that they had driven not, as originally planned, to Göttingen but straight home. An incredible evening, it had been. A bluish-black vertical wall of cloud. Buildings and trees looking eerily massive. Everything seemed to be dripping with heat. He had been told to drive out of town. Along the Eschersheimer highway. Then off to the right into a quiet residential area. His boss had gotten out and asked Xaver to get out too. Then in a low voice he had said: "Come along, Xaver, let's walk up and down for a bit." Xaver glanced back. Did the boss remember it at all? Xaver did. He had hardly ever known an evening with more extreme colors. It was the same with the heat. The same with the boss. Excited. Grabbing Xaver's arm. Pulling Xaver close. For a totally indeterminate time they had walked up and down the tree-lined sidewalk. The boss talking away to Xaver. The ground had been covered with little purple blossoms.

His arm around Xaver's shoulder, the boss had started talking about Königsberg. On spring evenings such as this, he had said, his mother, returning from her medical practice, had always leaned her bicycle against the white garden fence and announced her return by a few whistles produced by putting four fingers in her mouth. Did Xaver get the picture? Xaver nodded. But he felt like immediately retracting his nod because the boss went on to say that his mother had always worn a divided skirt of light gray flannel. In Xaver's mind, "divided skirt" clashed with "mother." Then his mother had always placed both her hands against the sides of her bobbed hair and waited until he—the boss—or his father, or both, appeared. It was a contest for who would have the privilege of lifting her doctor's bag off her bicycle carrier. Gradually it dawned on him, said the boss, that his father deliberately let him win the race. Even so, he had always run as fast as he could and always perceived his being the first to reach her as a victory. Besides, his mother had invariably treated him as the winner. Then she had cupped her hands around her mouth and shouted for Friedhelm. Whereupon they had all three waited until Friedhelm's grumpy voice was heard from the basement: "No time." Or: "I'm in the middle of an experiment." Then all three would go down into Friedhelm's lab and listen while he told them about all the inventions and discoveries he had achieved that afternoon for the benefit of mankind. Perhaps those front gardens in Frankfurt had suddenly reminded the boss of Königsberg. From time to time, while talking, the boss had looked at his watch. Xaver had the impression that the boss was trying to steal a look at his watch. And suddenly he had said that, if they wanted to get out of town before the thunderstorm, they'd better look sharp. And no sooner were they on the autobahn—they were already plowing through torrential rain—than a light showed up on the dashboard: the generator wasn't charging. Xaver reported this over his shoulder. Dr. Gleitze called out in alarm: "Do we have to go back to Frankfurt?" Xaver turned into the next pullout. One of the four belts had snapped. He had a replacement. Dr. Gleitze watched tensely as he put it on. When they drove on he said with a sigh of relief: "You did it, Xaver, congratulations!"

Xaver had told Agnes the whole story in detail. Unfortunately, one day at Konrad's he hadn't been able to resist telling it to him too. And on another occasion to his brother Georg and his wife when they had come over from Nitzenweiler on All Souls' Day. And also once to Aunt Klothilde and her son Franz in Bodnegg. It seemed to him that his listeners hadn't grasped the point of telling the story. Konrad's immediate comment was that the old man had been after a woman on that street, surely that was obvious. Xaver found this explanation absurd. Fortunately Agnes hadn't been present. As soon as anyone said anything against Dr. Gleitze, she would say: "And that's the kind of person you have to drive around!" He loathed that kind of pity.

What surprised Xaver most was that, whenever he told the story of that May evening in Frankfurt, one of his listeners would feel constrained to offer an explanation for Xaver and his boss walking up and down. The unfailing reaction was that Xaver had presented them with a question, a problem. And nothing could have been farther from his mind. He had merely wanted to tell them what happened. The early May evening, the vertical blue-black sky, the sultry heat, the kind we simply never have around here, the cars bumper to bumper, and the sidewalk more thickly covered with those blossoms than on Ascension Day, and then, of course, that walking up and down, Königsberg, the mother with her bobbed hair, the divided skirt, and then her tomboy whistle: wasn't that something worth telling? But after the third or fourth time he didn't think so anymore. He could have kicked himself. They must have thought he was trying to brag about his relationship with his boss. Did he really need to tell such stories? He now found it incomprehensible that he could have told a story that showed him up like that. If he didn't tell it, there was nothing objectionable about the story. It became fatuous only when it was told. After all, *he* could think of that May evening in Frankfurt as often as he liked, it was just that he mustn't talk about it. At the time, he had been Dr. Gleitze's chauffeur for three years. He remembered how, as they drove home through the cloudburst, he had been thinking that the worst was over. Anxiety, deep emotion, happiness. So his life would be quite a rewarding one after all. So everything hadn't been in vain after all. Dr. Gleitze had noticed him. Recognized him. Acknowledged him. Accepted him. After three years. After three very trying years. His constant display of diligence, zeal, loyalty, antialcoholism, antismoking—which had long been a torment because it was ridiculous—would no longer be necessary. It had really been high time for Dr. Gleitze to release him from all this jumping to attention, for Chrissake.

Xaver glanced back. There was nothing Xaver appreciated more than Dr. Gleitze's taciturnity. Xaver also spoke only when it was necessary. Dr. Gleitze even outdid him. There were a few things that it really was about time they discussed. Königsberg, for instance. Almost every time the boss happened to be sitting with someone else in the back, he would start talking about Königsberg. When the weather was fine, he would say: "When the sun shone in Königsberg . . ." When it was raining, he would start off with: "When it rained in Königsberg . . ." The boss still didn't know that Xaver's brother had been killed at the age of twenty in the defense of Königsberg. While they were still in Frankfurt, Xaver had wanted to tell him of his connection with Königsberg. But first the boss had talked so that it was impossible to interrupt him, and then he had hurried off and remained so silent in the car that it was impossible to speak to him. Oh well, if the boss was so attached to Königsberg, there was certain to be an opportunity soon of telling him that Johann had been killed there in April 1945. The boss would surely be amazed to learn that Xaver's brother had defended the city of Königsberg. With his assault gun. And his brother Jakob reported missing in Karelia. Up north there, too. The Zürn family really had done all it could to prevent the Gleitzes' native place from falling into the hands of the Russians. It almost made Xaver feel good to have these items of news in reserve. He had lost his brothers, the boss and *his* brothers had lost their native place. Whenever he recalled that he had been deprived of two brothers, he felt furious. He twitched with rage. He wanted to hit out. He would have liked to ask the boss whether he felt the same way—for instance, when he thought of the native city he'd been deprived of. To drive a person away from his native place, for Chrissake. Although, of course, the Gleitzes had gone much earlier. This was frequently discussed in the back of the car. Dr.

Gleitze's father had always owned a hunting estate in the Alps. On the Upper Rhine. Above Buchs. He must have been able to get away to Switzerland before the war started. Without his children. He must have been managing director of a textile factory there. Once when they had taken along Professor and Mrs. Rogall from Göttingen to Stuttgart, Xaver had heard that Gleitze's parents had even visited Wilhelm Gustloff, the National Socialist, in Davos, just before he was assassinated. The older Gleitzes were still living in Switzerland. Xaver had quite often picked them up from their villa above St. Gallen and driven them home again.

Xaver really would have had something to tell the boss. About Königsberg! In March 1948, a man, one of Johann's comrades, had turned up on a bicycle. He had propped his bike against the milk bench down on the road, removed his bicycle clips, taken his rolled-up raincoat and his rucksack from the carrier, and walked slowly up the path. Georg had turned off the buzz saw. He and Xaver had walked toward the skinny young stranger, who had taken off his green hat as if wanting to draw attention to his haircut. A prisoner's haircut. Just beginning to grow again. He introduced himself as Dr. Kuckuck from Tübingen. Xaver noticed a grin flit across Georg's face when he heard the name. Xaver was immediately aware that this doctor was a person whom Georg would later mimic. That was Georg's way. He was quite taciturn when a stranger came to the farm; but when the stranger had left, he would mimic his gestures, speech, movements. Georg found something to mimic in almost everyone.

By this time their mother was already standing at the kitchen door. On hearing that Dr. Kuckuck was one of Johann's comrades, she called out to Xaver and Georg in a voice that seemed to have lost its resonance, asking them why they were still standing around, why they weren't asking the doctor to come in. As soon as the doctor had reached the top step but one, she grasped him by the hand and shoulder and said: "Come on in, for God's sake, come on in!" She whimpered rather than spoke. It sounded as if the doctor were in dire straits and she had to help him. She drew him to the kitchen table and made him sit down on the corner bench. First he must sit down, for God's sake, sit down right away and have something to eat. God in heaven, she said, what a good thing he'd come, now that he had found his way here. And something to drink, boys! She was all muddled up. So she kept repeating: Just one thing at a time now, as if she were afraid that, before Dr. Kuckuck could tell them about Johann, something terrible would happen to him that would spoil it all.

When their mother's limp hands finally lay exhausted on the table before her, Dr. Kuckuck knew he could begin. In telling one part of the story he turned toward Georg and Xaver; in telling the other he turned toward their mother. And as he spoke he ate. She had insisted on that. He must be hungry. He admitted he was. From Tübingen to Wigratsweiler, by bicycle. He had been on the go for days. He had visited several families of fallen comrades. But mostly families living in towns. His explanation was unnecessary. In those days one knew that anyone arriving from far away was hungry. Dr. Kuckuck said he considered it his duty to inform these families about the fate of their sons. He had made up his mind to do this while a prisoner of war. He began by describing the situation in Königsberg in the spring of 1945. Xaver couldn't visualize what Dr. Kuckuck was talking about. The doctor sat very straight, his index finger, bent like a sickle, moving about in the center of the table. It was as if the doctor were seeing Königsberg and the encircling Russian armies from above. It was only when the doctor said that he had been in command of the infantry escort of Johann's assault-gun company that Xaver was gradually able to visualize what he was hearing. They had still been two hundred men strong. Assault-gun company and infantry escort combined. Assigned to the

Sixty-ninth Infantry Division. Then comes the order to with-draw from the Nasser Garten toward the center of the city. Staff Sergeant Schöne first sees that the dead are transported to the Alte Pillauer Landstrasse. Now the crossing of the River Pregel. Across the big swing bridge. Right into the billowing smoke of the city center. Until then they had been watching the Russian assault planes from the Nasser Garten. Full speed across the bridge. Johann astride the armored housing of the gun barrel. Even though the bridge was under enemy fire. His favorite posi-tion. All this Dr. Kuckuck had been directing toward their mother.

Before that, Johann had driven right over a Volkswagen. Onto it with the right-hand caterpillar tread, a quick turn, and the VW was a sort of pancake. Johann didn't want anything to fall into the hands of the Russians. Without casualties, onto Schubert-Strasse. Numbers 12 to 18. Now nothing but ruins and cellars, of course. First remove the dead civilians. By the time Johann had got off his vehicle, the dead had been removed. It sounded as if it had all been done for Johann's sake. One P.M. Work is resumed immediately. Tank mechanics, radio techni-cians, electricians, supply-service men. At the moment, no telephone or radio contact with the command post of the Sixty-ninth. A motorcycle and a car are dispatched. The car, driven by Lieutenant zur Mühlen, finds the staff adjutant. In the Pregel bastion at the Friedländer Gate. Orders: At five P.M. engage enemy on highway to Preussisch Eylau in scattered columns as protection against air attack. Infantry mounted on vehicles. The main gun is assigned directly to the bastion. At four P.M., new orders. Immediate move to seal off Russian breakthroughs at the Wrangel tower. Immediate departure for Post-Strasse. On each vehicle, one man with a big wire cutter. They had to cut their way through the dangling streetcar wires. Parade Square no longer passable. On Post-Strasse, enemy fire now coming from every direction. One impact drowned out by the next. A dispatch rider from the staff adjutant. One vehicle with infantry escort to head immediately for Hagen-Strasse. For close-quarter defense. Johann turns off. Dr. Kuckuck takes personal charge of providing cover. All quiet on Hagen-Strasse. Except for those Ilyushin 2's. They are flying in lower and lower. Suddenly two Stalin tanks ahead. And already they've fired. With their 122-millimeter guns. Direct hit in the frontal armor of the driver's seat. Johann and the driver, a cheery Rhenish boy, killed instantly. The radio operator, a solid Westphalian, dies on the way to Schubert-Strasse. The gunner, a calm Pomeranian, dies there in the cellar. Xaver could hear his mother trying to sob as quietly as possible.

Since Dr. Kuckuck had so far eaten only the smoked meat, Georg urged him to have some of the cheese, too. Dr. Kuckuck frowned at Georg, then started eating again. Xaver has never since seen anyone eating like that. The only word for it was reverently. It was somehow appropriate to the dark kitchen, to the four motionless people at the round table, and to the almost inaudible, high-pitched keening of this mother. Suddenly Dr. Kuckuck asked for the light to be switched on. Out of his rucksack Dr. Kuckuck dug a small bundle of papers still tied up with wartime paper string, checked it over, placed it on the table in front of their mother, and said those were the letters Johann had received. The motor-transport sergeant had given them to him shortly after the capitulation, while they had been getting ready for their departure to the prisoner-of-war camps. Their main concern had been to salvage the personal belongings of the dead. Each man had to promise to pass on to the families whatever he took with him. He, Dr. Kuckuck, had managed to get through. Since it hadn't always been easy to keep these letters out of the hands of Russian looters, he had taken the liberty of reading them and smuggling through only those written by the families. He had destroyed one pile of letters and notes from a somewhat flighty East Prussian girl. Georg nodded. Xaver nodded because Georg had nodded.

The doctor stood up, saying he still had to get to Primisweiler that day. His trip was carefully mapped out. Their mother stood up and sent Xaver to the smokehouse, Georg down to the cellar. She insisted that the doctor take along two slabs of smoked meat and two bottles of kirsch. When Georg brought up only one bottle, she sent him down again. Georg wrapped both bottles in newspaper and gave them to Dr. Kuckuck. Later he told Xaver he had given him ordinary fruit brandy, not kirsch. What next? Georg had said. For a bottle of kirsch he could get three pairs of shoes.

Three years later another comrade had turned up. During the summer. On a BMW 250. Roaring right up to the bottom step. Traugott Bierle from Sindelfingen. He had been a tank mechanic. In Johann's company. Now with Mercedes. Xaver had felt immediately attracted to the fat, red-cheeked, bespectacled man, who had immediately put an arm around their mother's shoulder and said he had lost a brother, too. He knew what it was like. He wouldn't accept anything to eat now, he would join the Zürns later for a meal, since he was going to spend the night here. And tomorrow too, if it was all right with them. They didn't know their Traugott Bierle if they thought he would drive almost two hundred kilometers just to say hello! While Königsberg was collapsing around him, he had made up his mind to look up the family of his comrade Johann. After all, he had always personally seen to it that Johann's three-hundred h.p. Maybach engine had obeyed him without a murmur. And it had. It hadn't been engine trouble that had caused Johann's death. And they'd always fooled around together. And made plans for after the war. He was going to do the inventions, and Johann, if by that time he had completed his law studies, would legally secure Traugott Bierle's brilliant patents.

The main difference between him and Dr. Kuckuck was that Traugott Bierle hadn't come with any idea of telling them about Johann's last hours. He wanted to meet Johann's mother and Jakob, Georg, and Xaver. When he heard that Jakob was reported missing in Karelia, he said: For Chrissake. He preferred to tell them about the living Johann rather than the dead one. That girl who had written the letters Dr. Kuckuck hadn't brought along—he had known her too. Henriette. Blond Henriette. A blondness that didn't exist in these parts. Blond as the sun, he said. What a girl, he said. Simply fantastic. She had been a refugee, staying with an aunt in Königsberg. Then she had run away from her aunt and moved in with the company. More and more the men were sharing quarters with the civilian population anyway. Toward the end she had tried to prevent Johann from moving into action. Really scary, the way she had stood her ground. It was just as well the National Socialist Front Organization hadn't happened to be passing by when that girl was talking. As early as the beginning of February, when everyone was still thinking in terms of defense, she had said that Königsberg was doomed. She had yelled so loudly at the divisional interpreter, a gaunt Balt who wanted to defend every fence post one by one, that he had been speechless. Domnoddy! she called him. God only knew what that meant. And clodpoll! She was a country girl, after all. From the Baltic coast someplace. At any rate, from a farm. Breakfas' for de men, she used to say when she brought them their morning coffee. And she had spent the evenings with them, too. Johann had leaned his shoulder against hers, she had hummed a folk lullaby. No one else was allowed to lean against her. Only the boy from the cloister school. Johann had blushed brick red when someone had pointed that out. Johann had called her Mergele. Everyone else had to say Henriette. Even the officers had done whatever she told them. Except capitulate. She hadn't managed to achieve that. But as time went on she had been running around like crazy, urging everyone to put an end to it. As if she had known that otherwise it might be too late for her and Johann. Johann had always said: The First Division is coming. The Fifth Panzer Division is coming. The Kurland army is coming. They won't fail us, Mergele. By that time they had hardly been able to leave the cellars what with all the artillery and planes. A thousand planes had been unleashed by the Russians against the fortified city of Königsberg, so he heard later in prison camp. There was almost no more engaging of the enemy. They just sat in the cellars, bandaging the wounded and giving them schnapps because it was no longer possible to get through to the main field hospital. The cellars reeked of sweat and blood. One of the men always stayed outside in a vehicle. Once when Johann had been outside, a building had practically fallen on top of him. They had heard the impact. Everyone rushes outside. All they can see is a huge pile of bricks, and from it comes the noise of rumbling and rattling. Then the engine revs up. And then Johann crashes out with the gun! Hatch opens. Johann grins. No harm done.

But each day turns out to be exactly ten times worse than the previous one. And suddenly their Russian volunteer, a man from the Caucasus, comes in and shouts: Königsberg has capitulated! And he's chalk white. Starts flailing around. They have to tie him to an old iron laundry mangle. Someone untied him that evening, whereupon he dashed outside and shot himself. In spite of the capitulation, the bombardment continued for several hours. They had packed their gear in preparation for the departure to prison camp. Henriette had put on a uniform. Johann had already cut off her hair some days earlier. The top sergeant had issued her a paybook. Then Johann had gone outside one last time. He had wanted to dismantle the radiotelephone set from his gun. Whyever had he wanted to do that? Georg and Xaver had asked almost angrily. Right, they had asked Johann that too. It would be a shame for the radiotelephone to fall into Russian hands, Johann had said. He wanted to bury it here in the cellar, maybe he could pick it up again on the way home, then he could try to locate them all. Everyone had laughed. Henriette had been across the street, saying good-bye to the civilians. Hardly had Johann gone outside when there was an explosion. He—Bierle—had run outside. Johann had lain beside his gun. The tractor tread ripped from the leading wheel. Johann facedown on the ground. Shell splinter. So he hadn't had to suffer. Their mother went on sending Traugott Bierle smoked meat and apples long after everything had become available again.

Then, later, a third comrade had turned up. According to his story, Johann had lived one more day in the emergency hospital in the government offices on Schön-Strasse. No one contradicted Comrade Number 3. He, too, was given two slabs of smoked meat and two bottles of kirsch. Once again Georg turned these into fruit brandy. This man had come by car. As far as the family was concerned, Johann had died neither on Hagen-Strasse nor on Schön-Strasse but on Schubert-Strasse. About an hour after the capitulation of Königsberg. From a shell splinter that had struck him from behind, killing him instantly.

After that, Traugott Bierle came almost every summer. He only stopped coming after he married a woman from the island of Juist and had to spend his annual vacation with her parents. But he had turned up for their mother's funeral. And spent another night with them, too. He and Xaver had left the funeral meal at the Happy Prospect early and walked out to the hop field. It had been a cold April day. Traugott Bierle had said that, whenever he thought about it, he felt uncomfortable at not having been strictly truthful in describing Johann's death. Because of their mother. Now he could say that Johann hadn't died immediately. Johann had gone outside to remove the radio-telephone, there's an explosion, he—Traugott—out like a shot—sees Johann, a bloody hole in his back, he dashes off to divisional headquarters, finds Dr. Bentele from Ulm in the cellar—Traugott had once repaired his jeep at Lake Peipus, otherwise the doctor would have fallen into Russian hands back there—Dr. Bentele comes with him although the wounded are lying around everywhere and screaming, but Traugott has grabbed hold of the doctor by the collar and says, I *insist*, so he comes along with an orderly and a stretcher. They put Johann on the stretcher. Johann's eyes are open. Dr. Bentele says his spine is actually still intact. And lowering his voice, for Traugott's ears only: But his intestines are ripped, in many places, his feces are floating in his abdominal cavity. Just then Johann says: Water. Traugott brings some water. Believe it or not, there was still running water. Traugott can see from Johann's eyes that the water makes him feel better. Then Johann lies motionless. Then he says: What a stink. It sounds, says Traugott, as if he wanted to say it louder. Then Johann turns his head to one side. Traugott can see only the tip of his nose. They have already lifted up the stretcher. Traugott never saw Johann again. Never heard what became of him.

And Henriette? Traugott said: Oh, sweet Jesus. Henriette had accompanied them as far as the repair shed of the railway maintenance works at Ponarth. The evening before, Johann had bandaged one of her arms and half her head to simulate wounds. Henriette hadn't spoken a word since Johann was gone. When the Russians had burst into the cellar, shouting Urr! Urr! *Davei! Davei!* and Woman come!, she had remained undetected. Even on their march through the city. But when they reached the repair shed of the maintenance works, Henriette had stumbled over a rail and let out a scream. One of the Russians standing there to give the prisoners one more frisking must have heard the scream. Woman! he had yelled and with two others had grabbed hold of Henriette. They had dragged her off into a railway car. A whole horde of raucous drunks had immediately followed them. The next day Traugott had looked for her in the first-aid station that was set up in the shed for rape victims. He had found her lying on a stretcher. At every word spoken to her, she was shaken by a dreadful trembling. As for her lips, they weren't lips anymore, just swollen tatters. Her eyes had been enormous, with a fixed stare. She hadn't recognized him. She must have lost her reason. A doctor had told him that it was completely impossible to force so much as a single drop of fluid through her lips. On the fourth day the doctor told him she had died. The doctor had said it was better that way. Simply died. And Henriette had been no featherweight but a big strong girl. Shall I clobber that little shrimp? she was liable to shout if someone pestered her. That was some woman, said Traugott, and still Johann had called her by the diminutive Mergele. And why not? said Traugott.

That's what was happening in the first half of April 1945 in your native city, sir, Xaver mentally told his boss, who was studying his pale green score. Xaver was pretty sure it was a Mozart score. If it had been Schubert, he could have said that there had been a Schubert-Strasse in Königsberg. How do you know? Dr. Gleitze would have asked. What do you expect? Xaver would have said. After all, my brother Johann died on Schubert-Strasse. Well I never! Dr. Gleitze might have exclaimed. I was born on Schubert-Strasse! Why didn't you tell me that right away? Xaver would have said. At some point or other there will be an opportunity to talk about the role of Königsberg in Xaver's life and the life of his boss. But Xaver already knew that, of the three reports on Johann's death, he would use that of Comrade Number 1 or that of Comrade Number 3. He wouldn't say that his brother's last words had been "What a stink." He hadn't told Georg that, either. Sometimes he thought he would have preferred Traugott not to have told him the truth abaout Johann's last moments. His thoughts simply returned to them too often. And then this urge. This wanting to lash out. And not being able to. You were lucky, sir, weren't you?

The boss and his brother had been antiaircraft gunners. The boss frequently mentioned this when talking to his employees, having spent the greater part of the war on the target-tracking team of an antiaircraft detachment in Vienna and at a tracking device on the island of Jersey. He had once stated: Anybody who's anybody in television today was with me then in Jersey. His brother Friedhelm must have performed the same function in Nuremberg. Apparently he had even assisted in the development of the tracking device 40. But, if Xaver had heard correctly, the principal inventor must have been a Bavarian brewery owner. They were all from better-class families and must have spent their war years very comfortably. The third and oldest of the Gleitze brothers, whom Xaver had to pick up every year at Kloten airport in Zürich, had gone to America in 1937 to attend university there. Yes, sir, my brother would have married a girl from East Prussia. You brought home a girl from Vienna. Your brother Friedhelm brought back a girl from Nuremberg. That's the way the cookie crumbles, isn't it, sir?

The boss had stopped reading. Xaver straightened up. Glanced back. Unfortunately they were almost in Munich. Too late to talk about Königsberg. For Königsberg we need time, don't we, sir? Maybe tonight, on the way home.

"To the Bayerischer Hof, please," said the boss. Xaver learned that they weren't going to drive home that day. For Chrissake, he thought. Words failed him. He merely noticed that he sagged a bit in his seat. The boss said he was sorry. *Figaro* conducted by Böhm, with Fischer-Dieskau, Hermann Prey, Janowitz, Fassbaender . . . Xaver knew the names, for they were always the same. He felt obliged to nod at each name. That was what his boss expected. Only then could his boss say that this would give Xaver an evening in Munich. Xaver was to drop him off at the Bayerischer Hof, then he could go off on his own. Xaver swallowed. If the boss still had a real home, thought Xaver, he wouldn't always be chasing after Mozart operas.

He dropped off his boss and drove out to Gauting, to Mrs. Bauer's, where he always took a room when the boss didn't need him anymore. She had a vacancy. She was glad to see him. "We're just a small guesthouse," she said, "but we're glad to see you." Room 10. A chocolate on the pillow. The rain had stopped, so he walked to the station and phoned Agnes. Agnes said: "Too bad, we were so looking forward to it." Why didn't she ever say: "I was so looking forward to it!"? We were . . . mother and children. . . . He felt like saying: What a load of hogwash. He couldn't say that. But he couldn't say anything else either. So he said nothing. The timer ticked away. He could feel a rage mounting in him. There he stands, paying for every second, Agnes talking a whole lot of nonsense. He gives her time to say something intelligent instead, but she lets the time go by. As a precaution, he dropped in another mark. When would he be arriving tomorrow? she asked. "As if anyone could tell," he said, adding: "With those fellows." Oh well, it wouldn't be long till tomorrow, she said. "Really?" he said. It will be for me, he wanted to say, but not for you, of course. He only thought that. He dropped in another mark. He would go on dropping in coins until she said what he wanted to hear. There they both stood, he in the booth, she in the living room beside the new buffet—surely she could be a bit more explicit in her regret, couldn't she? The two hundred kilometers between them! For Chrissake! No, he wasn't going to waste another mark. He said, as wearily and crossly as he could, "Well then." Agnes asked where he was. He told her, again said, "Well then." "Well then," said Agnes, "just come as soon as you can." They would be looking forward to it, she repeated. "All right," said Xaver, "good night." No sooner had he hung up than he was afraid of having given Agnes the wrong impression. He collected three marks from the coin return.

When Xaver stepped outside, a woman came toward him with a face like a frog being tortured; this face, apparently prompted by Xaver's expression, tried to smile at him in passing. He gave a loud curse as he splashed into a puddle. At the butcher's he bought some sausage, somewhere else some mustard, bread, and beer; then he went back to his room. Room 10 had a tiny winter garden, apparently the result of some arbitrary construction. In it a sofa, two chairs. Xaver began to eat. The fact that it was raining again seemed just right to him. Only it was raining much too gently. He would have liked to see torrents of water cascading down. Suddenly he was aware of his right hand fiddling with his empty left ring finger again. Just as the tongue can't stop probing a new gap in one's teeth, the fingers of his right hand were rubbing his empty left ring finger up and down. Apparently they couldn't grasp the fact that it was empty. Xaver was mystified. Now, after so many years. He freed his left hand from the persistent right hand. Oh, Agnes.

Next morning in the cramped little breakfast room, the monotonous peevish voices of an old couple got on his nerves. He took them for Hungarians because that peevish tone reminded him of Mrs. Gleitze. He was glad when Mrs. Bauer dropped a plate in the kitchen and called out loud and clear, "Hell's bells!" As he left, Mrs. Bauer repeated: "I hope you've been comfortable, we're just a small guesthouse." As soon as he was out of Mrs. Bauer's sight, Xaver could feel his face sagging again. It had stopped raining. Today they really would be driving home. To come home on a May afternoon like this, I ask you, was there anything more wonderful! And a delayed homecoming is even more wonderful than the planned one. Couldn't he look forward to the moment when he would round the top of the hill and see all seven red roofs of the Wigratsweiler farms floating among the dense foliage of the fruit trees? He couldn't lift his spirits. He felt that his every movement required effort. As soon as he sat behind the wheel, his one desire was to make no further movement. Release the brake, turn the key . . . Having to do something. To counter his condition. He shifted the automatic

to low gear. As he approached the Bayerischer Hof, he raised
and lowered his eyebrows ten, twenty times. He couldn't very
well pick up Dr. Gleitze with that kind of a face. When he was
close enough to see the hotel beyond the little park, he found
himself in a traffic jam; as long as he couldn't move on, he
watched an old man with a cane walking along the sidewalk
toward an iron garbage receptacle. The pensioner's rubber-
tipped cane was aimed, as if for attack, at a newspaper hanging
over the edge of the receptacle. He poked the newspaper down
into the receptacle and went on grimly poking away as if he had
a score to settle with the newspaper. Before traffic started up
again the pensioner had apparently had enough and was able to
walk on. That was a very satisfying experience. Xaver noticed
that his face had now become more relaxed; he was fit to pick up
Dr. Gleitze.

No sooner had he entered the lobby than he heard, loud and
clear and Bavarian: "Mr. Zürn, we have a message for you!" Evidently the hall porter had identified him from the time of day
and his chauffeur's uniform. A message from Dr. Gleitze to say
they would not be leaving for home until the afternoon. Xaver
was to pick him up at two-thirty at Hahn's. Xaver smirked
automatically on hearing this, seeking to act out, for the hall
porter's benefit, a kind of humorous superiority over the absurd
notions of his boss. It was all he could do not to take a swing at
that clown of a hall porter, pick up the nearest ashtray, hurl it
through the nearest window, and yell at the top of his voice. He
could feel his bowels contracting into a knot, getting harder and
harder. Still smirking, he left the hotel. Out on the street he
cursed aloud. He parked the car in the Königshof Garage, then
strolled aimlessly about the streets. Finally, in the Old Botani-
cal Garden, he looked for a place to sit down and eat the lunch he
had bought along the way, but he was unable to find a dry spot
and had to consume his sausage and bread and orange while
standing and walking about.

One minute before two-thirty, Xaver entered Hahn's and walked straight through the store into the restaurant. It wasn't the first time he was picking the boss up from here. Dr. Gleitze was the only customer. Two waiters were in attendance. Xaver was told to sit down opposite Dr. Gleitze. On the small table stood a large silver tureen with a lid. Next to it a small bowl of mayonnaise with dill. Xaver must order something for himself, since he—Dr. Gleitze—couldn't very well sit here eating alone in front of Xaver. What Xaver had in mind to say was that he would be happy to have his boss recommend something from among all these delicacies; but unfortunately he heard himself saying he had already had lunch. "Too bad!" exclaimed his boss. "Then bring him some ice cream, he likes that, but make it a big one, with whipped cream, a nice big dollop of whipped cream, right?" As he spoke, the boss tilted his head to one side as if to shake water out of his right ear, looking at the waiter with his head, so to speak, askew. His hands held little silver tools. When the boss lifted the lid off the tureen again, Xaver saw a thin broth with a reddish jumble of crayfish pieces floating about in it. His boss kept patiently filling crayfish broth into crayfish shells with his little spoon, then slurping the broth from the shells. Xaver, who couldn't stand it when anyone slurped at home, didn't find the boss's slurping unpleasant. That surprised him. The boss sat hunched behind his little table, his soft white hands hanging limply from the wrists. Those little hands were not very adept at handling the little forks and hooks. It took him quite a while to slit open another crayfish leg and pry out some more meat with a little silver hook. He remarked that with this dish one used up more calories than one consumed, that's what was so good about it. "You know how my wife keeps track of calories!" Xaver nodded. The boss had long and almost dirty fingernails today. Xaver had never noticed such a thing before. He wished he could shake his hand. But then, of course, the boss had never looked so much like a baby, either. If only because of the big white bib they had tied around his neck. On the bib were pictures of objects from kitchen and garden, like those in modern paintings, which Xaver didn't like. And on top of that the boss's lower lip was drooping moistly as never before. Expecially when he sprinkled spices from an assortment of little containers. Xaver felt the next thing would be the sound of a baby's rattle. When the boss picked up his glass of white wine, his expression was like that of the priest in Gattnau during the transubstantiation. His eyes almost closed, he murmured reverently, drawing in his lower lip: "Niersteiner." Xaver applied himself to his ice cream. If it hadn't been for this ice cream, he would have been enjoying himself. Much more than that. Why, this was a situation almost like the one in the forest outside Tuttlingen! Or on the suburban street in Frankfurt. Here he is, sitting companionably with his boss in a gourmet restaurant in Munich and having something to eat. Ice cream! Oh well, that was his own fault, wasn't it. It wasn't. It was. It wasn't. It was. . . .

As they were driving out of Munich, Xaver was still thinking about his boss's long, really quite dirty fingernails. Normally the boss always looked as if dirt couldn't even touch him. When they were on the road for a week, the boss, although his suitcase was no bigger than Xaver's, wore a fresh clean shirt every day, whereas no shirt of Xaver's stayed clean even for a day. He often had the impression that dirt was constantly seeping out of his pores. No matter what he put on, all he did was cover up his sweaty, dirty bodily self. The boss in his babylike cleanliness and inordinate grooming often seemed to him like a "white" man. That's what he sometimes called him in his mind. And today the "white" man in the back of the car had dirty nails! Hallelujah! Glory be! Once again a day for rejoicing. Never mind the ice cream. The way the boss had explained how to eat crayfish! The man could be incredibly nice, he really could.

Before they reached Landsberg it was raining again. Xaver

was glad. Unfortunately the boss had once again disappeared between his earphones. There he sat in the backseat, boneless, his lower lip drooping although no longer quite so moist. Xaver would have liked to stop, get out, and say: Drive on alone, for God's sake! Or put those things away, for God's sake! Xaver could have told him without hesitation that it was Mozart again, for Dr. Gleitze's expression never stayed the same for very long. As if Dr. Gleitze were standing on a hilltop and in the sky overhead contrasting types of weather were chasing one another. All that remained constant were his dimples. The right one deeper than the left.

Xaver drove up as close as possible to the truck ahead of him. It was a gravel truck, and its tires were spraying a thick, muddy goo. When the whole windshield was dripping with wet mud, Xaver passed the truck as slowly as possible to make sure that the right side of the car got a good drenching; the deflection caused by the roof post in this new model made it necessary for Xaver to pass three gravel trucks slowly until his right side was reasonably dirty. Then he let the three trucks pass him and gradually drench the left side of the car. Xaver enjoyed the feeling of being coated like that. He was waiting for the boss to tell him to switch on the windshield washers. The dirty goo dried, turned paler. Xaver made sure of further coverage. There was no shortage of trucks. By now he was seeing the traffic only in gigantic outlines. That pleased him. When cars approached from the opposite direction, he felt an urge to change lanes. The larger the oncoming vehicles, the more he had to restrain himself. He hoped he was merely toying with this thought. Cross the center line, he thought, go ahead, cross it—you wouldn't dare, you're chicken, aren't you? How wonderful it would be to step on the gas now, right down to the floor, making the cylinders wail, then with all 225 h.p. full tilt into a truck. Or rather, just into the trailer. After all, the other driver . . . Or into a concrete wall. First accelerate to 200, then head on into it. . . .

To drive through Memmingen, Xaver turned on the windshield washers. The boss had just inserted another cassette. Once again Xaver felt that tiny stab under his rib cage. He could see Waldburg-Zeil Castle. He recalled his ancestor who had been duped by the noble Georg von Waldburg. Whenever Xaver drove past that unscathed castle of the descendant of this peasant butcher, he perceived the course of history as a personal defeat. Wangen lay wet in the sun. Xaver was determined to take his favorite route. Not the great curve of the federal highway but the narrow, winding old highway from Niederwangen via Primisweiler, Pflegelberg, Goppertsweiler, Uhetsweiler, Neukirch, Bernried, and Dietmannsweiler to Tettnang. A route that was at the moment totally obscured by the May grass growing all the way up into the blossoming treetops. Xaver was happy. He was now driving straight toward Agnes. He wanted to do more than was possible. If he had been alone, he would have sung. This really was something, all around here. There was simply twice as much going on here per square foot as anywhere else. And today everything was freshly wet. And now in the sunshine! And all this while driving home. The blossom petals brought down by the rain were trimming both sides of the road with broad white frills. If this wasn't a wedding road! And it was even steaming, too, from the recent rain. This was the ultimate. If only he would take those blocks off his ears. For Chrissake. That fellow never lives where he happens to be.

Xaver let his great car glide into the steep curves, deliberately wrenching it out again each time just a fraction too late. It was incredible the way this car responded. How it dived down without softening. The way it immediately shot up the next hump, with no sign when it reached the top that actually it would rather take off. It just held the road beautifully at all times. Almost too beautifully, Xaver felt. He was really driving like this to evoke some reaction from Dr. Gleitze. At the very least he should utter his now-now. Or bitch because Xaver had chosen these back roads. But Xaver knew it was all right for him to take this route. The boss had postponed the trip home three times. This gave Xaver a kind of credit. And if not, okay, say so, sir, speak up. Dr. Gleitze said nothing. Xaver drove faster and faster. The boss began to sway in the curves.

Not until he had got out of the car outside the front door in Tettnang-Oberhof—the garden gate was open, indicating that Xaver was to drive up to the house—did he say: "Hm, so the horse sniffed the stable, didn't it!" Aloisia appeared at once and took the boss's things from Xaver as if she had to stop Xaver from entering the house. There was no sign of Mrs. Gleitze. Dr. Gleitze wished Xaver a good weekend and disappeared into the house. Aloisia, before going in, said: "Wait." When she returned she took a deep breath and made a face to indicate it wasn't easy to convey to Xaver all that she was now supposed to convey to him. So first a slip of paper with an address in Friedrichshafen where he was to take the two cases of wine from Ungstein. The car was to remain in Markdorf over the weekend. Whenever Aloisia had any messages for Xaver she would look up after each sentence with a frown, as if doubting whether Xaver understood everything as fast as she was saying it. She didn't really mean it, she just liked to pretend that Xaver was slower than she was. She regarded herself as being particularly quick. Quick-thinking. She always said she could think quicker than she could work. Needless to say, to put out her hand toward a drawer as slowly as Mrs. Gleitze did was beyond her. She often used to say to Xaver: "We fat guys must stick together." Xaver thought she was fatter than he was but didn't say so. She was certainly much shorter. His usual reply was: "Now, now, you little twerp." And she would say: "Little toads are full of poison too." She could be considered a living proof of this maxim. It embarrassed him that she spoke to him in such loud, broad dialect. By replying to her in his best High German he demonstrated that it wasn't necessary to address him in dialect.

So, now to the main thing, a request by Mrs. Gleitze, she couldn't insist, that she knew. . . . Aloisia grinned as she said this, jerked her head in the direction of the villa, and tapped the side of her little head with her stubby forefinger. In short: Could Xaver drive on to Hottingen, near Zürich? It was Dr. Gleitze's fiftieth birthday on Sunday, but the present was in Hottingen. Mrs. Gleitze had been expecting Xaver home earlier, of course. She hadn't, to be frank—Aloisia jerked her head again and tapped it with her finger—wanted to entrust the transportation of this gift to anyone else. Ready and waiting in Markdorf were a factory van, two Turks, and an employee who specialized in the transportation of fragile instruments. They had more or less been waiting for Xaver since yesterday, Mrs. Gleitze having, you know . . . head-jerking, head-tapping. "And what am I supposed to tell my wife?" asked Xaver. That was the least of his worries, said Aloisia; the later Xaver got home the happier his wife would be. That was another of Aloisia's jokes, a fact that Xaver first had to let sink in. Because he didn't react, or reacted too slowly for her, the quick one, she pinched his arm. Xaver said: "Okay, you phone her."

He drove to Hoch-Strasse in Friedrichshafen, delivered the wine; surprise was feigned, no tip was given, for which he was glad. The offer of a tip was something he was always prepared for as if for a blow that he was not free to return. The only person from whom he had ever accepted a tip was Dr. Gleitze's brother Albert, whom he had to pick up once a year at Kloten airport. He always got in the front seat beside Xaver and began oohing and aahing about the beauties of the towns and villages and forests and meadows between Zürich and Tettnang. He always arrived from Cleveland, Ohio. Xaver's first job was to drive to the Star in the little town of Kloten and have some draft beer with him. "I've been waiting for this swig for a whole year," Albert Gleitze would say every year after drinking down the first glass, slowly and ceremoniously, at one go. And Xaver must call him

Albert! He always said Xaver. Naturally Xaver didn't say Albert, but he didn't know how to refuse the five-dollar bill that Albert always pressed into his hand. Xaver still had all Albert's green bills at home. Maybe the day would come when one would have to emigrate to America, and then one would have some seed money.

In Markdorf he found the transport employee and the Turks in the cafeteria and drove them to Zürich in the van. Xaver chose the route via the Thurgau. He liked the Thurgau villages. The farms still looked the way they had at home before all that new building had started. Xaver pointed out the typical barn doors to his companions. He didn't dare point out the greenness of the meadows. But in his opinion, the green of the Thurgau meadows was something special.

"Nice country," said Hermann Lustig, the transport man, who looked more like an old watchmaker. He added: "I've come from Silesia." He said it as if he had arrived from Silesia right now, last night, instead of thirty years ago. Xaver felt rage immediately piling up inside him again. Why can't they leave people where they belong! And his cousin Konrad has the gall to defend such measures! It was time to start a new chapter, said Konrad. It was all our own doing. . . . Whenever Xaver ran into one of those displaced persons, he felt he ought to offer him something. He felt guilty.

The man from Silesia said the instrument to be picked up in Hottingen was a grand piano. A hundred years old. Made of mahogany. Built in Königsberg. By a famous Königsberg instrument builder. Brought to Switzerland by a composer from Königsberg. He'd had TB. Died in 1876. At the age of thirty-six. All the time Hermann Lustig—who had received this information from Mrs. Gleitze—was reeling this off, the Turks kept nodding as if to confirm what he was saying. Lustig said he had already explained the situation to the two Turks so they wouldn't act like lummoxes. The Turks went on nodding eagerly. "But," said Hermann Lustig, "I'd be a liar if I said it'd helped any. Those two guys mean well, they got good hearts, but otherwise . . . oh well, I won't say nothing no more. A person can feel real sorry for them. They haven't the foggiest what a grand piano is. Well, I say, listen carefully and I'll tell you: A grand piano, like the one this trip is all about, is an instrument that the composer Hermann Goetz used for his work. But they don't know what a composer is. A guy who writes operas, I say. They shake their heads. He wrote *The Taming of the Shrew*, I say. Shakespeare! But they've never heard the name. What am I supposed to say to that? Start a long sermon about Shakespeare? When that happens we got a saying in Silesia: The happiest people are the ones who know everything or nothing. To cut a long story short: I spelled it out to those two guys, I told them we'll get along fine together if they look damn sharp when they handle the instrument. Like lynxes, I told them, like lynxes, or they'll find I can be as tough as the next guy."

Xaver silently hoped they knew what lynxes were. He also felt sorry for the Turks, living as they did in a foreign country. In his eyes it was a crime to lure people away from their homes. That's the new way, simply. To that extent he could agree with Konrad. And where there's a crime, there are criminals. Now they act as if they were benefactors. He felt almost dizzy with rage at the thought that the two fellows beside him might be married and wouldn't see their families for God knows how long. And he would soon be driving up to Wigratsweiler, where Agnes, Magdalena, and Julia were lying in clean, soft beds, gently breathing away in their sleep. And these fellows! They had already told him. They lived in foreigners' quarters in Unterraderach. Six to a room. Why do you put up with that, for Chrissake! Mrs. Gleitze had told Hermann Lustig that, in bringing back this mahogany grand piano, they might be returning to German soil the last surviving instrument built in Königsberg. Hermann Lustig nodded. The two Turks nodded.

In Hottingen, all was in readiness. The grand piano had been swaddled in cloths, blankets, and planks in such a way they had only to lift it up and push it into the van. The legs were packed separately. In securing the piano inside the van, Lustig wouldn't let anyone help him. "The way things go sometimes, it'll take a bit longer than we expected," said Mr. Lustig. "I'll tell you something—why don't you go across the street to the inn? You're only in my way here." But Xaver insisted that the Turks and he must be allowed to remain as helpers, otherwise this enthusiastic expert would lose all sense of time. "That's done," Lustig said finally; now it was only up to Xaver whether the last surviving Königsberg grand piano would reach German soil.

Shortly before midnight they were in Tettnang-Oberhof. After parking the van behind the studio, they got into a VW that Mrs. Gleitze had arranged to have waiting. In the VW to Markdorf, transfer to Xaver's Renault. Then he drove the Turks to their quarters in Unterraderach, shook each by the hand, and clapped each on the arm. He was at a loss for words. He drove Hermann Lustig to his cottage in Eriskirch. Lustig thanked Xaver, adding that Xaver had done a good job. Today they had salvaged a piece of the German past. He expressed his thanks as if he were the German Reich. Maybe he is, thought Xaver at the sight of Lustig's puny figure standing there in the moonlight. "Well, I never," said Lustig, "the cherry tree has blossomed overnight. Look, over there, among the treetops, already a pale stripe. You know, I'd be a liar if I said I hadn't enjoyed our little outing. But then when you've shut your garden gate behind you, you can't help being glad you're still all in one piece. With all those damn trucks. It's not so bad at night. Oof, my watch says almost one o'clock. I have to get up at six-thirty, we leave at eight-thirty. We have to make long trips, a lot of things are different from the way they used to be. That's another day behind me. Disappeared like an old hat, I might say. It takes as long as it takes, that's what my dad always used to say. Have a safe trip, young fellow."

As soon as Xaver was sitting in his Renault, it occurred to him that he was paying for bringing the transportation crew home out of his personal kilometers. Otherwise he would have had to drive the factory VW from Eriskirch back again to Markdorf and from there drive home in his R 16. If Mrs. Gleitze had an ounce of brains she would realize this and would ask him about his expenses. At times she was almost insultingly punctilious. When he drove to the villa on summer evenings with strawberries, cherries, or red currants from Agnes's berry patch, she paid not only for the strawberries, cherries, and red currants but also for the mileage. She insisted on having it that way. Xaver would have preferred to have such trips remembered as favors. Agnes said: "You're nuts." Agnes wasn't ambitious.

A moonlit night. He swung his way voluptuously up the curves to his plateau. After the Mercedes and the van, his R 16 seemed like a mere toy with soft, rubbery hips. Dr. Gleitze was going to be fifty. So Gleitze was exactly ten years older than he was. Like Johann. Johann would be fifty now. For Chrissake, that was the excuse he'd been waiting for! My brother Johann, who was killed while defending Königsberg, would also be fifty now. No, that wouldn't do. It sounded as though Xaver meant it as a reproach to the boss. You're still alive, whereas my brother . . . Well, that was how he meant it. No, it wasn't. Dr. Gleitze had lost his original home, hadn't he? A birthday wasn't the right occasion after all. The important thing for Xaver was to let the boss be aware that Xaver wouldn't have become his chauffeur if Johann hadn't been killed in the war. Johann wouldn't have stood for that. Bet you anything. That was another of those bets that no one could accept. But Xaver was absolutely certain. So the boss had only Johann's death to thank for having Xaver for a chauffeur. Oh well, he'd simply have had someone else. Xaver realized that this wouldn't get him anywhere. In any event: Johann would have directed the course of the whole family history into other channels.

At the age of sixteen or seventeen, Johann had already been considering what each of them was to become. Jakob would take the farm. Xaver was to become a teacher. Georg a vet. Johann himself a lawyer. It was extraordinary how, as soon as Johann came home, life intensified. Everything Xaver remembered about Johann was somehow vital. Johann had come home only during school vacation. He used to be picked up at Kressbronn station with the runabout, a lightly built buggy that had a bench with a back to it and a hand brake up front. And an iron collar to hold the whip. They felt as if they were riding in a carriage when they drove in the pale, light, springy buggy. On the way home from Kressbronn, Jakob would hand over the reins to Johann; on the short flat stretch between Kressbronn and Gattnau, Johann would give Moritz his head. The days when Johann came home from Wurzach were higher holidays for Xaver than the high holidays themselves. Even Jakob, who all year round referred to Johann merely as that inkslinger, would be seized on such days by a crazy excess of zeal. The previous evening he had always rubbed the harness with a colorless grease and used a blue-black one for the hand brake and a yellow one for the axles. Their father, as long as he had been alive, had always made sure the wheel pins were secure before they drove off. To be able to bend down far enough, he had held on with one hand to the little railing that ran around the buggy.

"Let's go!" Jakob used to shout, cracking his whip. "Watch out now!" But he waited with that until their father had bent down to the fourth wheel. Then Moritz had yanked them off, making the gravel spray in all directions. Jakob would yell: "Giddyap, Moritz, giddyap!" He kept on cracking his whip until they were down on the road, then up on the ridge and out of the village.

Each time Johann had stepped down from the railway carriage, Xaver had been shocked to see how thin he was. Xaver still remembered the sensation of his own palms resting on the pale green paint of the wooden barrier. As if his shock at Johann's terrible thinness had made the palms of his hands sensitive. Jakob used to say when taking Johann's carton and suitcase from him that one had to look twice to see Johann once, he really was as thin as a rail. It always took a few days for Johann to come out with any details about his life in Wurzach. In return for reduced school fees he had to work afternoons doing odd jobs at the site where an extension was under seemingly interminable construction. But he was given no more to eat than those who were only studying. And they weren't getting enough either. Just once a year, when the Prince of Waldburg-Zeil, the patron of the monastery, turned up to receive homage, there were extra rations for each boy after the ceremony. But when the boys from grade 8 on were trucked out to the prince's fields to help with the harvest, the food was again a mockery. Windfalls and a slice of bread plus a morsel of cheese that one also had to look at twice to see once.

Xaver switched off his headlights. The moonlight, the blossoming trees, and his almost white car made a more harmonious whole without light. And he could see just as well at night as during the day. And at this hour there wasn't a soul on the road. Yes, there was—Friday! The customers from the Happy Prospect. Reluctantly he switched on his lights again. Now he could see only what the light sawed out of the darkness. Turning off the motor he glided down into the village with just enough impetus to bring him up the rise to the farmhouse. Tell was standing there as if he had been waiting day and night for a week. Xaver thrust his hand into the dog's fur and caressed him. Tell tried to tunnel his way into some part of Xaver. The dog snuffled and whined as quietly as he could, but Xaver had to ask him to be even quieter. Tell groaned. Xaver hugged him. Tell trembled. Xaver dug his fingers into the fur. Suddenly Tell knocked Xaver over. Dorle came running out and rubbed his leg with arched back. As Xaver approached the kitchen door, it opened. Agnes said in a whisper: "How late you are." "Yes," he replied. Because he had only said yes, she had to say something. She asked if he was hungry. Every sentence he now spoke was designed—almost against his will—to conceal his state of mind. Every movement he made served only to conceal his true mood. He avoided close contact with her. He made his way past her into the kitchen, turned on the light, and said: "Your feet are bare." He said it lightly, a bit reproachfully. He could feel the pulse in his neck. He was afraid Agnes might notice what mood he was in. Now that the light was on, he dared not meet her eyes. He felt that she could immediately tell from his eyes that he was almost fainting with longing for her. Only if she came to him of herself, because she couldn't stand it without him either, would he confess that earlier on, a few minutes ago, he had almost fainted.

She made him a green salad, fried eggs, and some fried potatoes. He brought up a bottle of white wine. But he put only one glass on the table. If she wanted to join him, she only had to take one step to reach a glass and put it on the table, too. Because he hoped so passionately that she wouldn't let him sit there and drink a whole bottle of wine by himself, he couldn't do or say anything to encourage her to join him. It was up to her to want to sit down with him at the round kitchen table and put down another glass and say: I'm thirsty, too. But how, since she had just got out of bed, should she be thirsty? While busy at the stove she told him what had been happening during the week. Julia had yet another new boyfriend. Herbert was leaving the day after tomorrow for Persia. From Stuttgart. He and a friend were driving in a secondhand truck to Persia. Xaver said: "I'd like to

see him drive a truck to Persia." This answer prompted Agnes to
tell him everything she had heard from Julia and Herbert about
the project. Used trucks are driven by young people to Persia.
He didn't want to know a thing about it right now. He felt the
knot forming inside him because that young punk, that good-
for-nothing who at some point or other had graduated from
high school and had been sitting around ever since, was now—
for a lark and out of sheer boredom—trying to play at being a
truckdriver. And to Persia, no less. Well well, Mr. Zürn, and
where are you off to? Oh, all the way to Munich, to Cologne
even? You don't say! Well, the day after tomorrow I'm driving
to Teheran, with a buddy, just for the heck of it. . . . Agnes,
Agnes, why don't you notice how little I want to hear that! The
only good news is that Julia has acquired a new boyfriend even
before Herbert has left. That pale, skinny character with his su-
percilious manner had been getting on his nerves long enough.
And the way when he stayed for supper he used to grab the
whole cheese in his fist to cut himself a piece. In math Julia had
had an E. In French, too. Languages were his department. The
new boyfriend was again much too old for Julia. Twenty-three,
just imagine.

"It's one-thirty," said Agnes, "and she's still not home."
Xaver began to feel dizzy. It was as if a mainstream of life were
suddenly clamped off. She should have been home by ten. Herbert was having a farewell party tonight. Last night she'd got
back at two in the morning from Bregenz. Today, this afternoon, saying she was off to Kressbronn, to Bärbel's to do home-
work, and simply hadn't come home again. And the night
before that at one-thirty in the morning. And that's how it had
been since Monday. Agnes looked too exhausted to cry. She suspected that Julia wasn't at Herbert's tonight at all but already
with this fellow Mick. Just imagine, twenty-three. Agnes
propped her head in her hands. She had asked Julia what she was
up to with this fellow Mick. The same thing she'd been up to

with Herbert, she had said. He has a job at your Markdorf plant
but wants to quit because he wants to be a photographer. He
was taking pictures of Julia every day. Every day she brought
home new ones. Agnes went off and came back with some large
photographs. Julia in front of blossoming fruit trees, under
blossoming fruit trees, among blossoming fruit trees, Julia beside the lake, Julia beside the pond, but mostly: Julia on the
motorbike. And in every one of them she wore an expression
he'd never seen on her before.

Xaver didn't spend much time looking at them. He had
reached the point where he really must make it clear to Agnes
that her problems with the kids weren't of the slightest interest
to him. But she had been telling him only about Julia. Now she
had to tell him about Magdalena, too. The very fact that she
always called Magdalena Leni annoyed him. He was the only
one in the family who always used her full name. To no avail.
The others said Magda or Lena or Leni. And because these days
Agnes almost always said Leni, Leni it was. Xaver got the impression that Agnes, by this least attractive abbreviation, was
taking her revenge for the problems she was having with Magdalena. Agnes maintained that Magdalena hated and despised
her. Now the child wouldn't even let her help with her math.
Xaver could point out that she didn't allow him to help her either, but still he didn't say she hated him. But then Leni didn't
hate him, said Agnes, she hated her, Agnes, and how! Okay,
perhaps it was more contempt than hatred, in any case Leni
hadn't addressed a single word to her all week long, and she had
answered every question, even the most cautious, merely with a
shrug, although mostly she had said "Balls," in a pained voice.
Shrug or "Balls," that was all she'd had from Leni all week.
Once Agnes had been about to place a hand on her shoulder, but
Leni had turned away with an expression of disgust and the single word: "Pest."

Xaver looked cautiously at Agnes. Her face seemed to have

sagged. Only the eyes were still in the same place. But because the face had sagged somehow, the eye sockets had become larger. The eyes stood in a sort of void. Did it only seem so, or was there a downy fuzz covering the pale, lifeless-looking skin of her face? He couldn't remember ever having noticed that downy fuzz. And now there it was on the pale skin, as if Agnes were dead and the decaying of the skin had brought a fuzz to the surface.

Agnes had fetched herself a bottle of mineral water. From time to time she took a sip without seeming to be aware of it. Actually this mineral water was kept for Xaver's benefit. Somehow he resented the sight of her drinking it now. She was staring straight ahead. When Xaver also stared straight ahead, their lines of vision intersected at right angles over the middle of the old round table, the sole remaining item from the former furnishings of the Hungerbühler Farm. Everything else had been replaced. Mainly by Agnes's dowry. She came from a large farm and had brought along more household linens and furniture and stuff than anyone had ever brought to the small Hungerbühler farmhouse. Consequently she had felt entitled to have everything that didn't go with her own things either ripped out or thrown out. The old mustard-yellow paneling in the parlor, the old wooden ceiling, the buffet, and the ancient leather sofa in the parlor, the grandfather clock encased in similar paneling, the wooden floor in the parlor and the passageway, and so on. Even the tiled stove had to go, to make room for her piano in the little parlor. For Xaver it was a kind of one-upmanship over the other Wigratsweiler farmers, and especially over Margot, that there should now be a piano at the Hungerbühler Farm. The first piano in Wigratsweiler. The Prospect didn't have one until Margot and her husband added on the banquet room.

The only part of Agnes's face that still had some color was the edges of her nostrils; they were purplish. Inflamed. The point where they met her face, in the corners, was where the purple

was most intense. Maybe, at that point, if one looked more
closely, it would blend into pus yellow. Oh, Agnes. She was
wearing her dark green nightgown: it made her look even paler.
Xaver seemed to see each one of her dark hairs springing indi-
vidually from her pale scalp. The two dark grooves from the base
of her nose to the middle of her forehead were familiar to him.
She nearly always had those nowadays. Sometimes he would try
to stroke them away, carefully and slowly, with his thumb. After a short time they were back again. Around the little mound
of her chin that had once sat amiably under her mouth, there
was a hard, colorless zone, as if the little mound, now deeply
scored, were being pressed up by a bloodless zone. And the
mouth: two downturned strokes. A black-and-white face. Tonight the ever-visible dark fuzz on her upper lip turned her into
the exhausted little Corsican soldier at the gates of Moscow
whom Xaver remembered from a movie.

When he had finished his meal, Agnes cleared away the dishes, leaving bottle and glass on the table. Xaver resented her going barefoot. Half the kitchen had a stone floor. Later on she'd
have ice-cold feet again. All through the night, too. The touch
of her cold feet cut like a knife. For God's sake, why can't she
put on some house shoes! At the thought of her little blue bedroom slippers, he remembered his Indian perfumes. This was
not the right moment to produce them. Agnes stood beside
him, laid a hand on his shoulder, and said it was getting on
two o'clock. He couldn't move. Besides, he hadn't finished his
bottle of wine yet. So he refilled his glass. She sat down on a
chair, her knees spread wide apart, her hands hanging down on
both sides. Xaver thought of Mrs. Trummel. He was totally at a
loss. Agnes drew up her legs, put her arms around her knees,
crouched behind her knees, rested her chin on her knees, and
looked at him. He was aware of this but didn't look toward her.
He drank up, poured again, emptying the bottle so that he was
sitting in front of the last glass.

Suddenly Agnes went to the kitchen counter, brought back
the bowl of oranges, sat down with the purple bowl in her lap,
took an orange, and peeled it. He watched her hands. It was
wonderful the way those hands dealt with the orange. Once
again he became aware of the pulse in his throat. Agnes offered
him half the first peeled orange on the palm of her hand. He
resented that, too. She quickly peeled three more oranges, one
after another, and ate them. He resented this guzzling of oranges more and more. What a ridiculous situation! There he sat,
swilling down his white wine while she guzzled oranges. How
idiotic. Suddenly he realized he must watch his step. If she was
to conclude from his behavior that he had some grudge against
her, she wouldn't let up until she found out and removed the
cause of his moodiness and changed his mood. Since she had
made no overtures of her own to him, he didn't want to provoke
her by a display of ill-temper. He must be as gentle and weary as
she was herself, so that, without sounding any alarm, they could
find their way past each other to bed and to sleep. If she had
wanted his return home to turn out differently, she should have
managed not to serve up that eternal litany of problems with the
kids the very first night. She should have managed to threaten
or bribe Julia so as to make her be home before midnight. With
a new blouse, Julia could be made to do anything. What was he
saying, blouse! A hair clip would do it! And Agnes hadn't even
tried anything like that! *She* hadn't been looking forward to anything! *She* didn't want anything! She was worn out. Exhausted.
All in. Finished. Amen. But watch it, don't look angry, or
she'll get right back at you. Your best bet is to pretend a similar
total exhaustion; she respects that.

He brought it off. The light was out. He lay in his bed, she in
hers. He was wide awake. She had said good night. He had said
good night. In a whisper. They always whispered in this bedroom, something that went back to the time when the kids had
slept in the same room with them. In those days they had rented

out the two rooms on the second floor not only during the summer but all year round. For the next few years, the kids had
continued to share the room only in summer. Xaver was thinking that, if she could have her way, the kids would be sleeping
in the same room with them to this day. No question. Unfortunately Agnes had every reason, every right, to be permanently
exhausted. She worked harder than any woman he knew or had
ever heard of. But that was the very thing that was so bad, that
pathological addiction to work. Or put it the other way around:
everything else was more important to her than he was—her
work, the kids, everything. Each one of her movements is work.
One doesn't own a farm for a few hundred years without every
movement being work, that's obvious; idlers soon clear out.
Only those who sweat their guts out survive. But surely not in
this day and age! Agnes and he might have been the first to take
life more easily. If only they could have—taken life more easily.
The boss—now he, he of course came home to a wife who had
used a minimum of movement all week long. During the day
she was so lethargic that most likely at nighttime she positively
bounced! From pent-up physical need. Or at least she got into
bed as lethargically as she always sat around. That might be
something too, a lethargic woman like that with flesh that was
inwardly highly alert. He could easily picture that. The main
thing was that she dominated her husband. He didn't know
what was behind it, but he had noticed a thousand times that
this was so. She steered the boss. She even ordered him around.
She kept him on the run. She sent him away. She made him
come. Probably at this moment she had arranged herself in some
treacly yellow light and was saying: Come along now, hurry up
if you don't mind, otherwise . . . Whereupon she would hoist
her lower torso into the most cloying part of the light. Xaver
longed for a woman who would order him around like that. He
really shouldn't have married a mere chance acquaintance. No
question, that's all Agnes was. At the International Lake Con-

stance Fair, that was where he had met her. Met her indeed!
Been taken in, was more like it! In front of the Brockhaus Encyclopedia booth stood three young bullyboys who thrust a piece
of paper into the hand of anyone who wasn't watching out. And
those who allowed the piece of paper to be thrust upon them
were then maneuvered into the booth, where a somewhat superior team continued to work over the captives.

Xaver had noticed that one of the three characters had
grabbed a dark-haired girl and propelled her inside. That
looked so violent that he couldn't help watching. She seemed
helpless. He had never seen anything more marvelous, either
before or since. The way she was being shoved in there. The way
her resistance delineated her body. Gradually she raised her
hands. He felt irresistibly drawn to the scene. Just then a piece
of paper was thrust into his hand, and he found himself being
propelled inside, his staring into the booth having been interpreted as interest in the encyclopedia. He felt he had to protect
her. But then he merely watched her hand as it was signing.
Agnes Guldin, she signed. He preceded her out of the booth.
Waited. Said: "Miss Guldin, I'm sorry I couldn't help you."
She said—blushing to the roots of her hair—that she had signed
only because he had been watching. That was a statement that
shot through him like an avalanche of fire. The very sight of this
girl had made him instantly feel strong. They had walked hardly ten yards side by side when suddenly trumpet music blared
from all the loudspeakers, flooding the huge hall. Military taps
converted to a hit tune. A booming voice announced that it
was almost six o'clock and that the fair was closing its doors.
With the music sloshing about over their heads, they left the
building.

Outside it was spring. When Agnes told him later that she
had really intended to spend that Sunday at the fair with her
friend Maja but Maja hadn't shown up at the bus stop, she and

Xaver agreed that their meeting had been an act of Providence. Maja, Agnes said, would have protected her from those Brockhaus touts. But if she hadn't been dragged off like that, Xaver would never have looked her way. If Maja had been there, he wouldn't have had a chance anyway, said Agnes, because Maja had picked out Agnes for her brother. . . .

The more often they discussed that Sunday afternoon, the more they embroidered upon the unmistakable nature of that act of Providence to which they owed their marriage. At some point they had begun to call the act of Providence a coincidence. After that, they spoke less often of that Sunday afternoon. They had never, for instance, talked about it to their children. Xaver would have been afraid they might say it was a fine thing to know they were the products of a coincidence. Perhaps he still wouldn't have spoken to Agnes if he hadn't also seen that her name was Guldin. He had immediately remembered Guldin's Theorem. At vocational school he had earned praise for knowing it: The Volume of a Body of Revolution is equal to the Product of the Area of the revolving figure and the length of the path followed by the centroid of that area. $V = A2\pi\bar{y}$ (where $\bar{y}$ is the distance from the centroid to the axis of revolution).

Oh, this woman, this woman. She was awake. He could tell. She was waiting for Julia. She never went to sleep before both the girls were home. It felt as if he'd had a row with Agnes. That's the way they were lying there now. As if they'd had a row. If one of the kids was sick or not home yet, they always lay as if they'd had a row. Completely separated.

So one drives a whole week toward a single moment, a single person, and then there's nothing. And he resented even more that he had to admit she was right. As long as Julia wasn't home, they were separated. Agnes was right. Agnes said in a low voice: "The worst part is that this fellow Mick rides a motorbike." But even if Julia had been at home, they might well have been lying separately side by side. Oh yes, she'd never understand what it meant to him to come home. Each time the same estrangement.

Sometime during the night there was a knock. Agnes was up and running. He followed her. Agnes and Julia were standing at the back door. He sat down at the round table. At his place on the drawer side where his father had sat and *his* father probably also. Julia came through the kitchen. She seemed to be walking on stilts. She held her head so high that it was impossible to meet her eyes. She stalked through the kitchen, jacked up her head another few notches, curled her lips back from her teeth so that the most one might expect from between her closed teeth was a hissing sound. Agnes was standing by the door in a more or less humble attitude. Or she merely seemed that way, barefoot, in the dark green, ankle-length cotton nightgown. Or she seemed that way because Julia walked like a hundred peacocks rolled into one. And on platform shoes. And anyway was a head taller than her mother. Her shoelaces were tied crisscross all the way up to her knees. A little rag of a dress hung on her large body. She really shouldn't have been named Julia, Xaver thought. That was Agnes's fault. Just because a daughter of a cousin in Überlingen was called Julia. Xaver had protested, saying it looked as though merely by giving a child that name he wanted to put her on the same level as the daughter of the first doctor in the family. But Agnes had pointed out that the Überlingen Zürns had copied them with a Magdalena, so what had been wrong with borrowing a Julia from them?

If Xaver hadn't called out to her to stop, Julia would have walked through the kitchen without so much as turning her eyes or saying a word. Xaver said: "Where have you been?" She stopped, then turned with extreme affectation toward her father. Looked at him. Through her eyelashes. He did not have the impression that she saw him. Her eyes sparkled. Her face glowed. Her lips gleamed. Her enormous mass of hair seemed to seethe. For him simply to stand there was disconcerting. "I'm asking you, where have you been?" Xaver shouted. He didn't really want to know. But he had to. He was beyond being able to distinguish anything. Everything, absolutely everything was rushing together inside him to form a rock-hard knot. Julia jacked her head a little farther up on her long neck and said calmly, in broad dialect: "We really tied one on." The fact that she spoke dialect didn't bother him when no one else was around. But her slang plus the dialect was too much for him. "Who?" shouted Xaver. "Who?" "Why're you yelling your silly head off?" she said. "If you really want to know, it leaves me absolutely cold." He moved toward her as if about to hit her. But all he wanted was to drive her away. He wanted her to be afraid of him and run away, up to her room, to get rid of her. But someone who walks and stands the way Julia walked and stood that night can't turn around and hop away like a rabbit. Xaver was aware of that as he approached her. She didn't run away. She stood her ground, waiting for him, looking at him as if she were much taller than he. So he had no option, it seemed to him, but to hit her. If only she had run away! Surely she could see he was coming to hit her! What a fool he would look to rush up like that and then not hit out. So he hit her. She jacked up her head a little farther so that all he got was her chin. He lacked the willpower for a second blow. She looked at him now as if she had proven something to him. She had evaded him just enough for the blow to reach her, but barely. Yet also enough for the blow not to hurt much. But a blow it had been. It was proven: he struck his children in the face. Her lips peeled back entirely from her teeth. Evidently she could use this peeling-back-of-lips-from-teeth, which he had just seen in those photographs, for any occasion. The sparkle in her eyes turned hard, her eyebrows rose precisely by the one millimeter necessary to add the quality of contempt to her entire expression, and she said, without raising her voice: "Asshole," and left the room.

Agnes seemed to feel a little better than before. Xaver's behavior had made up for all she'd gone through during the week.
But Xaver now felt worse than before. As if, through his shouting and hitting out, he had done violence to himself. Agnes
suggested they go to bed. He could only say that he'd be coming. He sat there so rigidly that he felt powerless to move. At
some point Agnes returned, stood before him, and said she
wasn't going back without him. He went with her. He got into
bed. Agnes stretched her feet across. They were ice-cold. He
didn't care. Agnes's hand came across. He didn't react. He tried
to breathe like someone asleep. The idea that she might try to
resolve everything by intercourse scared him. But Agnes didn't
want that either. She fell asleep.

Suddenly the birds were singing. It wasn't quite light yet.
The night is a barrel, he thought. A huge barrel, in fact. Xaver
listened intently. He raised his head. Sat on the edge of the bed.
Now that's singing, sir, that's pretty close to yodeling. Suddenly he heard a chair being moved. Overhead. In Julia's room.
Footsteps. She was going to bed. At this hour. Xaver lay down
again. The thought of Julia's having been awake all this time
haunted him. He hadn't the faintest idea how he was going to
fall asleep again. Under his right rib cage the little stab, fine as a
hair, made itself felt. With thumb and forefinger he pressed his
lids more firmly shut, to produce complete blackness and ab-
sence of imagery. But the harder he pressed, the more flashes
leaped out of the darkness. So he dropped his hand again and
just lay there.

He had a dream: Agnes and he had a large house. A villa. In
the garden a shed like at Tettnang-Oberhof. The gate, too, was
like the Gleitzes'. Suddenly someone rang the bell insistently.
Agnes had gone outside. She had succeeded in leading the man
away from the front door. He had even allowed himself to be led
out through the open gate. Across the street: the woods. There
the man stops. Two giant machine-gray spider beetles, as if

made of leather strips, approach the gate. Agnes leaps forward and simply turns the beetles around as they run. Now they run away from Agnes and Xaver just as fast as they had at first run toward them. As Agnes is about to return to Xaver, who is standing by the gate, the man, who is still standing across the road among the trees, draws a pistol, holds it with both hands, and aims at Agnes. He presses the trigger twice. Agnes collapses before reaching the gate and calls out: Help me, please help me! Xaver is rooted to the ground. That woke him up. He looked at the clock: twenty-past five. He was glad to be awake. He put his hand on the knot in his stomach. It would dissolve.

When Agnes awoke, she was ready to get up right away. He just managed to catch her hand. It was shortly after six. He told her he wouldn't let her go until she had listened to his dream. Then she'd have to tell him *her* dream. Then they could get up. He told her his dream. Then it was her turn: She had dreamed that Dr. Gleitze had given a party just for Xaver. In a big ballroom a towering buffet dinner had been carefully set up. Suddenly she had the feeling that people couldn't see each other at all because the light was so dazzling. She had to do something about it. Just a moment, she had called out, just a moment! And she had run to the windows and closed the heavy, dark green velvet curtains shut. But in doing so she had knocked over the buffet. Most of the towering, costly spread lay on the rug, smashed, oozing, ruined. Several waiters had instantly come running up to her and Xaver and written down in detail what everything had cost and how much she and Xaver would have to pay. Whereupon she and Xaver had fled to Dr. Meichle's, who had told them to wash their hands and take their time over it. Then he had placed a fine antique pitcher and basin in front of them. Gilt and purple. He had added that the set was over a hundred years old and had been made by the world-famous Saarbrücken company of . . . Unfortunately she hadn't caught the French name. But with her very first movement she had knocked the pitcher and basin from the dresser, causing both pieces to smash onto the stone floor. Then they had fled up the hill. But she had dropped everything she was meant to hold on to. Finally Xaver's binoculars, which she was supposed to hand to him so he could observe their pursuers. When the binoculars tumbled down onto the rock and were dashed to pieces, he had cried out in horror, and that had woken her up.

Xaver got up, opened the heavy, dark green velvet curtains, and said: "The weather is better than you'd imagine."

June

1

X A V E R sat on the sofa feeling like a waxworks figure. He really wondered whether his eyelids would ever move again. At any moment Agnes might come in. Then he would have to do something. For him just to be sitting on the sofa wasn't good enough for her. If he were to have a newspaper in his hands, everything would be all right. At the moment he didn't yet feel capable of picking up the newspaper. As soon as her footsteps approached on the stone floor, he would probably find it easier to pick it up. He could never explain to the continuously active Agnes that what he liked best was simply to sit there. The only thing that somewhat justified his sitting there was Dorle, who, as soon as he sat down on the sofa, came stalking up and settled down comfortably on his lap.

Suddenly Agnes was at the door. He hadn't had time to pick up the paper. Immediately her face acquired those deep grooves of dismay. On a wonderful June afternoon, her husband is sitting in the parlor, doing absolutely nothing. She dropped onto a chair. Then she must have felt obliged to respond to her husband's inactivity with redoubled activity. She sat down beside Xaver. Then she said he must promise her not to get upset. That told him what was coming. She intended to mow the grass. That was his job. But in her view he always left it too long. She was embarrassed before the people of Wigratsweiler. She knew that he couldn't allow her to do the mowing. So with the request that he let her do the mowing she forced him to get up and mow the grass. She couldn't stand the sight anymore, the grass was so high it simply made her sick, it looked so awful. . . . Tomorrow, he said, when he came back from the doctor's he'd do the mowing. That would fix her. That served her right. Yes, he's going to see the doctor. There, now she wouldn't say anything more about mowing, would she! Now it's up to him to reassure her. It's not all that bad. Just to be on the safe side. He was absolutely certain there was nothing to worry about. As he said, just to be on the safe side.

He went over to the telephone and dialed Dr. Meichle's number. Busy. He dialed again, and again. He might have to go on dialing for a whole hour with no success. Gradually he felt that the rapid sounds of the busy signal seemed to be directed against him personally. Was there anything nastier than this concentrated ten-numeral dialing and then the mocking beeps in reply! He had to tell himself that, of all the people trying to reach that number at that moment, only a single one would hit the jackpot. He told himself this, but it had no effect. When he got through he shouted at the receptionist that he must have an appointment with Dr. Meichle today. She couldn't fit him in that soon, said the receptionist. She said it so cheerfully that Xaver longed to throw the receiver at her head. Okay, then, tomorrow, but it's got to be tomorrow, on Wednesday he'd be out of town again, for Chrissake! She was intimidated. Tomorrow morning at seven-thirty, she said in an almost lifeless voice.

When Xaver walked in at seven twenty-five, the waiting room was already jammed. He just managed to find a place to stand against the wall. A room full of wilted people. A man came out of the X-ray room, his mouth daubed with white barium meal. He went over to the little newspaper table. The man sitting at the table drew his attention to his clown's makeup. To apologize for interfering, he added in a low voice: "Just thought you'd like to know." The man he addressed immediately came toward Xaver. Only now did Xaver notice that he was standing in front of the mirror. He had to step forward into the room to allow the other man to wipe away the caked white gunk. When Xaver had to swallow the gunk in the X-ray room, he was very careful. He didn't want to look like a clown when he returned to the waiting room. Twice he was told to swallow the gunk. Twice Dr. Meichle affixed himself to his apparatus like the U-boat captain to his periscope in a movie. Again and again he poked the rubber prow of some contraption into Xaver's abdomen, called out "Stop breathing!" There was a click followed by a whirring sound. Xaver waited outside until he was called into the consulting room. He might begin by wiping his nose, said Dr. Meichle, directing Xaver to the sink. Xaver saw in the mirror that he had an absurd white dab on the very tip of his nose. But not one of those decrepit old crocks in the waiting room had taken the trouble to tell him.

When Xaver was seated on the white chair in front of Dr. Meichle's desk, the question came: "Do you feel ill?" How pleasant it would have been if Dr. Meichle had asked: "Do you feel well?" This question would have been easier to answer with a no than the other with a yes. Somewhat uneasily, Xaver answered "No." That pleased Dr. Meichle. "So let's take a good look!" He examined Xaver with all the skill at his command. Dr. Meichle was an athlete. Xaver felt as if he should be putting up some resistance. Moreover, it occurred to him from time to time that Dr. Meichle might be playing tennis later on with Mrs. Gleitze and telling her all about Xaver. Xaver had more than once had to pick up Mrs. Gleitze from the tennis court. She liked to chat at the net as often as possible. Then she would walk slowly back and go on playing as if her racket were made of lead and every stroke were an ordeal.

After the examination, Xaver had to go to the nurse to give specimens of blood and urine. That was the worst part. The nurse was from Retterschen. One of the Grabherrs girls. Although Klara now lived in Ailingen, she still often came to Wigratsweiler to visit her sister, who had married one of the

Fiegles. Another of Klara's sisters, Maria, had married a colleague of Xaver's, formerly chauffeur to a chocolate manufacturer who had suffered a horrible death; now he was chauffeur to one of the divorced wives of that manufacturer. Xaver was always worried when this Heini Müller and Maria came to the Fiegle farm. Whenever he was in the village he would rush into each house, grab the women—on one hand he had only one finger left, the thumb of course, and he would dance around like a madman with the screaming women, asking them whether they would like to plait the hair on his chest into little braids. He was bald, but everywhere else he was covered by a thick fur. Oddly enough he was popular. Nevertheless Xaver was afraid that this holy terror would give the people of Wigratsweiler a false impression of what a chauffeur was like.

As Xaver approached Klara Grabherrs' door with the glass three-quarters full, he tried to think of some humorous remark. He felt that it would be better for him to be the one to make the jokes. He couldn't think of anything. But as soon as she saw him Klara said: "Come on now, Xaver, let's have that apple cider." He immediately felt relieved and was able to say: "Better than turnip soup, anyway." She laughed, he laughed.

Then once again he was sitting across from Dr. Meichle, who sat at an angle to his desk. Well tanned. He really did resemble an actor whose name Xaver couldn't remember. Perhaps because he resembled not merely one but many, if not all actors. Since there were still a lot of people in the waiting room, it embarrassed Xaver that Dr. Meichle should spend so long talking to him. He's probably doing it for Mrs. Gleitze's sake, Xaver thought. Sitting on his chair, he felt small, rigid, incorrigible, fragmentary, guilty. Dr. Meichle explained that there was nothing wrong with Xaver. Nothing for which Xaver wasn't himself the best doctor. "People come to consult me," said Dr. Meichle, "and think that's all there is to it. They hand themselves over to the doctor, and that's that. The rest is up to the doctor. Just as they're always screaming for more government, so they're always screaming for more doctor. And some even want the doctor to act in the capacity of a civil servant, so that there would be only one single voice. Well, Mr. Zürn, that's not how it works. One can't just hand over one's body to the doctor the way one hands over a defective automobile to the repair shop. If a person won't help himself, no one can help him. When I observe the lack of interest people have in their own health, I am shocked. They sit down in the waiting room, wait their turn, point to the place where it hurts, then lapse into a kind of trance from which they don't want to be brought back until the pain's gone.

"In your case especially, Mr. Zürn, self-help is more important than any medication. Your metabolism depends on mental effort. Tell me, who do you think this complicated metabolic system between mouth and anus is listening to? To you, Mr. Zürn. *You* call the tune. And if you produce only discordant notes, you mustn't be surprised at the discordant notes with which your digestive apparatus—which is more than a mere apparatus—answers you. And the belching, my dear Mr. Zürn, that seems to upset you so much—according to the latest research that's nothing but the return of air swallowed while eating. So just don't gulp your food, eat carefully, chew once in a while, my dear fellow, then instead of having to press down your food pneumatically you can let it slide down in your saliva. You should be ashamed of your lack of interest in your body. How can a person be such a stranger to himself? The point is, you're not interested in your digestion, my dear fellow. Right? Don't talk to me about your travel irregularity. As a partner, biology plays fair. Even on a trip. But you seem to take a peculiar pleasure in letting your body suffer at your own hands. To whom do you want to display this suffering? We are always out to impress somebody. That's the strongest of all motives. So come on, let's hear it! Whom are you trying to impress? Are you trying to get the attention of your wife? Are you jealous of your children? It's hard to imagine that you have any problems connected with your job. Dr. Gleitze's chauffeur! That's to say, chauffeur to one of the finest, cleverest, most humane human beings alive today! Highly educated, versatile, such a wide range of interests! And his wife, kindness personified, a paragon of altruism! But who am I saying this to! Chauffeur to the Gleitzes, what a stroke of luck! Or is there something more? Since I can't imagine it, you'll have to help me. Yes? No. Just as I thought. So what is it, my high-strung friend? Your children are now sixteen and eighteen. That can be tough. I know. But this kind of conflict is beneficial. It keeps you on your toes. So there remains your wife. Perhaps you feel neglected by your wife. And now you're reacting to this by working it off on yourself. You get stomach pains. You don't complain, if I know you at all. But you sit there demanding that your wife notice how you are suffering.

"Well, my dear Mr. Zürn, you won't get a gram of medication from me. I refuse to burden our national economy simply to spare you having to face yourself. You have to face yourself. You mustn't wait for your wife. Probably your mother is to blame for your present condition. You're an only child? No? But the youngest? You see? There you are. So come along now, enough of this carrying on like mother's pet. Please don't keep waiting around for your mother. Here you are, pick this up at the pharmacy. Belladonna. To bring you down from your high horse. And switch for a while to more meat. Shy away from the carbohydrates. But you know all that as well as I do. The main thing is: kill that mother's pet in you, accept the fact that you're an adult, and things will work out. . . ."

Xaver thanked him very much. The doctor shook him warmly by the hand. Even clapped him on the arm the way Xaver had clapped the Turks on the arm. Looking at him with those blue-gray eyes, to make Xaver feel, and Xaver did feel: I like people like you, Xaver Zürn, people like you never prove to be a disappointment. Once again Xaver felt he was a fraud. Without looking at anybody, he walked out through the waiting room.

Seated in the car, he found he couldn't drive off immediately. The doctor, while he had been talking, had kept his eyes fixed on him, to see how Xaver was reacting. Xaver gradually became afraid that the doctor would thus find out all those things that Xaver could discuss only with Dr. Gleitze himself. It would really embarrass him if Dr. Gleitze were to be told, by a doctor of all people, that their relationship wasn't as harmonious as Dr. Gleitze assumed. After all, Xaver was merely waiting for the right moment to tell the boss that he, Xaver, wasn't the healthy, frank, unspoiled person the boss took him for. Nor was he the teetotaler Köberle had made him out to be. Nor the anti-smoker. And least of all, German champion in small-bore shooting, for Chrissake. The boss forced him to behave like the person he assumed him to be. He still had to behave toward Dr. and Mrs. Gleitze as he had during the first year. They expected him to carry on for decades as the willing, cheerful, virtuous employee he had pretended to be during that first year. When he behaves as they want him to, he realizes he isn't like that. That he'd never been like that. He behaved toward them more like a dog. Which was how they praised him, too. Exactly as he praised Tell. When they showed their satisfaction, he felt he must move very carefully or he might break something. It was a matter of urgent necessity that he get around to telling the boss the truth. And if the boss couldn't take it, okay, that would be the end.

The doctor liked to preach. Everyone knew that. Xaver was glad to have wrested the term *dyspepsia* from the doctor. For this he had been given a prescription. He couldn't understand why he was now so depressed. Would he have preferred Dr. Meichle to discover something sinister in the troublesome area? At times, when someone he knew or a fellow employee at the factory suddenly turned out to have some terrible disease, Xaver had felt envious. How could he be such an idiot! Such an idiot! The doctor hasn't the foggiest. Xaver is ten thousand times worse than the doctor suspects. A hundred thousand times. The thought of everything going on in the same old way makes him gag. Incidentally, Dr. Meichle, what about my stomachache? Your lecture was fine, but the stomachache, which used to bother him only in the small hours, can now occur at any time. Like right now. Who or what causes such a hard knot to tighten in the very front of his stomach? There is no point more central than the one formed by this pain. And everything that happens now—visually, acoustically, or in any other way—hits this very spot. Only after it has reinforced the pain at that point does it reach his head as a sound or an image. This dutiful stomachache, Doctor, I'll pass on your regards to it, Doctor. The tireless stomachache, Doctor. The industrious stomachache. The faithful stomachache. The unswerving stomachache. The consistent stomachache. The stubborn stomachache. The ardent stomachache. The ruthless stomachache. The constant stomachache. The unassailable stomachache. The mulish stomachache. The unyielding stomachache. The inaccessible stomachache. The unattainable stomachache. The unapproachable stomachache. The glorious stomachache. The lonely stomachache. The eternal stomachache. The dear stomachache. The painful stomachache, Doctor. He must stop this litany.

That night, when he was again wakened by his stomachache, he realized why he hadn't been able to make himself understood to the doctor. Whatever he found to say about this stomachache failed to include the one vital factor: its persistence. If he said: two hours of stomachache, or eight hours of stomachache, the specifying of elapsed time conveyed nothing about its persistence. Yet the persistence of this stomachache is the only thing that matters.

He focused on the location in his brain that reported this pain and tried to persuade it to react differently. Why shouldn't a person be able to perceive this unchanging report as something pleasant? It is called pain. Mightn't it be possible to try and perceive it the way one listens to music? Dear brain, you don't agree. That's only natural. But if the pain were to go on like this for another month or for three months, we should have another talk about it, right? Maybe at the moment it's enough to realize that at any given time each body contains a fair amount of pain. So spread around as to be hardly perceptible. But when, for whatever reason, this pain is summoned from the entire body to concentrate on one spot, the result is the sensation he now has in his stomach. So he'll wait until it spreads itself around again. It's as simple as that. Or he'll imagine that life is an inflammation that wanders around inside a person. It hurts more here than it does there. It's as simple as that.

A moment later he felt no longer capable of such strategic considerations. Suddenly he perceived his stomachache as an agonizing skin stretched over his stomach; it must be torn away at once. But he told himself just as quickly that this pain wasn't at all the kind that called for screaming out loud or running away. So why was he incapable of perceiving this stomachache as music? For there is no difference whatever between a pain and music. That's just a matter of habit. One should try to hear the pain. That would be a beginning. When the boss sat between his earphones and lost all his bones, his face looked as if pain were something beautiful. Stop that business about music and pain. Music is the boss's concern. Yours is the pain. That's to say, the stomachache. After all, the boss is asleep while you are lying awake thinking of the sleeping boss. The fact that the boss slept well every night was often mentioned in the backseat. He was thinking of the boss, but the boss wasn't thinking of him. The boss seemed to him like a victor. He was the vanquished. Quite obviously the victor would be asleep. Naturally he can't think of this or that vanquished person. And the very fact that the victor is asleep and not thinking of the vanquished makes the vanquished person grow smaller and smaller. Put simply, the victor is the center. Everything works to his advantage. The very fact that he is asleep renders him superior.

When Xaver tossed and turned during the night, trying to find a position in which he could fall asleep, it seemed to him that even sleep became a kind of exertion. And he was no longer surprised at waking up tired in the mornings. Assuming one could call it waking up. Now he also recalled what the two women on the sidewalk had been talking about when, after his conversation with Dr. Meichle, he had been sitting motionless in his car, quite unable to drive off. One woman had asked the other: "What was it?" The other woman had answered: "Cancer." The first woman: "Yes, sure, but what kind of cancer? That's what I'd really like to know." The other woman: "Stomach." The first woman: "And here we've been thinking for years that his wife would go first. And now he's been the first to go after all." The other woman: "Right, so now there's one shoemaker less." After this remark, Xaver had no trouble starting the car and driving home.

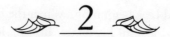

2

F I R S T, drive the boss to the plant, then pick up the boss's parents at Villa Säntis View and drive them to St. Gallen, to their house on the Rosenberg, then do some shopping in St. Gallen for Mrs. Gleitze: seven kinds of cheese on Neugasse; her favorite chocolates, *truffes Champagne*, on Multergasse. Konstanz–St. Gallen, one of his favorite routes. The road was still one of those designed for horse-drawn vehicles and discouraged speeding. And the farms! Each barn door different, but never to be found fifty kilometers farther on.

When he had old people like that sitting in the back, he drove more slowly than the road actually required. This was to imply his respect. They were returning from the boss's fiftieth-birthday celebration. He had had to pick them up the day before, on the Saturday. The boss had phoned him personally. In his Saturday voice, which, of all the boss's voices, was Xaver's favorite; one could actually sense that the boss wasn't wearing a jacket.

Xaver could never drive without observing his passengers in the back. He must have a sense of contact with them. Otherwise he might as well be driving around beer or gravel. In the case of the old Gleitze couple, he had the impression that they were making two different trips simultaneously in the same car. Old Mr. Gleitze sat upright, his cane between his knees and both hands on the crook. Facing straight ahead, impassive. He looked as if he were weeping. But without tears. She looked as if she were planning some merry prank. She still wore her hair as short as in the days when she had dismounted from her bicycle in her divided skirt and smoothed back that same hair. But he couldn't imagine that this lady had stuck four fingers in her mouth and whistled. Or could he? Her eyes looked as if she could have. But the mouth, that little wizened thing. Anyway, she could whistle like that only in Königsberg. Putting one's fingers in one's mouth and whistling like that is something a person can do only at home.

Mrs. Gleitze senior was telling her husband what she was seeing during the drive. Just look at that half-timbered house, isn't it charming? Oh, what a charming church! These cherry trees here are really charming! This Meersburg is always so charming! When for once she was saying nothing, she kept an eager, roguish lookout for something charming. Whether her husband heard what she was saying, it was impossible to tell. He had been traveling around as Hitler's *commis voyageur*, his furious daughter-in-law had said. In spite of his knowledge of French, all Xaver could gather was that it was meant as an insult. Might the boss's wife have been offended by his taking her husband's side in that argument? She had certainly noticed it. For a time it had seemed to him that the argument was being played out in his presence so that he might act as referee. And anyway Mrs. Gleitze is brighter than her husband. More alert. More aware. Her husband wouldn't have noticed in a hundred years that when Xaver was on duty he invariably wore shirts with cufflinks. *She* had already noticed that in the third or fourth year. And those had been his finest cufflinks, too. The ones from Marseilles, from rue Paradis, where the women call out *Fais-moi tout*, where he always stayed when the boss went to his operas in Aix-en-Provence. Mrs. Gleitze had even asked, a year or two later, why he never wore those gold cufflinks with the red stones anymore. He hadn't been able to tell her that those cufflinks had been appropriated by a certain Marlene on a side street off the Kurfürstendamm. Marlene Goldbach, believe it or not. He had forgotten the name of the pension. It had ended in -*itz*. Xaver had never had finer cufflinks than those. And they'd been easier to put on than any others. But he didn't consider them too high a price or too great a penalty for that night. A year later he had looked in that store in Marseilles for another pair of those finely wrought little golden knucklebones set with red stones. No luck, of course.

Old Mr. Gleitze's face always looked as if he had been suffering nothing but injustices for eighty years. This was just the kind of face Xaver didn't want to acquire. It showed lack of awareness. It's up to each of us to analyze *why* such and such things happen to us. Otherwise we'll sit around with that kind of a wizened, cry-baby face that's only fit for a laugh. Taking

part in that carnival procession in Markdorf in which Mr.
Trummel had been depicted as MONA LISA WITH GALLSTONES,
there had also been a band of mummers all wearing old men's
masks. Each mask differing slightly from the next, all one family yet two quite distinct groups: those who wept and moaned
and those who grinned and cursed. And all the mummers from
that village were walking as if their right legs were made of
wood all the way up to the buttocks. They must have made good
use of their experiences. And their masks proved that grinning
and cursing was superior to weeping and moaning. How ridiculous old Mr. Gleitze made himself with that face! Who the hell's
interested? What a miserable kisser! Don't try and impress me
with that. He refuses to sympathize with that parade of misery.
Mr. Gleitze senior might impress Agnes with that, but not
him, not Xaver.

Agnes was always dreaming about whatever personalities
happened at that moment to be under the sharpest attack from
the general public. When there was no one left to come forward
and say how much better he was than that fellow Nixon, the
globally destroyed Nixon would on one of the following nights
crawl into Agnes's dream, coming from the northwest across the
slope, into the berry patch, assuming a bird's voice that only
Agnes understood, calling for Agnes with his birdcall, begging
Agnes for food and drink, was given food, water, and comfort
by Agnes, until she heard the children crying out in the house,
whereupon she wanted to hurry back, but the house was no
longer there. A few weeks later it was Willi Brandt who, thrust
out of office and an object of mockery, appeared in Agnes's
dream crawling down the slope and into the berry patch, calling
for Agnes with a bird's voice, begging her to feed him and
stroke him. Then it had been Andreas Baader and Ulrike Mein-
hof crawling down the berry patch and wailing to make Agnes
come out and feed and stroke the condemned couple, until she

heard her children crying out, tore herself away, and, to her horror, discovered that where house and children should have been there was now a void.

Every time Xaver drove this couple home, the old lady would take out the enormous steel key ring from her handbag and give it to Xaver. Fifty or a hundred keys. The property was surrounded by a hedge and a fence. The upper part of the fence was barbed wire and bent outward. The barbed-wire part towered above the recently clipped beech hedge. At the garden gate there were three locks to be opened. Two on the gate itself. One on an iron bar that ran directly behind the gate connecting the two gate posts. The porch of the front door was closed off by an iron grille that had to be unlocked. In front of the door itself, an iron shutter was let down and secured by two locks. Outside all the windows there were grilles as well as shutters secured by locks. Inside the house it was much the same. Mr. Gleitze stood looking the other way without moving. As soon as they were inside, Mr. Gleitze sat down in an armchair, placed his cane between his knees, put his hands on the crook, and looked straight ahead. Before leaving, Xaver filled the refrigerator and the deep freeze with what they had brought from the Villa Säntis View. As Xaver drove off, Mrs. Gleitze started locking up from the inside.

Down in the city, on his way from the parking lot to Neugasse, Xaver passed a bookstore displaying secondhand books on the sidewalk. They were priced at only one franc each. Very soon, as he picked over the volumes, he found himself holding a book, pale green like his car, with a soft cover but what a title:

From the Diary of a Long-Distance Driver. Experiences and revelations of a Swiss private chauffeur employed by a National Socialist German manufacturer. Travel impressions from Berchtesgaden and Godesberg. The strange letters written by "Swiss" citizens for the defense of a rich Nazi. By John Frey. Privately published by the author in

*Buchs (St.G.). Parts of this material appeared in the fall of 1939 in
the* Auto-Courier Bern, *resulting in a warning from the censor's office and a ban on any further publication. People's Voice Printers, St.
Gallen.*

So this author lived in Buchs. Didn't old man Gleitze have
his hunting preserve above Buchs? Xaver bought the book. He
would have been glad to pay ten francs for it. A brother chauffeur had written it, if you please! He sat down in the nearest café
and began to read. On page 60 he had to tear himself away from
the memoirs of his colleague and drive his favorite route, St.
Gallen–Konstanz, faster than the old highway really permitted.
On the ferry between Konstanz and Meersburg he turned to
page 61, the chapter headed "National Socialist Winter Season." It suddenly occurred to him that, with all this reading, he
had forgotten to go to Neugasse and buy the seven kinds of
cheese for Mrs. Gleitze. Should he go back again? At least across
the border to Kreuzlingen. There were bound to be cheese stores
there too. But she would see from the bill that he hadn't
shopped at *her* store. And what should she do with cheese if it
hadn't been bought at *her* store in Neugasse in St. Gallen? And
he hadn't bought the *truffes Champagne* on Multergasse either.
Without *truffes Champagne* she simply didn't want to live, she
had once said. He should have driven back to St. Gallen and
then told her the whole story. She would have appreciated it.
She would have found it hilarious. Xaver drives from Meersburg
back to St. Gallen to pick up seven kinds of cheese and her
truffes, which, when he was supposed to pick them up, he had
simply forgotten. But why had he forgotten? Because of a
book. . . . At that point he was stymied. He couldn't say that
on account of the John Frey book he had forgotten to buy seven
kinds of cheese and *truffes Champagne.* The National Socialist
manufacturer for whom John Frey had driven had been not old
man Gleitze but a Mr. R: with a diabetic wife and several

daughters. And these R.s had moved to the upper Rhine valley not from Königsberg but from Thuringia. But while reading the first sixty pages Xaver still had to think of the old Gleitzes. He sensed that he mustn't tell Mrs. Gleitze about this book. Even though she had spoken of "Hitler's *commis voyageur*." She would resent Xaver reading a book written by a chauffeur who with every trip learned to hate his boss more and more. Involuntarily she would assume from this that Xaver felt a similar hatred toward the Gleitzes. Perhaps he could try to dissociate himself from his colleague. Such duplicity, driving people around and later betraying them! Such lack of integrity! . . . No, he'd never bring it off. So he would have to tell Aloisia that he had simply forgotten her errands. No reason. No excuse. Simple failure.

Aloisia was tickled pink. But she insisted that Xaver tell Madam himself. Aloisia always tried to pronounce *Madam* in a mocking Viennese accent. She dragged him along to the terrace, where Mrs. Gleitze was lying on an extensive combination of chaise longue, bed, and sofa, looking at nothing in particular. Apparently a brand-new lounging apparatus. A sun roof, supported by two poles that looked like ivory, arched over the head end. No sooner had Xaver reported his lapse than Mrs. Gleitze's face crumpled as if she were about to burst into tears. Her lower lip was buried in her teeth. Her eyelids squeezed up as if under unbearable pain. Exactly the kind of face people get on receiving news of a disaster. Then she seemed to feel embarrassed at her face. She covered it with both hands. Then she detached one hand slightly and waved it in such a way as to convey to Aloisia that she and Xaver were to leave. Obviously she wanted to be alone with her sorrow. Outside the garden gate Aloisia said it served her right. And the best part about it was that it had been done to her by Xaver, of whom she always said that he might not be the brightest but he was certainly the most loyal. Aloisia rubbed her hands and danced from one foot to the other. Xaver laughed and walked off.

As soon as he was in the car, he began his conversation with Aloisia. What justification did Aloisia have for claiming that Mrs. Gleitze *always* said that? Did it mean that she *always* said it in so many words? So that the phrase was *always* worded: Xaver may not be the brightest but he's certainly the most loyal? And who did she say it to? And what was the reaction? Above all, how did Dr. Gleitze react? Or was it a typical Aloisia invention? It does sound much more like Aloisia than like Mrs. Gleitze. The brightest . . . would one even put it that way in Vienna? There one would be more likely to say: the smartest. . . .

He had to break off his conversation with Aloisia, now feeling that it was absolutely necessary to review the scene on the terrace. He was bothered by the fact that no excuse had come to his mind when facing Mrs. Gleitze. That nothing whatever had been said. That she hadn't said anything, he hadn't said anything. All the way home he had to keep going over the scene in his mind. But in the way that he wished the scene had taken place. Above all, he saw himself taking the floor and speaking with fluency. The biggest mistake had been to leave the announcement to Aloisia. Naturally she had chosen the most impudent, the most frivolous tone for the unpleasant news. It implied: Now then, no moaning and groaning about a few morsels of stinky cheese and fattening chocolates! In his mind's eye, Xaver kept scanning Mrs. Gleitze's face, her hands, the way she held her head. Hadn't she been smiling behind those shielding hands? Might she have squeezed up her eyes like that, bitten her underlip, because otherwise she would have laughed out loud? Remembering that Aloisia had led him up to her by the hand. And since anyway she regarded him as some kind of dope, she had thought: My God, is that ever a funny sight, Aloisia leading him like that, I must say he's much funnier than I thought. And then she had tried to control herself, as best she could. . . . Or had it really meant a kind of pain for her? A profound disappointment? Maybe she had invited some guests to whom she had wanted to offer seven kinds of the finest cheese straight from St. Gallen? Which way did he prefer? He couldn't make up his mind.

As he drove up to the farmhouse he could already see what was in store for him. Master Köberle. For miles around, nobody else still drove a Mercedes 170S, vintage '51. Five marks was all Master Köberle had paid for this car many years ago. Since then he has been saying that he has three occupations: workshop superintendent at Gleitze's; building contractor for his wife, for whom he has annually to add on a room to her pension for summer vacationers; and spare-parts obtainer for his 170S. For several years he had carried on such an intensive search for spare parts at all the wreckers' that soon he had three or four of everything appertaining to this car. Using hand-cleaning paste, he would remove the rust from the parts and put them in storage. Xaver noted that Köberle had fitted new front fenders. The rounded ones from the old 220S with the sunken headlights. Perhaps Köberle was trying gradually to transform the 170S into a 220.

He was obliged to greet Master Köberle with a loud laugh and say how nice it was for Master Köberle to have taken the trouble to come all the way up to the farm again. Master Köberle took this trouble three times a year. In June, July, and October. To get himself some strawberries, to get himself some red currants and cherries, to get himself some apples. This was a tribute exacted by Master Köberle because, when Dr. Gleitze had been looking for a successor to Schorsch, he had told Dr. Gleitze that of all the men working in the automotive workshop he thought there was none more suitable than Franz Xaver Zürn. No one had the same healthy, frank, unspoiled qualities as Xaver. No one was such a teetotaler or antismoker. And German champion in small-bore shooting! So he'd never find anyone with a sharper eye. As well, he was a member of the church choir.

Whenever Köberle turned up, Xaver drank mineral water. He felt he mustn't make a liar of Master Köberle after the event. This time the daughter was along. When the Köberles had loaded their harvest, they stayed to share the supper that Agnes set out on the big table under the pear tree. In Xaver's opinion, Agnes always went to far too much trouble for the Köberles. Master Köberle reported on the problems he was having with the building permit and the construction of the most recent addition. Then came the 170S's turn. What spare parts he had just recently acquired under what circumstances. He continued his search for spare parts, although it was foreseeable that he would never be able to use up all those parts himself. It was his hope that Daimler-Benz would buy the 170S/220S after his death as a museum piece.

He was forever totting up his investment acquisitions. The pension now had fourteen rooms, nine of them with shower, five with bath. After the 170S he got around to his main topic: Sabine. This time Köberle had every reason to put Sabine in the limelight. She had just taken her final exams in high school. She might still have to do an oral in German. She was counting on an average of 85 or 80, which would entitle her to enter university and study pharmacy. This information relating to herself was delivered by Sabine personally. With lowered eyes and in a high, droning voice she recited the list of her successes, clearly striving not to hurt anyone's feelings.

"I always say," said Master Köberle, "that she needn't be conceited, she can't help being clever." Agnes said that was really something to be conceited about, 85 for heaven's sake!

"No, no, none of that," said Master Köberle. "She should be glad she's so clever, but she mustn't be conceited about it, because we're not the kind of people who look down on others, you know." They weren't the least bit stuck up just because Sabine was at the top of her class. To him it was just as important that every Saturday afternoon she gave German lessons to Turkish kids, and that she had started a music group with the kids from the special school because she believed that playing in an orchestra would encourage a development in those kids that nothing else would. She practiced with them twice a week. She'd even been offered full-time work at the special school. She wouldn't want to do that, of course, said Sabine in a high, thin voice, her real interest was in psychology, but since that was such an overcrowded field with no chance of a job she was going into pharmacy, where one could do the least damage. It was all a matter of willpower. "I just simply worked my head off," she said, "otherwise I'd probably have had an average of seventy or maybe even sixty-five, so you see there's nothing to be conceited about because I have absolutely no special talent."

Xaver saw that Magdalena was twiddling her left eyebrow again. She always did that with her right hand, reaching over the back of her head with her thin, long arm. Her elbow high over her head, her long thin hand reaching down from there. Her bobbin fingers twisted and twirled the thick eyebrow hairs not as if just to pass the time but with an insectlike, incomprehensible energy. Master Köberle, too, threw frequent glances her way. Sabine didn't. She merely looked at her own hands as they lay in front of her on the table, folded.

Before anyone expected it, Sabine suddenly stopped speaking. Master Köberle broke the silence by saying he regarded Sabine's modesty as her greatest asset. That was the quality upon which he placed his greatest hopes. There were more than enough geniuses blowing their own trumpets. What we needed was modest people, he said. Once again, silence reigned. Modesty is penalized nowadays, he said. Nevertheless, he was happy about Sabine's modesty, he said. She would have much more of it, if it were up to him. But unfortunately his wife had already put a few bees in her bonnet. Was there anything more beautiful than a person who was not aware of his or her value? Without a doubt, that was the highest to which human beings could aspire. When they went on their regular Sunday hikes in the mountains and came across a solitary fir or larch tree and stopped in awe in front of it—why did they see so much beauty in that fir or larch tree? Because that tree was entirely unselfconscious. That was the sole reason. And where were such people still to be found? Nowhere. Each person knew everything better than the next. One show-off drowned out the next. Each person took pride in selling himself as dearly as possible: it was not his true value that interested him, only the price he succeeded in getting for himself. These days, all the world's affairs were ruled by bogus claims and fraudulent hyperbole.

Xaver felt that Köberle's concluding sermon applied directly to himself, Xaver. All he could think of was: Look who's criticizing me while he's guzzling the schnapps *I've* distilled and stuffing himself with meat from *our* smokehouse.

Father and daughter left. Xaver asked after Julia. She'd been gone by four, he was told. On the motor scooter, having pinched the key from Leni. By the time they heard the motor scooter starting up, she was already on it and away.

"So neither of you knows when she's coming back," said Xaver. Magdalena said: "What do you mean 'neither'? It's your problem if you two can't control your own kids." Agnes said that Julia had informed them at lunch that she would probably fail her exams. Xaver could only stare at Agnes, begging her, as it were, to retract what she had said or at least qualify it. In the ensuing pause Magdalena said: "So what else is new?" Xaver looked across at Magdalena, who was picking her nose. She had been doing this ever since the Köberles had left. As soon as there were no outsiders around, her right hand would automatically go up to her nose and into it. Her nostrils were almost always inflamed. Xaver's imploring gaze at her fingers failed to move her; it seemed rather to fill her with satisfaction. She was probably remembering the confrontation of the day before yesterday when, unable to stand it another minute, he had said in a low, urgent voice: "Do stop picking your nose." Her retort: "I'll pick my nose whenever I feel like it." He had turned on his heel and left. Apparently she had looked upon that as a victory.

It was necessary for Julia to be flunked, she said, it was essential, and not only once but twice, so she would finally grasp the fact that high school was no place for her, no place at all. Since her parents were incapable of recognizing this fact, it was really up to the school to react in a less ambiguous fashion. For years now, Julia had been occupying the place of someone who might give anything to be allowed to attend that school. School was there for people like Sabine Köberle, or herself. She was glad that he and Agnes had at last been hearing from someone outside the family, too, what the proper attitude was these days. But most likely Sabine, who in her eyes was an absolutely fabulous girl, had been utterly wasting her breath. No doubt they would continue to let Julia get away with anything, until one day she would be too far gone to be fit for any kind of training.

Magdalena didn't wait for an answer. She went upstairs. And she refused to come down again, saying she had work to do.

Xaver didn't believe that Julia would fail. The fact that she had mentioned it herself meant she was aware of the danger. And surely that meant she would now do her utmost to prevent the worst from happening. Surely it wasn't necessary to have a heart-to-heart talk with one's kids about this. Failing one's exams was something quite alien to the Hungerbühler Farm, where up to now there had never been anything but first-class reports. And that went for high school, too. Of course, it wasn't necessary to overdo it like Magdalena, who exaggerated the Zürn family's sense of duty. But that someone who day after day makes the long trip from this farm via Gattnau and Kressbronn to school in Friedrichshafen *can't* fail, because failure would mean that all that traveling was just a lousy stupid joke—Julia knew all that. And the fact that she was still gadding about could only mean that the situation was not quite as serious as Agnes believed. Nevertheless, this gadding about was impossible. He wanted to have a talk about this with Julia rather than with Agnes.

He looked in the TV guide for a Western. Austria II had one. Agnes stayed in the kitchen. Unfortunately it was a comic Western. He hated those. But by now he was incapable of switching it off. After that they sat in the kitchen and read and looked at the clock. Finally they went into their bedroom, which was next to the kitchen, leaving the door to the kitchen open. They lay there in the dark. Once he asked: "What time is it?" She answered: "Twelve-thirty." After a pause she said: "She won't be back before one." But at one she wasn't back either. Only something absolutely terrible could have prevented her from coming home. Why, she wouldn't get into bed with someone, sleep with him, and then just lie there! Obviously it would occur to her that they would be waiting for her at home, and she would jump out of bed and come.

Xaver sensed that again he and Agnes were lying side by side as if they'd had a row. It was totally inconceivable, under these circumstances, for one to approach the other. Their waiting for Julia separated them. The longer they waited, the greater grew the distance between them. If either of them should break the silence now, it would be only to reproach the other. At some point Agnes got up and left the room. He lifted his head from the pillow. Agnes is talking. Someone is answering. He can hear voices. Yes. Those are voices. So soft as to be woven to the point of inaudibility into the silence of the night. But still they are voices. Or are they figments of his hearing? Agnes returned. He listened for Julia's footsteps on the stairs. Agnes said: "Nothing." But he had heard voices. So they had been voices in his head.

He thought of his mother, who once, when he had come home at seven in the morning from a dance, had said to him: "I hope your children never do this to you." At half-past two Agnes took a Valium and offered him one too. She knew he never took anything like that, he said. That sounded as if he were furious. At three she took another Valium and said she wished she could take a hundred. At that he immediately reached out a hand to her. He pushed one foot across. Her feet were icy. She had gone out barefoot. He pushed his other foot across and pressed her cold feet between his warm ones. His feet grew cold, without hers getting any warmer. She said she couldn't bear this sense of having failed. "We've done everything wrong, every-thing." He agreed. But he said nothing. He thought of Mag-dalena, who for the past two years had had no boyfriend and no girl friend, whose demands for a rigid daily schedule with set times for eating, working, and sleeping were becoming ever more stringent. When Agnes brought her home a blouse, Mag-dalena would grimace with disgust. Whatever Agnes placed in her room, she would put outside the door again. Her mother, she said, was a pathological spendthrift. She herself wore only things that were more than two years old. She looked odd in those outgrown garments. One dared do no more than hint at how odd she looked. She couldn't care less. The moment the TV was switched on, she would run up to her room as if the Devil were at her heels. She hardly ever washed her hair anymore.

Two years ago she had still radiated such charm that people had stopped on the street to let their eyes dwell on her a little longer. In those days she did cartwheels, uphill and downhill, played the guitar, let her hair flow around her face, singing through it in a high, delicate voice. A voice as if made of light and honey, the visiting church choir conductor had said. Five years ago she had still come racing down between the currant bushes, arms outspread, calling out that she was the wind. Now she never walked upright anymore. Her head always hung down at an angle, as if she were being bent over by some invisible force. Her crooked posture made her look almost like an old crone. At times her compulsive nose-picking seemed defiant. Her eyes looked out from under her tilted gray face, calculating, critical, cold. Her mouth grew more and more pinched. Probably Agnes was also thinking about these things. Mentally he was saying to Agnes: It's not your fault. If it's anyone's fault, it's mine. He hoped she had fallen asleep. Outside the birds were starting up. A mocking sound.

When Xaver drove off at six-thirty, Julia still hadn't come home. When he returned late that afternoon, she was there. He felt relieved. So he couldn't yell at her. So he felt he was making one mistake after another. He suffered from the look in Magdalena's eyes. She had stayed downstairs until he came home. No doubt she wanted to witness her sister's chastisement. But when he walked into the kitchen, Julia was the first to get up; she offered him her cheek. And it was quite obvious that she was offering it not for a slap but for a kiss. So he kissed her. But even as he did so, he knew what this was doing to Magdalena. He was rewarding *depravity*. It was as if he were punishing Magdalena for her diligence, her self-discipline, her capacity for dedication. Immediately after the kiss he looked across to Magdalena. Her mouth had shrunk to a small, hard spot. Her eyes were black with bitterness. Now they were all looking at Magdalena. She ran up into her room. When Xaver and Agnes stood outside her door, she said she was busy, she had work to do. She said this in quite a normal voice, only barely tinged with disgust. At any rate it was clear that now he must go downstairs, must yell at Julia, otherwise Magdalena's life would simply be meaningless. He went down the stairs and mustered his strength for his first loud words.

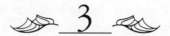

3

X A V E R read the book by his brother chauffeur, John Frey, pencil in hand. And the more he read, the more sentences he underlined. Sentences such as the following:

The constant night-driving, the irregular meals, fatigue, and the continual changes of temperature have made me ill. I have been confined to bed for four weeks with pneumonia, and during this period not a single member of Mr. R.'s family has visited me. It strikes me as strange that, whereas on such trips one entrusts one's life, as it were, to the chauffeur, one does not bother to make inquiries when the chauffeur himself is at death's door.

For some time now we have been driving every day to Chur to check out this prospective maidservant. How can one expect to find anything suitable here when one is not even capable of keeping trustworthy German girls from one's native Thuringia? By chance I discover something about the doings of Mr. Gustloff in Davos. During those long waits while parked in Zürich, Konstanz, Ulm, etc., all kinds of scraps of information can be picked up. Nagl has publicly declared himself to be a Nazi. But Mr. R. the manufacturer wishes the same thing about himself to be kept as secret as possible. He wishes to go on playing the innocent to the Swiss in order not to affect sales of his products to Jewish wholesalers.

The maid from Chur is leaving! After only a few weeks, this first Swiss maidservant of the R.s, a competent person, is fed up with her job.

At the hotel I am told that R. has applied for permission to visit the Führer on Obersalzberg. A few days later R. himself let fall that he had been to see the Führer. My colleague B., who is from Upper Bavaria, calls these fellows "VIP crooks." Moreover, B. is friendly with a girl who is on very good terms with members of the Führer's bodyguard. In fact, Schreck, the Reich Chancellor's personal chauffeur, is a particular friend of hers.

Everywhere in the Lake Constance area, on the German side, police gangs are racing through the streets.

Next come many kilometers when the stale, used-up air is freshened by squirting eau de cologne around. The boss hates open windows, he can't stand the wind.

For a change, the order goes out for musical kilometers. A portable phonograph starts squawking in shrill tones behind me, until a sudden bump flips the record onto the floor with a loud scraping sound.

Often, very often, my thoughts revert to my former occupation in the United States, where in California I was employed as a surveyor's assistant and chauffeur to the chief engineer of a large concern. Mr. Crowley was a fine man with strong principles.

All those long trips gradually caused a certain comradely relationship to evolve between us.

One evening, after a drive through the German Lake Constance area with guests from Thuringia, my boss R. urges me to visit the building of the German Labor Front in Lindau, where a "Strength Through Joy" rally happens to be going on. The big hall is swarming with flags, Storm Troopers, SS men, members of the Labor Front, "Strength Through Joy" tourists, brass bands, and Hitler Youth. I'm hungry and want my supper before driving home that night. There must be a thousand people here. The show is more than 90 percent propaganda, something that doesn't interest me one bit. So when they start singing the Horst Wessel Song and everyone instantly gets to their feet and stands to attention with the Hitler salute, I pick up my cap and walk toward the *exit. A Storm Trooper guarding the door asks me what I think I'm doing. I have to drive, drive—that's what I tell him!*

The car glides like a shiny, dark blue, silver-winged giant beetle swiftly over the rise before Bregenz.

During a leisurely drive around the well-known Nürburg Ring, Germany's great car-racing track, I meet another chauffeur from Upper Saxony, who tells me, among other things, that he has four relatives in various concentration camps. He is a Socialist.

Mr. R.'s brothers, relatives, friends, all of them factory owners, and their families, the bankers of the little industrial town of M., put on quite a party with plenty of beer and carp. One of the participants, a tipsy bank manager, needled me about Switzerland. Yes indeed, one fine morning Adolf, with his concept of Greater Germany, would swallow up that little Switzerland before breakfast.

In the morning I am summoned to my boss, who, without looking at me, announces that I am fired on the spot. To justify this abrupt step he accuses me of having ordered him around for the past three years. He was fed up, he said, with having to obey me.

DR. SCHWENDENER'S DEFENSE

"My actions were based, and continue to be based, on the principle of serving justice and humanity, thereby restoring justice to someone who, in my opinion, has been unjustly accused, a matter in which the community of Buchs, which I represent, has the utmost economic and financial interest.

"During the twelve years of his residence in Buchs, and in my official association with him, I have known Mr. Rösel to be an eminently respectable, high-minded, and exceedingly helpful person, who in my opinion is incapable of any action that might run counter to the interests of our country. Bern, June 21, 1945."

We soldiers do not agree with this attitude, for anyone who has given financial support to the Germans in Switzerland has also helped organize and develop the National Socialist Party, the Fifth Column with

*its athletic clubs, et cetera. For this reason we regard these financial
supporters as worse than "lukewarm" party members who had joined the
party under duress.*

Xaver took the book with him to Efrizweiler. It was Sunday.
As soon as he turned into the driveway, Xaver could see that
Konrad still hadn't stuccoed his house. Apparently they already
had some paying guests, people who were lying around in chaise
longues like corpses. Xaver walked as quietly as possible to the
front door.

He found Konrad in the kitchen, in the company of a skinny
man with a sallow face, his eyes squinting to keep out the smoke
rising from the cigarette in the corner of his mouth. Both men
were smoking fast and furiously. Both men were sitting in front
of a couple of transistors, one tuned to Frankfurt and the other to
Munich. They were following two soccer games. Konrad was
sweating. Especially on the top of his bald head. By now the tips
of his moustache reached all the way to his ring of wavy, dark
hair. At the moment the ring of hair was serving as a drip-
catcher. When the games were over, the stranger tucked one
transistor into his bag and said good-bye. His grin showed only
too clearly that the games had ended in his favor. Konrad explained later that he really wasn't a Bayern fan—mainly because
of that club's methods of trading in human beings; but all his
paying guests from North Germany were so anti–Bayern-Mün-
chen that he gradually found himself willy-nilly becoming a
Bayern fan.

Anni had gone to Bodnegg with the kids, he said. Aunt
Klothilde was in a bad mood after what had happened in Ra-
vensburg. Konrad wouldn't believe that the news of Cousin
Franz's attempted suicide hadn't yet reached Wigratsweiler.
How far out in the sticks can you be—really! But not to worry,
their cousin hadn't brought it off. That nitwit, says Konrad.
Why not go the whole hog? He was fed up with people who

pretended to do away with themselves but then didn't bring it off. He was sick and tired of those people. All they wanted was to squeeze out some sympathy. Unfair competition, that's what it was. And a highly unfair criticism of society. Darn right. All they want is to convey a reproach. Just never admit that they're sapheads themselves, and nothing but. Yet in this day and age anyone can make a go of it. If only a person wants to. He defied Xaver to say when opportunities had been more favorable. Never, never, never! No one's more aware of this than Konrad and Xaver. How people used to work their asses off on those little farms that Xaver and Konrad came from! Even in their fathers' generation! And now? Well, at the next elections Konrad was going to be a candidate for the Liberals. Starting at the community level. But the regional level isn't out of the question either. He's past forty now, it's time he did something. Farmer, gardener, parachutist, insurance, appliance salesman. He knows his way around, all right. He'll show those fellows a trick or two. And nowhere, he's discovered, is a psychological gift as important as in politics. And that's the very gift he has. He can always size up whoever he's talking to. What how where when, he has a nose for that. Those fellows in the Free Democratic Party have noticed that. They're counting heavily on him. . . .

Without interrupting his flow of words, Konrad brought out another bottle of wine from the closet. Since having an eye on a political career, he said, he prefers to drink his wine at home. Every mouthful swallowed in the taverns produced nothing but a lot of guff. That was something he could do without, just at the beginning of his political career. . . .

Xaver was looking for a chance to mention his Swiss colleague's book. But what was more important was to tell Konrad what he had heard about him on the drive to Cologne. By way of leading up to the subject, he asked how things were going at the plant. Couldn't be better, said Konrad. He had just scored a victory over that unspeakable Trummel. Trummel had had to take back his allegation that he, Konrad Ehrle, had been charging personal kilometers to business expenses. Unbelievable, the things that reptile dared to come out with! But he'd shown him who was who, all right! If there was anything that disgusted him more than cheating, it was to be suspected of being a cheater. He didn't need to explain that to Xaver. Nowhere had integrity been dinned into one so drastically as on the little farms that Xaver and Konrad came from. Konrad Ehrle charging personal kilometers as business kilometers! Ha! By rights this should have cost that pasty-faced bastard a million in damages, but, fool that Konrad is, he had merely demanded a scrap of paper containing a formal declaration. No compensation! But Konrad can wait. If his political career turns out the way it promises to now, he may meet that gentleman in very different surroundings. Unless he simply forgets about him. Who's Mr. Trummel, after all! Chances are, he believes, that in another three years he won't even be able to remember that repulsive pasty mug. Konrad is far too positive a person for anything like that.

With a huge old-fashioned, yellow handkerchief he wiped the sweat from his head, opened the window, turned on some loud music on the radio. They didn't need to overhear every word, he said, pointing outside. So what's up? Has the cat got Xaver's tongue? Good God, Konrad didn't think his decision to go into politics was all *that* sensational. Actually, such an idea would never have occurred to him if a customer hadn't suddenly said to him: "I wonder why you don't go into politics." Those were his very words. While he, Konrad, was explaining the new C-6 type, which is the most advanced alarm affair you can imagine—while he was explaining that the owner of a C-6 system could open his windows even when the system was switched on, this magnetic field doesn't worry about some window being open but takes care of everything else, thanks to the miracle sensor, the so-called movement reactor, which doesn't miss a thing even if some lout should have managed in some completely unimaginable way to worm his way into the interior of the house without triggering any of the magnetic fields at the windows and doors . . . that's where the customer interrupts him and says: "I wonder why you don't go into politics, Mr. Ehrle." And at that moment the scales fall from Konrad's eyes. Fancy someone else having to say this! And indeed, why *doesn't* he go into politics? He will, and how! It's a sheer miracle that Xaver finds him at home today. The first time in weeks. And then someone like Trummel comes along and tries to brand him a chiseler. Never mind, forget it. Basically everything is so infinitely depressing anyway! The more insight he gains, the more . . . the more . . . Konrad waved the thought away. Wiped sweat away. Possibly he might one day overturn a table. Or even two. Or all of them, Xaver. Yes, all of them.

He stopped, groaned, brought out another bottle. What a very good thing that Xaver had come today, otherwise he'd now be forced to drink with his people from Dortmund. Not that he had anything against the people from Dortmund, they were all right. They knew more about soccer than he did. But they were a bit conceited, and unfortunately that tended to show up when they drank. And he had no idea what they had to be conceited about. At home all they had was too few windows and too many kids. But stuck-up. Especially the ones this year. Not those who were here last year. And anyway, he preferred most people from Dortmund to some of the folks hereabouts. Actually one could feel sorry for them. All year round in Dortmund! But the way they bore up under that. He must say that many a person hereabouts could take a lesson from them. And the way they talked was amusing. More amusing anyway than the sounds produced by the people from Bayreuth who always stayed at the Widenhorns' in the house across the street. Mrs. Widenhorn made out she was so fond of the Bayreuth dialect that she wished she spoke it herself. She actually tried to. Even in fall, long after the last Bayreuth people had left, she might suddenly come out with something in pure Bayreuth dialect. Most likely only because she believed it annoyed him. But actually it didn't annoy him at all. The only thing that annoyed him was that Mrs. Widenhorn always behaved as if she could annoy him with her Bayreuth business. Or to put it better: it would annoy him if he didn't have such a positive attitude. His motto had always been: Every man to his own taste. Liberal, if you know what I mean.

He stopped speaking, but it was clear that this wasn't the moment for Xaver to bring up the subject of Trummel or the book by his colleague Frey. Konrad was actually groaning, wiping away the sweat with the enormous handkerchief. Then he said: "Xaver, d'you know what kind of a soup I want for my funeral reception?" "Of course," said Xaver, "liver dumpling soup." "Right!" said Konrad and laughed in relief. The telephone rang. Konrad grimaced, as if the ringing caused him pain. It was Agnes. She spoke in a low, hurried voice, as if something terrible had happened. Dr. Gleitze had turned up. With his wife. Xaver said: "I'll come right away." He told Konrad he had to leave for a conference with his boss. Konrad said: "You're nuts." Xaver ran out of the house and drove off. Konrad had run out with him. He had tried to stop him. Then he had called him a slave. Get-going-now. Xaver had laughed. It occurred to him that everything Konrad had said was impaired by the fact that Konrad still hadn't stuccoed his house.

Not the brightest, but the most loyal. That was what Xaver thought about all the way home. The first thing he saw was Dorle lying on the whetstone. Very close to her left eye a tick already so bloated it looked like a big shiny ball. Later, Dorle, later.

Dr. Gleitze was sitting at a table under the pear tree. Even at a distance Xaver could hear Mrs. Gleitze's Viennese voice dragging out all the words. And the ticktock of table tennis. As soon as he turned the corner of the barn, Julia and Magdalena stopped

playing table tennis. They seemed to have been merely waiting
for him to arrive and release them from the game. The faces of
both were flushed but glowering. Probably the boss or Mrs.
Gleitze had said as they came around the corner with Agnes:
Don't let us disturb you. And after that the two girls hadn't
dared stop. That annoyed Xaver. The way they stood there,
looking embarrassed, and then tried to get out of sight as quickly as possible, was even more annoying. And the boss's first
words were enough to tell Xaver that Agnes had revealed
Xaver's whereabouts to the Gleitzes and his relationship to
Konrad Ehrle. Really, this woman hadn't the slightest gift for
diplomacy. She always blurted out everything exactly as it was.
She didn't even know how to be cautious.

Xaver immediately tried to turn "cousin" into a very general
term of relationship that was always used hereabouts when there
was no real term available to describe the remoteness of a relationship. He couldn't be explicit because Agnes might have said
that Konrad's and Xaver's mothers had been sisters. Since he
wasn't considered the brightest, he didn't always have to express
himself very clearly. Agnes was in the midst of showing Mrs.
Gleitze her herb bed, which she had recently transplanted to
this part of the garden. One look was enough to tell Xaver that
Mrs. Gleitze positively suffered from her lack of interest in herb
beds. Obviously Agnes was totally unaware of this.

The boss immediately asked whether Xaver could pick up
Professor Meister and his wife at eight thirty-six P.M. and drive
them to the Trummels'. As if it were important to win Xaver
over, he added that the couple was exceptionally easy to recognize, especially at the Lindau railway station. A man of forty,
white hair like a bonnet, down to his shoulders. Wide-apart,
protruding eyes. His wife: eyes so close to her nose that from a
distance one might think the eyes touched each other. Xaver
enjoyed the manner in which the boss focused all his attention
on him while giving these descriptions. One certainly doesn't

talk like that to a person one considers stupid. It couldn't have been the boss who had used that phrase. Xaver eventually said that he had already picked up the professor and his wife twice before. Ah well, all the better. The return trip from Lake Deger to Tettnang would be taken care of by Wenzel Froidl, so fortunately Xaver wouldn't have to worry about that.

It was always a matter of surprise how talkative the boss could be on Sundays and holidays. The women couldn't tear themselves away from the good earth, he said. What charming daughters Xaver had, he must say. Dr. Gleitze looked across to the Ping-Pong table as it stood abandoned on the trampled lawn. The one with the loose hair, said the boss, she would know and demand and obtain what she was worth, no question. The other one—he looked over to where Magdalena had been playing—she wouldn't only remain self-contained, she would withdraw farther and farther into herself; she would deliberately reduce her opportunities because every opportunity would seem too risky to her; in practical terms she would seek dwindling, more modest opportunities. Success on a minimal level, that was her ideal: play it safe. So Xaver didn't have to worry at all: she would never let go of the minor position she had achieved. The other one, of course—she would tackle things quite differently, oh yes, men would be standing in line to make her offers, but she would be choosy, she certainly wouldn't be one to throw herself away. Xaver was to be congratulated. "Susanne, how much more of Mrs. Zürn's time d'you intend to take up!"

Dr. Gleitze and his wife drove off. To the Trummels'. Mrs. Gleitze at the wheel. Xaver returned to the table. He sat down with his back to the barn wall so he could look uphill, where the sun was just sinking behind the hump. Agnes and Magdalena came out carrying the food. Julia came out empty-handed. Xaver didn't feel like talking. He couldn't tell his daughters what Dr. Gleitze had said. He was furious. With Gleitze. That fellow had sized up his daughters like a veterinarian. Xaver

went on drinking from the bottle of Müller-Thurgau that Agnes
had opened for the Gleitzes. When Agnes was about to pour
back into the bottle Mrs. Gleitze's glass of wine, which stood
there pristine and untouched, he snatched the glass out of her
hand and with a grand gesture tossed the wine out into the garden. "That'll be the day," he said. Agnes pointed out that Mrs.
Gleitze hadn't even touched her glass. He didn't care. He
thought of the Gleitze youngsters, Jakob and Judith, whom he
had to pick up three times a year from their boarding school on
Lake Geneva. They would speak French to each other. He had
never given a thought to *their* future. It had simply not occurred
to him to size them up in that way, for Chrissake. He had always
tried to understand what they were talking about. He had been
far too much impressed by them. He must admit he wasn't entirely without animosity toward them as he drove them from
Nyon to Tettnang. Actually he had always been thinking of his
own youngsters while driving Jakob and Judith. His kids
seemed to him like losers when he compared them to this loudly
chattering sibling pair. To tell the truth, he was really furious
with Jakob and Judith. He wished that one day they would have
to clean Magdalena's and Julia's shoes. For Chrissake. On the
other hand, Dr. Gleitze had expressed his opinion about Magdalena and Julia with a kind of admiration. While he, Xaver,
wished he could spend hours railing at Jakob and Judith
Gleitze. The way Frey the chauffeur had at the R. kids. That
Frey book was the appropriate continuation of his favorite fairy
story, "The Gardener and His Masters." The favorite phrase of
the gardener's masters in his favorite fairy tale was: *This year
things didn't work out, my dear Larsen.* How happy the masters
were when they could say once again to their gardener: *This year
things didn't work out, my dear Larsen.* And right away again the
feeling that he was being unfair to his Gleitzes. Although he
knew that he wasn't being unfair to them at all. Not nearly unfair enough, anyway. If there was something he had to aim for,

it was how to be unfair to his masters. Overturn a table, Konrad
had said. That one under the pear tree couldn't possibly be over-
turned. . . .

Agnes said that Dr. Zürn had been there too. Just after Xaver
had left. In one way Xaver liked hearing her call his cousin "Dr.
Zürn"; in another way it annoyed him. With Johanna, Magdalena, Julia, and Carolin, said Agnes, who liked reminding him
that two of Dr. Zürn's daughters bore the same names as their
own two daughters. Dr. Zürn was still of the opinion, she said,
that Xaver would sell the house one day. Or at least the property, or a piece of it. Once again he had figured out for her benefit
how much money she was making with her fruit and berries and
how much money could be made by selling and investing the
proceeds. Xaver said: "He's nuts." That wasn't meant as a criticism. Xaver was glad for his cousin to come up from time to
time from Überlingen and to confirm that what they were sitting on was worth something. Unfortunately, the doctor cousin
had already left by the time the Gleitzes arrived. Xaver would
have liked to see his boss's face: May I introduce my cousin, Dr.
Zürn from Überlingen. . . .

Julia scarcely touched the food. Magdalena was eating her
own blend of cottage cheese, herbs, and raw vegetables; she
hardly ever ate what Agnes made for the family. Julia went back
to the piano. Magdalena went to her room. Agnes still had some
seedlings to water. Xaver wouldn't allow her to clear away the
dishes. He would look after that. Later. He went on with his
meal. Home-cured meat, Emmental cheese, a salad of cucum-
bers, lettuce, kohlrabi, and radishes, with a dressing of sour
cream, mint, rosemary, chervil, parsley, and lemon balm from
Agnes's herb garden. Plus Agnes's homemade bread. Plus the
Müller-Thurgau from Hagnau. From something he had read in
school he remembered the words "glory and gluttony." "Glory"
he conferred upon this June evening. Himself he saw as "glut-
tonous." Eating, he thought, is all that's left. Hunger's not

needed for that. Not even appetite. What was that anyway, appetite? His desire to eat wasn't to be expressed by that windy word. His desire to eat was a craving, a mighty one at that. He could have sat down at any time and started eating. As far as the craving of his mouth, palate, and gullet was concerned, he could have gone on forever. Once again he cursed his stomach, which was always far too quick to signal that his eating had to stop. He would ignore it. Not this time—this time he would go on eating. He had the feeling that he was eating in the name of centuries. Never before his time had there been as much food available on this farm. Now the day had come: there was as much food as one wanted. There was more than one could eat. He would start training. Spend more and more time eating more and more. Eventually do nothing but sit and eat. Eat himself to death. Die eating. Collapse with his mouth full.

From the house: Schubert. Julia played well. In his opinion. With her, timing was never in danger. The most delicate nuances of tempo were clearly perceptible. Against a basic tempo. That was something she had mastered. There seemed no possibility whatever of her making a mistake. With her, everything had its tempo. Julia is a thousand times more than any Dr. Gleitze can know. And Magdalena too. How could Dr. Gleitze have the slightest inkling of Magdalena's perfectly soundless strength?

Xaver ate even more greedily. From sheer enthusiasm. Food and music. Nothing goes together as well as food and music. He couldn't understand why Agnes felt compelled to belittle Julia. Saying that there was nothing whatever behind her piano-playing, that Julia played only to get out of stripping beans, washing dishes, drying dishes. Agnes was much more musical than he was. He enjoyed Julia's playing, behind which there was supposed to be nothing whatever. Especially when he could eat at the same time. The only thing that can stand up to music is eating. Schubert, sir, and tucking into a good meal. Why hadn't Julia played while the Gleitzes were still there! Just like her mother! Completely devoid of diplomacy. They both knew how keen Gleitze was on music. Why couldn't Agnes have whispered to Julia: Schubert! And Julia gets the picture, nods unobtrusively, an opportunity offers, and suddenly drops of wistful melancholy come welling from the house, Gleitze looks up: Schubert! But no: now, when the boss has left, now she plays. Or Agnes herself might have played Mozart. Agnes could play Mozart. That's right, sir, in this house you'll find we have Mozart too, believe it or not! However are they going to manage if they don't make use of all their assets, don't constantly present all they have, don't constantly summon up each and every talent! So they want to get ahead without the slightest use of strategy, do they! Oh, my poor dears. Schubert, sir, listen.

Whenever Xaver listened to music, he had to imagine something. He would have liked to ask the boss whether it was permitted to think of all manner of things while listening to music. Otherwise he simply couldn't have listened. Now once again with Schubert he took off very nicely. A kind of leaping began . . . bounding, uphill. At the top, some rapid little steps. For a long time on one spot. Trying over and over again to repeat the same movement. But the movement invariably turns out a bit differently. Plunging up and down on one and the same spot. No success whatever. One simply gets lost. Stopping in the midst of a movement one has hardly begun. Suddenly charge off. Catch-up attempts on the part of the spot where one last was. As soon as one taps the same spot three times, it becomes soft. The third time it already feels quite unstable. Yet it still produces a kind of echo. An unstable echo. Schubert, sir. And now try to finish it off toward the top, if you don't mind. Be brave, begin again. Stamp about a bit. Turn around. Dance. Shake. Climb up and down. Without noticeable effort. Now something passes over one. Pensively allow the dance rhythm to glide through one's head. Foundation vibrates in time. Try out a step everywhere. What is the effect at a great height? Or right at the bottom? Break up the step with movement. Once more up and down. Know your way around. Let the movement look in the mirror. Which puts an end to it. Start all over again, bravely hammering away at the top. No impact can last. Each touch is flung back. Insist on touching. Summon rhythm to aid. Start much more gently. A weeping willow with branches hanging upward. Weave about. Glide about. Let firmness take shape. Even if that means becoming quieter. Try to escape certainty by submerging. Having to rise like bubbles of air. Upward, but down again. Be content to stare upward. To stay. To stay submerged.

Xaver fancied that his listening was being guided ever more accurately by the music. At first he always floundered. But at some point he felt himself to be totally under the guidance of the music. The beautiful thing about Schubert, he thought, was that he sounded as if no one were listening.

He heard Agnes calling. From the vegetable and flower garden that extended down to the road from what used to be the manure heap. She was pointing to a flower whose bell-shaped petals started out deep purple and became paler and paler toward the edges, ending up almost white. "My columbine is lovely, isn't it?" she was saying as she pointed with a finger that curved upward in pride and pleasure. "Underwear of that color would also be very pretty," said Xaver. With her, he always had to pretend to make fun of flowers. From the very beginning, Agnes had always exaggerated the emotional impact of flowers. Gradually he was coming to like her flowers a little better. Especially when Agnes told him that they were beautiful. His mother had had nothing but dahlias. And only along by the fence.

Xaver went back behind the barn to collect the remains of supper and carry them into the kitchen. Luckily he didn't run into either of the girls. They would have noticed from the leftovers how much he had eaten. How he had let himself go. Without discipline, the children are lost. If he lacked self-discipline, the children wouldn't have any either. If they had seen him sitting there guzzling away, they would never have forgotten it and would always have had an excuse for self-indulgence, laxity, weakness. In order to perform yet another duty, he picked up Dorle and twisted the bloated tick from her face. While doing so, he tried to fight off a mental image of himself as being comparable to the globular tick. He threw the tick to the waiting Tell.

He recognized the guests from Munich because they were the only ones to emerge from the first-class carriage. But even if he hadn't recognized them at all, a mistake would have been impossible; he had put on his uniform jacket and cap, so the white-haired gentleman, who incidentally seemed to be less than forty, walked straight up to Xaver and asked: "Are you Dr. Gleitze's chauffeur?" "Yes," answered Xaver. At that the professor turned around and called in a low voice: "Gisi," whereupon the tall, slender woman approached the professor and Xaver. Her eyes really did seem to overlap. And as she walked, she placed one foot in front of the other rather than parallel to it. At each step she seemed to sway a little. She wore strap shoes the color of unripe tomatoes. She walked as if she were trying out her steps. The torso came later. At first came only the shoes, the knees, and so on. She kept her eyes almost closed until she reached the two men. At the last moment the professor held out a hand to her. Much too casually, in Xaver's opinion. A bundle of nerves like that has to be handled much, much more protectively, for God's sake! He, at any rate, drove all the way to the gate of the Trummels' villa as if he were conveying a load of swansdown on the roof, not fastened, and mustn't lose a single speck on the way. And besides, a June evening had something to offer on the way from Lindau station to Lake Deger. The scenery is glorious, Xaver thought once again. So the drive became something of a ceremony.

When Xaver dropped his passengers off outside the entrance to the Trummel villa, his impression was that this woman had sensed that he had driven in this way for her sake. And when she and her husband noticed all the cars belonging to the Trummels' guests, they looked at each other. Xaver simply remained standing beside the car. This implied: I'd be happy to take you along to my place if you don't want to stay here. From the terrace hidden behind green shrubberies came the sound of a strident medley of voices. The tall slender woman drew down the shutters of her eyelashes again, although during the drive she had kept them wide open. The professor thanked Xaver; he had enjoyed the drive, he said. The woman nodded. For a woman of her appearance, it was too sudden, unattractive a nod. "My wife is a painter," said the professor, who apparently found it necessary to explain his wife's exaggerated nodding.

Xaver walked ahead of the couple as he carried up their bags in the direction of the dense confusion of voices. At the top Ursula, the Trummels' maid, saw him at once, hurried toward him, and relieved him of the two suitcases. The first person to come from the terrace was Mrs. Trummel, wearing on her bare skin two pale straps with something attached to them, her hair a single curve landing in front of one shoulder, on her free ear an attention-getting golden hemisphere, et cetera. As if to say: Kneel down, worm, and retract what you've been thinking about me. Xaver couldn't just stand around. Where were the Gleitzes? The Munich couple was swamped in embraces. He felt he had already been looking on too long.

Down below he drove off, scattering the gravel. The Hungerbühler Farm already lay in nocturnal-seeming shadow. Dorle, Tell, Agnes, Magdalena, Julia . . . a colorless family that would never rise up . . . no . . . it wasn't that . . . he didn't know why he was so . . . depressed. . . . Was he annoyed because Wenzel would get to drive the Gleitzes home that night? Wenzel would have another chance to see the woman painter. Gisi. Could a name say more? Was that it? It was simply something to do with the region. One was practically a half-wit if one came from hereabouts. It had always been that way. He really couldn't say anything against Gleitze. That's what it is. You can't say anything. If your load is hurting you now, it's only because you've overeaten, you pig. We're all the same here, all one mess, one great almighty muddle that goes on reproducing itself, on and on and on. . . . He felt like a barrel swaying on two legs. Not the brightest, but the most loyal.

Julia was still playing Schubert. Agnes was still out in the garden. Magdalena's light was on. He went into the living room and drove Julia away from the piano. It was time for a Western. There was none. But something almost better: a movie with his favorite actor, James Cagney. Unfortunately he had so far seen him in only two Westerns. Now he was going to see him in a movie with a title he liked: *The Oklahoma Kid*. Tell lay down in front of him. Xaver slipped off his shoes and thrust his feet into Tell's fur. Dorle carefully settled down on his lap. Now something enjoyable was awaiting him. He felt a kinship with James Cagney. The way Cagney always had to fight for himself was something Xaver knew from his own life. High-Country Kid.

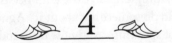

4

SOLEMNLY in a way, in a way collectedly, Xaver drove through the familiar woods, through Malspüren, Stockach, Winterspüren, Liptingen, Tuttlingen, toward Tübingen. At nine o'clock he was to report to Sister Gabriele on the third floor of the clinic on the Schnarrenberg. Xaver had had quite a shock when Mrs. Brass phoned to say that at Dr. Gleitze's request she had made an appointment for him for next Monday at nine A.M. with Professor Amrain, a friend of Dr. Gleitze's. But what on earth . . . ? "You should be pleased that our boss is sending you to a famous specialist." Mrs. Brass always warbled into the phone as if she had been instructed by Dr. Gleitze to spread sweetness and light. This function seemed to have become second nature to her. Xaver had to admit that he invariably found himself somehow caught up in her enthusiasm. Nevertheless, the very fact of her warbling sometimes made him think how grim her expression must be when she entered her apartment in the evening. Some instinct that he couldn't account for led him to regard her as anything but lighthearted. He thought about her quite often, because she had at least as much to do with Dr. Gleitze as he did. One should be able to have a talk with this woman someday. Unfortunately, inconceivable. Aloisia, yes, he could have a talk with her. He made up his mind to do this. Not the brightest, but the most loyal. He wasn't going to let her get away with that.

Yes, but what had Dr. Gleitze to do with all this? That much he felt compelled to ask Mrs. Brass. The boss had discussed it all with Xaver's wife. "You don't mean it," said Xaver. "I *do* mean it," replied Mrs. Brass.

Agnes claimed that, while they were waiting for Xaver on Sunday, she had merely told Dr. Gleitze that Dr. Meichle hadn't found anything but that the pain persisted. Dr. Gleitze had said he would do something about it. Agnes had taken this to be a manner of speaking. And now he's sending Xaver to his personal friend, who is a famous specialist. That's Gleitze for you. Poor John Frey, for whom the R. family hadn't done a thing even when he'd been in bed for a month with pneumonia. Gleitze inquires about one's health and then acts without wasting another word. And then things happen. You're given an immediate appointment. Monday morning, nine o'clock, Sister

Gabriele, if you please. Just conceivably it had been a favor arranged by Mrs. Gleitze over the phone.

Once again the precipitous bend in the forest before Tuttlingen. The pullout where their breaths had mingled in the cold air. It felt good to curve around tongues of forest on an early June morning. He loved roads that curved as if they were anxious to get home. The sun glinted from the tops of the fir trees. Tall grasses nodded inward from the sides of the road. A horse was standing in the meadow. Grazing. Two crows stalked across new-mown hay. A buzzard hovered over an unmown field, dropped, lunged. Then Xaver's favorite pond between Wellendingen and Schömberg, triangular and neatly edged with alders. And because today there was no Ruckhaberle, no Trummel, and no Dr. Gleitze with him in the car—maybe also because he was heading for a clinic—his stomach wasn't acting up.

As he walked across the parking lot outside the Medical Clinic, he heard one man calling out to another: "Mr. Bernhard, just a second—any further report on the Yugoslav?" The other man: "Just that there's no internal hemorrhage. . . ." Then the only other word Xaver could make out was *shock*.

In the lobby, right between the two elevator doors, stood a stretcher with a man lying on it on his side, motionless. A young male white coat approached, accompanied by a young female white coat, and said: "That's Mr. Birn, isn't it, Mr. Birn?" Mr. Birn, in a tone not appropriate to the tone in which he had been addressed, said he was in pain. The white coats told him that someone would be coming for him. Then a young nurse passed by, muttering to herself: "There's that Mr. Birn still lying there." Each time Xaver thought he heard his name.

Sister Gabriele displayed great pleasure. Xaver received the impression that she must have decided first thing that morning to be especially nice to that Mr. Zürn coming in from the uplands. She jumped up, left her glass cubicle, shook hands with Xaver, led him into room number 2. Xaver would be allowed to occupy this two-bed room all by himself. Sister Gabriele extolled the view, the window, the toilet. Xaver felt he was supposed to be delighted. So he nodded and smiled as best he could.

A little black-haired woman arrived and said she was Mrs. Born, did he want tea or coffee, and did he think he could pass some more urine, they needed just a little bit more. She asked as if he had already passed some. He wanted to say: But I haven't passed any yet! However, she went right on to ask: "I take it you've had no food?" He wanted to say that no one had told him not to eat anything but that of his own accord he hadn't; but all he said was: "That's right." With a roguish grin that started right at the door, in came Dr. Michel. He knows all about me too, thought Xaver. Still smiling, as if to imply that he knew very well what he was smiling about, Dr. Michel drew blood from Xaver's arm for a number of little glass vials and then, becoming more serious, questioned Xaver about his history. After him came a girl with no name who asked in a shrill, brassy voice directed toward the ceiling: "Are you Mr. Zürn? I'd like to take a drop of blood from your ear." Obviously no one had told *her* that chauffeurs from the uplands had to be constantly smiled at because otherwise they would promptly throw themselves out the window. Then came a Turkish woman who explained to him how to adjust the awning with a crank. Then came the professor himself. Even as he came through the door he stretched out both hands toward Xaver, beaming with pleasure at meeting the chauffeur of his friend Dr. Gleitze. It sounded as if the professor very rarely had a chance to meet a chauffeur personally and treat him. Furthermore—and now many things began to fall into place—Professor Amrain was from Wilpoltsweiler. I see, thought Xaver, from Wilpoltsweiler, that figures. Xaver had to tell the professor all over again what he had already told Dr. Michel. The professor and Xaver were seated; Dr. Michel didn't sit down until the professor invited him to do so. It looked as if Dr. Michel had Xaver to thank for that.

At one P.M., off for the ECG. At one-thirty, tea, pulse, and temperature. At two, a syrup, labeled "Purgativum." He'd bet anything he knew that word from his church choir days. Again no one around to bet with. These stretchers on wheels are so high that one's feet dangle in the air when one sits on them. He can look out on three mountain ridges. At four P.M. he is examined by Dr. Michel. It turns out they plan to keep him until Friday. He had thought until Wednesday. Oh, Agnes. Outside a cloudburst.

At seven-thirty the professor comes along and does what Dr. Michel has done, all over again. But only what can be done with bare hands. Xaver has to count backward from a hundred because he's too tense. Wiens, the young orderly, smiling—also well informed—brings three tablets and a suppository. Again Xaver notices that in this private ward, with all this attention, he is expected to feel as if it were Christmas Eve. He would have especially liked to tell the bearded youth Wiens that at home he didn't eat off the floor either.

Next morning, naked onto the tilting table. A Dr. Nägele fills Xaver with white guck through an enema tube. On the screen, Dr. Nägele and Xaver watch the contrast medium, a black mass, work its way upward in tortuous convolutions, stop, shoot ahead, stop again. Shift of position, encouraging massage by the gloved hand. Dr. Nägele says that Xaver has a fantastically tense bowel. He goes on: "The spastic condition of your colon makes things difficult." The stuff being pumped in backs up near the exit and forms a solid wad. The more is pumped in, the harder it is for you to hold it in. It feels almost like on that trip to Düsseldorf. And again it's the boss's fault that he has to go through this, for Chrissake. With his X-ray-glove hand, Dr. Nägele keeps trying to massage the stuff upward. And keeps sighing about Xaver's spastic colon. *Tone* and *spastic*: Xaver will never forget those words. As soon as all the guck is inside, it can be let out again.

Now air is pumped in. Xaver goes rigid. He wants to shout: Dr. Gleitze, that's enough, stop it! The Stag! What they're doing to him is what was done to the Stag in the apprentices' workshop. The Stag came from Torkelweiler. Doing his apprenticeship at the same time as Xaver. Because he kept breaking off his work with the file in order to stretch up his neck—craning it back and up as far as possible—they had called him the Stag. Although this craning and stretching took place without a sound, it made one think of a belling stag. One day they jammed his wrists in two vises and tied up the ends of his trousers and sleeves. One of them came with a pressure hose; they were going to inflate the Stag's clothes. The familiar neck-craning was expected of him. Inadvertently the boy with the pressure hose came too close to his behind, the compressed air shot into his bowel, ripped the bowel apart, and an hour later the Stag was dead. A death like Johann's in Königsberg.

Dr. Nägele said they couldn't go on like that. Xaver was given an injection. To slacken the tone, said the doctor. To relax the bowel. Like Konrad, the doctor said everything twice. Now for the X-ray photographs. Xaver is tipped this way and that. Sometimes he is almost standing on his head. He can still see his bowel on the screen. Now that the guck is outside again, the bowel is beautiful. Beautifully transparent. Like a very old drawing. My bowel looks as if it were drawn by Dürer, thinks Xaver. Shaded. Three-dimensional. Beautifully spacious. At appropriate intervals, one of those elegant narrowings. The lines flow with the utmost beauty in the airy brightness of the overall picture. Xaver can't get enough of looking at his bowel. And everyone was saying that this beautiful bowel was harmful to Xaver because it was so high-strung. Xaver wished it were possible to talk to his bowel. One should be able to preach a sermon to that beautiful bowel on the screen. Starting with: O my beloved bowel, listen to me. . . . But no matter how long he looked at that bowel, he simply couldn't imagine that it would listen to him, respond to him. On the contrary! That bowel hadn't the faintest idea that it belonged to him. *Did* it belong to him? Hey, listen, bowel! Who *do* you really belong to?

Then once again he was at leisure to look at the straight mountain range with its serried ridges behind it evaporating into the blue distance. With shrill cries, swallows swooped across the picture.

The thorax X rays. For a time there is presumed to be a problem. The technicians are whispering together. Xaver is aware of an ominous roaring sound about to mount in him. False alarm, however. It subsides. Are you so attached to life? You should be ashamed. And his first thought is always of the children. They must supply the justification for wanting to go on living.

In the intervals between procedures his thoughts revert to his expressive bowel. At first black. And constantly twitching. Like something noble, sensitive, persecuted. Then light, transparent, three-dimensional, a precious drawing. The very fact that he's seen his bowel! Perhaps it's a good thing after all.

Dr. Michel comes with a form. Xaver must sign his consent to the gastroscopy tomorrow. There is a risk of the tube interfering with breathing. Of abdominal hemorrhages. The latter unlikely in Xaver's case. It's expected to take twenty to thirty minutes. And supposing they find nothing after all this? Dr. Meichle will be annoyed anyway that Xaver has consulted a higher authority. Yet it had all been Gleitze's doing. However, if they find nothing it's Xaver who is the impostor. Talks and talks, and then they find nothing! But will they really find nothing? His stomachache certainly can't be caused by nothing.

At eight-fifteen A.M., atropine injection. To reduce secretion and promote relaxation. Wehmaier, an orderly looking like a sick man himself, comes to wheel him away. They want the patients to be brought in while still in bed. Xaver can no longer breathe through his nose. For half an hour his bed stands in the corridor outside the gastroscopy room. This mouth-breathing doesn't come at all naturally. A young nurse and an orderly walk along the corridor arm in arm. Singing—in June—a Carnival march song, stamping their feet in time. Inside the room the young specialist asks a woman assistant: "Lying down or standing up—how does Professor Amrain do it?" "Lying down," she says. This means Xaver must lie on a special table. It has two black knobs. The young specialist puts on gloves and sprays Xaver's throat three times as far back as possible. "Normally, twice is enough," he says reproachfully. But Xaver hasn't asked for three times. Xaver has merely said that, since receiving the injection, he hasn't been able to breathe through his nose. That made the young specialist laugh out loud; what a joke, he said; the atropine was supposed to do exactly the opposite! Isn't that dandy? thought Xaver. On the other hand, he was glad that this unpleasant inability to breathe through his nose wasn't intended.

Once again the professor, even as he comes through the door, stretches his hands out toward Xaver, clasps Xaver's hands in his own for an inordinately long time. The professor nods wordlessly at Xaver. There follows a discussion between the young specialist and the professor as to whether the professor wants to use the Olympus instrument or the other one. He'd like to use the other one. But the young specialist says the professor is more than welcome to use the Olympus instrument. "No, no," says the professor, "the other one." To Xaver it sounds as if the professor were now also convinced that the Olympus instrument was the better one, but in order not to lose face he couldn't go back on his decision. Or, thinks Xaver, he intends to try out on Xaver whether he can do it with the other instrument, which he has never used before. Sure, with a chauffeur he can do that. On the other hand, he does come from Wilpoltsweiler. And those people have nothing against the ones from Wigratsweiler. If anything, they have something against the people from Dabets-weiler.

A black tube is placed in the professor's hands, which are already gloved. The tube is no thicker than Xaver's middle finger. But it is not particularly flexible. The front end is equipped with a shiny metal head. The end held by the professor's hands is the control brain. It has to be explained to the professor: This button, rinse! This button, drain! And everything else about the remote control of the metal head. He has the metal head placed on a piece of bandage paper and tries to see whether he can move it. His fingers play on the control part as if on a clarinet. He has delicate fingers. That man can play the clarinet. Xaver is instantly convinced of this. The people of Wilpolts-weiler have always had good music. The head on the tube moves like a snake. The tube is greased, the professor places the metal head in Xaver's mouth and pushes it down his throat. The light goes out. The professor tells Xaver to swallow. But as a result of the spraying there is no sensation anywhere inside there. Xaver has no idea how or where he is supposed to start swallowing. He tries. But he doesn't know whether he is swallowing or not. There's no longer any reaction inside there. The professor pushes the stiff tube farther in, saying in a consistently and noticeably kindly tone that Xaver should go right on swallowing. Xaver can't. Willy-nilly, a hiccup starts inside him. A rapidly increasing retching.

Xaver is reminded of his mother's grandfather. In the Franco-Prussian War, during the siege of Paris, a music teacher from the lowlands taught him to play two instruments, the flute and the trumpet. The Ehrles are the type that like being conspicuous. One Sedan Day, in Tettnang, this Ehrle great-grandfather has had too much to drink and the conductor can't allow him to go on playing in the band. This is too much for an Ehrle. He has to try to pay back the conductor for the disgrace for which he has only himself to blame. So he waits until the conductor, a teacher from Hemigkofen, is sitting at a table in the Bear with some of the local bigwigs; then this true Ehrle goes to the kitchen door, where there is a basin seething with little eels, grabs one, dashes back into the front room, puts the squirmy little object into his mouth, pretending to play the flute, but when he draws breath the wriggly creature slips into his mouth and halfway down his throat. Johann Ehrle is transfixed, turns red and blue; the men laugh because they know he is a prankster; but the prankster gulps and gulps, tries in vain to pull out the eel. The eel disappears entirely. Johann Ehrle feels a momentary relief, then screams, grabbing his stomach. Dr. Moll, the regional health officer, jumps up, presses Johann Ehrle against a corner of the table, pushes him repeatedly against the corner, holds on to him no matter how much he screams—the screams were such that even thirty years later people were known to say that the worst thing they had ever heard in their lives was Johann Ehrle's screams while he had that eel in his stomach. Suddenly the eel finds its way out; Johann, deathly pale and drenched in sweat, puts his hand down the back of his pants, grabs the eel, gives it to the landlord of the Bear, and tells him to cook it for him. *Au bleu*, but without the trimmings, Ehrle is alleged to have said, and this afterthought suddenly made a hero of him again; back at the table he had proceeded to eat one little eel after another.

Xaver already knew that he would never tell a soul how in a totally darkened room in a Tübingen clinic he had had to try to swallow a plastic tube as thick as his finger and with a metal head. Compared to that, what's a flexible little eel wriggling its way down one's gullet! But that's what the Ehrles are like. Show-offs! The Zürns may be ambitious, but they don't thrust themselves forward. If a person insults them, he never gets to hear about it. Xaver hoped he had also inherited something from the Ehrles. Otherwise Dr. Gleitze would never find out what he had done to Xaver by sending him to this institute of torture.

"Swallow," Xaver hears. He shakes his head. He raises his hand. Waves it as if to say: It's no use, forget it. You can see it doesn't work with me, not this time, another time maybe. But in the darkness the professor sees only what he wants to see. They've almost reached bottom, he says. He has told the truth. Xaver can feel it. The metal head is at the bottom. The retching stops. Xaver is now lying on his left side. Hadn't the boss been lying like that at the Carlton? Like a helpless animal? "Beautiful!" says the professor. Would Xaver like to have a look? An attachment is brought. Xaver is given something to look into. He is awestruck. The vault of his stomach appears gloriously pink and shiny before his eyes. He looks up the shiny walls as if he were standing below them. "Now we'll move along the stomach wall," says the professor. Xaver feels the profoundest reverence as the journey moves along the pink, shiny, mucous vault. "These are the peristaltic waves," says the professor. Xaver immediately feels as if he were in a subterranean Bosporus. If only he could ask the professor to turn out the light in there for a few seconds! He'd like to spend a few seconds in the natural lightlessness of his inside. But the professor has an objective. Can Xaver see that black spot? Xaver can. In the middle of the marvelous pink that glistened as if freshly painted, a totally black spot. "That's the pylorus, the opening of the stomach into the gut." Xaver feels relieved. "We're now approaching the pylorus," says the professor. They approach it. Unfortunately this fantastic journey reminds him of a stupid movie with trick shots that were very similar to this reality. The pylorus grows larger. Recognizable as an exit. "Here we are, now watch," says the erudite guide from Wilpoltsweiler. "We are leaving the stomach." And, incredibly, they are able to disappear into the pylorus. "We are now in the duodenum." But

here the professor's voice betrays some excitement. Xaver can't
go on looking, there is suddenly such an acute pain. He hands
back his apparatus. The young specialist takes it. He and the
professor discuss whether the blood they have just noticed could
be iatrogenic. Xaver makes a mental note to look the word up at
home in Agnes's Brockhaus Encyclopedia. Iatrogenic, iatrogenic. Tone, spastic. Iatrogenic. He must be sure not to forget
these words.

The young specialist now takes over. He points out a bulge to
the professor, something called pulvus. Pulvus, too, Xaver
thinks. Now the pain becomes almost unbearable. He kicks out
a little. Immediately he feels a hand, the professor's. It is stroking him. At once Xaver feels like an animal. Xaver is told to bite
on the plastic sleeve through which the tube enters his mouth.
This is said by the young specialist. Xaver finds this brutal.
How dare he offer this plastic teether! The professor says: "Hold
on, we're almost there." The young specialist asks with undeni-
able malice whether they should make a side trip into this or
that part. Fortunately the professor each time says no. Tissue
specimens had still to be taken from three different places. Otherwise what would have been the point of the whole journey?
Each time a sounding probe was introduced through the tube,
equipped at the front end with a device for cutting out and re-
trieving the snippet of tissue. Three times came the order:
Open—shut. This was carried out by the female assistant. Now
Xaver bit on the mouthpiece that only moments ago he had rejected. The professor stroked him again. It was true, he was
really stroking him. Firmly. Or sympathetically. In any case,
perceptibly. After the second stroking Xaver stopped kicking.
He didn't want to give the impression that he was kicking merely for the sake of being stroked by the professor.

Then it was over.

Xaver was wheeled upstairs. He still couldn't breathe
through his nose. He couldn't remain in bed. He sat on the edge

of the bed. He couldn't stay there either. He stood up. He had to steer his breathing as carefully as his car through the traffic of Milan. He was overcome by restlessness. He didn't know where to put his hands. He wrapped his calves in cold compresses. Marched around his room with slipping compresses. The professor at the door. Xaver must lie down for two or three hours. Xaver lay down. As soon as the professor had left, he got up again. He saw the boss. Not in reality. Nor as a single image. His whole turmoil-driven consciousness produced Gleitze images at breakneck speed. Parts, full views, fragments. At the same time Xaver noticed that his own face became as distorted as the face of an infant that is about to let out a howl and burst into tears. A muglet, they called it in Wigratsweiler. He knew exactly what he looked like now. Grotesquely ridiculous. And meanwhile the ruthless Gleitze images chased through his mind. How brutal the boss could look! He really does have quite a different chin from what one always imagines. And how that horned forehead glistens with ruthlessness! And the hair on the crown of his head reveals how hard it is for anything to grow there. The dimples . . . ah yes, the dimples . . . the one on the right more distinct, darker, than the one on the left . . . in this face there's nothing endearing about them at all . . . because of the mouth . . . when it's closed . . . when the boss isn't listening to music that mouth is a sword lying straight across the face. And the dimples look black. Nasty. And you with your infant's mug ready to start bawling. For God's sake, man, hide somewhere. Hide. Little screaming sounds escaped him. It was clear that Dr. Gleitze could do whatever he liked with him. Xaver always put up with it. Xaver never hit back. Never. Never.

Dr. Michel came and said something. Xaver told him that his nose was still closed up. Dr. Michel said that old people could often breathe only through their mouths. That silenced Xaver. Among the Japanese, Dr. Michel went on, who were known to have eight to ten times as many stomach ulcers as we did, a gastroscopy was a routine annual examination; this ensured a reliable early diagnosis of all carcinomas and thus the possibility of a prompt operation. Xaver felt ashamed. After Dr. Michel had left, his restlessness resumed immediately. He went downstairs, took off his shoes, walked barefoot across some meadows, then through the Upper Steinen woods. Barefoot. All he wanted to do was walk barefoot. My God, he had never known that walking barefoot could be so wonderful.

Two hours later he came back, his restlessness with him. That evening the professor told him he had lied the day before in saying that with the bowel X ray the worst was over. Now he was telling the truth in saying that with that hellish business today the worst was over. That made Xaver want to touch the professor, so grateful was he for his way of putting it. Hail, Wilpoltsweiler, hail to thee!

As Xaver, returning from his walk, had approached the clinic, he carefully averted his eyes so they wouldn't look into the ground-floor wards. He couldn't stand the sight of patients. Suddenly he found patients hideous. Only doctors were nice-looking. And nurses. The entire clinic staff, in fact. But those patients! They aroused sheer disgust in him. The way they were sitting around laughing. Or, looking ghastly, lying in their high-legged beds. As soon as a patient appeared in the corridors, Xaver would immediately look at the floor.

That night Xaver dreamed that Wenzel Froidl, the chauffeur of Dr. Gleitze's brother, kept punching him in the kidneys, saying how typical it was that for the past two years Xaver's children had come to nothing. Having been born in Trautenau, in Bohemia, Wenzel Froidl never did anything without music, or rather, he never forgot to use music for his own purposes. So he not only said, while pummeling Xaver's kidneys, that for the past two years Xaver's children had come to nothing, but actually sang—repeatedly as in an opera, over and over again—how typical it was that for the past two years Xaver's children had come to nothing, come to nothing, come to nothing, all the time thumping merrily away at Xaver's kidneys.

Next morning, the rectosigmoidoscopy. First came the young orderly with all that black beard. Xaver had already forgotten his name. But the young man apparently looked forward to Xaver's room more than to any other. He had been instructed to give Xaver a clysma. "An enema, Mr. Zürn, to clean out the bowel, you know." He spoke a very refined Swabian dialect that sounded as if it had been bequeathed to him by a great-aunt, together with a lifelong cold in the head. When Xaver had to permit the young man, whose front teeth kept reappearing between his moustache and beard—ah yes, Wiens, that was his name—to busy himself with his (Xaver's) behind, Xaver tried to imagine himself far away.

Bends of the Nonnenbach stream were what he saw, far below the Eckes grove, scattered meadows, alders. What dark, quiet places the stream creates, eroding the bank at some spots but then having to leave it behind again at the next clump of alders. Behind the matted roots of those alder buttresses, pure dark mirrors are formed. Down at the bottom, in layers, the fallen leaves of many years, three feet high. Each layer visible. As a child, Xaver had often spent the whole day down by the Nonnenbach; he had loved to lean out over the quiet dark places in the bends of the stream. Had dipped his arm in the water to watch the refraction below the surface. Had undressed. Looked. At himself. In the dark mirror. And counted the layers of leaves all the way down until they disappeared in the gloom. . . . But although he kept his mind fixed on the Nonnenbach, he also thought of Wiens the bearded Swabian. Even during the bowel X ray he had tried to keep his mind off the procedure. Then he had given up. It was hopeless. Clearly he had been brought here for all the world to busy itself with that part of his anatomy which he wished most of all to keep concealed from the world. Perhaps Dr. Meichle was behind all this after all. Wasn't he always trying to show Xaver how to achieve a more friendly relationship with his bowel? As if Xaver needed Dr. Meichle for that! He was the very person he didn't need. In fact he didn't need anyone for that: his relationship with his bowel was excellent, as long as he was left alone with his bowel. And if he'd been alone in the world he wouldn't have had even the slightest problem with his bowel. It was only because all those people were interfering that there were problems at all. The very fact that they didn't call anything by its proper name was suspicious enough. Suddenly it seemed highly likely to him that his being sent to Tübingen had been discussed and decided upon by Dr. Meichle and Mrs. Gleitze. Then, in order to keep up the pretense, the trip to Wigratsweiler had been made: their luck is in, Xaver isn't there, the conversation is brought around to Xaver's health, then everything goes like clockwork and with the appearance of true concern and a genuine checkup. In reality, however, they intended to bring him to heel. . . .

Xaver brought himself up short. He noticed how once again pure megalomania was dictating his thought processes. As if Dr. Meichle and Mrs. Gleitze had nothing better to talk about than Xaver's bowel! You'd like that, wouldn't you? On the tennis court, during a tête-à-tête across the net, Mrs. Gleitze's first question to the U-boat movie captain's head with its blue-gray, silver-wire hair is always, isn't it: Do tell me, how is Xaver's bowel at the moment? Of course, of course, of course. That's enough. Forget the whole thing.

But there was no denying an increase in the demands being made on him in the way of self-exposure. The trestle on which he was obliged to kneel for this new inspection, the position he was made to assume . . . really, the very way a person simply must *not* be allowed to kneel ever since the human race abandoned the four-legged posture. And before the arrival of the professor, Xaver was told to put on white, incredibly drafty paper shorts. The woman assistant, with whom he was alone for some time, was probably also wearing nothing but that clinging little white coat over a clearly outlined bikini. Hardly has he survived this when he has to kneel down in the vilest possible way. The professor has arrived. And, with no explanation, rips the paper shorts to pieces. Then he compliments him on his sphincter muscles, his healthy rectal veins; he drains, rinses, snips. How can a person possibly keep his mind off that? After all, the professor is handling him the way a veterinarian handles cows when he pushes his arm all the way up their backsides. At the time, hadn't Xaver felt sorry for the cows? And wasn't he now being treated like a four-legged beast? But since man has learned to stand upright he has actually lost sight of his backside. Even the ability to reach it with the mouth has gone to hell. Where else! Only the hands, which are incapable of seeing and smelling, can reach it now. The result is an ever-growing alienation. You can't smell yourself anymore. And this head of yours, which refuses to have anything to do with its opposite end, becomes heavier and heavier the higher it is carried. Again Xaver behaved as if he were somewhere else. You can't do that, Dr. Meichle! Dr. Gleitze! Mrs. Gleitze! Not to him! You can all kiss his ass! In his mind, those Konrad phrases linked up with one another and talked their way through his head.

As soon as he was alone in his room he buried his face in the pillow. His one desire was not to have to think of anything for a while. How does one manage that? The very thing one wants to avoid keeps on coming. It seems one mustn't want to avoid anything. In other words, one must put up with everything. Right.

Suddenly the fountain outside was turned off. An audible silence ensued. It made him feel good. "That Elvis Presley, he's got something, you know," Agnes had—suddenly—said. She, the musical one, who suffered far more from the kids' records than Xaver did. Why did he happen to think of that at this moment? Why not? Surely he ought to be glad at having that particular thought. At the time, that remark had pleased him

very much. It had been the Sunday after Easter. A brilliant
April day. Behind the house. The radio was close to bursting
with Presley. A little later, Xaver had kissed Agnes on the neck.
He hadn't wanted to kiss her immediately after that remark.
That would have seemed stupid to him. From that time on, he
had quite often brought a Presley record home with him. And
he had found an occasion to mention that Elvis had also been a
driver, a truck driver. In Tennessee. They say that's hilly country, too. What Xaver had actually wanted to say, he hadn't said.
He had wanted to say: Only a driver can sing like that. He was
afraid a nondriver might not understand. So he said nothing.
Next Christmas, a whole Mozart opera had lain under the tree.
From Magdalena. She bought things like that with her own
money, earned by gathering elderberry blossoms. Next to the
album lay a slip of paper: For my father. Magdalena simply di-
vined one's thoughts. No one could do that like Magdalena. It's
fantastic, this ability to think not only of oneself but also of
someone else. On Christmas Day, Xaver had sat down on the
sofa. Dorle had immediately gone into her lengthy ceremony of
making a comfortable place for herself on his lap. Magdalena
changed the records. It was the opera *Don Giovanni*. Once again
he thought that Mozart's music was, quite simply, familiar to
him. It all sounded as if he had often heard it before. Perhaps
even sung it. In the church choir. Dorle's ears twitched in time
like an oscillogram. She turned her head to escape the music.
Toward the end a woman screamed. Dorle tried to bury her head
between Xaver's thighs. Then, at his final plunge, Don Giovanni himself screams. A really terrible scream. That was too
much for Dorle. She dashed out of the room. It was the first time
she had had such a fright in the family. After that, whenever
Xaver listened to those records he had always stopped short of
the final scene. He didn't want to inflict the violence of that
fearsome ending on Dorle a second time. Eventually he stopped

putting on that opera altogether, feeling that, without the ending, something was lacking.

When the professor arrived with Dr. Michel for the final visit, he held out his hands higher than ever; Dr. Michel smiled more roguishly than ever. "We know now, we know now for sure: there's definitely nothing! Our congratulations!" By beaming, smiling, shaking hands the two men demonstrated that a feast day had dawned for Xaver. Xaver nodded and smiled as best he could. And thanked them warmly. Packed his things, went downstairs, got into the car, and drove slowly down the hill. He felt like an utter failure. Agnes would be happy.

Suddenly—he was already driving through Spaichingen; just in front of him he saw the Seven Winds, the inn for which the road had to make a bend—suddenly he discovered a reason for his mood. His feeling about himself was not the same as the feeling those people had about him. The Gleitzes. And the difference between these evaluations was becoming larger rather than smaller. It was easy for Agnes to say he craved recognition. For only now—and for the first time—did he grasp the fantastic, unwearying energy with which she converted every movement into work. She had no Dr. Gleitze and no Mrs. Gleitze over her. Only now did he grasp why in almost every discussion about his job Agnes understood the Gleitzes' point of view better than his.

Agnes, too, regarded Xaver's job relationship as an especially good one. All his friends and relatives agreed. Whenever any conversation came around to his position with the Gleitzes, Xaver invariably struck up the same paean of praise. This harked back to the first two or three years. The most important thing, he now felt, was something he could never express: that he thought of himself differently from the way everybody else did. He knew no one, not a soul, who thought of him the way he thought of himself. There was no one whom he could ever have told how he thought of himself. The difference seemed to him too great. Worse still: now he couldn't even have said *how* he thought of himself. He was merely aware of the difference. He had so often, and for so long, agreed with the opinion of others about himself that by this time he remembered his true sense of self as something belonging to the past. It already seemed almost extraneous to him. But what had remained undiminished was the importance to him of his sense of self as distinct from whatever anyone else could say about him. Feeble though it was, there was nothing he would defend more tenaciously than this feeble, barely perceptible sense of self; this certainty, which he could no longer communicate, no longer substantiate, no longer even comprehend, that he was different from what all those other people thought. Maybe Magdalena had an inkling of who he was. Sometimes he suspected this. The Gleitzes didn't want to find out any more about him than they already knew. They wanted him to be a good, safe driver. That was really all he could expect of them.

So don't worry about going home. The Gleitzes won't laugh at you. They won't take you for a fraud who claims to have all kinds of illnesses and then, when they have him examined by a famous specialist, turns out to be the picture of health. Oh no, they'll say: What splendid news, Xaver—so, Monday morning at seven-thirty, Villa Säntis View. The boss sent him to Tübingen, to those machines, because he needs a man whose reliability has been scrutinized by every technological process. And if Xaver wanted to be that man, if he had himself given rise to doubts, it was up to him not to object to that scrutiny. The boss was entitled to be informed about every square centimeter of his insides, that was quite obvious. How many hundreds of X-ray pictures must they have taken this past week? They'd been snapping away as if they'd been using an old box camera. Now Gleitze knows what he can expect of me. Now you know what you can expect of Gleitze.

But now every thought that was unfavorable to the Gleitzes failed to convince him. Not even his rage. He couldn't escape from them. That scared him. What would he have to do? He remembered the knife in the glove compartment of the Mercedes. He gave a laugh. Shrill rather than loud. Then he said aloud: "Oh, Xaver," and glanced at himself in the rearview mirror. Then he drove a little faster. He was already moving down the Stockach slope. The fact that the employers of his colleague Frey had presumed to boss him around in a similar way cheered him up. However, the Gleitzes were incomparably better than the R.s. Yet in some ways they were very similar. In fact, you could hardly tell them apart. The next moment he again felt this was being unfair to Dr. and Mrs. Gleitze.

All he wanted now was to get home. To Agnes. Yes. But Agnes had never worked for strangers. As far as his relationship to the Gleitzes was concerned, Agnes had opinions that were almost as mistaken as those of the Gleitzes themselves. But Agnes . . . Yes, Agnes. But . . . In Fact . . . Yes.

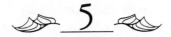

5

H I S mother would certainly have regarded a day like this as a reason for thanking God. One more homecoming. His mother had always acted on the assumption that everything would go wrong. If something didn't go completely wrong, she immediately fell on her knees to thank God. Gradually she reached the point where she thanked God even for what had gone wrong. Either because it might have turned out even worse or—if it was impossible to imagine it turning out even worse than it had—because she would thus be protected from imprudence. Although he had long since ceased to operate as directly under God's eyes and judgment as his mother had, he did feel that there was something about this boisterous June day to inspire a certain reverence. Uphill and downhill, the wind raced through the green treetops. But no matter how deeply it lashed about in them, they were green through and through. June is green, through and through.

The best part was always the moment when the seven red rooftops of Wigratsweiler showed up. Fiegles, Heners, Korroses, Späths, Zürns, Ehrles, and Gierers. Not higgledy-piggledy. Not in a row. Properly distributed. But he would never have stopped just to look. The roof of the Hungerbühler Farm was the only one that needed reroofing.

Xaver let the car coast down in neutral and up again onto the bluff where the Hungerbühler Farm and the Happy Prospect stand a little closer together than all the other houses of the hamlet. Maybe one should move higher up the slope one day. Stand higher than all the others.

Agnes said: "Well?" Again Xaver immediately felt it was humiliating to have to say: "Nothing. Sound as a bell." Agnes seemed happy at the news. She laid her cheek against his chest. But what is she thinking? There he is with his stomachache, like a truant. Or like someone who imagines things. At some point she is bound to wonder why he is always talking about his stomachache when a professor and a whole university clinic have established that there's nothing the matter with him.

Agnes had been waiting for the car. She had to go off to the nursery gardener's. Besides, the TV set is on the fritz. Young Philipp Fiegle took it down with him on Tuesday. It's supposed to be ready by today. In that case he'd go with her. And the girls? Agnes shook her head. The two vertical black lines rising from the base of her nose deepened. She sat down again. For a while she was unable to speak. For three days Leni had refused to come to meals. Out of hatred. She could sense that. Wasn't that rather inadequate proof for such a far-reaching assumption? She was quite sure of it. Leni no longer accepted a single mouthful prepared by Agnes. Leni was living entirely out of cans. When she was asked anything, she said she didn't feel like answering the same old questions all the time. And Julia was flunking her exams. Xaver wanted to go upstairs at once. Agnes said she was lying in the bathtub. She was always either out or lying in the bathtub. At the moment she was lying in the water with her jeans on, having emptied a few bottles of Coca-Cola into the tub. First, to fade them a little, second, to make the jeans cling to her body. Mick had done that too, his fit him super, she had said, in fact real neat. Mick? Herbert's successor, he'd be sure to come by today, to pick her up. "If she flunks her exams, she's not going to leave this house," Xaver said promptly. "And anyway, how come she's flunking now?" He simply couldn't understand it. Till now he'd always believed, he went on, that she was merely toying with this prospect. "If I know I'm shaky, I automatically steady myself." She's his daughter, after all. She must know what it means to fail. In Wigratsweiler. In the company. Surely she must know that she . . . that we . . . Xaver fell silent. He refused to believe it now. "Come along," he said, "let's get going."

As soon as they were in the car, Agnes wanted to go on discussing Julia. But first he scolded her for having described him to Dr. Gleitze as a very sick man. It was her fault that Dr. Gleitze had sent him to Tübingen. Now he looked like a malingerer, he said. He should be sending *her* now to Dr. Gleitze to confess that she had grossly exaggerated. He was ready to bet anything that she'd said she was at the end of her tether with her husband—that eternal stomachache! "Well," said Agnes, "and wasn't that correct?" "And," Xaver shouted furiously, "what's the matter with me? Nothing. There, now it's your turn! What do you say now?" "Doctors don't know everything," Agnes said in a low voice. From then on, Xaver calmed down. With those words Agnes had repudiated the judgment that he was a hypochondriac. She had admitted the possibility that there really was something wrong with him.

He asked after Julia. It all depended now on Mr. Wacker. "Oh my," said Xaver, "Wacker, Latin." "Exactly," said Agnes. There was nothing more to be done about the E in geography, Miss Merkelfinger, she said. They'd known all along that it would depend on Wacker and Merkelfinger. Till now she had regarded Wacker, Latin, as more of a threat than Merkelfinger, geography. And now it had suddenly turned out that Miss Merkelfinger had already finished marking, she had already announced the candidates for an E. Among them Julia. In other words, if there was any hope left at all they would have to pin their hopes on Wacker, Latin.

"Of all people," said Xaver. "Exactly," said Agnes. Xaver was reminded that he had undertaken to help the girls in languages. But Xaver, who had worked his way into English and French by gritting his teeth and with the aid of television, hadn't the slightest idea of Latin. And Agnes wasn't interested in languages anyway. But didn't Latin really belong more on her side, the mathematical side? Didn't people always say that Latin was based entirely on logic? He didn't mean to reproach Agnes. Neither of them had bothered about Latin. The school had discovered the Zürn family's weak spot, had concentrated its attack on that, and was apparently on the brink of victory. In her last report Julia had had a D from Wacker, Latin. Since then one E and one D-minus. So, Agnes added up, an E plus a D-minus equals an E-plus. That plus a D from her last report gives her an average of D-minus. But now the oral. That's why Julia is counting on an E. After the lesson she had gone up to Wacker, Latin, had written her calculation on the blackboard, and said she needed a D, with an E she'd be sunk. He had twitched the corners of his mouth. With Wacker, Latin, Julia had said, that meant a smile. His wife was known to have been dying of

bowel cancer for the past three years. It seemed to Xaver that
Agnes had said the words *bowel cancer* unsteadily. He, Wacker,
Latin, had said he would give it some more thought. He had
given Isabell a D, although her average was E-plus and Julia's
D-minus, but still he'd given Isabell a D. "Why doesn't she tell
him that?" Xaver exclaimed. That would mean that Wacker
would have to give Isabell an E too, Julia had said, then Isabell
would flunk too, and she didn't want to be responsible for that,
Julia had said. Even now, all the time she was in school, she was
thinking of the teachers' snide remarks about the kids who
hadn't made it. The way the teachers sneered at those kids all
year long, you wouldn't believe, Julia said. Just as if they had
criminal records. Xaver shouted. He couldn't help shouting.
He couldn't help shouting when he heard something like that,
he shouted. She, Julia, knew everything, saw through everything, foresaw everything exactly, only she didn't do anything
about it, didn't do a thing to save the situation, didn't even
make any serious attempt, she'd rather lie there like a dummy in
the bathtub and watch the disaster approach her, my God. . . .
Xaver could hardly go on driving. And there he'd always been
believing that he was living with his children in a remnant—
although an ever-diminishing one—of mutual understanding,
which for them meant they could rely on him not to do anything
they couldn't understand—for example, he would never burst
into the girls' room with a knife in his hand in order to stab
them, of that they could be almost certain, as they could about
disasters in general, as far as it was in his power; but this was the
very thing he had expected of his children too, just what was
normal, nothing exceptional. All right, so high school was not
the normal thing for his girls. The attempt of the Wigratsweiler
Zürns to move up a modest step in the world was being dashed
to the ground, he had to accept that, although by this time he
had learned enough of the world to know that what was happening now wasn't inevitable; it *could*, he said, more quietly now,

have turned out differently; there were not only laws, there was also blame, personal blame; one always had greater control over things than one cared to admit. . . .

Agnes said: "Maybe he'll give her a D after all." "Wacker, Latin!" Xaver shouted shrilly. "Never, he was a career officer!" He recalled how one of their daughters had once brought home a remark made by Wacker, Latin: There had once been a time, Wacker had said, when the occasional genius had arrived from the country; nowadays only scrap drifts in from there.

He dropped Agnes off at Kugel's nursery and drove on to Radio Franz's, where he walked straight up to Mr. Bippus, who was laughing as he approached. Mr. Bippus spoke Swabian dialect like the bearded orderly. Xaver was in no mood to chat; he wanted to pick up his television set. At his very first words he noticed that he must control himself. He had uttered them in a tone to suggest: I'm not the least bit interested in why you're laughing like that, and don't you forget it! The salesgirl was laughing too. She must have told Mr. Bippus something that caused him to laugh like that. Now he was all set to pass it on to Xaver. Then they would get around to Xaver's business. But Xaver Zürn has only entered this store to pick up his TV set. I couldn't care less why you and your salesgirl are in such paroxysms of mirth. Xaver really had to control himself.

"You've come for your TV set, of course, Mr. Zürn, obviously, tomorrow's Saturday, that's when a person needs his TV, isn't it?" And pressed a button and spoke into a mike: "Michel, Mr. Zürn's come for his TV. . . ." By way of reply came a mechanical squawking. Mr. Bippus translated: "You seem to be out of luck, Mr. Zürn, the set's not ready yet—we've ordered the spare part, but they don't have it even in Friedrichshafen—whether they have it in Ulm we don't yet—" "Just a minute, just a minute!" Xaver said much too loudly. "Who's out of luck here? Obviously it's you, let's get that straight, if you don't mind!" "You're so right, Mr. Zürn," said Mr. Bippus with a laugh, "so we're both out of luck!" "But I'm without my TV!" shouted Xaver. "Of course, of course," said Mr. Bippus, "that's why I say you're out of luck."

Xaver stood transfixed before this Mr. Bippus. Who the hell did he think he was! Xaver felt everything inside him concentrating once more on a single, hardening spot. Mr. Bippus seemed to be looking at him with a sneer. Gloating. In any case amused. He was grinning, wasn't he? Xaver had to turn away. He could think of nothing to say. He walked along beside the counter. Toward the door. But if he wished to reach that door alive, he must do something immediately. He felt the hard spot inside him rotating. Turning into a frantic knot. In his extremity, as he walked past the counter Xaver simply swept off everything he could reach without actually stretching out his hand. Mainly records. "Just a minute!" Mr. Bippus called out. Before Xaver was outside, Mr. Bippus had caught up with him. Xaver simply knocked him to the ground. As he fell, Mr. Bippus managed to pull down a rack of records with him.

Xaver was outside, and although he felt an impulse to run he checked himself and walked as fast as it is possible to walk without appearing to be running. He drove to the nursery garden. Agnes was still talking to Kugel the gardener. They were standing in the evening sunshine between flower beds, chatting about bedding plants. Mr. Kugel was pointing first here, then there, with his slightly bent index finger; Agnes was looking wherever he pointed. At last her eyes moved in the direction where Xaver was standing. Kugel and Agnes filled the trunk of the car with bone meal, peat, and bedding plants wrapped in newspaper. Xaver didn't budge.

On the way home Xaver's face was such that Agnes asked why he was making such a face. He said he'd had a row with the salesman at Radio Franz's. "With that smarmy bastard from the lowland, you know who I mean." Xaver knew he had to tell Agnes more about his tantrum at Radio Franz's. But he didn't

know how to explain that tantrum to her. He could hardly understand himself what had possessed him. At home they carried
everything into the garden. Xaver said he wanted to go off into
the woods for a bit. He walked so quickly that Agnes had no
time to ask any more questions. But not so quickly that she
might have felt obliged to run after him. He took his bicycle
and coasted downhill without using the brakes, just managing
to make the curve around the corner of Fiegle's farm. From then
on the road sloped down more gradually, but, since it became
rougher and stonier, Xaver got a good shaking-up. He quite
liked that. It reminded him of earlier days, when he had always
sung out one note and let the rough road shake it up. When he
reached the forest the road became smooth. As smooth as a parlor floor. Now he glided silently on his bike down through the
shady forest. In the past, no sooner had he dived into the forest
on his bike than the sound he was making leveled out completely. At that point Xaver had usually begun to sing properly in
the forest. The last bit down to the stream had to be taken at a
run. He used to run down to one of the spots where the stream
flows around a clump of alders in such a way as almost to turn
back on itself. Behind the clump of trees the stream was quiet as
a little pond, a dark mirror, and, above it, thirty years ago
Xaver had undressed so he could look at himself. Each time he
had resolved to undress for the sole purpose of looking. Each
time he had broken his resolve. Soon it became a fingering.
Then masturbation. He used to make his semen splatter onto
the dark reflecting surface of the water. Then he had pelted the
pale drops of semen with stones until he had driven the tattered
streaks into the current and the Nonnenbach carried them away.
Before sadness at his renewed defeat reached and paralyzed him,
he briefly imagined that downstream trout would be snapping
at his streaks and swallowing them. Then sadness became all-
engulfing. Light dripped dimly through the branches. He
trudged home.

His rapid heartbeat so long ago had been different from today's. Nothing would have been more remote to him now than to undress. He could still recall his pale reflected shape in the dark mirror. Now he would see himself from shoulders to thighs as a barrel. Why had he come today? Lash out, he thought. Konrad was right. At the moment, he refused to contemplate any other notion. Lash out, lash out, lash out. . . . Nowhere could he abandon himself so utterly to this notion as here. Lash out till he'd had enough. Till the urge had subsided. Till he no longer felt like lashing out. That he couldn't imagine. His compulsion to lash out seemed unquenchable. Eternally unquenchable. Lash out. . . .

It became dark and chilly. He could move again. He reached out for dry twigs, broke them into smaller and smaller pieces as if this were a labor he had to perform. Then he walked up into the forest. He remembered a phrase from the story of the Peasants' War: When the peasants were no match for their enemies, "they donned the cloak of the forests."

He wheeled his bicycle home, where he washed the sticky resin off his hands in the water trough beside the stable door. He must ask Agnes to phone Radio Franz. He would never set foot in the store again. He was never going to recognize that Mr. Bippus again. He must describe the incident to Agnes in such a way that, although she would phone the store, she wouldn't really be able to imagine what a fool he'd made of himself there. No need for the girls to hear about it. Nor did he want to be entirely sober when he told her about it. Which meant Xaver would have to start drinking wine right away at supper. Hadn't he just spent a week in Tübingen? Hadn't he been told there was nothing the matter with him? Well, wasn't that a reason to celebrate? At that point it occurred to him that Julia's new boyfriend was expected. Agnes would insist on inviting this stranger for supper. She could never get enough of the empty gabble of those fellows. She was insatiably curious about them. She herself was under the impression that the questions with which she plied Julia's swains were inconspicuous! Xaver had invariably been embarrassed when obliged to be present at one of those interrogations. Even though he didn't care for those young punks, when they were quizzed by Agnes he felt sorry for them. There was also the pain of knowing that Magdalena had to listen to all that.

The new boyfriend drove his motorbike right up to the coach-house. Julia ushered him into the room. "This's Mick," she said. Hair and beard a curly golden mass. Pointed nose. Inflamed eyes. At any rate, eyelids that were noticeably reddened. They showed up as the only color in all that pallor and blondness. From the moment he sat down he sat very straight and ate as if there were a contest: Who can eat the least conspicuously? Toward the end, not only did he not take the whole cheese in his hand to slice off a piece as his predecessor had done, but he responded to each offer with: No, thank you. None of the others had ever spoken that softly. He hardly ever raised his eyes beyond the edge of his plate. Julia sat up even straighter than Mick. But in her case it looked less like good manners than like gloating. Sometimes she gazed at him as if at something that belonged to her and with which she could be content. Magdalena sat as far back as possible from the table. So far that she had to lean forward to eat. Her chin barely hung over the edge of the table. She opened her mouth and with a soup spoon shoveled the corn kernels—which she had emptied from a can into a vinegary broth—from her plate into her mouth. She resembled some humpbacked, dwarfish, evil thing. She behaved as if she heard and saw nothing. Her ghastly posture implied that, no matter what was to be seen and heard here, she was prepared to give only one answer: her grotesque pushing back and leaning forward.

When the meal was over, Mick had eaten practically nothing. He had drunk two or three mouthfuls of mineral water. He had quietly refused any alcohol. That appealed to Xaver. My God, the way his predecessor, that snooty high-school graduate, had placed a naked piece of Tilsit cheese on his naked palm to saw off a slice for himself! It looked for all the world as if he were going to hang onto the Tilsit cheese and continue whittling bits off until there was nothing left. But no, he had put the Tilsit back onto the cheese plate. To Xaver, that behavior had revealed the butcher's son. For that's how a person whittles bits off a sausage when he doesn't have to pay for it. Actually, the father of this whittler had sold his butchery business to Gaissmaier and had been working for years—as a forklift driver—at MTU in Friedrichshafen. And his fine son hung around waiting for a chance to study chemistry, a chance that seemed to be a long time coming. On the other hand, he *had* graduated from high school. An exception, as far as Julia was concerned. All her boyfriends were laborers. But not proper laborers. Casual workers, unskilled workers. They called their work "jobbing." They were dropouts. The high-school graduate was also a kind of dropout, a loafer. That was Julia's specialty.

Agnes asked her questions very quietly today. Evidently this boy hadn't put her into a panic. A repro photographer. But why did he call himself Mick? Someone who works in the repro department at Gleitze's in Markdorf, photos that are then used to make switch panels for the construction of alarm systems, doesn't call himself Mick! For the last three months he has been working in alarm-systems production. Xaver can contribute that he knows from his cousin, who works in alarm-systems sales, how well that department is doing. But it didn't lead to any conversation. Mick only answered questions. And that as softly as possible. He didn't answer the question as to why he was called Mick even when Agnes asked it for the third time. He looked across each time with a shy little smile to Julia. Apparently she was supposed to help him. The third time, but not before, she does. In her particular way. She stands up and says:

"Before she gets around to asking a fourth time, basically, we'll bugger off, come along." They were expected at the Harbor Inn. They'd more or less promised, basically. "But tonight we won't tie one on. Just a few drinks, basically." Mick wasn't feeling all that hot, either. So they'd be back in no time, basically.

But it was more than forty kilometers there and back, they told her. "That doesn't mean a thing, basically, with Mick and his bike."

As soon as the couple had disappeared, Xaver and Agnes were very surprised that they had allowed them to go. Meanwhile, Magdalena had cleared the table, loaded the dishwasher, and turned it on. Agnes and Xaver confirmed their pleasant impressions of Mick to one another. Only that of course he was much too old for Julia, said Agnes. Only that again he wasn't one of her classmates, said Xaver. "Only that he smokes pot," came Magdalena's voice from the kitchen. "What do you mean?" Magdalena gave a thin, shrill laugh. Parents like that shouldn't be allowed to have children, she said. With such innocents for parents, a kid didn't stand a chance. If they couldn't see that he was a chronic pot smoker! With those eyelids. Hadn't they seen those inflamed lids? And, she was sorry to say, she knew all about that from the time two years ago when she'd also been stupid enough to hang around with such types— though she must say she'd learned her lesson once and for all; she knew that such scarlet eyelids and the bluish rings around the eyes were the unmistakable signs of a pot smoker. And since as a factory worker he couldn't afford the quantities that led to having such eyes, he must be a dealer too. That was quite obvious, wasn't it? So they had just had supper with a far-out pot smoker *and* dealer—how little he had eaten and with what contempt he had refused any alcohol was something they, simpleminded parents that they were, had probably also failed to notice—and then they'd handed over their daughter to him. She spoke as if she herself were no longer a daughter of these parents.

Agnes clenched her hands into tight little fists and rubbed her temples. Xaver coaxed Magdalena and Agnes into the living room. Then he set down their two glasses and poured some of his white wine. Magdalena pushed her glass into the middle of the table, saying she would fix her own drink. She always needed half an hour to prepare one of her herbal teas, for which she would gather whatever she needed from verge and hedgerow. As long as Magdalena was outside, Xaver tried to persuade Agnes that Magdalena's insinuations said more about Magdalena than about that fellow Mick. He didn't believe what he was saying. But he had to prevent Agnes from getting into a complete panic and sweeping him up into it as well. It had happened before: after ten minutes they had dashed off like firemen to the car, driven to Friedrichshafen, chased from tavern to tavern, making themselves ridiculous, and finally found them standing beside a jukebox drinking Coca-Cola. . . . A fine thing that would be. Magdalena was the most prone to panic in the family. Sometimes Xaver thought she was merely imitating him in order to show him what he was like. But then it always turned out that she was completely serious about it.

When she came in with her little earthenware teapot, she said she couldn't understand how in such a situation her parents could sit around in the living room drinking wine while their daughter was tearing around through the night in the clutches of a pot smoker. She sat down and, with the first and middle fingers of her right hand, drummed so swiftly and lightly on the tabletop that the fingers became almost invisible. She seemed scared. Xaver began to get scared too. On Agnes's forehead the two vertical black lines deepened. "That's enough now!" cried Xaver. He'd just spent a week in the hospital. Clinic! The most horrible machines in the world. She should first be put through an ordeal like that, then she could say her piece. Magdalena's fingers immediately stopped their antennalike drumming.

He went to get another bottle. He was glad Agnes was drinking too this evening. Magdalena, in one of her favorite poses, was now holding her teapot in both hands and pressing it against her right cheek. Xaver lit his first cigarillo, remembering as he did so that, in answer to the professor's question as to whether he smoked, he had replied with an unconditional no. Then the professor had asked: Alcohol? Upon which Xaver had managed an indignant-sounding no. And a violent shake of the head. The professor would be sending a copy of everything to Dr. Meichle, who in turn—because of Meichle's connections with Gleitze—believed Xaver to be a teetotaler. Once again Xaver saw in his mind's eye his beautiful, twitching, elegant, innocent, persecuted-looking bowel. At first totally black. Then—more beautiful still—suffused with light. As if etched in silverpoint. Was there such a thing? He believed he'd heard something of the kind.

First of all, he must confess that he'd had a tantrum at Radio Franz's. No, first he must tell them about the week. The farmers' wives pressing bits of white cotton to their earlobes as they stood around in skimpy nylon smocks outside the lab after a drop of blood had been taken from them. Where be ye from? I be from Grumbach. Ah, you be from Grumbach. I be from Urach. First of all, Agnes and Magdalena must be able to visualize how he had been received. A deluxe room had been reserved. The whole station had been practically waiting for Xaver Zürn from Wigratsweiler. They'd better believe it. Had it all been some kind of joke? Apparently, it had been very funny for all concerned, a chauffeur in a private ward, alone in a double room. Obviously they couldn't very well put a managing director in with a chauffeur. Hadn't he been treated all week long like one of those lucky people on TV who have won something they're clearly not entitled to? Gradually he began to grasp what had happened to him during that week. A fraud. The whole thing was a fraud.

Xaver believed he would be best able to explain his tantrum at Radio Franz's if he first described what kind of machines he had been exposed to for a whole week in Tübingen. But since he didn't want to start off with that subject, he would first talk in general about the family. About the Ehrle and Zürn families. Just about the old days. What it had been like hereabouts in the old days. At school he had always been waiting for some mention of Wigratsweiler or perhaps even of the Hungerbühler Farm. But then mention was only of the Montforts, of the people of Werdenberg, Sürgenstein, Waldburg, Fürstenberg, Summerau, of Ravensburg, Lindau, Überlingen, Konstanz, Vienna, Stuttgart, Berlin. Wigratsweiler had come up only twice in school: once because in the census of the year 1515 it had had eleven houses, in the census of 1789 thirteen houses, and in the census of 1910 seven houses; the other time in conjunction with the Ice Age! "The most attractive feature of Lake Constance is the surrounding hills, for which we have to thank the Ice Age," Mr. Reckholder the teacher had told them. And among the hamlets situated on these hills he had also named Wigratsweiler.

When Xaver started to talk about the old days, he invariably said the same thing. But always in such a way that it sounded as if he'd never said it before. He wanted his words to arouse astonishment. Whenever he talked about what it was like hereabouts in the old days, Agnes and the children were supposed to exclaim: You don't say! As late as the generation of his grandfather, thirteen children had had to grow up on this small property. Just try to imagine that. Thirteen. One room for the girls, one for the boys. There'd been no way of providing beds for them, even if they'd had any; that many beds just wouldn't fit into the two rooms. They'd slept on straw sacks. When they reached fourteen, they had to leave. Never mind how many years' schooling they'd had. And all the places they'd gone to! He didn't tell them that every time.

He stuck to the farm. To his grandfather. Whom he'd never seen. Because he'd hanged himself in the hayloft. Way back in 1912. With a piece of string for tying sheaves. Purple string. His grandfather, like all the Zürns before Xaver, had been a hunter. When he was only eleven he had taken his father's gun and shot and killed a boy his own age, one of the Hener boys from down the hill, Berthold by name. While playing. By mistake. Who knows whether it was a mistake? Xaver repeats the question as he has heard it. He also repeats the next sentence as he has heard it. His grandfather was not a happy person. And his three brothers were odd, too. What he had heard was: "queerish." He couldn't be sure that Magdalena and Julia would know what had been meant by "queerish," so he simply replaced it with "odd." Agnes, of course, knows what "queerish" means.

As two brothers had left the farm, he never mentioned them when he talked about the farm. He didn't say anything about Benedikt, who had stayed on with Grandfather as a farmhand; all he knew about him was that he had always waited to comb his hair until he had had his bowel movement, in order never to be uncertain as to whether he had completed his most important activity. Xaver didn't regard this as worthy of mention. So Grandfather—this was an item of information that never lost its impact—had hanged himself in the hay barn at the age of forty-four. But why? A Zürn family reason. In the old days—please remember that, in the old days—today things are different! Today no Zürn is exposed to want! Today a Zürn life can turn out well, very well in fact, there's every probability that today a Zürn life will turn out well or very well, but it seems that in the old days the Zürns were regularly exposed to want. In the year '12, in July 1912 I mean, Grandfather came in one evening from the woods. It was a Sunday. He used to go up into the woods twice a day. In the morning with his gun. In the evening without. So now without. And on the way home he went past the hop garden. Then along by the field. Then home via Engelschwand. Where the cherry trees are. And he noticed that the fruit crop was coming along better than he had ever known it. He stopped in the kitchen and told his wife that prices would be lower this year than ever before. Groaning as he said it. Then off to the barn to hang himself. His wife has thirteen kids and is thirty-nine years old. So there. And he hanged himself because he was afraid the fruit crop was coming along in such unprecedented quantities that it would fail to fetch a good price. Everything a bargain. Worth noting. Such a price collapse is something he doesn't want to live to see. So there. Xaver's father, in talking about the farm, used always to say at this point: In those days the hop Jews, the crop Jews, the fruit Jews, used to fleece the farmers left and right. In repeating that remark, Xaver would add that the dealers buying up those crops needn't actually have been Jews. In his youth he had known ruthless fruit dealers who weren't Jews. He was thinking of one from Lindau who had a gold eyetooth; when he was bargaining, he used to get so excited that long strands of hair would fall across his face, and, since he needed all his beringed fingers for bargaining, he had to keep tossing back his hair without using his hands; his brother Georg likes to mimic him to this day.

Those dealers, Xaver would say, used to beat down the farmers over crop prices just as the real Jews had done in the past. He felt obliged to say that. He wanted to be sure his children weren't infected with prejudices that might harm them. The Zürns must be careful, said Xaver. Of late they were always wanting to be right up front. Originally that hadn't been a flaw in the Zürn character. It was only through connections with the Ehrles that the family had acquired this urge to be conspicuous. Not with the Ehrles of Wigratsweiler, that went without saying, but with those of Horgenweiler. As far as was known, no Zürn had ever married someone from the same hamlet.

In saying that, Xaver was always reminded that all through his childhood and youth he had had no other desire than to win Margot Hener of the Happy Prospect. He had seen her get on her bike to ride off to the dance cruise where she met the lawyer from the Ruhr district who took her away and after two years sent her packing, so that, being pregnant, she had to marry Sepp Mehl, a cook in Lindau-Reutin. Xaver hadn't known where she was heading for that evening, but he had sensed that, if she was riding off on her bike all dressed up like that on a Saturday evening in June, she was up to something he ought to prevent. He stood there watching her get on her bike. She saw him. She said nothing. He said nothing. It was totally unnatural. Both feeling awkward. She didn't look back. He could perhaps have shouted: Come back! No, he couldn't. As soon as she was on the saddle she stepped hurriedly on the pedals, although the path used for leaving Wigratsweiler either on foot or by bicycle immediately starts to slope gently downhill. The upshot was that now her name was Margot Mehl and she was just as fat as her husband. Xaver still found her beautiful. For him she was attractive. Dizzyingly attractive. The simple fact was that there was something left over from the past. No one would ever hear anything about that from him. The Zürns know how to keep something to themselves.

That brought him back to what could be told. Admittedly the Zürns were ambitious, Xaver said to Agnes, but they weren't noisy. Quite different from the Ehrles. An Ehrle would tell you practically more than he knew. A Zürn who doesn't keep something to himself was quite unimaginable. His brother Georg, for instance, who never opened his mouth as long as anybody was around but had to mimic everyone the moment they were gone, was a Zürn as well as an Ehrle. He, Xaver, considered himself pretty much of a hundred-percent Zürn. To play the clown like his maternal great-grandfather on Sedan Day in

Tettnang, in other words to play the flute on little eels, was
something he would never dream of.

The eel story, told with as much pride as disgust about Johann Ehrle, his maternal great-grandfather, was always followed, in order to give due prominence to the Zürns, by the
story about his paternal great-grandfather, David Zürn, of
whom it was said that no one would ever have known what he
did in the Franco-Prussian War if a Gattnau comrade hadn't
found his way up to the Happy Prospect after the war and told
the tale of what the young fellow from Hungerbühler had done
in France. What had happened was that when, after the longest
siege of the whole war, the fortress of Belfort had finally been
conquered, the general, a Mr. von Tresckow, had ordered the
Prussian flag to be hoisted on the battlements of vanquished
Belfort. Just the Prussian flag. Not the flag of Baden or Württemberg or Bavaria, although the soldiers who had taken part in
that siege from October to February certainly came not only
from Stettin but also from Baden, Württemberg, and Bavaria.
In February 1871, shortly after the founding of the Reich, that
had been a bit of an outrage. And it had been David Zürn who
during the night had torn down the Prussian flag, ripped it up,
and then distributed the shreds among a few comrades from his
own area. When he got home, David Zürn had used the flag
material to make shoelaces for himself and his brothers. But
without the comrade from Gattnau no one in Wigratsweiler
would ever have found out how he had managed to lay hands on
any flag material. In repeating this tale, Xaver knew that he had
now destroyed any possibility of bringing up the subject of
Tübingen. After all, he wasn't one of those talkative Ehrles, he
was a taciturn Zürn. He wished the professor were sitting there
at their table, telling about how Xaver had kicked his legs a
little and he had stroked Xaver and all that. The Zürns weren't
cut out to be chroniclers, he felt that quite clearly. Apparently

he had enough Ehrle genes to feel some slight regret over the taciturnity of the Zürns.

"Jakob's case shows what can happen," Xaver said after a while. What he really wanted to say was: what can happen to us. But he didn't quite dare, it would have seemed presumptuous. But mentally he always added "to us." He suddenly realized how he missed Julia. True, she had heard everything he had to say, many times. He told it over and over again because it couldn't be heard too often. What can happen. What can happen to us, for Chrissake. And Jakob is a case in point, too. In 1941, in Berlin, during the Reich small-bore championship, Jakob had had fifty-nine twelves on his target and his rival from the Walther team of Zella-Mahlis had sixty-one hits on his, and the rival's worst shot was deducted from *his* score and the bull's-eye, the twelve, that Jakob had fired onto the wrong target was *added*. The dream was over. One year later Jakob was already on the Eastern Front, where he perished with the Schörner army. That's what can happen. To us.

In telling the story of Jakob's fate, the most important thing was that, as long as one was still telling it, the ending was again uncertain. Each time he told it, the insane hope would arise that this time Jakob would become German small-bore champion because *this* time he would place all sixty twelves on his own target. Even after he had once again recounted the miserable ending and described in detail Jakob's uncanny talent for calm and concentration and the firing method Jakob had invented, that hope of a happy ending would raise its head again. Jakob's stance as he took aim! The way that fellow stood there! When Jakob aimed, he kept both eyes open. One eye concentrated on notch and bead, the other on the target. He could really do that! That was his method! Xaver can still remember Jakob coming home from explaining his method to the Ravensburg Rifle Club for the first time. They'd laughed in his face. Until he proceeded to hit one twelve after another. And he became famous from here all the way to Berlin. The hardest test for the competitors was the twenty shots to be fired *kneeling*. Concentration depends solely on breathing. And to make one's breathing just as conducive to concentration while kneeling as when standing or lying—that happened to be Jakob's specialty. To kneel doesn't bother a Zürn. After all, Jakob had been an altar boy.

It had been wonderful to listen to Jakob talking about shooting. One had the feeling that his eye had possessed such accuracy and power of concentration that to that eye the bullet had, as it were, flown toward the target in slow motion. After each shot, he could immediately tell you the number of the ring before it was announced. And it had to happen to him that, after looking down for a split second, he had in looking up again mistaken the next target for his own and, his vision being so excellent, hit it as accurately as his own. After the war it had been proven that Jakob was no dreamer but a pioneer. Agnes nodded. She knew that. But Xaver still had to say it, for that was the only happy thing that could be added to Jakob's fate of being among those reported "missing in action." After the war the Russians suddenly became incredibly successful in the world championships. And with what? With marksmen who fired with both eyes open. So there. Xaver thought that Jakob might have revealed his method to one of the guards in a POW camp in Karelia. But he didn't say that. In any case that was the proof that Jakob Zürn hadn't been queerish, but a pioneer. One had to admit, of course, that Jakob inserted the right eye of a bat into his rifle stock, said Xaver. But that certainly wasn't what did the trick. That was simply part of the Zürn hunting tradition. People did it whether they believed in it or not. As a boy, Xaver had also rubbed his eyes with bat's blood, so as to see just as well at night as during the day. And to this day, even by minimal moonlight, he only switches on his headlights so as to be seen by other drivers, not so he can see; he'd find his way even without headlights.

To tell of what went wrong in such a manner that, second by second, it was possible to believe that this time it would end well was the idea Xaver strove for whenever he told the history of the farm. Nothing was so deeply embedded in him as the belief that everything must end well. But perhaps it was more of a need than a belief. That was why he could never get over Jakob's wartime fate and the various versions of Johann's death. He had to recite to his family, over and over again, what had happened to Jakob and what to Johann, in order, as long as the story lasted, once again to experience and to convey the feeling that everything was still in limbo and might still end well. Life *must* turn out well. Johann's fate in Königsberg, which today he was again telling in Dr. Kuckuck's version—direct hit in the frontal armor, finish—was always the penultimate story of his Zürn legend. Would Henriette today say good-bye to her civilian friends in the nearby cellars quickly enough to come back in time to prevent Johann from moving into the final action? Would Johann let himself be prevented? Or would he at least, when turning onto Hagen-Strasse—as the Dr. Kuckuck version had it—discover the two Stalin tanks in time for him to retreat? And, if that direct hit couldn't be prevented, did he then really have to be killed right away by it? Mentally gnashing his teeth, Xaver had then to confess the ending, the unhappy ending. But maybe . . . no, no illusions please, Jakob and Johann are not alive in Siberia. They are not alive anywhere. They are dead. For Chrissake. But it took a war for that to happen. Without a war, a Zürn life turns out well today, remember that.

Xaver felt he must din this into his daughters. He was always afraid they would suddenly confront him with reproaches at having brought them into this world. This accounted for his desire to prove to them by means of stories of the past that now things could turn out well for Zürns.

His final story was always the Peasants' War story, from a

book Johann had brought home. Actually there were three
books, very old ones; the binding had colors like the layers of
leaves in the Nonnenbach. Inside they bore the stamp of the
cloister school. Probably Johann had never got around to returning the books. Xaver spent less and less time reading the
legends and more and more time reading these three books,
which had been published by a certain Dr. W. Zimmermann in
Stuttgart in 1841, '42, and '43. Of all the stories concerning the
Zürns, this had had the worst ending. Xaver must have read the
pages describing the local events at least a hundred times. And
each time he had hoped that this time the peasant leaders Dietrich Hurlewagen and Eitelhans Ziegelmüller would not let
themselves be cheated by Georg von Waldburg, the leader of
the army of the nobles and burghers. Between Good Friday and
Easter Monday, in the year 1525, everything had been decided.
Against the peasants. But how was that possible? It simply
couldn't be possible. This time it really should have turned out
well. A just cause. Great superiority over the unjust attackers.
An excellent vantage point for the numerically superior cham-
pions of the just cause. The nobles' general, Georg von Waldburg, has only mercenaries under his command, and they have
already shown that they prefer merely to chase away the peasants
rather than kill them. They're from the same class, after all.
And yet everything goes wrong. Believe it or not. There's nothing to be done about it. But surely that's impossible. They
should've been able to pulverize that Georg von Waldburg. Together with his Wilhelm von Fürstenberg and his Froben von
Hutten. Pulverize them, ram them into the ground. Finish, the
end, amen. Victory for the peasants, the war won, once and for
all. No more serfdom or any other kind of domination. There'll
be elections. For the pastor as well as for the mayor. That's how
the Bible wants it. Christ wants free men. No way. Believe it or
not, it all went wrong. But how, how on earth, when it was

impossible for things to go wrong, when everything was in better shape than ever before or since, how could things possibly
have gone wrong? They couldn't have, surely you must agree!

All right, just listen to this now: With eight thousand men,
Georg von Waldburg marches from Wurzach toward Weingarten. On Maundy Thursday, on Wurzach Heath, he duped the
peasants by negotiating with them, then proceeded to attack
them, give chase, and kill several hundred of them. Now, because the peasant bands have fled southward, he worries about
the Waldburg properties. In Gaisbeuren he meets up with our
lot from the lake. Ten thousand strong. Under the command of
a squire by the name of Dietrich Hurlewagen from Lindau. And
overnight they're joined by the five thousand peasants from
Wurzach, led by their pastor, called Florian. (Although the
book says "blackcoat," Xaver can't say "blackcoat." That was
what the Nazis used to call priests.) From Markdorf another ten
thousand peasants are moving up, led by Eitelhans Ziegelmüller. Never before had there been such a night in the uplands
as that from Maundy Thursday to Good Friday in the year 1525.
Starting at two in the morning, the bells of one church rang out
to rouse the next. Eight thousand peasants from the Oberallgäu
were approaching from Leutkirch. In addition, four thousand
from Hegau were also marching toward Weingarten. Georg von
Waldburg was practically done for. One could almost feel sorry
for him with his eight thousand pros. What he had done to the
peasants in Leipheim and Günzburg was something he couldn't
even think of doing here.

On Good Friday the peasants managed to snatch Gaisbeuren
from under his nose. Back to Waldsee was all Mr. von Waldburg could do. But that night Count Wilhelm von Fürstenberg, in command of von Waldburg's horsemen, bribed three
farmhands—they were paid ten guilders—to sneak into Gaisbeuren and set fire to the village in a number of places. The
peasants immediately took this for a surprise attack, evacuated

Gaisbeuren, and moved off through Altdorf Forest toward Weingarten. So far nothing had been lost. On Easter Saturday, Georg von Waldburg was forced to send four emissaries to the peasants' camp in an attempt to improve his situation by negotiating. Somewhere in the forest—in the Löffel mill perhaps, or perhaps in the Foxhole—the peasant leaders consented to listen to the four emissaries, who were: Count Haug von Montfort, Baron Wolf Gremlich von Hasenweiler, and two Ravensburg city councillors. The message was that, if the peasants would hand over their arms and flags, he would approach no closer to Weingarten. If they did as he said, all complaints of the peasants would be examined by a tribunal chosen by both sides. Past events were to be forgotten.

On Easter Sunday the peasants, believe it or not, discussed this outrageous proposal. For the duration of negotiations, no military movements, so the peasants had demanded and the general had promised. Nevertheless, while the peasants were deliberating, von Waldburg moved his troops in order to improve his position. Whenever Xaver, coming from Ulm, reached Marsweiler, where there is a view of the Schussen valley, he would remember that the general of the nobles and burghers had advanced to this point on Easter Sunday. Contrary to the agreement. But the peasants twigged and proceeded to take up their own battle positions on the slopes behind Weingarten. On Easter Monday the four emissaries met their general near Baindt Monastery and reported that the peasants would actually accept mediation. But they were simply of no mind to hand over weapons and flags.

Georg von Waldburg realized that he was in serious trouble. The peasants had occupied the heights. A deep ditch in front of the peasants' position rendered the use of massed horsemen impossible; and these were the general's most effective weapon. Georg von Waldburg ordered eight hundred horsemen to parade in all their glittering panoply, so as to impress the peasants looking down from the heights. Weingarten would provide a fine blaze in the coming night between the two camps, he said. With this threat he sent the four negotiators back to the peasants' encampment. A second round of negotiations with these gentlemen was too much for the peasants. They gave up. Capitulated. But they did not deliver up their arms. And of the thirty-two flags that should have been handed over by six that evening, only five ever reached von Waldburg. With his own hands he ripped each flag apart.

But by this time the band of Oberallgäu peasants, who had not agreed to the treaty, were already in Schlier, less than an hour away. And the men from Hegau, who had also not yet knuckled under, were expected to arrive that night. So von Waldburg ordered a detachment to march past Weingarten and take up a position between the Oberallgäu and Hegau groups. His emissaries then succeeded in persuading all the various bands of peasants to accept the scrap of paper known as the Treaty of Weingarten. Thus Georg von Waldburg was out of the hole and could set about finishing off the peasant bands between here and Würzburg, one by one. That was how, because of a hundred thousand slaughtered peasants, he had been dubbed "Bauernjörg," or Peasant Georg. Not one of the promises he had given in the treaty was kept. It was nothing but a trick. But a trick that succeeds comes to be known as something quite different.

Xaver noticed that Agnes had nodded off a bit. Magdalena's face showed that she was determined to listen never mind how long it went on. She wouldn't fall asleep. Julia had on one occasion even begun to read the paper, when Xaver came to Easter 1525. Eitelhans Ziegelmüller and Dietrich Hurlewagen, he said, as if these two names must now keep them wide awake. Florian the pastor had fought, he said, no doubt about him. But Ziegelmüller from Bermatingen and Hurlewagen from Lindau, they were the rats. "Mind you, that wasn't recorded anywhere," Xaver said. What *had* been recorded, of course, was the cleverness and the genius of Georg von Waldburg. But the fact that Ziegelmüller was proud of having had dinner with the Abbot of Salem, and that Hurlewagen was only acquainted with the peasants because he had an estate in Gitzenweiler, that had been recorded. And that he was bankrupt in Lindau, as a merchant. Above all: it is recorded that on Easter Monday Hurlewagen himself rode down the gentle slopes to von Waldburg's camp, in the morning probably, when the peasants hadn't yet backed down. Rode there, jumped off his horse, and went on his knees before the nobleman, throwing up his hands, beseeching, imploring von Waldburg to be patient—he, the leader of the lake peasants, Squire Hurlewagen, would manage to persuade the peasants to back down.

At this point Magdalena had once said that in a similar situation a certain Vercingetorix, a Celtic leader, had also ridden to his enemy Caesar and placed himself at Caesar's feet just as Hurlewagen was said to have thrown himself down on his knees.

He, Xaver, said Xaver, had no doubt that Hurlewagen had received money from the coffers of the nobles and burghers. The fact that he wasn't entirely successful and even got caught up a little in the avenging orgies of the nobles and burghers—but really only a little—doesn't mean that he wasn't a rat. It only means that he didn't manage to bring the peasants around entirely, and consequently had to do a terrible lot of finagling until von Waldburg had finished off the peasants in the Black Forest, the lowlands, Franconia, and the Oberallgäu, band by band. As a result, he got into hot water with all of them. Later, when the peasants heard how von Waldburg had treated the peasants elsewhere, they must have clutched their heads in despair. But by that time they had already given their oath. A representative of each community had sworn that they would no

longer defend themselves but would wait for the tribunal. They
didn't notice what a swindle that was until the nobles were back
in their saddles and could behave as in the past. Of course there
was no point in cursing Hurlewagen, said Xaver. After all, it
was our own people who agreed to be led by such a character.
When they noticed how he was finagling, they could have killed
him a hundred times. But hereabouts we keep to our oaths.
That's the worst part of all. That made everything go wrong.
The whole Peasants' War. That's what Dr. Zimmermann
wrote. Anyway, he calls the Peasants' War a "People's War." If
the army of eight thousand had been defeated at Weingarten,
the nobles and burghers couldn't have raised another army. It
was right here that things went wrong. The joke is that the
Waldburg family still owns everything that was given to Georg
von Waldburg as a reward for killing off a hundred thousand
peasants. You see, crime does pay. And is respected. There's a
Bauernjörg-Strasse in Weingarten. Xaver made up his mind to
hang a pig's bladder on that street sign next Easter Monday.
Written on the bladder would be the words: "To the victims of
the bloody Waldburg swine."

Xaver could have stamped his foot with rage because once
again he hadn't managed to change the story of the Weingarten
fiasco. It really hurt to subject himself yet again to the yoke of
that old defeat. But every time he retold the story of the events
of the Peasants' War, his greatest disappointment was that,
even at this telling, he failed to understand why his people had
allowed themselves to be prevailed upon. And why do they respect treaties formulated by their masters? Why are there still
masters? Because everyone hopes to become one himself, said
Xaver.

Those were always his concluding words. Accompanied by a
sort of finagling gesture to urge upon his family sympathy for
this hope. But at the same time his face became distorted with
rage in a grimace that did not match the finagling gesture.

Agnes opened her eyes, felt a bit embarrassed, and said: "Julia should be home by now." Magdalena sprang up and, with teapot, cup, and an inaudible good night, hurried out of the room. She seemed merely to have been waiting for a subject to be broached that would not require her presence.

Xaver wasn't sorry to see her go. He would have found it more than difficult to explain in her presence what had happened to him at Radio Franz's. That explanation could no longer be postponed. Agnes would have to call them up tomorrow and account for Xaver's tantrum. The best thing would be to use the week at the clinic as an explanation. And in asking for the bill for the damage, she could hint that the amount would be reimbursed by the health insurance. Ye-es, that's how serious it is.

Because her anxiety about Julia was now turning into panic, Agnes let Xaver's vague description of his tantrum at the radio store pass without a question. Something told Xaver that there couldn't have been a more opportune moment for this embarrassing revelation.

They sat up until two o'clock. Then they lay down in their beds. Agnes kept reiterating how quiet, reserved, shy, polite, gentle, soft-spoken, endearing, helpless, et cetera, that Mick had been. There was no way he could keep Julia out all night when he knew she was expected at home. Besides, Julia wouldn't be capable, either, of simply staying out. She knows how her parents worry about her. So this time they felt quite sure there must have been some disaster. From time to time Xaver thought of his boss. In three weeks Xaver would have to pick up the Gleitze kids again from their boarding school on Lake Geneva. Judith and Jakob. Again they would speak French together all the way home. Xaver envied the boss. *He* was relieved of his kids for almost the entire year.

As always, while they were waiting resentfully for Julia, the resentment gradually became all-encompassing: they became resentful of each other too, heaped reproaches on one another, yelled at one another. This time, again, Xaver had had quite a different vision of his homecoming.

At five-thirty in the morning Mick pulled up at the back steps. Agnes let Julia in. Xaver was too tired to do anything about it.

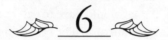

6

J U N E can be scorching. When Mrs. Gleitze instructed Xaver to paint the garden fence, she couldn't have known that that particular day would be such a scorcher. Xaver told himself this as he painted because he found himself looking for reasons for being furious with Mrs. Gleitze.

Each time Aloisia came out into the garden with drinks he wanted to ask her the origin of that phrase—that he was the most loyal but not the brightest. The best thing would be if she brought up the subject herself: How do the Gleitzes talk about Xaver? What do they think of him? Do they share the same opinion? How often do they talk about him anyway? And who brings the conversation around to him? Is it an effort for one of them to persuade the other to discuss Xaver, or is the other one also glad of the chance at last to be able to say something about Xaver? Do they laugh when talking about Xaver? Could she tell him, please, have they ever laughed when his name was mentioned? So what kind of a laugh was it?

But every time she came waddling up with her drinks, behaving as if besides heat and thirst there were no other problem, he couldn't find a way of getting her onto his subject. She suffered from the heat much more than he did. After all, she was fatter than he was: in her case there were so many layers on top of and beside each other that no air could get in between them.

Xaver invariably started to talk about the Gleitzes. So where are
they today? When are they coming back? Didn't she also have
the impression that Mrs. Gleitze was now taking the car herself
more and more often? Is she really always driving off just to visit
friends? Is she trying to impress someone? Or has she something
against Xaver? Yes? She has? Aloisia tilted her head to one side,
planted her hands on her hips, and said that frankly she felt too
hot to open her mouth about Mrs. Gleitze. If he didn't need her
now she'd be back in half an hour, so he wouldn't die of thirst.
With a groan she bent down for the tray and shuffled back into
the house.

Suddenly an eruption. An ear-splitting racket. The brush fell
from Xaver's hand. The racket was a medley of steely sounding
bird twitterings, steely insect whining, and vicious whistling.
But filling the world. Shattering the world. Supernatural insects, thought Xaver. Horror insects. This world's-end cacoph-
ony came from the villa. Up under the gable, a light was
whirling like that of a police car. Out ran Aloisia, gasping like a
fish and flailing her arms. Xaver ran after her into the basement
and tripped the fuse of the alarm system. The old one with the
American police-siren sound had been more to his liking, he
said into the silence. She agreed. This was the third time this
one had gone off without being switched on. "Keen," said
Xaver, conscious of using one of Julia's expressions. Xaver
should be that keen, said Aloisia and insisted: "A shock like that
requires a beer." Xaver drank his straight down. He didn't want
the Gleitzes to arrive and think he was fooling around in the
house. But he did have to make a quick trip to the toilet. Whenever he walked through the front hall of the villa he had to look
at the old, high-shelved, worm-eaten dresser standing against
the wall. Exactly like the one they had thrown out when Agnes
moved in with her glossy new furniture. In the toilet there was
nothing to remind him of Wigratsweiler. Here the lever to
work the flush was surrounded by a large metal plate that was a

sort of distorting mirror. Everything reflected in it was enormously magnified. When one passed water into the bowl, one's sex organ appeared very much bigger than was possible. From the very first, this installation had given Xaver an inkling of the scope of living in such a house.

Aware now that he couldn't talk to Aloisia today about the Gleitzes, he said he would take her for a drive someday to Lindenberg. Aloisia rolled her eyes up at him. Head at an angle, hands on hips. Lindenberg, of all places, Little Paris, what! Well, if she wasn't interested, he said, he'd never forced anyone to drive anywhere with him. That she could believe, she said.

The conversation had immediately acquired a tone that Xaver hadn't intended. At that moment they heard the Gleitzes driving up. Two cars. Xaver heard the cars long before Aloisia had. He ran outside through the basement door. As he hurried off he called out that his offer still stood.

Fortunately, while the Gleitzes were still absent, he had finished painting that part of the fence which could be observed from the terrace.

The confusion of voices turned into some that he recognized. Provided they hadn't seen his Renault, they wouldn't know he was close by. Mrs. Gleitze might have forgotten that she had told him to come today. There could be no better opportunity of hearing how they talked about him when they were among themselves. No. The Trummels! That spoiled it. The Gleitzes alone, that would be the thing. In the presence of the Trummels, the Gleitzes might not talk about him at all. He stopped painting in order to listen. He could make out almost every word. He could clearly hear that Mrs. Gleitze and the Trummels were comfortably seated or lying, while Dr. Gleitze went from one to the other, sometimes disappearing into the house; then whoever was speaking would raise his or her voice so that Dr. Gleitze could still hear. Xaver could also tell whether someone was going beyond the terrace room farther into the house. Then the voices would adjust to being audible only on the terrace.

So far what he was hearing was no different from what he also heard in the car. He was still hoping for the extraordinary. So they had just returned from a visit with Dr. Gleitze's brother Friedhelm. From his yacht *Albertina*. Mrs. Gleitze, whom they all addressed as Susanne, led the conversation. She was in a state of excitement. Anyone trying to say something was shrilly drowned out by her. She was the easiest to understand. She was intent on reminding everyone how Friedhelm Gleitze's wife, Inge, had described the vacation she and her husband had spent in Tunisia. Her sister-in-law had apparently enjoyed being treated with reverence by the native chambermaids. Reverence, Mrs. Gleitze repeated, her voice already shaking with laughter. At that they all laughed. Trummel, whom they all addressed as Ralf, was even more amused by the fact that Friedhelm had demonstrated his admiration for Bourguiba, the Tunisian head of state, with a single sentence about the labor market: "The way he keeps a tight rein on the labor market—hats off to him, I say!" Dr. Gleitze, whom they all addressed as Dieter, joined heartily in the laughter but defended his brother by adding that Friedhelm had also said: "A huge human reservoir, cleverly deployed—no one earns much but everyone earns a little." At this, still more explosive laughter broke out. At least two voices repeated more than once: "No one earns much but everyone earns a little!" Even louder laughter. But now Mrs. Gleitze tore herself loose from the laughter that was almost threatening to kill her, and exclaimed that the *best* part had been Inge's remark that on this trip she had had a few kilos of candies along, thus giving pleasure to many people. Now the voices reiterating Friedhelm's phrase about no one earning too much but everyone earning a little mingled with those reiterating: a few kilos of candies along, thus giving pleasure to many people. That wasn't only Gleitzes and Trummels. There were at least six voices, if not eight.

There had been one experience that Inge and Friedhelm had had in common on their Tunisian trip, had they noticed that? This comment was called out by a voice unfamiliar to Xaver. The question put by the unfamiliar voice was answered almost in chorus: Many, if not all, had noticed which experience Inge and Friedhelm Gleitze had had in common on their Tunisian trip. During the night the ordure carts come to remove the night soil from the hotels and take it out to the desert. Xaver waited impatiently for a new theme. But they were in no hurry. Like in an opera, he thought. During the night the ordure carts come to remove the night soil from the hotels and take it out to the desert. . . .

As soon as he became aware of the presence of total strangers, he lost all hope of overhearing anything about himself. He collected his things. Was about to leave. Just then he was brought up short by a name. Gisi. Was *she* there? No. Now they were talking about Gisi. About Bertram Meister and his wife, Gisi. The woman with the close-set eyes who places her feet one in front of the other and had been wearing shoes the color of unripe tomatoes. Now, suddenly, they were talking quite differently. In low-pitched, eager voices. They were talking about the evening at the Trummels'. Trummel himself was speaking. He knew for sure, he said, that Gisi was still a virgin. He mustn't say how he knew, but he knew. All she and above all he—Meister—required was for her to watch him at some distance while he masturbated. As the voices from the terrace were raised again, Xaver put away his things and left, without saying goodbye to Aloisia.

That night he dreamed that he was standing in the toilet of the Villa Säntis View with its shiny, gold-brown, textured wallpaper, and passing water into the beautifully shaped porcelain

bowl that was now the soup tureen. He sees his urine being suspended in colored streaks in the crystal-clear water, not blend-
ing with the water. Since the lever for the flush is surrounded by
a highly polished brass plate, he sees his sex organ and his hand
gigantically magnified in the golden reflection. The lever offers
no resistance as he presses it. Without a sound, the water immediately rises in the bowl. Xaver waits in vain for it to drain away
with a gurgle. He has long since let go of the lever. Nevertheless, the water continues to rise until the bowl is filled to the
rim. On the surface, the urine streaks drift restlessly around. He
hears Dr. Gleitze's voice outside. Dr. Gleitze seems to be furious about something. His angry voice resounds through the
house. Meanwhile he is coming closer and closer to the door
behind which Xaver is standing. Xaver feels himself rising on
tiptoe. He stands rigid and motionless. Any moment now he
expects Dr. Gleitze to bang on the door. All he can think of is:
Why doesn't Aloisia come to my rescue? Only Aloisia can help
me now. Why doesn't she help me? She should be distracting
Dr. Gleitze, holding him back, deceiving him, killing him! He
tried to call out to her. But he couldn't.

On Saint Peter and Saint Paul's Day he picked Aloisia up
from the station square in Lindau for their outing to Lindenberg. She had wanted him to pick her up in Tettnang, but he
had tapped the side of his head to indicate that she was nuts. She
had called him a coward.

Aloisia was wearing a sleeveless dress of pale yellow. He
opened the door for her from the inside. He put on an expression
that, in his opinion, was gloomy. He wished to appear unhappy
in order to make Aloisia aware right from the start that today
was no day for her incessant chatter. Not too unhappy, of
course. Otherwise she would begin to caress him out of pity,
and everything would go wrong again. So he lightened his expression a bit. He hoped he now looked like a person who,
though happy-go-lucky about some things, is not in the mood

for laughter. They had not yet driven across the bridge when Aloisia said that unless he changed his expression she would get out of the car. Did he imagine that on her day off she would go for a drive with such a sad sack? If she wanted to see a sourpuss like that she might just as well stay at Mrs. Gleitze's. That made Xaver laugh. And anyway, if she had known that in this car one could drive at only a walking pace she wouldn't have come. The Mercedes 450, that's what they should be driving, said Xaver, in order to bring up the subject of the Gleitzes. He accelerated his Renault as much as he could. There now, she said, stretching body and legs, that felt a lot better. She'd soon teach him how to take her out. To begin with, she wasn't as easily satisfied as a wife, she hoped that was understood. Xaver pretended to be highly amused at that. Well, did he imagine he didn't have to entertain her when he took her out on her day off? And where were they heading for, anyway? She wasn't one who'd let herself be led with closed eyes to the slaughterhouse. Xaver said: Couldn't she see they were driving up the Rohrach valley? Around Lindenberg there were all kinds of possibilities. Restaurants, he qualified. Did he think she wanted to spend her day off cooped up in restaurants?

Outdoor restaurants, he said.

Outdoor restaurants! Did he think she would drive to the Allgäu for the sake of outdoor restaurants?

Now he was forced to ask her what kind of an outing she had in mind. She replied that she'd rather hear that from him, since he had invited her.

He enumerated: go for a walk, or a short hike; panorama; the Scheidegg waterfalls; even crossing the border into Austria was one option, to be followed by a good meal. Not to worry, he knew a few places that had food Aloisia would really enjoy, he was willing to bet. And the wine, too.

She was thrilled to death, she said. My, fancy that! She was completely bowled over. She could tell he'd been married far too long. Dear old Xaver, he meant well. She was sure he wouldn't mind a bit if from now on she took charge of their outing. He could still do the paying, of course. So first of all they'd drive to Füssen. Neuschwanstein Castle. She'd always wanted to have a look at it. Keeps popping up in movies, and there she was, living close by and had never seen it. After Neuschwanstein, lunch. Then they'd live it up. In Lindenberg, Wangen, or Ravensburg—that was up to him. As long as there was something going on. No day off without some dancing, was that clear! Let's go! Step on it! Neuschwanstein!

If she wanted to spend most of the day in the car, that was fine with him. In that case the subject would have to be discussed while they were driving. On the Alpine Road that would be easy. At the moment, Aloisia was reacting only to outside attractions. Fancy, everything still in bloom here, while at home, down below, the blossom was all over! She was especially fascinated by the cows. Just look at that . . . , she kept on exclaiming. And there's even some snow left up there, just look. . . . Just look at those dear little calves! She was actually speaking High German today. That must have something to do with dress, handbag, and shoes. Just look at that chair lift against the green, it looks just about as at home in a meadow as a priest in a nudist colony. She wouldn't be caught dead on top of that mountain. Aha, that's the third BMW to pass them! Just look at that VW, it's passing them too. Doesn't Xaver want to do any better, or can't he? Not that she cares. She quite likes driving this slowly through the countryside. What she can't for the life of her stand is slow drivers in a dumb countryside or a place she's driven through before. Would he believe it, although she was born in Ailingen she'd never been in the Allgäu! Oh well, as far as Wangen, of course. But no farther. So today's a red-letter day for her. Always reach for the stars, that's her motto. He should be happy! Through her he would for once in his life see the most beautiful castle in the world. Just look at that little church spire, so adorable. . . .

Xaver said that of course he'd driven this route quite often with Dr. Gleitze. "But never yet with me!" she cried gaily, stretching again and placing one arm along the seat behind Xaver. Mrs. Gleitze was also a great admirer of Neuschwanstein, he lied at random. Maybe Aloisia had the idea of Neuschwanstein from Mrs. Gleitze? "Poppycock!" cried Aloisia. Hadn't she just told him? From movies! That handsome Ludwig the Second, she liked him! But Mrs. Gleitze also spoke with the utmost admiration of Ludwig and Neuschwanstein, insisted Xaver. Was he trying to ruin Neuschwanstein for her? In that case all he had to do was repeat for the third time that Mrs. Gleitze fancied Neuschwanstein too. But then, of course, she might get out and walk home, because on her day off she could stand anything except a Mrs. Gleitze memorial service. Only yesterday she'd again told Madam, but for the last time, that she—Aloisia—would give notice, final, irrevocable notice, if Madam ever again called her—Aloisia—Josefine. "Oh, of course, Josefine!" said Xaver with a grin. "Right, Josefine!" cried Aloisia. She regarded it as an insult to be confused with her predecessor. "Oh, come now," said Xaver. Maybe he also thought it was easy to confuse her with that woman? It so happened that she had met her, so she knew what she was talking about. But when she protested against the slur implied by this confusion, Madam would only groan that she hadn't meant any harm, it was simply that maids changed so often these days. Back home in Vienna, from the very first day to the last they had had *one* maid. Lotte. So it had been possible to concentrate on other things besides maids' names that were constantly changing. Lotte, for a lifetime. Lotte—ah yes, those had been the days. The fact that she was herself to blame for no one being able to stick it out with her—Mrs. Gleitze never mentioned that.

She was even too lazy to remember a name. Even that was too much for that lazy old bag. Just look at that dear little lake over there. Just look, the Wertach. But where is the Wertach? First it says "Wertach," then there's nothing.

In the parking lot, Xaver would have preferred to remain in the car. Whenever there was sightseeing to be done, he was always glad to be able to stay behind in the parking lot. It meant nothing to him to stand in front of some object for the sole purpose of looking at it. It always gave him the feeling of seeing nothing. Aloisia tapped the side of her head when he indicated that he'd rather stay in the car. Nothing doing, he was coming along. But she wasn't going to join the crowds crawling up the hill, she could tell him that right now. And already she was seated on the horse-drawn trolley, beckoning. Xaver followed. The driver ordered the Americans, Dutch, Japanese, French, and Germans to move over until he had twice as many passengers as there were seats. Xaver felt sorry for the horses. The road was steep. Gradually one could see each glistening vein clearly outlined on the horses' sweating bodies. The driver had to stop, twice. Once he stopped beside an old man with a white beard, dressed in Bavarian costume and sitting by the roadside, beside him a long hazel staff and a bottle of gentian schnapps. The driver asked him how business was. Bad, said the man, and croaked out a sad apology for a yodel.

For the last steep bit they had to get out and walk. Outside the castle gate a photographer was snapping away at the new arrivals. A sewage-pump truck was rattling beside the gate. The air was foul. It was hot. They had to stand in line. When they finally entered the courtyard they could see the lineup going around the courtyard and far into the building. It also became clear that the castle could be visited only by joining a guided tour. An argument ensued. Xaver had to admit, in response to Aloisia's shrill questions, that he had never been on a tour. He also had to admit that he knew precious little about King Ludwig the Second and Neuschwanstein. But he refused to stand in line just to learn something on a guided tour. Then he was nuts, she cried. During this altercation, while they stood in the lineup that curved around the stone crucible in the broiling courtyard, Xaver deliberately spoke in heavy dialect. He hoped the foreigners wouldn't understand him. He told Aloisia he would wait for her in the parking lot. She should take her time. He was never bored in parking lots. And off he went.

He walked down the hill. As he passed the old man in his Bavarian costume, the latter raised his bottle of gentian and emitted his croaky yodel. Xaver felt like slapping him. To make such a travesty of yodeling! When he saw that the old man was obliged to let himself be photographed for money, he no longer resented him.

Back in the car, he felt annoyed. He couldn't have behaved more stupidly if he'd tried. First to drive all the way here and then not even look at the most beautiful castle. Just like him. Of course. Typical Xaver, that was. Xaver to the very life, that was. How could he still stand himself? He looked at his dashboard. The dashboard pleased him. He recalled the days when he was still working in the repair shop and was allowed to sit in cars only when he'd covered the seat with a cloth. What had always attracted him most were the instruments. He could have stopped beside every parked car to look at the dashboard. He never ceased to be surprised at owning a car. And one that started without trouble, even in winter, and never had a flat tire. That was more than he would ever have expected.

Aloisia arrived with two trophies. A silver thread that she had pulled out of the back of the royal reading chair in the bedroom. It was something she'd had to do when the guide told them that everything in Neuschwanstein Castle was original and hadn't been replaced by renovation. So Ludwig had touched this thread. Just imagine that. Who wouldn't be turned on by that! And she also brought along a photo showing herself and Xaver in the front row of the new arrivals. She immediately snatched back the picture from Xaver's hand and stowed it away with the silver thread in her handbag. A man festooned with joke novelties passed in front of the car shouting in a Berlin accent: "The latest hit, the sensation from Darmstadt, illuminated ladies' garters, gentlemen's suspenders with TV, musical chamberpot, the latest hit . . . !"

Head down, he walked past the cars that were lined up in the sun, shouting down onto the hot asphalt.

Aloisia said, if only Xaver could have seen that bedroom! The roof of the canopy over the bed consists of the towers and spires of all the most famous cathedrals and minsters in Germany, each one a perfect replica carved in wood. Ah, and the washstand set! Gold-and-purple porcelain! Made by a firm in Saarbrücken whose French name she was sorry she couldn't remember, the firm still exists. It sounded as if she were soon going to order something of the kind for herself. Suddenly he recalled that only a few weeks before Agnes had dreamed about something similar. But Agnes had never been to Neuschwanstein! This wasn't the first time she had startled him in this way. She probably knew where he was at this very moment. Xaver turned the car slowly toward Wangen. Just before Wangen he turned off and stopped outside the restaurant in Staudach. It was time they had a talk.

Inside the restaurant he began by being annoyed because Aloisia found fault with everything and gave the waitress, who was doing her best, a hard time. Instead of telling Xaver she would like the pepper and salt shakers from the next table, she summoned the waitress. She sent back the soup because it wasn't hot enough for her. When Xaver mentioned in a low voice that the air at Neuschwanstein evidently hadn't agreed with her, she exclaimed loudly that this was her free day, that she demanded decent service, and if that wasn't available in this joint she'd go somewhere where it was available. Now she was

no longer speaking even High German but Viennese. She repro-
duced to the life Mrs. Gleitze's intonation. She grinned at
Xaver. She was putting on the entire act because she enjoyed
imitating Mrs. Gleitze.

Xaver stared down at the tablecloth. Among the other customers there were some who supported Aloisia, while others
laughed at her. Luckily the loin steak found favor with her. She
bade the waitress convey her compliments to the cook. Now
that she was using her stentorian voice to praise the restaurant,
Xaver was no longer quite so embarrassed by it. Actually he
would have liked to stay on here so they could drink and have a
talk, but now that they had attracted so much attention he was
eager to leave. Aloisia noticed this and announced in a loud
voice that on her day off she liked to be able to clean up her plate
in peace and quiet. . . .

By the time they drove on she was in a good mood. She'd had
two big glasses of Lagrein wine, Xaver one. The last thing he
wanted now was to go to a bar where there was dance music. He
drove toward Ravensburg. After crossing the River Argen, he
turned left. He suggested a short walk beside the Argen. She
agreed. Maybe the walk could be extended until it was too late
to go dancing. He liked the way she went on speaking in Mrs.
Gleitze's intonation. As soon as they had penetrated as far as the
bank, she wanted to take a dip. She insisted he turn around. He
did so willingly. In the water she stayed close to the bank. Was a
married man no longer allowed to take a dip, she asked? Or was
it that when one was married one didn't feel like doing anything
anymore? He undressed and let himself down into the water.
She was glad he had joined her. She couldn't swim. She'd never
had time to learn. Perhaps he could teach her? She placed herself
on his hands. Her breasts were always in the way. She kicked her
legs a little. Then very quickly she decided it was too cold. She
made her way to the shore and got dressed. Xaver had to look
away again. To warm up, they both ran back to the car.

She brought a blanket from the car, spread it out, and lay down on it, saying she wanted to enjoy a cigarette in the great outdoors. Was a married man not permitted to stretch out beside a single woman? And before he could move, she abruptly changed her tone and commanded: "Lay down now!" Then she demanded that he get up again and find some music on the car radio that was fit to listen to. He tried. She said that was impossible, got up herself, and in no time found some that so enthralled her that she had to cluck her tongue. I'm the Nick Neck man. . . . Then came a snicker that immediately reminded Xaver of Dr. Gleitze, then the words of the song said that the Nick Neck man sits behind when one's had a bit to drink and is driving. Aloisia sang along, snickered along, kicked up her legs with pleasure. Unfortunately her dip in the Argen had made her forget about Mrs. Gleitze's intonation. But she still maintained a High German distance from herself. He wondered how to bring up the subject of the Gleitzes. Now all she needed was a man, she said, and she'd be happy here. He gave no indication of having heard her. He felt the stirrings of apprehension. In his opinion Mr. Gleitze was a much nicer person than Mrs. Gleitze, he said, as if their sole topic had been the Gleitzes. "Aha, change of subject!" she said. "Why would I change the subject?" he asked. That's what she was asking him. Most likely because he wasn't a real man. Yes, she was stupid enough to have taken a liking to him. That was why he was married, of course. She'd never met a man she liked who wasn't married. If he didn't come a little closer to her right this moment, she'd freeze to death. Incidentally, to lie beside him in the great outdoors was quite enough for her. She could understand the things he wasn't saying. . . . She spoke as if she were about to burst into tears. Obviously he had to do something. Caress her. Then kiss her. Only superficially, of course. She reacted to everything ten times as violently as anyone could have expected. And in no time at all she was sitting naked astride him. And he was lying on his back also not wearing anything worth mentioning. Oh my God, he thought. Oh my God.

Against the golden-red evening sky he saw three globes of equal size, of which the middle one, above the other two, was her head. She did everything that had to be done. She also said what had to be said. That she had waited long enough for this moment. That he'd been stringing her along all this time. That she'd begun to wonder whether he really meant all his hints. But that somehow she'd felt he was a person who meant what he said. That she was no floozy either. That she needed quite a bit of persuasion before she said yes to a man, but once she'd said yes . . .

Then she fell silent and devoted herself entirely to intercourse. In the role of a rider, a rider being pursued by someone or pursuing someone. "You certainly don't take after your patron saint," said Xaver admiringly. And she had no intention of doing so, said the rider, panting and putting her hand two or three times between her legs and rubbing herself with what she scooped out and up from herself down there. She put her hand inside herself as if into a big jar and found enough to anoint her breasts and belly and thighs with a flick of her wrist. Agnes had never done that. He liked it. He wished he could convey this act of anointing to Agnes. Whenever he had seen anything of the sort away from home, all he had thought of was how he could convey it to Agnes. An almost impossible task.

While he withstood, as best he could, the exertions of his rider, he suddenly saw, quite close by, two deer slowly emerge from the forest. They walked right past Xaver and Aloisia, whom they may have taken for a single creature, and a harmless one at that. Xaver saw the two white scuts in the light of the full moon, which had meanwhile rolled in from the left as rapidly as if it had to catch up with the sun that had sunk out of sight on the right. In the white patch under the scut of the second animal, a dark spot opened to form a round hole, and at the same time the animal acquired a stilted gait; the hind legs especially seemed to stiffen. At each step the deer pressed a black pellet out of its white patch. The animal wore a look of pride and suffering as it stalked and pressed.

Now he must pay attention to his rider. He didn't want to be the one who wasn't a proper man. He did like her, after all. He really did. The way she had mimicked Mrs. Gleitze was good enough for TV. Moreover, he realized that what he was hardly able to appreciate right now was something he would want to relive with longing and nostalgia. One day, when this coupling, illuminated by the low full moon, existed only in his head, he would want to relive the moment that now meant nothing to him—remembering Marlene in the *-itz* pension in Berlin, how it was at the time and how he thinks of it now. He was aware of trying to egg himself on. Which wasn't necessary. Aloisia was first-class. She grumbled because he lay there doin' nothin'. He liked her better when she reverted to dialect: had he forgotten how to poke a fire, huh?

When after a lengthy and persistent approach she was about to take the last highest-most-blissful hurdle, she let loose a shout of pure joy, so he *also* let himself go, and the two startled deer bounded away in sudden, slow leaps clear across the moon. And were submerged in the hazy darkness. Aloisia immediately began voicing serious complaints in a jocular tone. Xaver was calculating, she said. Had taken advantage of her. He, on the other hand, after they had dressed and slowly made their way behind the headlights back to the road, found the courage to ask her the questions he wanted to ask. Somehow he had the feeling that he had earned this. She was really quite an actress, he began. Were there some more people she could imitate that well? Dr. Gleitze, for instance. No, not at all. There was nothing about him to imitate, he was just great. Well then, take his brother Georg, who also had this gift and who had seen Dr. Gleitze only a couple of times, very briefly and just by chance—

and many years ago at that—it was fantastic the way he could imitate him! So what was there about Dr. Gleitze to imitate, she'd like to know? Xaver gave as loud a laugh as he could. The way Gleitze shakes hands. The hand hasn't started to move. It hangs limply out of the sleeve. And those shirt sleeves, always a bit too long—Georg doesn't even have them, he has to pretend them. And then when Dr. Gleitze shakes the water out of his ear, that's when the handshake begins. That's to say, he holds out his limp hand to you. When his brother imitates Gleitze, one doesn't only recognize Gleitze, one actually sees through him. And what is there about Gleitze to be seen through, she'd like to know? Well, did she actually believe that she found out everything the Gleitzes thought about her—well, maybe *she* did, she was around the Gleitzes all the time, but he must say it would interest him to know: How did they talk about him? About him? She didn't quite understand. Why should they talk about Xaver? And if they did, why should he care? She must say, if there was something she couldn't care less about it was what the Gleitzes said about her.

It now seemed to Xaver that he wasn't sure himself of what he really wanted to know. He said he happened to remember a phrase she claimed to have heard the Gleitzes use: that he was not the brightest but the most loyal. Surely such phrases were of some interest. She hadn't the slightest recollection of this phrase, but of course her memory wasn't that good. Especially when it concerned such rubbish. If, on the other hand, he had said to her I-love-you, which he hadn't, she was sure she would never forget that. All the same, he said firmly, he would be interested to know whether and how the Gleitzes talked about him. She laughed. Okay, she said, so in future she would write down every sentence in which Xaver's name occurred, since Xaver-baby was obviously keen as mustard to find out what kind of a mark his teacher had given him for Conduct. Anyway, that they considered Xaver to be the most loyal—that much she knew without being able at the moment to give an example. And not the brightest, Xaver added. No, no, that wasn't the way they'd said it. Aloisia denied having either heard it or repeated it that way. It was just that Xaver wanted to have heard it that way, she saw that clearly now. At some time or other, Xaver had been mentioned in connection with a dog, she remembered that. . . .

What did she mean, a dog? What did he have to do with a dog?

That was just it, that was what she'd forgotten.

But how on earth can one forget something like that?

Good heavens, if it'd been something important—

Just a minute, now *that* he really didn't understand. That was completely illogical. If it had been utterly trivial, surely she would hardly have remembered that Xaver had been mentioned in connection with a dog. Maybe even more than once. That was why it had stuck in her mind. So she should also be capable of remembering in just what way he had been mentioned in connection with a dog. Might it have something to do with the Gleitzes' regarding him as the most loyal?

Really, she didn't know. But she did promise him to watch out, she'd write everything down, and then they'd go on another outing, and he'd be told everything, word for word, okay . . . ?

Oh well, it wasn't all that important to him. But if it amused her, he had no objection.

Just a minute! Hold everything! Why did she remember it only now? For it happened quite often—oh well, maybe not that often, but in any case it was mentioned more than once, perhaps not more than twice, in any case she remembered now, it stuck in her mind, most likely because she was so impressed that Xaver was German champion in small-bore shooting.

He drove straight to Tettnang-Oberhof and dropped Aloisia off near the villa. She would have liked to go on to some place with dancing. He said he mustn't get home too late. Oh well, she said, since he'd had his fun. . . . Then she kissed him in such a way that he began to fear everything would start all over again. He pulled away from her. He retreated into the car. She didn't budge. He had to drive off before she would move. Vaguely he had had to consent to another outing.

As soon as he was alone in the car, he stepped on the gas and extracted from the curves everything they had to offer. The words from the fairy story went round and round in his head: *This year things didn't work out, my dear Larsen.* Someone was whirling this sentence around mockingly in his head. Xaver smoked until he pulled up outside the Hungerbühler Farm. He was afraid he still smelled of Aloisia's ointment. But at home smells of quite a different nature prevailed. Late that afternoon Julia had fallen asleep on her bed, a lighted cigarette in her hand. The bedclothes had caught fire. Magdalena, who had been working in her own room, noticed an acrid smell. She ran across, woke up Julia, et cetera. They extinguished the smoldering bedclothes. One effect of the shock was that all three were able to speak to each other properly again for the first time in months. Julia was the rescued heroine. Magdalena was merely the rescuer. Agnes totally exhausted from the images that had besieged her mind when it was all over. But she was also blissful about the harmony.

All Xaver could think of while the three of them were telling him the story of the fire was that he was to blame for everything. He couldn't persuade himself that it was nonsense to feel responsible for the minor blaze. "As I opened the door, I saw the minor blaze," Magdalena had said, and Xaver had wondered where she'd picked up that phrase. But that's how it always was with Magdalena, she knew things that others in the family didn't know, and least of all did one know where she'd picked up such things. At her mention of the minor blaze he had taken her hand and held it. And Magdalena—this was the sensational part—hadn't withdrawn it immediately. If he'd arrived home at five-thirty he would have wanted, as always, to say hello to everybody, and Julia wouldn't have fallen asleep at all! He opened a bottle of white wine. But first he took a shower. Then when he sat all fresh and clean with the others in the living room, it annoyed him that he couldn't make his family listen to his complaints about the total failure of his efforts to find out how the Gleitzes spoke about him.

In the middle of a sentence Julia pointed to the moon, which had suddenly appeared above the pear trees. She said it was in great shape tonight. They all glanced at the moon, which looked as if it were too big for Wigratsweiler. The briefest glance was Xaver's. He merely made the kind of gesture one makes as if to say: I've seen it all before.

July

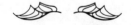

1

ONLY on the radio were Sundays still the way they used to be. On Sundays between two and four Xaver stayed close to the radio. He didn't have to sit right in front of it. As for the brass bands that are always trying to turn their ponderous stomping into a kind of soaring, he actually preferred to hear them through walls. His Sunday bands were those from Appenzell, the Walser valley, the Bregenz forests, the Allgäu, and the bands from hereabouts. Sunday was when the *Ländlers* came on and whirled around until one went crazy. As soon as he heard any yodeling, he came rushing into the living room. He didn't want to listen to yodeling through the wall, he wanted to hear it as directly as possible. Whenever he heard yodeling, he felt he'd made a mess of his life. Yodeling isn't intended to cheer a person up, that much he realized. When he heard yodeling, he became the one who was yodeling. Of course he also continued to be the one who was listening. A person who couldn't yodel. Although he was seated with his eyes open, he felt as if he were standing with his eyes closed. Standing and yodeling with his eyes closed: that was how he felt when he sat there with his eyes open, listening to the yodeling on the radio. He felt as if he were growing. Not bumping into anything. Yodeling seemed to offer a release from limitations. Longer and longer notes stretched over higher and higher arcs. Higher and higher notes were being drawn ever more slowly across wider and wider spaces. Until out of sheer lack of momentum the note came to a full stop at a point that was now no longer near to or far from anything. There was then practically nothing left. Apart from that note, of course. And the fact that it wasn't oneself who had produced that note. Xaver felt that the note stretched from Wigratsweiler across the two ridges of hills that lay between Wigratsweiler and the lake, equally far away from everywhere. And Margot, he thought, was looking out and up to the place where his voice was suspended, and she had to shield her eyes with her hand because such radiance emanated from his voice. Childish. Admittedly.

The next number: Wenzel Froidl with his Bohemian Trio. Xaver switched off the radio. Wenzel Froidl was to be heard more and more often these days. People were already saying he was going to give up being a chauffeur and devote himself entirely to singing. Xaver found Wenzel Froidl's style of singing with his Bohemian Trio affected, trivial. He sang only for an audience. He sang practically straight at one. Fancy people not noticing that! The more music existed for its own sake, the better Xaver liked it. Genuine yodeling exists for its own sake.

For the time being, Xaver's Sunday afternoon had been ruined. Suddenly there was only the heat. Why couldn't they have left the Bohemians in Bohemia? Then that fellow would now be singing in Eger. Everyone was raving about that jolly old Wenzel. Most of all Mrs. Gleitze. He felt pretty sure that she would rather have had Wenzel Froidl for a chauffeur than himself. She and Wenzel Froidl had almost the identical way of speaking. No doubt he had Mrs. Gleitze's patronage to thank for the recording of his pretentious singing. At Christmas all 497 Gleitze employees had been presented with the Froidl record. Xaver hadn't been able to bring himself to allow this record to enter his home. Because of Agnes. The girls would have rejected that kind of stuff anyway. But Agnes might have said: He's really quite musical, you know. He was afraid she would say, as she had when Elvis Presley had boomed through the house: He's got something, you know. Probably she wouldn't have said it. She was much too musical herself for Wenzel Froidl to remind her of Elvis Presley. But suppose she let herself be fooled? Suppose she reacted too hastily? And once one has expressed that kind of wrong judgment, one defends it later against one's better understanding with greater obstinacy than any correct judgment. He must prevent Agnes from reacting favorably to Froidl. After all, she wasn't familiar with his smarmy, mealy-mouthed ways. The three songs on the Froidl record that Wenzel had written himself were especially characteristic of him: "Now Wenzel Strikes Up!" "From Bohemian Hills to Lake Constance." And: "The Little Turk's First View of Säntis." Xaver assumed that originally Wenzel Froidl must have had a name that sounded less Bohemian. Then—perhaps from nostalgia—he had decided to take on his Bohemianness as a sideline, with the intention of developing it into a full-time profession. And to be a Bohemian—so he incessantly proclaimed—meant making music. Whenever he met Xaver he told him that for some years now he could have made a living out of music; he was merely carrying on as a chauffeur because the Gleitzes were such nice people. It was typical of them that a few nights ago they had allowed him—Wenzel—to drive their guests home. Probably on Mrs. Gleitze's insistence, so that, before driving them home, Wenzel had a chance to sing and play the guitar. And didn't Trummel come from somewhere around there, too? Only it wasn't that obvious from his accent. Xaver had no difficulty imagining how Wenzel held open the car door for Mrs. Meister. Wenzel could always put on a big smile and maintain that smile for as long as he wanted. Moreover, he had black, crisply curling hair. And thick, bushy sideburns. And a moustache, too, of course. A much thicker, denser, more luxuriant one than Trummel's. Xaver had often thought of going to Mr. Friedhelm Gleitze, the director, and suggesting that the latter relinquish Wenzel as a chauffeur to his brother Dr. Gleitze and take Xaver on in Wenzel's place. Wenzel would be better suited to Dr. Gleitze while he, Xaver, would be better

suited to the director. Xaver was quite sure of this, but he didn't
know how he was going to prove it. Whenever he heard Dr. and
Mrs. Gleitze discussing the director and his wife, he felt he
would be better suited to the other couple. The director resembled the American Gleitze, who was the nicest of all the
Gleitzes. The worst Gleitze was his Gleitze. If only because of
his beautiful, lazy, self-indulgent wife. The director's wife, on
the other hand, was a fat, deathly pale Franconian with a tiny
voice. When she was in the car and the others were talking and
laughing, she never joined in. She had one single wig, which
she wore at all times. Wine red and glossy. As if she were trying
to emphasize its artificiality. Xaver felt that, of all those he had
ever driven, he knew least about the director's wife. Yet he
probably heard more about her than about most of the other
people he drove. But she aroused in him the notion that the
absurd and humiliating tales about her were no more than the
sound made by the wind when something large and unyielding
stands in its way. She always held an old-fashioned handbag on
her knees. She always wore gray dresses with long balloon
sleeves. Closed right up to the neck. Apparently the director,
who was even fatter than his wife, kept a mistress in Zürich.
Wenzel had to drive him every Saturday to Zürich and pick him
up again Sunday evening. How Xaver would have loved to take
over those drives! How was it possible for the director's wife,
whose mouth looked as if it had never been opened, to stand that
smarmy fellow Froidl! There are some things that are so inexpli-
cable that the very thought of them can drive a person nuts.

The telephone shrilled. He didn't budge. Julia was already
dashing to it. But it was Mrs. Brass. First a warbled paean about
the wonderful July Sunday, and nowhere could it be more wonderful right now than in Wigratsweiler, and obviously Xaver
knew that, otherwise he wouldn't have stayed home, and she
congratulated Xaver on his wisdom, and so tomorrow he
wouldn't be going as planned to Basel but to Göttingen instead,

on Tuesday Dr. Gleitze had to attend the funeral of Professor von Lawin, it wouldn't be the first funeral in Göttingen, but it would soon be the last because soon there probably wouldn't be many former Königsberg people left there, and on Wednesday to Stuttgart, no change, and by next week he could relax, they'd be off to Glyndebourne again, wasn't it amazing how quickly a year could pass, and now she'd like to wish him, she envied him, he must believe her, she had a nice home, he had a lovely home, she has, oh well who was interested in her home, and she could tell from the nonsense she was talking that it was Sunday, so then, be ready to leave Säntis View at eight A.M., he'd be staying at Pension Sachse as usual, Dr. Gleitze, also as usual, at the Hotel Gebhard.

Xaver felt the twinge in his right side. It wasn't a stitch, it was a twinge or was it a . . . Stop it, stop it, stop it. He sat in his own fart. He was afraid someone might come before the miasma dissipated. His fear helped him to move. He walked through the kitchen. As he went outside, a pair of magpies happened to fly into the empty concrete box that had once contained the manure heap and started pecking about in Tell's food bowl for scraps. Usually this pair didn't come until the end of September. Xaver saw how the summer was plunging from its peak into autumn. Like someone dying at forty, thought Xaver. He went back through the kitchen and up the stairs. He would tell Julia to turn down her Pink Floyd music. But before he reached Julia's door, Magdalena yanked hers open and shouted: "She's smoking again, and she'll fall asleep again, and I can't work if I have to watch out all the time that she doesn't set fire to everything again!" Xaver nodded his agreement to do something about it, knocked, and opened Julia's door. She had taken all the scarves she could find and spread them out on her bed. And there she lay on the many-colored field. Naked. From the walls, the music makers whom she venerated looked down upon her. She was smoking and looking up at the ceiling. Xaver forbade her to smoke. To forbid is wearying. He walked quickly back to his radio and tuned into a Swiss station. There he was safe from unpleasant programs. A request program was on. People who had suffered some deprivation could request certain pieces. A girl who had lost her voice through a throat infection requested Sarastro's aria from *The Magic Flute*. Blind people described playing soccer using a ball with bells. One of them, blind from birth, asked for *Fair are the days of youth, fair is youth, it cometh never, it cometh never again, never ever again*. What Xaver liked best was the line: *And so I say again*.

Suddenly he heard Magdalena yell, in a needle-thin, all-penetrating voice, that she couldn't stand it anymore, all that radio racket from downstairs and Julia's record racket from next door. Xaver dashed to the radio and switched it off. Now only Julia's Pink Floyd came booming through the house.

If he didn't tell Agnes to come in she'd go on picking berries until midnight. She was apt to fall into a trance and be unable to stop picking black currants in the moonlight. In the bushes, cicadas were rasping. The moon was holding court in a golden haze. The hollyhocks were reducing their cups to trumpet shape. The heat was gradually cooling off. Xaver roused himself and brought the berry picker in from the garden. He carried the full pails into the barn and admired the gleaming blue-black harvest. And what had he done?

Mick came for Julia before supper. Agnes defended him against Magdalena's accusations. His red eyes—she knew this now from Julia—came not from hash but from his work as a repro photographer, which forced him to spend all day in the dark. How naïve could one get! Magdalena shrieked. Xaver let the two of them argue it out. If there was a Western, now was the time. There was. *The Plainsman.*

At some point the Western struck him as idiotic. Gary Cooper disgusted him. For the first time, the fact that the Indians were painted white people disgusted him. The movie-type speech of the Indians disgusted him. The fact that Gary Cooper, disguised as a buffalo, sneaked up with a herd disgusted him. Agnes came and asked in a low voice that betrayed a terrible anxiety: "What's the matter?" He said he was just too tired to go on looking at the movie. Since it was a Western, this information was unconvincing. For the last fifteen years he'd never been too tired for a Western. But what could he have said? The movie really had disgusted him. On top of that he had a general sense of loathing. He would have felt sick to his stomach at the very thought of ever looking at a movie again. Since he had many times reproached himself for looking at too many movies, he reveled in this sudden onslaught of loathing for movies. Never again a movie, he thought. Ah, that felt good! But not only good. It also scared him. What's the matter with me? It must be something pretty bad if you never want to see another movie again. So what. Never mind what it means, just never a movie, please, never, never, never again. Was something hurting him? asked Agnes. Was Julia back yet? he asked. That was enough to stop Agnes. She said she'd rather wait in the kitchen.

Xaver felt quite comfortable now that he was alone. He felt the twinge. Why not? He had a feeling he would soon be doing something. Killing a happy person, for instance. In his mind he could stare at this idea as at a distinct point: killing a happy person. Without any effort, just where a moment ago this point had been, Dr. Gleitze appeared. If someone kills someone who is happier than he is, he'll become as happy as the other one was. He felt much more comfortable than during those nights when he had tried to experience stomachache as music. To stab a happy person. He was entitled to that. He could rely on his conscience. School and church had made him steadfast. At home this steadfast conscience had undergone refinement and sharpening from his mother. If the idea came to him of killing a happy person without any protest arising within him, then he was entitled to do so. Probably even obligated. Dr. Gleitze. The

naturalness with which this name had taken the place of the
previous very general "happy person"! Surely that meant something too. He hadn't searched, fretted, contrived. Like a ripe
fruit, Gleitze's name had fallen onto that spot. Xaver saw the
knife glinting in the blackness of the glove compartment. He
pressed his eyes shut with two fingers. The glinting didn't stop.
He had wanted to be liked. There was nothing he wouldn't have
sacrificed for that goal. That had been the cause of all his tension. That was what he'd been reaching and stretching for. To
the point of rupture. The way the Stag had stretched. He had
probably also been a tense person. The Stag of Torkelweiler. Dr.
Meichle was right: Xaver must escape from his tension. It
would be enough if he were to kill Dr. Gleitze. Then no
one would be able to claim that he was trying to ingratiate
himself with the Gleitzes. A knife stab that was still coming
to Dr. Gleitze would be enough. Dr. Meichle and Professor
Amrain should be satisfied with him. Xaver felt like getting up
then and there and driving to Tettnang. He had to tell himself
to be reasonable. Such a beautiful idea mustn't be jeopardized
by irresponsible action. Stay in bed now. Sleep. Gather
strength. Tomorrow. Everything's going to be fine. That's clear
now. Look, you've taken all this time to hit on the right solution, you're not going to jeopardize everything now for the sake
of a few hours, for Chrissake. He carefully worked his way toward sleep. That was a labor of the spirit.

Once again he was awakened by the noisy departure of the
Happy Prospect's customers. Agnes was lying beside him. So
Julia was home. It struck him as outrageous that he should now
have to deal with the noise nuisance made by drunken customers
from the tavern. But he had no choice. Paragraph 30, section 1,
of the traffic bylaws. From newspapers he had collected all the
judgments he could find concerning noise nuisance. They all
mentioned how deep the ear went, how seriously mental health
was affected by the sensitivity of the ear, whose sixteen thousand

auditory cells were active even during sleep. One of these nights he would run across and shout at Margot and her husband, Sepp, that now he was going to take them to court, that they might consider themselves already sued. Antinoise bylaws! He tried to wrap himself up in these words so as to shut out the idiotic shouts being bandied about by the drunks as they said good night. Whenever he was awakened in this way on Friday, Saturday, or Sunday nights, he tried to shut out individual sounds in the overall racket. But above all he was trying not to recognize Margot's voice. But each time as he lay there his defensive tactics resulted merely in his hearing Margot's voice more clearly, sharply, and penetratingly than anything else. He heard only her. Then one mental image produced the next. Their day's work done, they go upstairs to their huge, recently enlarged bedroom, prepare themselves in their enormous bathtub, and then . . . Each time Xaver thought about that, he felt dizzy. Had he given Margot a kiss? The most insoluble problem that he had. Quite often he woke up convinced that he had given Margot a kiss. Just once, during a Carnival dance at the Happy Prospect—he'd been married less than a year—he'd succeeded in pulling Margot behind the cellar door and giving her the kiss he'd been saving up for twenty years. It was her reaction that even now made him feel dizzy when he thought about it. Everything about her had reacted. Nothing of her had remained where until that moment it had been. Everything shifted. Was it a rough sea? Whatever it was, he felt powerless against the force suddenly confronting him. It was as if Margot were being thrown against him by a raging storm, pressed against him and trying with all her might to get away from him, but with no success whatever. She was pressed against him without his embracing her or her clinging to him. Even more miraculous was the number of parts she consisted of. All making themselves felt. And how. But then he'd always known that. Suspected it. No, known. Otherwise he wouldn't have waited twenty years.

No, he hadn't been waiting at all, hadn't he only just gotten married?

It was at that very moment that Agnes had turned up. Practically at once. The kiss had begun, click, she was there. Like in a dream. And Margot had noticed her before he had. Agnes had already turned to leave. "Wait, wait! You're welcome to have him back," Margot had called out, and was gone. With a loud laugh. Agnes had turned away and run home. With him after her. Each time he let the Carnival episode run on to this point, he began to have doubts. And the more he searched his memory, the more unmistakably he realized that the kiss episode had never taken place. Over the years he had come to know in ever-growing detail just what had happened. But how, if it had never taken place, did he know that screwed onto the inside of the cellar door was a board with three projecting brass clothes hooks? And only the middle hook had a hat hanging from it, a silver-gray velour hat of the traditional type, narrow green cord plus fluffy feather! He had been the only one to stay behind at the top of the cellar stairs, and he'd had time to look at the cellar door from the inside. Nevertheless, shouldn't he admit once and for all that the kiss hadn't taken place anywhere but in his imagination? Only in a dream does frustration materialize as quickly as Agnes had appeared on the scene. He immediately felt that he was too weak to degrade this episode to the level of imagination. He had nurtured it too long for that. It must have taken place. How else would he know how soft her mouth was? And within a very short time the softness and depth of that mouth had increased fantastically. Never again had he been pulled so violently into something as deep and soft and moist. And that was supposed not to have taken place? It hadn't. It had. . . . During the day he was as good as safe from this phantom episode. Only when she said good night to her customers, when her voice resounded in the giant barrel of the night, was he no longer in control of what she awakened with her voice.

At break of day he woke up from a dream: In a narrow car someone is approaching him from above. It is almost totally dark. He can tell only from the other man's movements that he is drawing a knife. He aims the knife at Xaver, who realizes that the other man is miscalculating Xaver's left side. If he lunges in the direction in which he is aiming the knife, he will merely rip through the gray uniform jacket just above Xaver's shoulder. And that's what he does. As soon as the man has plunged his knife in above the shoulder, Xaver sinks his teeth into the man's arm. Xaver woke up from having bitten his own arm.

At breakfast Agnes said reproachfully that this morning he had again woken up so early, was there something the matter? Xaver shook his head. "Be sure and get home safely," said Agnes.

As Xaver was driving the 450 out of the garage in Markdorf, Wenzel Froidl came across the yard. As soon as he saw Xaver, he waved his respects so vigorously that Xaver not only waved back but involuntarily pulled up beside Wenzel and asked what was going on. Wenzel was surprised. Nothing, said Wenzel, except that he was glad to see Xaver. They were always just driving past each other, y'know. And it always gave him, Wenzel, a slight pang because he liked Xaver, y'know. Y'know, they should really get together someday. And now, have a good trip, what's the program, Göttingen, fair enough, he had to drive Madam home, to Nuremberg, and that was always painful for him because he'd like to drive on another two or three hours, to his own beloved native land, y'know, to the plum dumplings, to beer soup and potato pancakes, y'know.

All this while Xaver could do no more than nod. He was already starting up when he forced himself to utter a few words. Yesterday on the radio, fabulous! With a sweeping gesture Wenzel bowed. Xaver stepped on the gas. So now he's supposed to feel embarrassed at all the things he'd been thinking yesterday about this fellow. Wenzel knew instinctively that Xaver disliked him. But it was a matter of principle with Wenzel to win everybody over. The more a person disliked him, the greater the charm he displayed toward that person. In that way he won them all over. Or he accosted everyone today because he expected them all to have heard him yesterday on the radio and now exacted a compliment from each one. Xaver was glad he'd just managed to produce his remark about Wenzel's radio performance. Had he neglected to make it, Wenzel would now regard him as an implacable enemy whom he had to attack. But since Xaver had come up with the expected compliment, Wenzel would regard him as a fan and thus would take no action against him and, if Xaver's name was mentioned in his presence, would have nothing negative to say. This was the kind of calculation that thrust itself upon him after every encounter with other people. Had he harmed or benefited himself? Of course he had let Wenzel talk for a very very long time before coming up with the expected compliment. If Wenzel was to survey his haul this evening, he would find that no one had delayed the compliment as long as Xaver Zürn had, and that in no case had it proved to be so meager. So he was bound to realize without a shadow of a doubt: the true enemy was Zürn. And now the preparations for an inexorable blow must already be getting under way in Wenzel's mind.

Always, but always, Xaver made this same mistake. How pleased he would be feeling now, seated behind the wheel, if he had denied Wenzel the expected compliment! Confrontation. Let's just see who or whom . . . What a good feeling it could also be if he'd interrupted Wenzel after his first few words with an unparalleled onslaught of congratulations. Get out of the car. Embrace Wenzel, work himself up until the tears came to his eyes! Wenzel was from Bohemia. One couldn't lay it on too thick with Wenzel. But the worst possible thing was what he had actually done. He had congratulated him, had expressed homage, but in a way that was not only not beneficial but actually highly damaging to himself. Why, why did he never learn? Soon, he felt, his family would end up in misery and he alone would be to blame.

Aloisia came hurrying up with Dr. Gleitze's luggage and refused to let Xaver relieve her of briefcase, coat, or suitcase; she acted as if only she knew what to put where in the car. Nor was he allowed to call for Dr. Gleitze at the studio today. Aloisia came back with Dr. Gleitze from the studio as if he were her property. She had crossed her arms and was holding her chin quite unnaturally high in the air. Mrs. Gleitze remained invisible. Since she was known to stay in bed every day until ten or ten-thirty, this didn't mean anything. At the last moment, when Dr. Gleitze and Xaver were already sitting in the car, Aloisia jumped in front of the hood so they couldn't drive off, then flattened the tip of her nose with her forefinger, finally shook her head and said through the open window: "I just felt I mustn't let you drive off before giving you a message, but now I can't remember what it was." "From my wife, perhaps?" Dr. Gleitze asked. "No, no," Aloisia replied without hesitation, "it was something else." She shook her head, Xaver started up, she jumped to one side. Xaver could see her waving. Apparently Dr. Gleitze could too: he waved back. But only like someone imitating waving. "What a good soul," he said. Xaver had broken out into a cold sweat at Aloisia's strange behavior. Maybe she'd wanted to say something to himself rather than to Dr. Gleitze? That she was pregnant or something?

Today Xaver avoided meeting Dr. Gleitze's eyes. He had been thinking too much about the boss since last seeing him on Friday. But what he'd been thinking about Dr. Gleitze last night—killing a happy person—now seemed idiotic and alien to him. It wasn't he who had thought that. It was a nocturnal spirit. A joke. Yes, a joke. That's all it was.

Xaver felt as if today the car were sticking with all four wheels to the tarmac. Never before had any drive seemed so labored to him. He required all his willpower if the whole shining vehicle was not to grind to a halt. Every kilometer an effort. And the fellow back there believes in horsepower. If he believes in anything at all.

When they were already past Stuttgart, the boss suddenly asked what was the matter with Xaver today, why wasn't he driving into Stuttgart to pick up the Rogalls? Xaver hadn't known he was supposed to. He didn't see why he should take the blame for Mrs. Brass's mistake. He repeated word for word what Mrs. Brass had told him the previous afternoon about changes in plans for the week. And he used Mrs. Brass's words so pointedly that the blame for this mistake could be only hers. "She's a treasure," said Dr. Gleitze, "but she just can't cope anymore." As soon as Xaver had finished with his defense—by now they were driving into Stuttgart—he realized he had just missed an ideal opportunity to tell the boss about his brother Johann, for he could have said that, while he might possibly forget some instructions, he would never forget any that had to do with Professor and Mrs. Rogall. "How come?" the boss would have asked. "Well, sir, how does Professor Rogall address his wife when he raises his voice to repeat something that, in his opinion, his rather deaf wife hadn't understood?" "How? 'Johanna Henriette, let me tell you . . . ,'" the boss would have answered with a chuckle. "Right," Xaver would have said, and for that reason Xaver's favorite people from Dr. Gleitze's entire circle of friends were Mr. and Mrs. Rogall. He still didn't get it, the boss would have said. "Well, sir," Xaver would have said, "the thing is, sir, that I had a brother called Johann who defended Königsberg, and he had a girlfriend, from East Prussia, sir, called, and I'll give you three guesses, yes, correct, she was called Henriette, and if the two of them, my brother Johann and his girl Henriette, hadn't been killed in the defense of Königsberg, sir, I'll guarantee their first daughter would have been called Henriette Johanna." That's what Xaver would have said. He was really looking forward to seeing old Mr. and Mrs. Rogall again and hearing that Dear-Johanna-Henriette-let-me-tell-you. . . .

The old couple, who looked as if they might have been blown away by a puff of wind, were toddling back and forth on Wernhalden-Strasse outside their garden gate, which they had long since locked. They had simply refused to believe that Dr. Gleitze, their best friend's son, would forget them. Old and forgettable though they were, they had found it impossible to believe that . . . but now everything was twice as perfect. Now the air in the car both in front and behind was filled with Königsberg. As always on a drive to Göttingen. Normally the trip to Göttingen was made only once a year, from April 21 to 23. For the birthday of the Königsberg philosopher. Xaver had read up about him in Agnes's encyclopedia. Whenever he drove Gleitze's compatriots in Göttingen from their hotels or to the Small Auditorium or to Stern-Strasse, whenever there were other people in the car going to or coming from Göttingen, Kant was always the topic. Xaver gradually learned that Kant must have taught that it was best to be good. It was really amazing how often they talked about a man who had been born more than two hundred years ago. Every year in April they elected a "bean king." That must have something to do with the philosopher's eating habits. There was nothing about that in the encyclopedia. Moreover, they calculated exactly what percentage of Kant's blood was German, how much was Lithuanian, and how much the rest was. Xaver had felt quite hot with pride on hearing that it was only because Kant's paternal great-grandmother had come from the Lake Constance area that there could be no doubt whatever that Kant had had more than 50 percent German blood. In fact, the ancestress of the great Protestant had been called Anna Maria. The rest of his family apparently came from up north and for that reason had to share in the philosopher's blood with all those other types up there. So one thing was indisputable, that 50 percent was from hereabouts. Bravo. And, what was more, from Hödingen. Whenever the boss had Königsberg visitors, a drive to the ancestral home of the Nothhelfer family was taken for granted, to the Cross in Hödingen, the inn that, while no longer belonging to the Nothhelfers, did belong to some refugees from Königsberg.

Whenever Xaver heard a broad Königsberg accent, he saw in his mind's eye a kind of woodland. He saw slender brownish tree trunks, almost red. Because he always saw something when he heard something. Standing close together, many rosy tree trunks. He saw sand-colored leaves. And amber-colored blossoms. And in the midst he saw Henriette. Heard her. Heard her more clearly than he saw her. And the dandelion-light old Königsberg couple—he saw them toddling among the tree trunks of their language, endlessly repeating to each other the latest news about Königsberg.

Who had last been to Junker-Strasse? Ah yes, Junker-Strasse! The luxury storefronts that had collapsed onto the street from both sides have left only a narrow footpath down the middle. On Junker-Strasse? Yes!! As late as February 1947 it was still firmly in the hands of robber bands. Russian deserters, remnants of German soldiers, children running wild. A kilo of potatoes, nineteen rubles, you must have heard that. The great forest of the Elch marshes, destroyed, oh yes. Not a tree left intact in Methgeth Forest. It's the truth. Not a tree. Finally trying to get to the station across Honig Bridge or Green Bridge. I'm telling you! They could still get to the cattle market over High Bridge. The Schindekopp Bridge, gone. That great Ponarth Bridge, gone. Ponarth, that sounded familiar, that's where Johann's girl Henriette had fled with Traugott. The two voices that sounded like damaged stringed instruments recited antiphonally what Dr. Kuckuck, Traugott Bierle, and Comrade Number 3 had recited not nearly as well: Woman. Urr. *Davei. Bistra.* Kenigsbyerg. Great heavens, how much better things had been in

1914, now what was the name again of that colleague of yours who made a note of all the atrocities committed by the invading czarist armies in East Prussia? What, you don't know about that? He counted every slaughtered chicken. Every damaged fruit tree. Every slap in the face. *One* rape. The guilty Cossacks were shot on the spot. *One* case of manslaughter. And in 1945 what good was the Rokosovsky order that threatened looting and rape with death? That was the harvest of Ilya Ehrenburg's seed. You know, of course, that at first Strasse-der-SA was known for a while as Königs-Strasse? But Erich Koch Square is still Erich Koch Square ha-ha-ha. But General Litzmann-Strasse is Sovetsky Prospect. You know, don't you, that the Hinterross Garden is now called Minskaya Ulitsa? But the extension of the Kantgraben is still standing. Without the bronze gates, of course. By the way, in Danzig someone turned up a tailor by the name of Johann Kandt, without doubt a Scotsman, died before 1681. By the way, one must admit that it was wrong to change the name of the village of Judtschen in 1937 to Kanthausen, simply because Kant was a tutor there before he became a professor. Tell me, in Moditten, does the tiny little cottage still exist that belonged to the forester's cottage where Kant's friend Wobsär lived? Wobsär, yes, who let Kant live there in the summer of 1763 so that Kant could write down his observations on the feeling for the beautiful and the sublime? In *that* tiny damp hole? Yes, right there. It was only in such a place that sentences like the following could be born, said Professor Rogall and proceeded to chant in a cracked voice: "Temperaments possessing a feeling for the sublime are gradually drawn by the calm silence of a summer evening, when the trembling light of the stars breaks through the brown shadows of the night and the solitary moon is above the horizon, into lofty sentiments of friendship, of disdain for the world, of eternity."

This time a main topic of discussion was the boss's birthday present, the mahogany grand piano of Hermann Gustav Goetz, who was prevented by tuberculosis from making use in Winterthur of the instrument he had brought with him from his Königsberg home. Whatever the boss heard from Königsberg people, he passed on to other Königsberg people. Perhaps everyone from Königsberg did that. Quite often the boss pretended that he had always known something which, as Xaver well knew, he had heard only the day before or even during the past hour. What he was now being told by Professor Rogall about a certain Ehregott Andreas Christoph Wasianski—a man who had managed Kant's household, written his biography, and supervised the construction of the first piano in Königsberg—he would be telling every group of Königsberg people to whom he gave rides during the next thirty hours from the Hotel Gebhard, the Hotel Central, or the Hotel Sonne to the cemetery or one of the castellated villas in the richly treed eastern suburb of Göttingen.

But each former denizen of Königsberg was himself an expert, which meant that the boss invariably learned more than he related himself. Just as by mentioning that birthday piano he had learned much more about the instrument builders of Königsberg. In Göttingen he asked everyone to whom he gave a ride whether in 1945 the piano built by Wasianski and Garbrecht had still been in the palace museum. No one could tell him. Everyone told him something else instead. The Kant monument by Rauch had disappeared, only the pedestal remained and was now in Maraunenhof. And where had that inscription *Juste et sincere* been? Do you remember that? And what was the inscription on the former courthouse near the north station, do you remember that? No, no, I'm sorry I don't. And yet one walked right by it on going to pick up one's permit in order at last to get out of the city as medical officer in charge of a transport. When they'd had their first meeting in Göttingen, remember? That was before Stern-Strasse. That had been in a white-tiled former soldiers' lavatory. Enlisted men's lavatory, I ask you! Hadn't it been in Mr. Hoffmann's living room? In any case, Nicolai Hartmann had been there. Really? Yes. And Stavenhagen and Kammlah. Now who was it again who gave that lecture about Kant's teacher Schultz? On the moral meaning of the world, you mean that one? That was when that American was there for the first time, what was his name again? At any rate, it was during the session at which the return of the German eastern territories was declared the primary and principal aim of all future German policy, remember . . . ? That was the wording of the federal government. We still believed that a moral-humanitarian attitude would suffice, all that was necessary was to proclaim it, *urbi et orbi*. Then when it began to be called the Oder/Neisse problem, it was already much too late. It was just that we weren't aware of that at the time. By the way, you know what's now standing on the pedestal that used to support the bust of Kant? A bust of Thälmann, believe it or not. By the way . . .

It was the biggest jigsaw puzzle imaginable. Pieces that showed where they belonged, next to quite haphazard pieces, but the people from Königsberg knew they were part of the puzzle. The sequence simply didn't matter. They were in a hurry. The largest number of pieces had to be put on the table in the shortest possible time, before it was too late. By the way, someday we'll have to admit to ourselves: our only hope is China. The fact that Chou En-lai had died was of course another great blow for the people of Königsberg. Chou En-lai had consistently refused to call Königsberg Kaliningrad. That's the truth. And with good reason. His son had been killed in the defense of Königsberg. Xaver thought: So had Johann Zürn. In response to a general expression of amazement, the knowing one explained that Chou had studied at Göttingen and got a local girl, also a student, in the family way, and had kept abreast of everything that happened to his son, who was born in 1927.

It made Xaver feel good to listen to the Königsberg voices.

These people had their problems too. And he would have felt even better if he could have remarked at some point that his brother had been killed at the side of Chou's son. He was sweating with excitement. Should he cause an accident as he drove off from the Hotel Gebhard onto Berliner-Strasse and then explain to the police that he had been distracted by the conversation about Königsberg because, you see, his brother . . . Then it would have been out. Once and for all. On the other hand, he told himself at times, it was quite a good thing to keep this piece of information up his sleeve. Should the boss ever find out that Xaver was not German small-bore champion at all, that even his brother Jakob had only almost become German champion, then Xaver could say: You're right, that's quite true, and I've been wanting to tell you this for ages, only you never let me get a word in. I didn't even have a chance to tell you that my other brother, Johann Zürn, was killed at the age of twenty by a shell on Schubert-Strasse, a few hours after the capitulation of Königsberg, sir! I think we're quits! If not, I'll take a swing at you. You see, for quite a while now I've been unable to control myself all that well. I have the feeling that it's my turn now to land a punch. Or else . . . or else . . .

On the trip back to Stuttgart there was less conversation than on the drive to Göttingen. The Rogalls were exhausted. Having to attend a funeral, at that age.

Xaver wished to drive his favorite passengers to Wernhalden-Strasse without their feeling anything of the drive. He could foresee that another drive to Stuttgart was in the offing. Double funeral. In one coffin. If people had any sense of piety left, they would place this couple in *one* coffin. Dr. Gleitze had told them that today he was going to indulge in his vice in Stuttgart. "Mozart," Professor Rogall enlightened Johanna Henriette. She violently rejected this tutelage. As if she didn't know that herself! Finally they asked Dr. Gleitze, please, in spite of Mozart, not to forget to convey the very warmest regards of Johanna Henriette and Albert Rogall to his father. Dandelion fluff, thought Xaver. A pallid young man with dark hair hanging down to his shoulders stopped to watch the Rogalls disappear into their house, then continued to drag himself uphill by holding on to the fence.

Xaver drove to the Schlossgarten Hotel, where the boss always changed his clothes. Xaver was told he would have more time than usual that night since the boss would be meeting some of the artists after the performance. Departure twelve-thirty A.M. If Xaver would like to take a room so he could lie down until then, the boss would have no objection. Xaver said he would think about that. It was midafternoon. He didn't feel like lying down. As he left the hotel he was joined by a fellow chauffeur who had also just dropped off his boss. How long d'you have? Four hours. And you? Midnight. That's tough. Xaver was glad to be able to take a walk through the park with his colleague from Osnabrück, who today had driven only from Karlsruhe. But yesterday from Aix-en-Provence all the way to Karlsruhe. For Xaver that was nothing new. He had driven at least seven times from Aix to Tettnang. Straight through. And next week to Glyndebourne, he added hastily. Glyndebourne didn't interest the man from Osnabrück, but Aix did. In fact, the whole Midi. Montpellier? Of course, said Xaver. Had he ever had a cup of coffee on rue Foch? Xaver, a little too quickly: *Un grand café crème.*

His colleague steers him to a table at a park café, orders a beer, and Xaver, who actually would rather have had mineral water, also orders a beer. Gerd—as his colleague is called—spreads out a map on the table and points to the cities he has circled with a thick felt pen as if they were a lot of fortresses to be conquered. What Xaver found less attractive was that Gerd immediately took off his jacket and hung it over the back of his chair, although he was wearing a shirt with short sleeves. Not that he expected everyone to appear with such choice cufflinks as his own. But men with white, hairless arms, even if with only a scattering of moles, shouldn't wear short sleeves. The fellow from Osnabrück had white, thin, hairless arms. Covered with moles. He told Xaver that the route he drove from Osnabrück to Marseilles and back had been worked out by his son rather than himself. In fact, he had his son work out all the routes he drove. "That way he's sure to get an A in geography," said Xaver, for the sake of saying something. "Listen, amigo, I'd have a thing or two to say to that boy if he came home with an A in geography only—he gets A's in everything, you name it." He was raising this boy, he said, deliberately as a co-pilot. There were quite a few cases of chauffeurs calling themselves pilots. Xaver didn't approve of that. He indicated as much, remarking that it sounded as though it weren't enough to drive a car if some people found it necessary to pretend they were airplane pilots. No, no, the colleague from Osnabrück had neither said that nor meant that. He simply felt that whoever was sitting up front was the pilot, that was all. But if Xaver preferred to be a chauffeur, he was welcome. The colleague from Osnabrück laughed, raised his glass to Xaver; Xaver admitted to himself that he was pettier than Gerd. Hadn't he just been highly critical of him? And his fellow chauffeur had listened with a laugh and not taken offense. Xaver was prepared to admire his easygoing colleague.

After folding up the map with a circuslike flourish and stowing it away in a black leather pouch he carried slung over his shoulder, he pulled out of this pouch a flat, transparent plastic box containing some squares of heavy white paper; these squares were perforated in the middle with a hole about two centimeters across, and could be removed, his colleague explained. That was his serviette. Right now he had to find a john. He would stick the serviette onto the skin around his artificial anus and do his business through the opening. Never heard of an artificial outlet, had he? He held the container out to Xaver. It was marked "Coloplast." Xaver thought of Tübingen. "My friend," his colleague said in the loud voice he used for everything, "you wouldn't believe how I'm looking forward to a decent German john. I needn't tell you, eat in France, go to the john in England, the other way around would be a tragedy. Now show Dad where to go," he said to the waitress and disappeared. Xaver finished his beer, paid for both beers, and told his Osnabrück colleague when he eventually returned that he had to leave; unfortunately he'd promised to look in on some relatives. "I'm not holding anyone back," said his colleague. Xaver wanted to say: Your beer's paid for. But he couldn't get it out.

He walked off toward the station. The main thing was to get away from that fellow from Osnabrück. He quite liked him, but he shouldn't have been so graphic about his bowel situation. At the railway station he ordered another beer. He needed another beer. Because of that "artificial outlet." He listened to two foreigners—one seemed to be a Turk and the other a Greek—arguing in recalcitrant German about whether a relative who had died here should be transported home or buried here. They yelled at each other. Suddenly the Greek ran away. The Turk ran after him, swung him around by the shoulder. Just as the first blow was about to fall, a policeman's arm separated them.

Xaver went off in the direction of the Old Town, where he walked slowly past the women who had taken up their stations for the evening's business, and listened to what they called out to him. Their language here in Stuttgart wasn't nearly as way out as in Marseilles. He studied the photos in the display cases as thoroughly as he always did. Finally he looked for a respectable tavern outside the quarter and ordered a grilled Swabian rump steak with dumplings. With it he drank some mineral water. Then he wandered back into the lanes again. By the time he had walked everywhere three times, the night life was in full swing. Xaver was afraid the women might take offense at his snooping, so he walked out of the Old Town again and sat down in a respectable tavern. To his own surprise he ordered a beer again.

After that another. And another. But because he thought each beer was his last, he paid for each right away. He was seated. A few customers were standing at a high table. At some point, two of them started an argument. One of them, about thirty, had no jacket on but was wearing a shirt whose long sleeves he had folded back two or three times, revealing powerful, hairy forearms. The other man was wearing a jacket and tie. Xaver noticed that the poses and gestures of the two men were becoming more menacing. Because of the noise from a crime movie on TV, he couldn't make out what their argument was about. The one with the jacket might have been as old as Xaver. The younger man without a jacket finally tossed a glass of beer into the face of the man with the jacket. To anyone watching, this came as no surprise. The one with the jacket took the glass from the hand of the younger, stronger-looking man—that he allowed it to be taken out of his hand was very surprising—and tried to slam it down onto the head of the jacketless, younger, incomparably stronger man. But quick as a flash the latter intercepts the raised hand of the forty-year-old; the glass flies through the air and smashes to pieces across the floor. The high table falls over. The two men with it. Evidently more force has been involved than was apparent. But now pretty well all the customers rush up to the two combatants. They are separated. Everyone talks at once. The one in the suit loudest of all. He demands the MP immediately. He shouts that over and over again. Not the police, the MP! Xaver now being close beside the younger, jacketless one and holding on to one of his wrists—for which he needed both hands and the acquiescence of the man he was holding on to—he began to berate him. Everyone was berating the two men. "You don't have to throw a glass of beer into a man's face, right off," said Xaver. The younger man said the other fellow had laughed at him. "You're nuts," said Xaver. "What've we come to if we're going to throw beer in a man's face for something like that? So I say you're nuts." Thereupon the man in shirt sleeves roared much louder than was warranted by the pitch of Xaver's voice: "Listen, we're not in East Germany." And with these words he shook off Xaver's hands. On all sides voices were immediately raised: "Right, right, don't let 'im get away with it!" Xaver has to watch out now, or he'll become one of the warring parties. "You're nuts, all of you," he said under his breath so that hardly anyone except himself could hear it. And, as if he'd had enough, he walked straight back to his table.

The innkeeper's wife had wiped up the broken glass with a large wet rag, the high table was upright again, the two men had been released by their custodians. Before anyone can intercede, the man in the jacket walks up to the jacketless younger man and punches him in the eye. The younger man doubles up, holding his eye. Blood oozes through his fingers. Everyone comes to his aid. Xaver is alarmed. He remains seated. Back comes the woman with a pile of large serviettes. With fantastically inflated movements the man in the jacket walks up to Xaver. Xaver tells him off, saying that he had originally taken his side because the other fellow had thrown beer in his face. But now *he* was first to use his fist. Xaver had seen it all, plain as plain. The other man had been standing there completely off his guard. The assailant was pale and sweating, but he grinned and nodded at every word of Xaver's, extending the hand he had punched with. Xaver said: "Anyone who wears a great clunky ring like that doesn't punch a person in the nose anyway." "That's an ornamental ring," the man said fondly, holding the ring right up to Xaver's eyes. "I'd be ashamed if I were you," Xaver said. "Would you now?" said the man, swinging back his arm, but Xaver ducked out of the way. Before the man could take another swing, Xaver had simply pushed him over. Just like Mr. Bippus at Radio Franz's. The man struck the floor with the back of his head. Xaver walked past him and out. He could still hear someone shouting that no one was to leave the place, the police would be there right away, his friend here had lost an eye. Xaver ran, and stopped running only after he had turned a few corners. It was eleven-thirty. He didn't have time to act as a witness. Dr. Gleitze would hardly have appreciated Xaver's becoming involved in a brawl while on duty. Besides, he had had three or three and a half glasses of beer. Although that had no bearing whatever on the matter, it was true that he'd been in a tavern, and things had happened that wouldn't have happened if he'd gone to a café and had an ice cream. The idea of the boss standing outside the Schlossgarten Hotel and Xaver failing to show up because he had to describe the details of the brawl to a police officer typing with two fingers involuntarily distorted Xaver's face in a grimace of pain.

It was one-fifteen A.M. when the boss emerged with a largish group. After they had all been distributed among two taxis and Xaver's car, they drove off toward the Killesberg. Dr. Gleitze was drunk. He introduced Xaver to the two ladies and the gentleman riding with him. One of the ladies shrieked "Xaver!"— how clever of Dieter to have a chauffeur called Xaver! Since the others were baffled by her excitement, she shrieked that Xaver was the patron saint of travelers and it was no use Dr. Gleitze telling her he hadn't known that when he'd employed a Xaver as his chauffeur. Dr. Gleitze was able to point out that he was a Protestant. He couldn't care less what kind of a patron saint he'd engaged, the important thing was that Xaver was, had been, German champion, yes indeed. But in what? Formula Two or what? No, in small-bore shooting. Oh, small-bore shooting, isn't that darling. But she finds it even more darling that Xaver is called Xaver. Then the singer—Xaver took it for granted that the members of this trio were all artists—shrieked that even as a Protestant Dr. Gleitze couldn't avoid being blessed. And that anyway a person who had to live with the name Dieter would be well advised to assure himself of the support of a Xaver.

They stopped on the Feuerbach side of the Killesberg. Xaver should by all means take another forty winks, said the boss.

Whenever Xaver slept in the car he was afraid his lower jaw would drop, that he would snore and rattle, that the boss would come and, instead of waking him right away, first watch him at length. So he tried to sit in such a way that his lower jaw could not drop. The junk coming out of the radio seemed to him an insult. Fancy having to talk to people that way! Should he even try to fall asleep? He recalled his thoughts of the previous night. It's a mistake to think such things every night. You're licked if you keep thinking of such a thing and never do it. Anyway those had been nothing but idiotic night thoughts. The important thing is that a problem should find its own solution. In any case, those are the nobs whom you never see sweating, or waiting, or trembling, or foaming at the mouth. In their lives, things take care of themselves. They lie on chaise longues, sit on high-backed chairs, raise cups of tea to their lips, enjoy the pearly raindrops, the palm trees' rustle, their affairs progress, it's all taken care of. At the only appropriate moment, one of them gets up, goes to the phone, says something, jots down something. No sooner has he done that than he sees the young woman in the doorway. She is carrying a cocktail in either hand. Gleaming teeth, lustrous eyes, silk. She congratulates him on having done it again. At his merest touch she moans sweetly and says urgently: Don't, don't, dooon't. In the evening some friends, whose day has passed equally successfully. One of them says: Today everything went right for me. They laugh uninhibitedly. Touch each other playfully. Alcohol. Then they separate, retire for sexual intercourse, which occurs in unconventional surroundings. At last they all fall asleep and breathe with complete regularity through their unimpeded nostrils. There are no sounds. Only certified dreams are permitted to enter. When the time comes, they kill themselves. But perhaps they can have even that done

for them. Whereas he must do everything himself. Otherwise
nothing would progress. And everything he didn't do turned
out to his disadvantage. He could no longer take himself quite
seriously. Once the imagination plays a bigger role than reality,
you're done for. A few days ago his check to the German Automobile Club had been returned with the comment: *Your remit-
tance cannot be completed because the account in question is carried under
the following designation*: And this was followed by exactly what
he had written and by what appeared on the rejected check. He
was shocked. It's not so bad when a person gets dizzy looking
down from the platform of a high tower as long as one can hold
on to a firm railing. But when, as one looks down, the railing
suddenly comes away in one's hand, then . . .

It was shortly after three A.M. when the boss reappeared,
bringing another gentleman with him. The two men were accompanied by the lady of the house. She was exactly the kind of
woman whom Xaver had just been imagining. She accepted ca-
resses from the two men. "Well, it's a bit later than I expected,"
said the boss. "But tomorrow, or rather today, there's nothing
on." Xaver said that Mrs. Gleitze wanted to leave at ten o'clock
for Teuffen to see her doctor. "You mean her quack!" Dr.
Gleitze said with a snicker. And the gentleman he had brought
along and whom they were taking to Tübingen snickered too.
That meant a slight detour. Xaver didn't mind. The boss and
his companion snickered more than they spoke. After they had
dropped off their passenger in Tübingen, the boss said that next
week Xaver would be able to stretch out on the green lawns of
Glyndebourne. Then the car raced silently through the moonlit
countryside. Past the camel profile of the Alb range.

What made Xaver suddenly think of the Stag? Because they
had just passed through Tübingen and the last time he had
thought of the Stag was while his bowel was being inflated? But
now he was seeing the Stag rushing over from the lathe, holding
the thumb of his right hand between thumb and forefinger of

his left and showing it to everyone, the thumb with a long piece of tendon hanging from it. That looked so funny that a few of them burst out laughing. But the funny part was that the Stag still hadn't realized that the bloody thumb with the piece of tendon was his own. He'd found this in the lathe, he said, with an expression of dismayed surprise. Until someone yanked him off to the first-aid station. All the things one remembers, at night.

In Schömberg Xaver turned left for the shortcut via Wellendingen. A better road takes priority over a shorter one! To hell with that. He was dozing anyway back there. Until the Day of Judgment. Xaver grimaced. Suddenly he heard his boss's voice saying would he please stop as soon as convenient, he had to go behind a tree. Go behind a tree, he said. Xaver could have stopped right there at his triangular pond. But the pond seemed too good for that. He didn't stop until after Wellendingen, when the forest reached almost all the way down to the highway. The boss walked unsteadily to the edge of the forest and let his water splatter randomly on the leaves of the bushes. Xaver saw him standing there in the light of the waning moon. Xaver's fantasies began to race. But in perfect sequence. It was as if suddenly everything had become possible and, because it had been prepared so far ahead, could now run its course, without haste but swiftly and surely. There was no longer a problem. At last everything will automatically run its course. Take the knife out of the glove compartment, leave the leather sheath in the compartment, walk toward the boss's back as it catches the full moonlight, swing back your arm, knife and cufflinks flash together in the moonlight. Then stab two or three times below the left shoulder blade. That's the only real effort: your right hand would—quite mechanically—rather stab below the right shoulder blade. So, over to the left. No chance of missing. First place the knife point against his back, then immediately plunge it in all the way. The boss topples forward, inevitably, so follow up, follow up, follow up. Stab again. And each time say to yourself: There had to be an end. It couldn't go on forever. I've lived long enough. It's always too soon. So what. Okay, so I'm crazy, otherwise I wouldn't do it. You have to cling to this. So that, whatever happens, this feeling of being crazy will never leave you. A feeling like a skin-tight hood. No matter how quickly you move your head, it stays tight. In fact, it's become your head. Okay. Go on stabbing. Into that dead Gleitze. It makes wet, almost sighing sounds. That was to be expected, that was to be expected, that was to be expected. Faster. Operaopera. It's lucky you're wearing your driving gloves, for now you have to do something that gives you some distance from this and that. The best thing is, first cut off one of Dr. Gleitze's ears and, after you've turned him over, place it on his mouth. As if he were listening very intimately to himself. And now his genitals. That's right, cut them off too. To give yourself some distance. Luckily you have your lunchbox with you. Empty. You'll put them in there, but then clear out. Wait a moment. You still have to have a crap. Right beside the dead man. Perhaps his nose is still alive. If so it could report to the boss: What a stink. Just so the boss still has a chance to experience that. Then clear out. A good wheel sings. You can yodel. At last. For the first time you can yodel, for Chrissake. Too bad that as a driver you mustn't close your eyes. But you yodel until the spiraling column of sound finally comes to a stop in the midst of the dazzling nocturnal light above the valleys at the edge of the Black Forest. For God's sake, no accident now. Never was there a more precious cargo. And don't ring the bell. If Aloisia were to come to the door, everything would be ruined again. Climb up over the terrace. Onto the balcony. Don't try to go inside. The alarm system. Just knock. On Mrs. Gleitze's window. Keep knocking. Even if it takes an hour. She mustn't feel the slightest bit scared. She must think it's her friend, Dr. Meichle. You see, now she's coming. Appears in the doorway. Excuse me, Madam, Xaver has something to hand you. The rosy light of dawn is favorable. Look, here in the lunch box, does this look familiar? Think this question more than say it. Step aside a bit so she doesn't have to look at the genitals in your shadow. Go on standing there until they come to take you away. You'll remain silent. From now on you'll remain silent. The police officer will state that no sound had come from you: but if the movement of your lips had produced a word the moment the cell door closed behind you, that word would most likely have been "Thanks." Then off to Weissenau. The institution swallows you up. Under the trees you are a king. For the visiting Agnes you write on a slip of paper: The coat is still too small. Every year in the fall you write a note like that. So as not to sacrifice distance. Every year she brings you an even bigger coat. You sew all the coats together. The huge train of coats drags along the floor. Keep your distance, people. The mighty trees are already saying: At last a king again. Shouldn't you place your left hand on Dr. Gleitze's left shoulder, gripping his left shoulder so that the knife meets resistance as it stabs?

Xaver was quite calm. The knife lay in his hand. It passed through his mind that the boss was taking a terribly long time over his peeing. He felt he had known this in advance, too. At this moment it was impossible for him to make a mistake. Just as Xaver was about to leave the car, Dr. Gleitze let out a fart as he urinated. Xaver gave a start and instinctively turned aside. If the boss happened to look his way he must think that Xaver couldn't have heard the disgusting sound. Dr. Gleitze was already on his way back to the car. Xaver threw the knife into the glove compartment. Was there a searching look on Dr. Gleitze's face as he turned it away while addressing Xaver? "Were you thinking of whittling a flute?" asked the boss. "No, no," said Xaver. They drove on. Dr. Gleitze hummed some cheerful Mozart arias that Xaver also knew. Never before had the boss hummed arias that loudly. He was almost singing. *The*

Magic Flute, thought Xaver. Probably *The Magic Flute* had been on in Stuttgart. In Tettnang-Oberhof, Dr. Gleitze got out with a yawn and instead of saying good night said "'night." As Dr. Gleitze walked away Xaver wished he could walk away from himself too.

When he was lying beside Agnes without moving, her hand came across. Xaver stiffened. But he just managed to say: *"This year things didn't work out, my dear Larsen,"* whereupon Agnes drew back her hand. She soon fell asleep. He lay awake, unable to prevent his mind from trying to recapture, over and over again, the splattering sound made by Gleitze's peeing on the leaves. He tried hard to push himself away from the edge of the forest, from the Black Forest, from the ground itself. He longed to think of something destructive. Nothing would have pleased him more than to be able to imagine a universal and complete destruction in which the victors would necessarily suffer more than the vanquished. On reaching this point he felt warmer. He had a feeling of mohair.

Xaver sat close beside Konrad's bed. Since they had rented out too many beds, the Ehrles had had to provide sleeping space for several children in their own small bedroom. Konrad spoke as if his lips mustn't touch each other because it would hurt too much. His voice, which used to sparkle under the sweep of his moustache, was now no more than a plaintive whisper. But when Anni, who stood the whole time at the foot of the bed, wanted to speak for him, his forehead would wrinkle in a frown that instantly silenced her. His arms lay stretched along his sides, palms upturned. While loading straw—Anni still owned the meadow, and every year he got a few boxes of potatoes for the straw—he suddenly says: "Anni, I can't go on, I can't stand up anymore." But instead of dropping the loaded pitchfork, he hoists it up again. The pain had been such as no one could ever imagine. But then he no longer feels it. It's already subsiding.

He is still aware that he's lying down or has fallen down, in any case he's lying down. Then Anni is there with the car. How she manages to load him into the car he simply doesn't know. Anni tries to say something, he won't let her speak. The rough track toward home is even more agonizing than hoisting up that last forkful of straw. Each bump is a knife-thrust right into his body. At home he notices he is wet. The wet meadow, he thinks. You've been lying on it. Then he undresses and sees that he's soiled his pants. He had time to feel embarrassed, but only for a second. After that he can't remember a thing. Three days later he's told he's had a heart attack. Fortunately he can prevent them from taking him to the hospital. You know yourself what they did to your father, Xaver! Shoved him into that tiled room, done for. That's not going to happen to him. None of the Ehrles has ever died of a heart attack. They all have enlarged hearts. Didn't the last fellow who looked at Konrad's heart on the screen say: It almost touches your ribs? In our family the heart has always been too big, but never too small.

On the fourth day after his collapse in the meadow, something happened that Anni needed to tell about. But only outside, after Xaver had pressed Konrad's completely limp hand. Xaver had been told to go and see Mrs. Brass at two-thirty. He was glad to have a reason that Konrad would understand. With a movement of his finger, Konrad managed to stop Xaver just as he was leaving. "Xaver, you know what kind of a soup I want for my funeral reception?" Xaver said he knew but even if he'd forgotten Konrad would have a chance to tell him again a hundred times. "You've forgotten," said Konrad. "Liver dumpling soup," said Xaver. "So that's all right," said Konrad, looking up at the ceiling like someone who has finally put all his affairs in order and can now die in peace. Typically Ehrle, thought Xaver. That was Konrad's way of trying to make him stay. Or is Mrs. Brass more important than his death? Xaver left.

Outside, Anni insisted there was something she had to say to

him. Not that she wanted to send Konrad to the hospital against
his will, but there were times when she didn't know which way
to turn. On the fourth day after the heart attack she hears him
locking the bedroom door. Turning the key twice. She goes to
the door, knocks, then he falls down inside, she hears that quite
distinctly, so she runs to the phone to call the doctor, and when
she comes back the door is open and Konrad is gone, out
through the kitchen door. The doctor arrives, notifies the police, woods and streams are searched, finally with flashlights. It
is almost midnight when Konrad's brother Philipp arrives and
reports that Konrad turned up at the old home in Horgenweiler
around eleven o'clock. Barefoot and in his pajamas. But wearing
a coat. They had made him lie down on the sofa. Anni immediately drives back with Philipp to Horgenweiler. There they are
met by Hedwig, who tells them that Konrad is gone, having
left a note to say he was going to disappear for a while, it was no
use trying to follow him. But the next evening he knocks at the
bedroom window. More dead than alive. Since then there's been
an obvious improvement every day. But he knows nothing
about his expedition to Horgenweiler. Did Xaver think his
brain might have been affected?

Xaver said maybe it had been something instinctive, maybe
Konrad had merely wanted to try out whether he could still
manage to walk all the way to the family farm. Now that he was
satisfied he was improving. Xaver was disgusted with himself.
Anni was still standing there helplessly. And he walked away
from her.

By the time he knocked at Mrs. Brass's door it was five minutes to three. He apologized. She wasn't that interested in his
reasons, she'd rather just forgive him. "We're none of us getting
any younger," she said. She found exactly the same thing with
herself. More and more often she overlooked something, forgot
something; she was beginning to wonder at Dr. Gleitze's infi-
nite patience. She was soon going to suggest to the boss that he

transfer her to a less crucial position in the company. To know when to leave—something she'd observed all her life—was the highest and most difficult art in business life.

While she was speaking she made coffee, put some cups on the little table, and invited Xaver to sit down, but she kept stopping suddenly and, interrupting her flow of speech, would look at Xaver for a few silent moments. With a smile. The smile produced the same kind and probably the same number of little creases around her eyes as around her mouth. With her golden-blond hair that ended in a golden knot, she looked, when she smiled, like a golden Madonna. As soon as she was not smiling she looked as if she were crying. The treasure. Well, to come to the point, she hoped that Xaver felt as she did, although of course he was much younger than she; on the other hand, for a chauffeur he wasn't all *that* young anymore. Even so, Dr. Gleitze had found it hard to make the decision that now had to be made. Actually Dr. Gleitze hadn't said a word to her about Xaver's age. That was purely her own opinion. As a matter of fact, Dr. Gleitze hadn't given any reason.. She had merely noticed that it had been hard for him to come to this decision. Somehow he had indicated that Xaver himself would understand his decision better than anyone else. When a person gets older, regular working hours really are preferable. To drive a forklift in Number 2 Warehouse is simply less demanding than having to cope constantly with traffic that was becoming more dangerous day by day. Xaver, if she had understood Dr. Gleitze correctly, was finding it more and more difficult to do without his daily glass of beer. In fact sometimes, if she had interpreted Dr. Gleitze's tremendous discretion correctly, Xaver hadn't been able to wait for his glass of beer until he went off duty. What an effort that must have been for him! How well she understood him! Fortunately all that was over now. Now he was *free* to have it! For Xaver's sake Dr. Gleitze had had to decide to dispense with Xaver. There had been very few decisions, *she* could testify to that, that had caused Dr. Gleitze *soo* much an-guish as this one. He had, she *could* say that, really suffered. After all, one doesn't find a *German* champion for a chauffeur every day, does one?

She stirred her coffee. Now that she wasn't smiling she again looked as if she were crying. She had a tan. The tan of an apart-ment terrace. Then she looked up, smiled; Xaver raised his eye-brows and smiled back. He hoped what he was displaying was a smile. She stood up, picked up a file lying in readiness, and read out to Xaver that he actually had no less than sixty-nine days' vacation coming to him. So before he started in Number 2 Warehouse he had vacation, vacation, vacation! Oh, how she envied him! Then she wished him a good weekend. He wished her the same. At the very end she was *not* smiling anymore. So he didn't have to smile either. She shook hands with him. Would you believe it. First coffee and then a handshake, for Chrissake.

Xaver drove to his Lotto agent. Automatically. Standing there with the card in his hand, he was incapable of choosing any of the numbers. He had to pick one. He had been picking num-bers for the last fifteen years. If Gleitze should succeed in curing him of betting, then . . . Just imagine yourself sitting in front of the screen tomorrow night, the balls start rolling. . . . And you're not involved. Hadn't he always picked more numbers than he could finance? And now? And the 32. He simply couldn't imagine that the 23 or the 32 would come up. It was ridiculous to kid himself that the 23 or the 32 would come up just because he wanted them to. The 17, the 19, the 27. His numbers. He couldn't bear to look at them. They repelled him. Was there a more repulsive number than 32? Only an idiot could bet on the 32. Not he. Never again on the 32, the 23, the 17, the 19, the 27. . . . Let alone any of the other numbers. He had ceased to believe in anything. He had become as unbeliev-ing as . . . as Dr. Gleitze. Who never traveled by plane. Xaver found himself unable to bet. The realization shocked him. In order not to be too conspicuous, he bought ten packs of cigarettes. No sooner was he outside than he realized that there had never been a weekend on which it was more important to have a bet in reserve than the one coming up. Go back again. Or fill out the card in the car. He sat down and, using his briefcase as a support to write on, stared at the forty-nine numbers. He couldn't do it. To make little X's at random wasn't his style. He must have a palpable feeling of inevitability about the numbers he marked. A kind of force always emanated from him onto the numbers card. He invariably felt sure that at least four numbers were correct. And in fact three numbers had often been correct. But now he couldn't come up with a single number. He was beginning to wonder why he had come here at all. At the moment he felt incapable of driving on. His innards were apparently trying to turn inside out. They contracted and contracted as if they wanted to become one spot. That was on the way to being the hardest spot that had ever existed anywhere. He loosened up his fingers. It didn't help. Involuntarily he thought of hay. How beautiful hay is. So dry and light and fragrant. A rich fragrance made up of many things drifting together. Is there anything more beautiful than hay? And there's nothing cleaner than hay. To throw oneself into the hay. His hayloft was, of course, empty. He wouldn't go up into that hayloft to hang himself. Never. He'll fill up the hayloft again. With hay. So that he can let himself fall into it from above as in the old days.

By now the spot in his stomach seemed almost like a nail. One should wrap it up. In thoughts. For the stab of pain to assume a rounder shape. But he can do no more than wish for that. How a move such as Dr. Gleitze's saps one's strength! By making this move, Dr. Gleitze has produced in Xaver the feeling that at the moment he can do nothing. His sole point of existence is this sharp nail in his stomach. Everything else seems to have been emptied out. All the areas or places that are normally felt to be sources of strength have disappeared at one stroke. One has been reduced to a heavy empty mass. And, of course, this single point of pain. In order to do something, Xaver muttered the word *stab* to himself so often that he ended up not knowing what the sound was supposed to convey. After that, his thoughts proceeded at the same all-engulfing speed: Since God obviously doesn't exist, all that remains is the Russians. Why don't the Russians come marching in to do away with this whole gang and establish open injustice? Surely that's better than this hypocrisy—if the Russians don't make a clean sweep of them . . . if there's nothing to be done about that gang . . . then there'd be no hope, then they could do whatever they liked . . . after death nothing, before death nothing, nothing but nothing, then the only thing would be to wade right in and give them a fistful, make their teeth march out of their assholes, for Chrissake.

Xaver was panting as if he were lifting a load that was too heavy for him. He felt dizzy. Konrad, Konrad. . . . For a while he didn't know whether it was still daytime. Then gradually everything came back to him. He became more aware of himself again. No longer heavy. In fact he felt as light as in those dreams where he managed to leap high into the air and stay up above the treetops and gables of Wigratsweiler; hovering over everything, with the neighbors down below, staring up at him, incredulous, admiring. He saw how he displayed himself, publicly: baring his teeth and foaming at the mouth. Who wouldn't like to threaten! And not have to pay for it! To turn brutal, a person should be able to afford to do that, then he's arrived. That means being the master. Turn brutal and not have to pay for it. . . .

For God's sake no accident now. He drove to Wigratsweiler like a student driver. When he saw Agnes he felt his strength was inadequate to tell her immediately what had happened. It wasn't necessary, either. The reports were there. Julia had flunked. *Your daughter Julia cannot be promoted to the next class,*

Xaver read. Fine thing. I see. Well, hadn't he known it all
along? No. No idea. Or rather, now he realized that he had regarded it as utterly impossible. A blow can't be imagined. Only
when the blow strikes does one get an idea of it. Very gradually.

Mustn't he now retract everything he had been thinking
about Gleitze and his entourage? Suddenly Gleitze's move had
been placed beyond criticism. The school, the ultimate authority, had vindicated Gleitze. The Zürns are failures.

"Where is she?" he asked.

"She's gone out," Agnes replied.

He stared at Agnes as if he didn't believe her. "How about
looking at Magdalena's report too?" she said. He looked at it.
C's and B's. Phys. Ed., A. Religion, A. Music, A. Biology, A.
He went over to Magdalena and pinched her arm.

"Where is she?" he asked Agnes again. She had arrived with
Mick, had merely dropped off her schoolbooks and the report,
Mick hadn't even switched off his motor, she had called out that
they'd be back in an hour, but after an hour she phoned to say
they were going on to Sigmaringen, to the Revolution disco,
and would be home at eleven. Xaver took his bicycle and rode
off into the woods above the Nonnenbach. He walked down to
his alder bluff where he had dropped Wenzel Froidl's record
into the water, where he had dropped so much into the water.
Entrusted to the alder leaves. For them to accept into their
careful layers. For him to be rid of it. For them to keep.

"You're fighting something," Dr. Meichle had said. "Why
must you always put up such a fight? Why not be content for a
change, you're nothing but a bundle of nerves."

"Yessir."

Accept the fact that you're in the wrong. Enjoy being in the
wrong. Wallow in being wrong. Deeper. Much much deeper.
Your mistake has been to try and compete with Dr. Gleitze in
being right. Idiot. You should have competed with him in being wrong. You must beat him at being wrong. Snapping twigs

with his hands, he walked back to his bike. One always thinks the worst is over. That's the illusion that prolongs life! The worst is never over. That should be obvious.

Just as he reached home, Master Köberle drove up. With daughter. Xaver applauded his own instinct. He would have to siphon off Köberle's sympathy and comments on Xaver's demotion before Agnes joined them. Fortunately something had happened to Köberle that he considered worse than Xaver's demotion to forklift driver. Xaver would go on living in a paradise, whereas one third of his own garden was going to be wiped out by the new access road to the federal highway. And the access was going to be raised to a height that on his property would reach the level of the second floor of his house and run parallel to practically all his extra guest rooms. That meant that the rooms he had built on for summer guests during the last twenty years were virtually worthless. Yet on the other side of the present road, the one that connected the village with the federal highway, there was no one living at all. Nothing but meadows on that side. So if they have to raise the new access road yet make it follow the gentle curve of the present road, they could take the necessary widening from the other side, where it's all meadows. But no, they have to design the new access road straight as a die. Straightening out curves, that was the ultimate for those people. And the mayor says that it was all finalized under his predecessor. Too late for an appeal. The bulldozers were already there. "The human being," said Master Köberle, "no longer counts." "In our part of the world," his daughter Sabine corrected him severely. They just wanted to pick up a few cherries today, said Master Köberle, he was sorry they couldn't stay for supper, he hoped Xaver and Agnes would understand, but ever since the dredges and bulldozers had been parked in their garden Mom had been sitting in the kitchen in a state of shock, so they mustn't leave Mom alone a minute longer than necessary.

Xaver sent them off to the orchard and told them to help themselves. Agnes was busy canning. He told her what the Köberles were up against. It would be better not to talk to them at all today.

Agnes merely said: "She'll do well." She was obviously referring to Köberle's Sabine.

Agnes looked pale, limp, exhausted. She had taken Julia's failure harder than he had. Because it involved math, she felt guilty. So suddenly it wasn't Wacker, Latin, at all who had dealt the blow, but Wagnerberger, math. And Julia had thought she was safe with him. Somehow it reassured Xaver that the blow hadn't come from Wacker, Latin. He would have found that much harder to understand. But Wagnerberger, math, well! He was an unapproachable person. At parent-teacher meetings he illustrated everything by means of his personal mountaineering experiences. It seemed he spent every free second on an overhanging north wall and always conquered it in an exemplary manner. He was tough, jut-jawed, inaccessible. He was spiteful. Cold. Apparently open to sensation only on overhanging north walls.

Xaver's face felt crooked. Lopsided. Swollen. He would have liked to help Agnes. But he couldn't say anything. For the last little while, Magdalena had been standing beside Agnes. She had taken over the cherry-stalking. Probably because she had her eye on the stalks, which she dried to make tea from in winter as a remedy for chest colds. As if she knew that each of them was thinking only about the school, Magdalena started to talk about it. What she said was a reply to what Xaver had been thinking. She refuted him. Wagnerberger, math, was one of the best teachers in the school. Of course, he wasn't the type to be won over with mascara. Merkelfinger, geography, was one of the most popular teachers in the school. Because she was so patient. It was practically impossible to get in her bad books. She always gave a person a second chance and then one more. A student would have to spit right in her face for her interest in him to decline appreciably. And anyway, all this moaning and groaning about the demands made by the school! It was the most ridiculous thing she'd ever heard! For nowhere, as far as her experience with reality was concerned, was there more justice than in school. If the school could be accused of anything, it would be its almost successful striving after perfect justice. Any student who was in a position to experience this almost paradisical accomplishment of justice on the part of the school could look forward only with horror to the realities of life approaching him. Nowhere so far had she met with a more credible confirmation of herself than in school. So if her mother and father now intended to run down the school, then kindly not in her presence. She couldn't stand that. Julia had brought it all on herself. She, Magdalena, refused to destroy her one and only solid basis merely in order to pander to any more of Julia's delusions. She felt that her parents, who until now had been living their heedless lives without even trying to realize the extent of their responsibility, should hear this from her so that, when the consequences of their heedless life-style became even more drastically apparent, they would not be able to say that they should have been told sooner. She was convinced that there was nothing to match the ignorance of parents, but this was not enough to exonerate them. She had always been deeply disgusted by her parents' reading aloud to each other from the newspaper those hypocritical politicians' speeches deploring "school stress," oblivious of the fact that those politicians were simply exploiting the limitless sniveling sentimentality of parents in order to gain popularity for upcoming elections.

She stopped. Because she had been speaking more or less in a low monotone, one couldn't be sure whether she had said all she wanted to say or had stopped because she had now collected all the available cherry stalks. In any event, the cherry-stalk speech did not continue. When Magdalena was outside, Xaver said: "She'll do well too." Agnes said: "If she doesn't die of scabies first." Xaver protested. Agnes said she wasn't saying that in order to disparage Leni but merely from fear, because Leni—why, Agnes didn't know—simply had not the slightest aversion to dirt. That went farther than she dared tell Xaver. Then she'd better be quiet, said Xaver.

He had the feeling that, with this slur on Magdalena, Agnes was only trying to get at him. What she really meant was: Although Julia has flunked her courses and it's my fault, she will survive it all as a somehow normal person. Whereas Magdalena. . . .

He went into the living room. Then realized that he was still incapable of looking at anything on TV. He wanted to shout at Agnes: Why did you let Julia go! She flunks her exams and you let her clear out! But he also felt glad she wasn't there. He simply felt too weak to shout. Or: he didn't feel like shouting. Only the other night he had been shouting at Julia in a dream, whereupon a girl he didn't know had immediately come running up and stabbed Julia repeatedly with a knife, looking at him as she did so with eyes seeking praise.

The phone rang. He was sitting six feet away from it, but he couldn't walk across and lift up the receiver. At last Agnes came. He said: "Don't." She said: "What if it's Julia?" He shouted: "Leave it alone!" She hesitated, then lifted the receiver. Xaver rushed out of the house. First behind the house to Tell. Then, with Tell, he walked up through the orchard. Among the currant bushes he admitted to himself that he had still been convinced he would never be called upon to face a truly serious challenge. And if he wished to be honest he must admit that even now he didn't believe the situation to be all that serious. So what else had to happen to make him take something seriously? Was this because of the currant bushes? Whenever he

stood among these bushes, he was suffused with this terrible
contentment. Contentment with everything. Apparently there
was absolutely nothing stronger than the soothing power of
these currant bushes. What a notion. Yes, if one could only
stand here indefinitely. Anyway, he no longer had to drive to
Marseilles to the Hôtel Européen, room 209. The beetle, last
year, in the bathtub. An inch long. Long, serrated back legs.
Short middle legs. Semilong front legs. Gigantic antennae.
Each time the beetle discovered that the tub was too smooth to
climb up, it started to flounder wildly; all its legs drummed on
the smooth surface of the bathtub simultaneously. Even the antennae were whipping, too. But because of these fits it kept slipping back again to the bottom of the tub. Then it would work
its way up again as far as it possibly could. Its optimum climb-
ing performance, although not sufficient for ultimate rescue,
was achieved by moving its right back leg and left front leg simultaneously. Xaver held out the cord of his electric shaver to
the beetle. It couldn't hold on to it. All right then, the chain of
the bath plug. That was almost as good as a ladder. The beetle
managed to get only its left legs onto the chain. Its right legs
continued to slip. Xaver had an empty paper bag. The beetle
immediately crawled into it. Xaver placed the bag on the window ledge and closed the window. On going to have another
look ten minutes later, he found that the wind had blown down
the paper bag. The window gave onto an inner courtyard. At the
level of the second floor a corrugated asbestos roof with kitchen
chimneys and ventilator ducts. The bag beside one of those
ducts. Probably the beetle had fallen into the duct. Xaver suspected that Magdalena would have condemned his behavior toward the beetle.

Since there were never enough rooms in Aix-en-Provence, he
usually had to find accommodation in Marseilles. At the Hôtel
Européen, all the guests and staff had always given the impres-

sion that, the moment one stopped looking at them, they were being tortured. He could really feel happy that he . . . But he couldn't even tell Agnes that he . . . In fact, even he didn't actually believe that he . . . To be honest, he had to admit that he believed Dr. Gleitze would send for him within a very few days. Konrad had said that Franz, their cousin in Bodnegg, had been rescued by his boss.

Xaver told himself he had to be careful. The best thing would be to regard nothing as possible. His worst mistake, after all, had always been that he regarded too much as possible. That was not a mistake, it was more like a quality. His worst quality, in fact. His fevered imagination. You are going to be rescued. You of all people. Berta Fiegle has some little nodules on her ankle, is given the wrong radiation, the leg has to be amputated, forty thousand marks damages; upper-class people are paid a million when it is falsely reported that their fifth marriage is their sixth; but you won't be treated like the higher-ups, you'll be treated like Berta Fiegle, for Chrissake. You still don't believe it. You think you're going to be spared. Last year, in that little place the other side of Aix, you had a row in the parking lot with another chauffeur because you told him you would never put up with what he had to take from the wife of his Düsseldorf boss. To drive without her all the way from Düsseldorf to Marseilles merely to drive her the few kilometers from the airport to Aix and in and around Aix! You would, you'd said, tell your boss that, if he's going to fly down there, he'd better use taxis when he gets there. Which the Düsseldorf chauffeur found totally unreasonable. Since he preferred to make that long trip alone rather than with the old cow. You shouted at him that he hadn't a spark of decency in his body or a grain of common sense, otherwise he'd simply refuse to make such an idiotic trip. The chauffeur again: Those were his favorite trips of all; when the old cow flew to Salzburg or Hamburg, he'd drive there alone, pick her up at the airport, drive her to the hotel. . . . Xaver was reduced to yelling at him. The chauffeur had looked up at the Hôtel Moulin, grabbed Xaver, and said if Xaver didn't stop at once he'd beat him up. Xaver knew drivers who reacted exactly as he had. He didn't want a job that made no sense.

At supper, Xaver went on eating as if he would never stop. With a certain sense of dread he noticed that Magdalena was doing the same. If he went on eating, she would also go on eating, bringing in more and more cartons of buttermilk, emptying them into her soup plate, slicing pears into it, adding fresh-ground wheat to it, stirring it all up, and eating it. At the same time eating one half-washed carrot after another with her fingers. Agnes had finished long ago. She looked on while Xaver and Magdalena were eating. Xaver drank white wine. His stomach felt as if about to burst. His head felt as if he were going to topple over. That was a pleasant mixture, this feeling of being about to topple over and about to burst. But then he did stop. He could no longer bear to see Magdalena falling into his habit of mindless stuffing. He was now convinced that he would never reach the point of taking his and his family's situation really seriously, although their situation was completely hopeless. Everything will go wrong. But you don't care. You are immune. You gorge yourself. You booze. That's it.

Later, when he closed the bedroom door, Agnes asked him to open it again so she could hear Julia coming home. He said he didn't want to lie in a draft. Agnes got out of bed and opened the door. The exchange of words had immediately taken on that tone of resentment which always prevailed when one of the girls still hadn't come home at night. He dreamed of a long, wearisome path to be traveled. Gradually it ceased to be a path and turned into a permanently hostile pathlessness. At every second they were on the point of collapse. It got steeper and steeper. His legs had become mere pillars of pain that balked at every movement. In this world of mountain peaks they were steadily moving toward the lowest spot of the no-longer-distant south ridge. A spot clear of snow. They could tell each other how love-ly it would soon be. They reached the spot. They looked out. From here on it was downhill. An easy path. Sheer reward. They sang. Under chestnut trees they spent the night. In the morning sunshine it was warm. The ordeal was over. With nimble steps they followed a stream downhill as it tinkled over pebbles. No leap seemed to faze them. Impossible to imagine that one of them would sprain an ankle. They kept looking at each other. We've actually made it. You see, if we'd given up? It just goes to show, one should never give up. Haven't I always said so? There was a loud rumble. They all looked up simultaneously. On the other side of the stream a scree slope rose up to the base of a vertical wall. Down that wall plunged a dark mass. They stood rooted to the spot. The rockslide came straight at them. Should they run upstream or downstream to avoid it? The rockslide was too wide. Maybe it would come to a stop on the other side of the stream. The stream bed was deep. The mass of rock and scree sprayed, thundered, filled the stream bed in no time, surged up onto their side. Two were immediately crushed to death. The others were merely buried in scree. They managed to keep their heads free. But because too many of their bones were broken, they could do nothing to free themselves. They died of thirst, one after the other. Xaver felt the pain and woke up.

It was already light outside. His stomach hurt all over. In-temperate fool. You should have stopped eating half an hour earlier. No, wrong. Get up, right now. Eat some more, drink some more. Of course. Just go on eating and drinking. If he got out of bed, Agnes would wake up. Maybe she had waited for Julia until three o'clock. So he had to postpone the resump-tion of his eating until six or six-thirty. It promised to be an odd kind of Saturday. And an even odder Sunday. As for Mon-day . . . ! Somehow the right thing would have been, Xaver thought, for everyone to turn up today. Georg and family from

Nitzenweiler. Philipp from Horgenweiler. Dr. Zürn with wife and kids from Überlingen. Konrad and Anni and the kids. And the Ehrles from Unterreitnau, and Aunt Klothilde, married to a man in Bodnegg, and . . .

He saw himself lying in bed. They were all standing around him—oh, even Professor Amrain from Wilpoltsweiler was there, well isn't that nice, Professor, of you to come too—some of them took his left hand, the others his right hand, one put his hand on Xaver's shoulder, children rubbed their noses against him, one child stroked him, they all talked at once, but softly, and although they were all talking at once there was absolutely no confusion but rather a perfectly intelligible singing, something that floated and was pleasant. Then Xaver would tell them what had happened to him. Then Georg would mimic Dr. Gleitze. He remembered how, when Gleitze had left the room, Georg had instantly leaped up, run to the door, and then come back from the door as Dr. Gleitze. In the middle of the room he had turned around, looked back and up under his left arm, shaken water out of his ear, and somehow held out his limp hand. Everyone laughed: he was Gleitze, he really was. They all asked Georg to do his Gleitze act again. Ever since then, Gleitze entering a room and turning aside to shake hands was one of Georg's best performances. Xaver reveled in the feeling of being able to call up Georg anytime and ask him for the Gleitze performance. Oh yes, Mr. Gleitze, we have some good times here in Wigratsweiler.

Strange, waking up for the first time after such an event. The still wholly unknown unpleasantness. The way it surges up inside one. He's no longer Gleitze's chauffeur.

It was as if this news had been waiting for him to wake up because, as long as he was asleep, it hadn't had a proper chance. Now with all its pent-up force it hurls itself upon you. No matter what you try, you won't be able to think of anything else. You have to go along with it. Give everything free rein. You can feel your brain racing. What's racing through there are the reasons in your favor. Just like blood corpuscles racing to the spot where you've been injured. Yet the biggest help would be if you could forget about that spot. Everything drawing you toward that spot saps your strength. Even when it takes the guise of help. But you are that spot. And nothing else. There is not a single bird to be heard in the pear trees today.

Xaver put on a shirt with button cuffs. Once Agnes had grasped the extent of the change, he would ask her to sew up one buttonhole and sew a button on all the cuffs of his work shirts.

At breakfast Xaver forced himself—for Magdalena's sake—to utter a few harsh words against Julia. He pointed out to her that she was totally depraved. The disaster at school was merely a manifestation of her overall total depravity. She was the most depraved creature he knew because she made no effort but instead actually enjoyed the condition into which she had sunk from pure sloppiness, oh, yes, instead of turning the deterioration into a change for the better she was reveling in her total corruption. Julia said: "My ass." And calmly went on eating. He then made a gesture that swept her bread off the table. She stood up and said: "Can't you keep your asshole shut?" Then she picked up the bread, examined it, and threw it in the garbage pail.

Xaver jumped up. He felt like sweeping everything off the table with a single movement. But he mustn't do that. Only after reaching the door could he do something. Slam the door shut. As he did so, he could hear Agnes going for Julia. She was screaming at Julia in a shrill, exhausted voice. Slapping her too. But these were no doubt slaps for which Julia hardly needed to raise her chin. He ran behind the barn, up into the orchard. Tell ran after him with flattened ears and tucked-in tail, cowering a bit and whimpering the way he did when he'd done something wrong and was afraid of being punished. Evidently he thought Xaver's shouting had been meant for him.

When Agnes appeared, he sent her back. He went over to a cherry tree and ate some cherries. As fast as he could. In all the cherries he saw Julia's eyes. How accurately she could aim. How accurately she found her mark. Admirable. He stuffed so many cherries in his mouth that he could hardly munch. Later, Agnes appeared with Julia. Agnes said Julia wanted to go to Venice for the weekend with Mick. Returning Tuesday. She disapproved. By motorbike to Venice. In the middle of the tourist season. Xaver shrugged his shoulders. He couldn't say a word. Imagine her so quickly having the guts to face him, to hope he would take her side! What a gal. If *she* didn't get on well! Agnes asked whether he didn't disapprove too. Again he pretended that whatever concerned this daughter simply didn't interest him. Julia concluded brightly that he approved. Even more brightly she called out "Thanks!" and ran off. With Tell after her. Agnes's face was crisscrossed by a spider-web pattern, which meant that she was at the end of her tether. He drew her to him. Incredible how he could feel every little curve of her body. He could have copied it in any material. Preferably in white linden wood.

Agnes said there was something she must do. Xaver thought: How typical. He wanted to tell her now. If anywhere, then here among the currant bushes. Agnes said that, since Xaver was allowing Julia to go, she, Agnes, would have to see to it that Julia dressed warmly enough. He walked slowly after her. Mick came roaring up to the house. Julia stowed away her bag. Then they drove off at a slow, hypocritically slow speed. Julia raised a happily waving hand high above her head. Leather outfit and safety helmet for Julia were to be picked up in Nonnenhorn at Wiltrud's, Julia's predecessor with Mick. Was she sure it would all fit her? Agnes had asked anxiously. "Don't worry, it'll fit," Mick had said, casting a shy, practiced look over Julia's body. "I s'pose you know what you're doing," said Magdalena from the top step, as soon as the sound of the motorbike had died away. Magdalena never uttered her critical statements in a loud, let alone reproachful voice. It was clear that she was controlling herself, leaving most of it unsaid, as if whatever became audible welled up out of her against her will. Xaver walked over to her and pinched her arm. He was glad Julia had gone off to Venice on that motorbike. The way he used to go to Glyndebourne, to Aix, to Braunschweig. To drive long distances, that's the thing. Perhaps they will die. On a steep mountain-pass curve. In an instant. At twelve noon. Without suffering. A flash from the darkness. Finished. Poor Agnes. In any case he was glad Julia would be out of the house until Tuesday. He preferred to be alone with Agnes when he told her what he had to tell her. He saw Julia and Mick flying through the air. Leather dummies. . . .

He quickly reached for the newspaper and read it from beginning to end. That helped. In Friedrichshafen, in the lakeside park for which he felt responsible, Wilhelm Grübel, a municipal employee originally from Selmnau, walked up to thirty-six-year-old Wilfried Weissflog, who was sitting on the back of a bench instead of on the seat, placed his rabbit stun gun against the chest of the musicologist from Munich who was vacationing at Lake Constance, pressed the trigger, the musicologist died on the spot, the municipal employee gave himself up to the police. Xaver knew Willi Grübel. Many years ago he used to go to his place for rabbits. With Magdalena and Julia. In Selmnau, Willi had fenced in a huge enclosure where the rabbits could practically run wild again. There had once been a picture of the enclosure in the newspaper. But even without the newspaper, Willi would not have been unknown in Wigratsweiler. The Grübels of Selmnau were a family one knew. Why? he wondered. Because they all had such a thick thatch of hair and such red faces? And such big heads. Willi was a familiar sight at the Happy

Prospect. He was known as Willi the Mole. He liked watching the people dancing. During the Third Reich a brother of his had been killed in the Grafenwöhr mental institution. Another was still in an institution. The father and mother were no longer alive; even by local standards they had been considered particularly devout. The newspaper article surmised that the long-haired musicologist had drawn Willi's wrath down upon himself by insisting during the past few days on sitting on the back instead of the seat of the park bench. It was assumed that on preceding days there had been arguments between Wilhelm Grübel and Wilfried Weissflog. Anyone having witnessed such arguments was asked to report to the police. Since giving himself up to the police, Wilhelm Grübel had not uttered a single word; his silence was such as to indicate that he would not speak again.

Xaver felt somewhat relieved after reading this article. People would rather talk about what Willi had done than about his own demotion. There was also an article about Glyndebourne. This year's *Figaro* had received rave reviews. He read this as an old Glyndebourne hand. Next Thursday . . . He must tell Agnes. Another article was devoted exclusively to Mr. Trummel. Mr. Trummel is leaving the Gleitze enterprise to become head of the Euro-Aero-Space Corporation, a subsidiary of the American WTW concern. One would do well, the article said, to contemplate Trummel's career and principles, which were equally instructive. His desk, completely cleared every evening. Himself, ice-cold in his calculations. An intellectual with a razor-sharp mind. There have been no setbacks in Trummel's career. He decided on the study of law because of the abstract clarity of the subject. Tennis player, skier, yachtsman. *But the executive stays behind at the factory gate. On the tennis court—when his busy schedule permits—the rules of the court apply to him as rigidly as to any minor employee.* A mere fourteen months had sufficed for him to pass through each commercial department at Osram in Munich and become assistant to the president. At Gleitze's he first specialized in production, organization, and efficiency. Later also in sales. There was no mistaking the high level of personal dedication accompanying Trummel's success curve. *Not once during my career have I asked for an increase in salary.* Trummel was never satisfied until a department manager told him: *What you are now demanding is beyond our capability.* No wonder they are sorry to see him go at Markdof. But they all wish him . . .

To Xaver it seemed as if black shadows were flying past in the glittering southern sky. He cut out the Trummel article and put it in an envelope that he addressed to Konrad. As he moistened the gummed flap with his tongue and tried to close it, he noticed that the flap wouldn't stick. Apparently his saliva lacked something today that would activate the gum. It occurred to him that he could mail a newspaper article in an open envelope. He heard a car and ran outside. A young fellow jumped out of a vintage Porsche. He was wearing a red-and-white check shirt with short sleeves. But then *he* had arms like a boxer. He was Sepp Bräu, he said. First of all, here was the knife that Xaver had left behind in the glove compartment; secondly—and with best regards from Mrs. Gleitze—a box of chocolates. Xaver saw at once that they were *truffes Champagne.* In all probability some he had picked up himself. Xaver immediately steered the fellow away from the house. He put down chocolates and knife on the old milking stool beside the water trough. "I'm your successor, see?" the fellow said. He wouldn't mind finding out why Xaver had quit like that, from one day to the next; after all a guy couldn't know too much about what to expect from the boss. As for himself, he had landed with Gleitze by pure chance. And now he had to go right off with him to Glyndebourne. Actually he had already more or less accepted a job with a gentleman in Augsburg, who then turned out to have cancer; apparently a friend of Dr. Gleitze's. The Augsburg boss, when he still thought he was going to recover, had paid for Sepp to take the skidding course in Osogna. Had Xaver taken that course? Probably not, it was really only meant for very young drivers. He put you through the mill all right, that Unnus Hendrichs. Xaver might know him from his rally days, zigzag driving, skidding, 180-degree turn on the spot. He thought it was crazy, of course, but it sure was fun. And if our bosses happen to be more scared of gangsters than of cancer, we don't mind learning for their benefit how to make a fast getaway. Xaver seemed to be more interested in in-fighting, to judge by the knife. But these days knives mightn't be quite enough; oh well, he'd better get going now; what a way to start, picking up some guy at Kloten airport: Passenger Mr. Albert Gleitze, please come to the information desk. . . .

Xaver was about to say, Give him my best regards, but fortunately he was able to check himself. When the fellow was back in his old Porsche, he called out: "Aloisia sends her regards," winking as he said it, then glided slowly away. Obviously he had forgotten his desire to find out more about the Gleitzes. Or he had never really wanted to find out. Xaver thought of his predecessor. Schorsch. Who had been demoted to messenger because of a glass of beer. Xaver had made a point of always going up to Schorsch when he'd seen him anywhere in the plant. He'd had a guilty conscience about him. Once, maybe three years after Schorsch's transfer, Schorsch had rubbed his left side and made a face when Xaver met him. It hurt like hell there, he had said. "Then why don't you go home and lie down?" Xaver asked. "Come along, I'll drive you." "Nonsense," said Schorsch, who had started drinking after his transfer. "We'll go and have a schnapps first, come on." On the way to the cafeteria the pain had increased. "Nothing doing," Xaver had said, "now I'm going to drive you to Dr. Meichle."

Schorsch put up no further resistance. Dr. Meichle had asked: "Do you feel ill?" Schorsch had said: "Not a bit, I just have this pain in my left shoulder." Dr. Meichle had asked: "How long have you been a chauffeur?" "Twenty-eight years," Schorsch replied. Well naturally, it was an attack of rheumatism in the left shoulder, common enough among chauffeurs. Schorsch grinned. Xaver drove Schorsch home. Walked with him up the stairs. His wife comes to the door: when she sees her husband, her eyes open wide. "What's wrong?" she asks. Schorsch points with his right hand to his left shoulder and grins. But then falls over. Xaver doesn't even have time to catch him. And is dead. His wife says: "Oh my God, Schorsch."

Agnes came out and asked who that had been. Someone from the plant who'd come to tell him that his request for leave had been granted. Then he explained to the astonished Agnes that he hadn't meant to tell her about it until the evening, but he might just as well tell her now. He had asked Personnel to figure out his accumulated vacation time and to let him know whether he could take his vacation this summer. That young fellow was the substitute they'd found for the sixty-nine days of vacation Xaver still had coming to him. He was simply fed up with gadding about between Glyndebourne, Vienna, and Marseilles and leaving Agnes to do all the summer work. "Just think, next Thursday off to Glyndebourne!" Agnes was already biting her lower lip. He was wondering—this was something they would have to discuss thoroughly, of course—whether he shouldn't try to have himself transferred to an inside job. To the warehouse, for instance. Regular working hours. No risks. No excitement. Of course no expense account either. They might talk about it sometime, right? Agnes bit deeper into her lower lip. Out of a pleasurable emotion. Or because it struck her as unlikely. Or incredible. For her husband to become sensible—after all these years how could she have expected that? Or was something the matter with him? Tell me! Is it your stomach-ache? No, it's pure reason. He thought of those people from Königsberg, who often used that expression.

Agnes clasped her hands around his neck, leaned back, and clung to him the way she used to do twenty years ago after they had reached the top of the slope. "Dear God!" she said. It turned out that for a long time she had been thinking that the job with Gleitze was bad for him, but since Xaver had always seemed so devoted to Dr. Gleitze she hadn't dared say anything. Although she'd always had the feeling that that job was poison for him. "Oh, come along," said Xaver. Truly, that's how she had felt. "They aren't good people," said Agnes. "We'll talk about that later," Xaver said. If Xaver was going to spend more time at home, they might be able to improve the yield of the orchard. Maybe they could buy back a few acres from Georg. Before she could repeat that she would make a farmer out of Xaver yet, he said he would like to go up into the woods. She let him go, it being well known that his father and grandfather, that all the Zürns, had gone into the woods every day.

Before getting onto his bicycle, he took the knife into the bedroom and put it in the bottom drawer of the bedside table, where—hidden under socks—lay the five other knives. Now he had six knives. He couldn't imagine ever buying another knife. What did he want with knives? He took all six knives out and placed them in a plastic bag. Outside he also put the chocolates in the bag, then rode off. Again he felt exhilarated by the violent shaking up. Then, with no jolting at all, along his smooth woodland path. Into his green retreat. When he dropped the knives and the *truffes Champagne* from his alder bluff into the Nonnenbach, he got goose pimples. The chocolate sank right away. The knives flashed as they descended, then were obliterated. Like comets. Too bad he didn't have his cufflinks with him. Even the newest ones, of mother-of-pearl. He'll sink them here. All of them. He'll sink everything here that has to do with the Gleitzes. Everything there is. He wondered what his ancestors could have consigned to the layers of alder leaves that looked so carefully arranged. One should have a look sometime in those leafy archives. Or had they really taken their daily walks just for the sake of game and the forest? What a mistake to sink the knives and the *truffes Champagne* here. That turned his alder bluff into a memorial to Gleitze's victory and to his own defeat. In that case he shouldn't even have broken up the Wenzel Froidl record here. In that case he . . .

Why should he try to duck out of it? After all, what is a victor? The difference between victor and vanquished is merely that the victor thinks of the vanquished only when he wants to, whereas the vanquished has to think of the victor whether he wants to or not. You know that, you know that. If you do away with yourself, for example, that will be the best thing that could happen to them. They have fixed everything in such a way that it proceeds automatically. As if they weren't the least bit involved. Let alone interested. If you do away with yourself, that means you have acknowledged the situation you are in. You have taken things to their logical conclusion. Like the Bodnegg cousin in Ravensburg. Then what they'd like best would be to go to extremes to rescue you. So get on with it, do the Gleitzes a favor and kill yourself. Get on with it.

When light approaches us, Pastor Dillmann had preached, we throw a black shadow. When darkness approaches, we throw a white shadow. This white shadow is God. According to Pastor Dillmann. Think of Gleitze, and you'll immediately cast a white shadow. And *what* a white shadow you'll cast at the mere thought of Gleitze! Now just concentrate on that snicker Dr. Gleitze produces as soon as he's managed to make others snicker. Isn't that a vile snicker? Although Agnes tends to say less rather than more, she has a sensitivity for people that is comparable with the absolute pitch that some people have for music, and Agnes said that the Gleitzes weren't good. You could never say such a thing. But Agnes can say it. His colleague Frey had a point of view. If one lacks Agnes's sensitivity for people, one needs a valid point of view. Especially toward such established people. Gleitze is a bishop. Of course he is. And you never noticed. Gleitze has just as complacent an air as the gentlemen in old portraits. Lord High Steward Gleitze, Prince Gleitze, Dr. Gleitze, for Chrissake. And you his Hurlewagen, for Chrissake. Xaver snapped twigs into little pieces and threw them into the Nonnenbach. O John, pray for me. O Willi, pray for me. O thou white shadow, if only it were possible to destroy something!

When he pushed his bicycle out of the forest, the western sky was almost black. The wind was riffling through the trees as if furious at not being able to find something it was looking for. It was ripping them apart. Long before he reached the house, Xaver could hear Agnes playing the piano. For the first time in how many years? And it wasn't even Sunday! Sure to be Mozart again. Whenever Agnes played, he saw the notes running through the house. Running up and down the walls at great, orderly speed. He saw Agnes driving the notes in front of her. She made them skip. He crept in. There she was, actually sitting at the piano in her defiant posture just like in the old days. Tense, thought Xaver. When she plays she's tense. It's almost fanatical the way she perches on the chair. That way of sitting upright and leaning forward. He was glad she was playing again. He hoped all Wigratsweiler could hear it. He hoped Dr. Gleitze would drive slowly through the village one day and hear Agnes playing Mozart. He wanted her to play for sixty-nine days until there wasn't a spot left in or around the house from which notes didn't leap up. On every one of those sixty-nine days he would, like his grandfather's brother Benedikt, not comb his hair until he'd had his bowel movement. The telephone rang. Xaver answered it at once and, holding the receiver, walked out into the corridor. He didn't like telephoning because he had inhibitions about saying his name. He felt strongly that his name was something that only others could use for him. For himself he found his name unusable. Above all when he was supposed to say, as was customary: This is Xaver Zürn. For him it would have been natural to have said: This is Xaver, in dialect. He could also have added: of Wigratsweiler. But he didn't like saying: Xaver Zürn. That seemed to hang in the air.

It was Aloisia. She had tried to phone earlier. She just wanted to tell him she'd given her notice. She was fed up with kowtowing to that silly old cow and listening to herself being called Josefine. That old bag had actually believed that she, Aloisia, had only been joking about not liking to be called Josefine. He should've seen her face when Aloisia handed in her notice! That face alone was worth the two years she'd spent there. She, Aloisia, had applied for a job in the post office. Her chances looked good, letter carrier, an old ambition of hers. Fresh air! Of course she'd keep in touch with him. Hullo? Was he still there? Yes. Well then. He could be glad he was rid of his job. Well then. She said good-bye.

As Xaver hung up, he was sweating. Magdalena came running down the stairs, uttering shrill screams. Probably they were meant to mean: Look . . . look . . . look! On her palm lay a little pile of butts of hand-rolled cigarettes. Found in Julia's religious-studies book. Apparently she had made a thorough search. In the textbook she had at last found these butts and positively identified them as marijuana butts. After all, she'd also once smoked pot. But just the once. To find out what it was like. Okay. Now she hoped her dear parents were aware what kind of a guy their daughter had gone off with. Okay.

At Magdalena's first shrill cry, Agnes had stopped what she was doing. She and Xaver now stood before the butts that Magdalena had thrown onto the table. Agnes sat down, placed her head in her hands, and assumed her expression of exhaustion. Which now included a look of total bleakness. She no longer seemed to have the strength to weep. Out of the silence came the sound of an approaching car. Xaver went to the door. "Georg," he said. They all walked out onto the steps. Georg got out, raised his eyebrows, pursed his lips, nodded, and made a gesture as if to say: It's no use trying, or, It's useless. Had those fellows from the highways department been here yet? Well, they'd been to his place. Yesterday around lunchtime. Two cars, four gentlemen. At the word *gentlemen* he automatically became thinner, his neck grew longer, he carried his head noticeably higher, his chin rose and went on rising. On one of the car hoods they had spread out a map and shown him that in future the B31 would go past his stable. That's right, past his stable. They're taking away two thousand square meters from him. For a pittance. Naturally he'd asked them right off what they were going to do with Wigratsweiler. From then on, Georg's imitation was limited to the tallest of the men, who apparently also headed the group. Georg's arm grew longer and longer. The hood of the car seemed farther and farther down. And as superintendent of highways he started scraping around with a stiff, crooked forefinger on a map spread out over the hood, without bending down to look at the map. And he not only scraped, he tapped here and there with that crooked finger, circled something, enlarged on something. Georg looked up from his performance with a quick grin. Had Xaver caught on? No? Once again. The long arm, the crooked finger, way up top the small head. Dr. Kuckuck! Yes, of course. Dr. Kuckuck from Tübingen. The beanpole with the bullet head. Almost as skinny as all those years ago. But he'd been so preoccupied with announcing that the hearings on the planned routing according to Paragraph 16 of the Federal Highway Statutes had been concluded, that the hearings on the execution of the project had been initiated, and that no further objections would be tolerated—Georg really hadn't felt like reminding him of the report he'd brought up here more than twenty-five years ago. And no schnapps, no smoked meat, no supper. He doesn't remember us. And what he's bringing us now is not much better than what he brought us then. Wigratsweiler is going to be hit twice. Down below, fifty meters below the Happy Prospect, the new B31. Up above, only partially following the present little road, the new county road. It will no longer wind around the top of the hill. The top of the hill is going to be removed, twenty thousand cubic meters are going to be shaved off. What else? "There won't be much left of the slope," said Georg, dropping his imitation of the beanpole. "The orchard," said Xaver. "You're going to lose sixty trees," said Georg, "and three thousand square meters. They'll start construction whether you agree or not, but if you do agree, you'll be paid at once, six marks per square meter for the county road and eight for the B31, plus a hundred and fifty marks per tree. There's a meeting next week of the village council. Just a formality, of course, they're all in favor, those teachers. They have all the say in the village council. The teachers and the mayor. All they have in their heads is highways, those teachers."

Before leaving, Georg once again switched to being Dr. Kuckuck the beanpole; his arm grew long again, up on top his head was shaking, down below the crooked finger scraped and mowed. Georg gave this final installment of his performance without a word. Then he grinned and said that the two thousand square meters he was losing hurt him more than the three thousand would hurt Xaver. After all, nothing could happen to Xaver. On the contrary. He was one of those people who needed more and more highways. That was Georg's only consolation, that one member of his family was on the winning side. Xaver had a momentary vision of *his* sublime 450; but now the incomparable car seemed to him like an invulnerable science-fiction insect. Georg called out that he had to move on, to Horgenweiler, to demonstrate to Philipp and Hedwig what they would have to face. "You're looking at George Zürn's Traveling Disaster-Show!" he called out, and roared off.

"Come with me," Xaver said to Agnes, and walked up with her into the orchard. "Why don't you come too?" he called back to Magdalena. She shook her head and went into the house, walking more erect than usual. As if trying to prove something. Probably all she wants to prove by walking erect is that she is walking erect, thought Xaver. But that's enough, he thought. It made him happy. Xaver sat down with Agnes at the table under the pear tree. They gazed up the slope. It'll look pretty funny when they saw off the top of the hill. *The most attractive feature of Lake Constance is the surrounding hills, for which we have to thank the Ice Age,* Mr. Reckholder the teacher had said. Xaver went on to think about the soothing power of the currant bushes. He'd lose about half the bushes.

That evening Xaver drank two of the six bottles of rosé that Dr. Zürn had brought with him from Überlingen when he came over for some apples in February. Since he and Agnes weren't saying anything, Magdalena spoke up. She explained how and what a person must think so as never to mind anything. She spoke as she always did. Through almost closed lips. Actually she spoke almost inaudibly. One was surprised to understand everything that small voice was saying. No longer was it a voice of "light and honey"; now it was more like a voice of stone, of a little stone, but one that gives off a tiny sound. Personally, for instance, she regarded herself as undiscoverable, she said. And that's the way she'd like to stay. A person mustn't want to be found, she said, or she's finished. It embarrassed Xaver to listen to her. At first she'd been open, had reached out for contacts and wanted to be cooperative. Luckily she'd soon noticed that, wherever she looked for contacts, only accomplices were wanted. Then she had encountered herself. At the moment she was existing as an egoist. She didn't intend to stay that way. She still had to learn to cope with her parents. The biggest problem for kids was their parents. No matter what those parents were like, they were the greatest threat. Once they had been coped with, nothing really bad would ever have to be faced. Parents represented principles that were totally divorced from reality. Nothing was so debilitating or so misleading as whatever was associated with parents. The longer one lived with one's parents, the less likelihood was there of ever recovering from them. By the skin of her teeth she had avoided becoming a victim of her parents. But a recognized danger was like a cool bath and a juicy apple in summertime. Now she's talking nonsense, thought Xaver. She was lucky enough, she said, to be able to exist standing on one leg in the snow. Barefoot. Go ahead, thought Xaver. When she's through with her parents and her school she'll apply for a job in Radolfzell. At Schiesser's. She kind of felt in her bones that she'd be comfortable in a plant with a thousand female workers. Provided she managed to start at the bottom and stay at the bottom. She would regard even the slightest promotion as a defeat, as her destruction.

When Magdalena stopped, she immediately stood up and said—almost inaudibly: "Good night." Agnes, later: "If only she wouldn't pick her nose like that all the time she's talking. Can you explain that?" Xaver said: "Oh, let her be." But he thought, too, that everything Magdalena said would have sounded better, if, while she was speaking, she had stopped picking her nose just once. It also didn't seem to bother her to transfer what she had picked out on nimble fingertips almost with a flourish into her mouth. She actually tossed it in. Or was that all very deliberate? Was that her way of trying to prevent

him and Agnes from becoming her proud or sentimental listeners? Xaver had managed, before she left the table, to pinch her
arm. "Oh, Magdalena," he had said, as cheerfully as possible.
He wanted very much to call out to her: Good luck. Take care.
You'll make it. You're the first one of us whom they can't kick
around the way they've kicked the rest of us around. You want
to go down, not up. You'll make it. But he didn't trust himself
to say anything. He could only pinch her arm. She smiled in her
critical way, and enigmatically.

Agnes took Julia's diary out of the drawer. Xaver protested.
Agnes said Julia had left the diary lying around so openly that it
might be taken as an invitation. "When she leaves her underwear lying around, you say she's sloppy," said Xaver. "Just listen to this," Agnes said impatiently, and read out: *What I really
want. . . . If I knew that, I wouldn't always have to be glad about
what I don't like. Australia. Sounds neat. Australia. That would do
it. Australiaaustraliaaustralia. And then the nose in the flower till
they fuse. Oh Australia.*

Agnes believed that Julia and Mick were on their way not just
to Venice but to Australia. Xaver was shocked, but he protested. Agnes, you're talking nonsense. Australia, impossible. A
Zürn doesn't go to Australia. Not even an Ehrle would. But a
Guldin would, Agnes said grimly, almost menacingly. They
searched the diary for further clues. In vain. *And then the nose in
the flower till they fuse.* Did that have something to do with the
butts? He fetched the butts he had put away at lunchtime and
used them to roll a cigarette. Agnes refused to take a puff. So he
had to puff away by himself. They had no perceptible effect on
him. Then they went off to their bedroom. Like a crew that had
been taking part in a totally exhausting but unsuccessful rescue
operation. Without Agnes's putting it into words, all the blame
for Julia's trip to Venice fell on him. He had let her go. With a
pot smoker.

They undressed. Each preoccupied. Over the dresser was a

mirror in which Xaver saw himself when he had almost finished undressing. He immediately stepped aside. As soon as he saw himself it seemed to him incredible that Agnes could still put up with him. Although there were times when he believed that there was no woman alive who could put up with him as well as Agnes did. But maybe she wasn't putting up with him well at all. No, all wrong. She can put up with him very well. She's excellent at putting up with him. But she doesn't like him. In other words, he has no effect on her. He senses that whenever he is aware of how she affects him. Of how he longs for her. Of how he would like to pull her about. Tear her to pieces from sheer can't-get-enough-of-her. If she felt the same way about him they would really have to tear each other to pieces from sheer can't-get-enough-of-each-other. But she doesn't. He knows that. She puts up with him. She puts up with him gladly. He's not at all repulsive to her. He hopes. Today it seems to him even more incredible that she should put up with him gladly. He simply doesn't believe it. He, a barrel swaying between shoulders and thighs. On his face that embarrassed grin, permanently doming his cheeks. He finds himself more and more repulsive.

Xaver got into bed as inconspicuously as possible. Again there seemed to be that animosity in the air which prevailed between them when something was amiss with one of the children. But surely this rapidly escalating mood of disaster is merely a product of Agnes's mother-hysteria. Either she sees some dirt that she can't ignore or she anticipates disaster for her children. In both cases her expression is the same. For Chrissake. After all, it was a long time since things had gone as well for them as they had today. Magdalena has worn herself out with an impressive speech. Julia is strolling along by the lamplit waters of Venice. Arm in arm with a boy who is as pleasantly unknown to us as life after death. All right, so maybe he does smoke that stuff. Which has no effect. So okay, for Chrissake!

Why couldn't Agnes show now that she, too, regarded the

present situation as bearable? The prospect of his being here for the next sixty-nine days and nights seemed to mean nothing to her. They were simply no longer able to cope with the daily dose of dirty tricks in a way that would allow them to touch each other at night as if they were still carefree. This means that Dr. Gleitze continually triumphs here in our bedroom, for Chrissake. Xaver felt his innards contracting to a hard point. He saw his bowel as he had seen it in Tübingen. Saw it twitch, as if pursued. Ah, thou noble creature of the wilds! he thought. To loosen up, he moved all ten fingers.

Agnes asked whether he couldn't sleep. He shrugged his shoulders. That was much too strong a reaction. If he didn't want her to come to his aid like a nurse, he should merely have let out some barely audible routine sound. That wordless shrug alarmed her, as if he had shouted for help. It was too late. She was already there. To help him. He resisted. That made her all the more vehement. Now he had to offend her. He had to shout at her, although softly. Now she shouted at him, also softly. It was as if within a few minutes they had been torn farther apart than ever before. But as a result, because the bond between them seemed not to have torn, the pull toward each other had also increased enormously. Which was why they were propelled toward each other. They were virtually flung against each other. And at the moment of impact they were still discussing— breathlessly and in detail—the blame that each, according to the opinion of the other, carried for the terrible growing separation of the last few minutes, no, not minutes! Weeks! Yes, the last few months! Each disparaged the other as hotly as possible, proving that the other was solely to blame for the minutes— hours—weeks—months—of glacial estrangement, trying to wound, to punish, to torment the other as spitefully as possible.

At the last moment Xaver groped in his bedside table for the Indian perfume that had been lying there since his trip to Hei-

delberg. He poured it recklessly over Agnes. She spread it carefully over herself but forbade him ever to bring such sickly stuff
home again. He said that anyway he was never going to be in
Heidelberg again. This prospect delighted Agnes. The Indian
stuff was so strong that Agnes had to get up and take a shower.
Xaver had to wait for her. He didn't mind. When it was all
over, Xaver wondered why it was that intercourse still produced
the only sense of well-being that he knew. Must be some happy
relic of early days when it was still necessary to propagate. But
what gave him this feeling that through Agnes he felt more justified than without her? Through Agnes he was more possible
than without her. Without her he would feel more obnoxious.
She makes things right again. And already he was suffused with
the lovely heaviness of sleep.

When he awoke, there was still no daylight showing through
the heavy drapes. But the songs of the birds were already so in-
terwoven that Xaver felt as if he were looking into a single web
of twittering.

If only Agnes could give up those heavy curtains! He would
have liked to look at the outline of her body now. On one occasion they had been staying at a hotel in Zürich where the street-
lights had shone through the thin curtains. He could see Agnes
lying beside him. She lay on her side, turned away from him,
covered with only a thin sheet. A flowing line as of white mar-
ble. Like a recumbent statue meant to display one hip, that was
how she had looked. At home she insists on its being dark at
night. He saw that Agnes was no longer asleep, so he quickly
got out of bed, pulled back the heavy curtains, and lay down
beside her. The weather was again much better than he had
thought. Like two fields under the sun they now lay side by
side. Whenever he looked at her, she looked at him. Her eyes
were not yet quite open, not yet quite clear, still full of sleep and
night; her expression was soft; whatever met those eyes now

must sink into them: eyes not for seeing but for receiving. There was no mistaking that Agnes was remembering last night and wanted to remind him of it. They didn't look into each other's eyes for long. They never did. They couldn't. He listened to her breathing. She had fallen asleep again. Proof that she didn't need it to be all that dark. Since he couldn't listen to anything but the gentle puffs of her breath, he also fell asleep again.